F

Doms of the FBI

Michele Zurlo

www.michelezurloauthor.com

Doms of the FBI: Re/Viewed
Copyright © March 2017 by Michele Zurlo
ISBN: 978-1-942414-24-7

All rights reserved. This copy is intended for the original purchaser of this e-book ONLY. No part of this e-book may be reproduced, stored in or introduced into a retrieval system, or transmitted, in any form, or by any means (electronic, mechanical, photocopying, recording, or otherwise), without the prior written permission from the copyright owner and Lost Goddess Publishing LLC. Please do not participate in or encourage piracy of copyrighted materials in violation of the author's rights. Purchase only authorized editions.

Editor: Nicoline Tiernan
Cover Artist: Anne Kay

Published by Lost Goddess Publishing LLC
www.michelezurloauthor.com

This e-book is a work of fiction. While reference might be made to actual historical events or existing locations, the names, characters, places and incidents are either the product of the author's imagination or are used fictitiously, and any resemblance to actual persons, living or dead, business establishments, events, or locales is entirely coincidental.

Warning: This e-book contains sexually explicit scenes and adult language and may be considered offensive to some readers. It is not meant for underage readers.

DISCLAIMER: Education and training are necessary in order to learn safe BDSM practices. Lost Goddess Publishing LLC is not responsible for any loss, harm, injury or death resulting from use of the information contained in any of its titles. This is a work of fiction, and license has been taken with regard to BDSM practices.

Reading Order

Re/Bound

Re/Paired

Re/Claimed

Re/Defined

Re/Leased

Re/Viewed

Acknowledgements:

I'd like to thank Sherry Dove for patiently beta reading this, Misha McDavid for troubleshooting issues, and Wife for her tireless—but not thankless—work as my editor and numbers lady.

Chapter One

Wind rushed over her cheeks and roared through every fiber of her being. Every time she jumped from a plane proved better than the last, but this was going to eclipse even that experience. The roar of the burner had diminished, and the colorful envelope—the balloon itself—cruised on currents of air. Looking down at the squares demarcating patches of land, Tru thought about her best friend, Poppy. The two of them were so very different, and yet she had never felt closer to another human being. Poppy didn't understand Tru's need for thrill-seeking, but she accepted it.

For her nineteenth birthday, Gram—the only other person to whom she was close—had taken her skydiving. At the time, neither of them had been sure she'd live to see her twentieth birthday. Not only had chemo been kicking her ass, but Tru had been too tired and depressed to care. Gram had stumbled upon a bucket list Tru had made as a response to her therapist's suggestion that she make plans for the future, something she'd stopped doing. The list had been full of crazy ideas and experiences, none of which she would have considered if she'd thought she'd live for much longer.

But sometimes life's a bitch, and since Tru fully expected to die, she had no interest in fighting back. When Gram first suggested that she jump out of a plane, she hadn't argued. If the chute didn't open, then she wouldn't have to endure the pain and sickness of cancer treatment anymore. The skydiving instructor had expected her to be afraid, but she hadn't been. Jumping from the plane into a vast expanse of atmosphere had been liberating. Well, it had been liberating after she acclimated to the wall of wind that smacked her body the moment she leaped from the bay doors. It had sucked the air from her lungs.

But after that, it had been wonderful. Tru's apathy had turned into a thirst for adventure, and that's what drove her to this day—mostly alone because Poppy didn't have an adventurous bone in her body. Now both Poppy and Gram thought that Tru was adrift in her life, roaming from one experience to another without a plan or destination in mind.

Adrift. There was another word Tru loved. It had a lofty, floating sound that made her envision nameless possibilities with momentary glimpses of rainbows and the occasional unicorn. Some might consider it a hopeless and aimless kind of word, an unintended journey through a vast sea of nothingness. Perhaps it was, but Tru saw the nothingness as the unknown, and the curious part of her nature loved accidental journeys and exploring the unfamiliar. Adrift was the perfect place to stay.

"Nervous? You don't have to jump if you don't want to. This can just be a nice afternoon sailing over the countryside." Elvis Zee, the young co-owner of the company that let people jump from their balloons, interrupted her thoughts.

Tru threw him a grin. She'd first encountered Elvis when he'd commented on one of her posts, and that had led to a spirited back-and-forth about the merits of various beers. Eventually they'd moved their conversation to email, and they'd become friends. She felt very comfortable having him supervise her first dead-air jump. "Back out? Are you kidding me? I've been looking forward to this for weeks." Once Tru latched onto an idea, she generally made it happen. Base jumping was in her future. This was one step closer to realizing that dream.

"There's nothing like it." Elvis returned her grin. At 5'4, he was one of those shorter men who made up for his lack of height with an outgoing personality and a perpetually sunny disposition. He had a great smile, and his handsome face had been weathered by a lifetime spent outdoors. When Tru had first met him, she'd pegged him at around forty, but when she found out he was actually thirty-one, she was glad she hadn't mentioned age at all in conversation. She hadn't bothered to try to guess his business partner's age. James, who also worshipped the outdoor life, wore his weather-beaten appearance proudly.

Elvis motioned for her to turn around. He checked her equipment once again, tugging at the latches on her parachute to make sure it was securely fastened to her body. She'd packed this one herself.

Tru wasn't afraid of death. It happened to everyone eventually, and it was what you did with the moments between then and now that mattered. She climbed onto the edge of the basket. From this height, she knew she could get at least a ten count out of it, but the daredevil part of her wanted to push for longer. "I count twenty, and then I throw the pilot chute."

Well aware of her love of adventure, Elvis shook his head and chuckled. "Ten, fourteen if you want to push it, but don't go longer than that. We're not that high up. You have an altimeter, so don't forget to use it. Don't push past 250 feet.. If you're panicking, it's okay to pull it early, better to be safe than a pancake. If you really open up in your batsuit, you'll definitely get 10 seconds of flight time." He pointed to a field in the distance. Two trucks, tiny like toys, were parked on the road next to it. "James is waiting for you there."

As she threw a leg over the edge, Tru winked at Elvis. "See you on the other side." She jumped straight out, careful to keep her eyes on the horizon so that she didn't become disoriented. It was different than skydiving from an airplane. The wall of air was missing, and she found that she loved the complete lack of sound. She spread her wings. Wind whistled past her ears, but it was the kind that enveloped her in silence and wrapped her in a singular cocoon. This mindless nothingness, these moments of pure delight, was the sweet bliss she spent her life chasing. She was gloriously adrift.

Ten seconds might not seem like a lot of time, but with the absence of everything, it stretched to an eternity. Even the ground rising up to meet her took on a surreal quality. It was deaf and blind, shades of green and brown that meant nothing and everything all at once. It was breathless beauty, earthy and elemental in its stunning simplicity. And it was the void, that great, black nothingness where she stored her most precious parts. She lived a lifetime in those ten seconds, but a check of her altimeter showed that she'd run out of time.

Reluctantly she pulled the pilot chute to open her parachute. With a tremendous *whoosh*, it deployed, jerking her from the freefall and delaying the moment of death. The ground still rushed at her, but it came slower, and it seemed suddenly real. As she fell, she used the handles to steer so that she didn't end up in a tree or an awkward bush. Soon she felt her feet make contact, and she ran a few steps until the chute touched down as well.

Her hands shook as she tried to unlatch the pack that had held the chute, and James was suddenly there, helping her.

"How was it?" His smile told her that he already knew the answer.

"Wonderful." Her words sounded breathy but steady.

James nodded. "When do you want to go again?"

Tru laughed, a joyful, trembling noise. "This afternoon."

> E + J Balloon Rides
> Ease of scheduling....................5
> Friendliness of crew..................5
> The ride itself............................5
> The jump..................................5+

Five-thirty in the morning, and the dining room was still dark and deserted. Tru's stomach grumbled in protest. Two weeks at home in Northport, Michigan meant that her stomach was not used to the Pacific Time zone schedule. She crept through the empty dining room of The Abiding Tide, the B&B where she was staying, snagged an apple and a banana from the fruit bowl, and headed outside. Pink and orange stained the sky to the east and glittered softly on the water to the west.

The pieces she'd done on three bed-and-breakfasts a few weeks ago had been well received, and now Tru found herself on an extended tour that would take her up the coast of Northern California and into Oregon.

This place was located near a picturesque cliff that overlooked a turbulent patch of the Pacific Ocean. Last night when she'd arrived, she'd spent time looking out over the wet beach, as they called it when the water met the cliff. Lacking sand and a real shore, in Tru's mind, it didn't qualify as a beach. This early in the morning, however, the tide was out, and a narrow strip of rocky, boulder-filled shore peeked out.

Dressed in a warm sweatshirt to cut the chill of a Northern California summer, she made her way along a circuitous path that led down the cliff, stopping every few minutes to stare over the vast expanse of sea. It seemed to go on forever—immutable and secretive while promising newness and adventure. In the distance, calm swells rolled and flattened out. Closer to shore, the water lapped in some places and crashed in others. Tru began mentally composing her next blog post.

The path terminated suddenly, and she was forced to be careful in the placement of her feet. The rocky shore wasn't there for a pleasant stroll. She trespassed in this world at her own peril. She put the banana in her pocket and held the half-eaten apple in her mouth, and she used her hands to climb up and down rocks unevenly worn by the passage of time and elements. Pools of water, teeming with life, swirled here and there. She stopped to watch a small crab foam at the mouth to appear larger and threatening. Green anemones, snails, barnacles, and mussels clung to rocks, waiting for the tide to bring water, and with it, food.

After a while she found a rock with a flat enough surface and nothing growing or crawling on enough of it to fit her butt. She found a toehold and rocketed to the top. The perch gave her a great view of the ocean and the cliff. For the first time that morning, she stopped looking at the ocean and concentrated on the details of the cliff. The black basalt of the rock face seemed so solid and strong, yet eons of wind and water had battered pits and personality into it. Feeling a bit of camaraderie, Tru smiled. Life had battered her, and she had the scars to prove it. Like this cliff, she hadn't bowed under the relentless pressure.

She snapped pictures of the cliff, the ocean view, and the temporarily exposed shoreline. Then she took some time for herself, munching her fruit while soaking in nature's perfection. Today's agenda included a visit to a vineyard. Tru wasn't necessarily looking forward to it. If she'd seen one vineyard, she'd seen them all. *Look at the grapes. Buy some wine.*

Tomorrow, though, that would be more fun. She'd booked a kayaking trip that explored caves near the shore. By this time, the sky had brightened considerably. Reluctantly she climbed down from the rock. A banana and an apple weren't quite enough to satisfy the grumbling in her stomach. She hopped down and headed closer to the cliff so that she could explore a different area on her way back.

Mostly it was rockier and offered a less hospitable path. She found herself clambering over even more precarious rock formations. That was okay. She'd long ago learned how to deal with curveballs, and this was nothing major. Still, it was a workout. She stopped on a long, flat spar of rock to catch her breath, and that's when she noticed a break in the cliff face.

Yeah, she was hungry and a little winded, but what the hell? Life was for living, and it had been years since she'd been spelunking. Though the opening was narrow, she squeezed in with no problem. The entrance proved deceptively small, but the cavern opened up once she stepped inside. Not much light penetrated, so she used the flashlight on her cell phone to look around. It was a good thing she'd sprung for the waterproof case. She wished her tennis shoes had the same protection as she splashed into one of the many puddles that dotted the floor. In no time, her feet were soaked and cold.

Crabs scattered from the sudden intrusion, and she found more anemones and mussels clinging to the smooth walls. The rocky room had a high ceiling along the right side, but the left side dropped down sharply, leaving only two feet of clearance. If she were spelunking, she'd have to belly crawl through that part. The room wasn't large, though it did seem to go back pretty far, and it stunk to high heaven—like the colony of harbor seals she'd passed on her way out of Monterey Bay. If she knew when the tide was scheduled to come in, she might have ventured down the corridor just to see how far it went. The smell was bound to diminish deeper in the cave. As it was, she walked the perimeter of the damp room, noting a lone purple anemone among the green.

As she approached the side of the room where the ceiling dropped to two feet, she noticed that someone had painted a picture of an eye on the cave wall with what looked like sparkly red nail polish. The shock of graffiti in such a beautiful place struck her as tragic, and she took a deep breath to deal with the grief and anger. The smell arrested her ire, and she breathed through her mouth to keep from gagging.

Before she turned away, she noticed several tentacles sticking out from the narrow crevice. That struck her as odd because she was under the impression that the water here was too cold for an octopus, and it didn't look like a jellyfish. Judging from the smell, it might be dead. Frowning, she crouched down for a closer look, and that's when she realized those weren't tentacles. They were a person's fingers, and they were still attached to a hand.

Dead people didn't scare Tru. As someone who had survived two matches with leukemia, she'd lost a lot of friends to the disease. However, they'd all died in hospitals, hooked up to machines.

She shone the light into the crevice, and the bloated face of a man greeted her. Though part of his head was bashed in, his lifeless eyes peered back in horror, and his mouth was open in a soundless scream. The horrible odor hadn't been raunchy or rotting sea life. It had been the smell of a decaying man being feasted upon by bacteria, crabs, and other small scavengers. Suddenly the apple and banana sat heavily in her stomach. She turned away and was violently ill.

Stumbling from the cave, she gulped fresh air. Tears burned her eyes, and she couldn't seem to get enough oxygen. Reflexively she pressed the button that would speed-dial the one person in her life who was always there for her. She didn't know how long it rang, but it felt like forever.

"Gram." The single word strangled in her throat, but she forced it out. She coughed to avoid throwing up again, and her breathing came through loud and shaky.

"Tru—baby, calm down. Breathe." The sound of her grandmother's voice had been the light that had guided through her worst days. She responded immediately.

"Gram, I found a body." The hazy world came back into focus. "I mean, I've seen dead people before, but not like this."

If Gram was shocked, she hid it well. She kept her tone friendly and conversational. "What's going on, Tru? Slow down and start at the beginning."

"It's early here. I went for a walk on the beach, and I found a cave. There's a dead guy in the cave. And, Gram, he looks like he's been murdered." She based her supposition on the fact that he looked like he'd been beaten to death.

"Murdered? Have you called the police?" Now Gram's pitch rose an octave. "How do you know he was murdered?"

"Part of his head is caved in, like he's been hit over the head with something." She looked around, noting the prevalence of hard, basaltic rock. "Or maybe he slipped and fell, and the tide came in."

Gram made a thoughtful noise. "That could account for many injuries. There—see? You can't jump to conclusions. Have you called the police yet?"

"No. I panicked, so I called you."

"I love you too, dear. But now you're going to call the police, and you'll call me back as soon as you can. Okay? That poor man probably has a family and friends who are out looking for him."

As always, Gram came through. Though she hadn't needed Gram to talk her out of a panic attack in years, she knew Gram would know exactly what to say. "Okay. I love you. I'll call you later."

She looked back at the entrance to the cave. There was no way she was going back in there. With one eye on the tide, she called the police.

The Abiding Tide/Day 1:

The room............4

Breakfast..........................2

Scenery............................5

Finding a dead body..............0

Crossed, bacon-patterned duct tape marked X-shaped spots in several locations on the mattress propped against the wall. Liam rolled his shoulders and focused his attention on a sequence of four. With a deep breath, he let the flogger fly. It landed close to the first mark and hit the rest dead center.

Clapping came from his left side. He glanced over to see if it was real celebration or controlled sarcasm. Sometimes with this crowd he couldn't tell. Malcolm leaned against the wall, arms crossed loosely over his chest. Dustin lounged next to him with Layla, his girlfriend, nestled in his arms. Darcy, Malcolm's wife, was the one clapping.

"Great job." She clasped her hands together in front of her chin. Her whole face glowed. "You've come far in two weeks. I think you're ready to practice on a real body."

At this Malcolm merely shook his head. "Not you, sweetheart."

Darcy's hopeful smile fell. "I'll wear protection."

Mal's laconic exterior didn't crack. "Call me crazy, but I'm not letting a newbie practice on my pregnant wife."

Layla laughed, a soft bit of music that put an end to Darcy's pout. "Under ten minutes. The evenings you have to work don't count."

"I was sure she'd hold off for longer." Dustin sighed. "I'm off tomorrow."

Liam eyed them curiously. "What was the bet?"

Dustin released his hold on his sub. "If Darcy offered herself to be flogged in under ten minutes, then I have to cook dinner for a week."

"Naked." Layla jumped up and down, and this time the clapping came from her. "And I get to feel him up."

For the past two weeks, Liam had been coming to Malcolm's house every day to practice flogging techniques. This was his first foray into the lifestyle. It had begun with a casual conversation and an invitation from Malcolm to train in his dungeon. Liam had been around the periphery of the BDSM scene long enough to know that it appealed to him, but he wasn't sure exactly what parts he liked. After watching Malcolm send Darcy to subspace, he knew without a doubt that he wanted to have control over a woman's pleasure like that. He had reserved judgment on other aspects, like D/s and bondage, for now.

Liam wagged his finger between Darcy and Layla. "You don't think the two of them cooked this up so that Layla would win?"

Dustin tilted his head to better study Layla. "They probably did. Of course, I never said she wouldn't be naked or bound."

At this, Layla gasped. "That's cheating. I have touching privileges."

Darcy pressed her front to Malcolm. "I swear I didn't collude on this."

He traced a caress up her spine. "I know, sweetheart. Don't worry—Dustin knows what he's doing, and you will get a spanking."

Liam was no longer shocked by the fact that Darcy's idea of a reward was a thorough spanking, and not necessarily an erotic one. "So, who am I going to practice on?"

"Layla." Dustin pushed her forward. "We'll see if you can make her cry."

Layla didn't protest. She dutifully crossed the room to stand in front of the St. Andrew's cross. She waited there in silence.

Liam motioned to her. "Where do I aim?"

"Aim for Domination." Dustin came to stand next to him. He motioned to Layla's still figure. "You've seen this done before. Secure her to the cross, but make sure that she understands, without a doubt, that you're in charge."

Liam studied the petite blonde doubtfully. She was standing there because Dustin wanted her to, not because Liam was throwing off Dom vibes. "Aren't you in charge of her?"

"Yes, and I temporarily give that duty to you for the purpose of this flogging." Dustin waited for three beats, his ice-blue gaze steady and reassuring. "You can do this."

He knew he could do it, at least theoretically. "I'm not sure I could share my girlfriend with another person."

"I'm not sharing her," Dustin clarified. "I'm loaning her out for a flogging. Sometimes I like to watch. If you did this without my permission or when I wasn't around, then I'd probably kick your ass. I'd definitely slash your tires and set your computer on fire. Now get to it. I want to see her suffer."

Liam wasn't sure if he had a sadistic streak. He kind of wanted Layla to enjoy it. With that in mind, he approached her. She stiffened as he came closer, and he put his hands on her shoulders. "Relax. Tell me what you like."

Her posture didn't change. "I like a thuddy sting on my butt and thighs, and more of just a thud on my back."

Searching his memory banks, Liam mentally selected the two floggers he'd use on her. He looked toward Dustin. "Shirt on or off?"

Malcolm shifted uncomfortably—Layla was his cousin—and Dustin grinned. "She's wearing a bustier underneath."

He wasn't going to undress his buddy's woman. "Take off your shirt."

Once she'd complied, he lifted her wrist and secured it in the leather cuff attached to the cross. He wasn't under the impression that she'd submitted to him. She was behaving because her Dom was watching. Something in Dustin's tone when he'd said he wanted to see her suffer had subdued Layla. Her normal effervescence seemed to have converted to a calm, peaceful bubble bath.

Once he had her bound, he checked the cuffs. "Color?"

"Green." Her steady tone exhibited a level of trust and confidence that calmed his nerves. Yep, this definitely was a two-way street.

He started with the deerskin to warm her up. After a time, her whole body relaxed. A shiver of satisfaction washed through him, and he awakened to the awareness that he was completely in control of her experience. It was a heady feeling, but he didn't know if this counted as a Dom experience. As he switched to elk, he glanced at Dustin to find his friend watching Layla's face, his expression both soft and firm at the same time. Darcy had snuggled up to Malcolm, resting her head on his shoulder as they watched the scene.

With a sense of purpose, he started slowly with the elk flogger. He beat a path up and down Layla's back, butt, and thighs. Her shorts covered her ass, so he hit a little harder there. Red streaks marked her skin, and he found that he liked the look of it. Flogging a person was definitely an art. She sighed, and her whole body seemed to fall in line with the rhythm he set. A sense of lightness invaded his mind. It seemed as if his arm belonged to another person. It flew through the air on a sadistic autopilot.

A hand on his wrist halted his actions.

"That's enough." Malcolm regarded him with a knowing look, the deep brown of his irises brimming with understanding. "It's called Dom space. While subs have the luxury of giving themselves over, a Dom, or a Top, has a responsibility to avoid losing control."

Alarm raced through Liam's veins, banishing the heady feeling. He rushed to Layla, one hand tugging at the buckle around her wrist and the other on her lower back, ready to catch her if she fell. "Did I hurt you?"

Pupils unfocused, she blinked at him. "I didn't safeword."

"She's near subspace." Dustin unhooked the other cuff from the cross. Liam helped by freeing her ankles. "The more you do this, the easier it will be to develop an awareness of what's going on with your play partner."

He couldn't see her face. "How am I supposed to know when she's in subspace? Why didn't you stop me earlier?"

Malcolm clapped his hand on Liam shoulder. "I stopped you when I saw that you were in Dom space. Dustin didn't stop you because Layla wasn't in danger. She's full of endorphins and in a happy place. You could have probably switched to something with even more bite, something she normally wouldn't enjoy, and she'd take it just fine."

Liam wasn't sure he wanted to push that line just yet. "We didn't talk about doing anything else."

"Which is a great reason not to do anything else," Dustin said. He lifted Layla in his arms, and she snuggled into his chest. "Never use an implement unless you've both agreed on it. Layla would freak if you tried to use something with more bite. I only push those boundaries with great caution and a lot of preparation."

Liam had been part of the team that had taken down Layla's ex-boyfriend and his human trafficking ring. He was aware of her history, and he admired her resilience. Many women would have given up the lifestyle after an abusive experience like that, but she'd found the courage to move forward with Dustin.

"It's time for aftercare," Dustin said. "Usually when I'm training a Dom, or in your case, a Top, I have him do this, but since Layla is my sub, you can watch me."

That seemed fair. From what he'd read, aftercare could be a very intimate activity. And so he watched Dustin rub ointment into Layla's back and thighs. He pulled down her shorts and massaged it into her butt as well. When that part was over, he wrapped her in a blanket, settled on the sofa, and held her in his arms.

Liam left them alone. He looked to Malcolm. "How did I do?"

"Fine." Malcolm grinned. "Want to spank Darcy?"

Liam wasn't sure. They'd talked about this, so the invitation didn't catch Liam by surprise. "Spanking seems like a punishment. I don't know how I feel delivering punishment to someone who hasn't done anything to me."

"She doesn't consider it a punishment. It's either discipline or a reward." Malcolm turned to Darcy. "Sweetheart, why don't you explain it?"

Darcy smiled, a gesture that reached to the depths of her clear, blue eyes. "It's in the tone and the intention. If Malcolm wants me to enjoy a spanking, I do. If I've let him down or upset him, then I can't enjoy it. You can read a thousand articles about how the body relaxes or doesn't, but at the core of it is the idea that I live to serve him. If I don't get the discipline I need, then I can't let go of whatever transgression I've made. I'll spend days beating myself up about it. And most importantly, this helps me process my sometimes debilitating anxiety."

Liam had read a lot about the philosophy of discipline. He knew it was different for everybody. Darcy fell into the category of the rarest of masochists—she was a Painslut. Her body interpreted pain differently from most people. Layla, he knew, represented a greater percentage of submissives. She endured pain because her Dom wanted to dish it out. Though she could—and did—enjoy it, she needed a slower build and more of a scene to get herself into the right headspace.

He studied her closely, noting how attuned she was to Malcolm's body language. Mal nodded his agreement with her explanation, and she beamed. Liam continued with a different question. "What's the difference between punishment and discipline?"

Darcy giggled. "That's up for debate. Some people don't differentiate. Others do. You'll get a different answer from every person you ask. For me, discipline is maintenance. It's how Malcolm shows he cares. He's not a fan of the idea of punishment, so if I've misbehaved—or he has—we talk about it. Layla would say that she doesn't need discipline. When she misbehaves, Dustin would say that he punishes her—even though it might not look a whole lot different from what Malcolm would do with me and call it discipline."

Much like his online searches, Darcy's explanation clarified nothing. Still, he nodded. "Spanking—is this discipline or pleasure for you tonight?"

Her grin grew. "Both. I'll be over there on the spanking bench while you two discuss Dom stuff."

Malcolm watched her go, his gaze glued to her ass. "It's pleasure. I'm the only one who can discipline her."

"I don't want to hurt her." Liam folded his arms over his chest. "Are you sure about this? I kind of feel like an ass for entertaining the idea of spanking a pregnant woman."

Malcolm laughed. "It's fine. I spank her almost every day. In all likelihood, you won't hit her hard enough to do anything but make her antsy for more. She has a very high threshold for pain. I remember the first time I used a belt on her. I thought I'd delivered some pretty harsh blows, but she asked for it harder. It's taken me some time to learn to meet her needs. You won't hit it out of the park your first time. This is just for experience."

They went to where Darcy waited. Before laying on the padded bench, she'd lifted her skirt to reveal a pair of very sexy white lace panties.

Malcolm swatted her on the upper thigh. "You couldn't wear plain underwear for this?"

Darcy peeked over her shoulder. She seemed to not notice that he'd smacked her leg. "Master, you picked them out. Do you want me to take them off?"

Malcolm rolled his eyes, and Liam chuckled. His buddy had his hands full. Ignoring his submissive's question, Malcolm faced Liam and held up his hand. "Cup your hand. Not only does it pack more of a wallop, but your palm won't go numb so quickly. For most subs, a bare hand is fine. For this one, you'll want a spanking glove or a paddle."

"Ooh," Darcy said as she wiggled her ass. "Goody."

Malcolm rubbed his palm on her ass. "But tonight we'll do it bare-handed so that you can feel what you're doing. You want to start by stimulating her nerve endings. Rub her skin to wake them up, that way it won't be a shock when you start the spanking. You did the same thing with Layla by starting with the deerskin."

As Malcolm had already flogged Liam—because anybody who was going to flog another person had to first experience it himself—he had an intimate knowledge of what the deerskin did. However, there was no way in hell that Liam was going to feel up Darcy's ass. He let Malcolm do the honors.

Motioning to Liam's pant leg, Malcolm said, "It also warms up your hand. Trust me when I say that you're going to want a warm up."

Liam rubbed his palm on the leg of his jeans. Suddenly the concept of delivering a spanking seemed too intimate to do with a married woman. "I'm not sure about this. I think I'd rather practice on a woman who isn't married to you."

"We can do that, but it'll take a while." Malcolm rubbed the other half of Darcy's ass. "In the meantime, I promised my sub another spanking. You can watch. Dustin can answer questions."

Before Liam could agree to the new terms, his phone rang, the X-Files theme whistling to life. Everybody in the room knew what that meant. Malcolm and Dustin waved goodbye, and Liam showed himself out.

Chapter Two

FBI crime scene analysts had been able to record the crime scene before high tide had come in again. Clustered in the cabin of the private jet, Liam's team studied the images during the flight from Detroit to McKinleyville, California. While Brandy, Jordan, Jed, and Avery committed every detail of the digital images to memory, Liam combed through the data a fingerprint search had turned up.

"Angelo Braithwaite, 47, single. Driver's license shows a residence in Encino, California. No criminal record, but he has a slew of parking tickets. I'm waiting on the warrant to come through for credit card and cell phone records. Unless you want them sooner?" Liam had no problem hacking the victim's accounts, but Brandy Lockmeyer did. His boss was a by-the-book kind of special agent with a pretty high conviction rate. It was generally best not to compromise evidence. However, the man was dead. He wasn't going to be on trial for anything in this lifetime.

A small frown creased the space between Brandy's eyebrows, but she didn't look up from the photograph she was studying. "Wait for the warrant. Check public records and social media first."

Liam had already done that. Angelo Braithwaite didn't have any social media accounts, not even a Linked In profile to brag about his accomplishments as part of a sales team. Braithwaite had been a sales representative for a beauty supply company, and he traveled as part of his sales position. According to reports, he'd been at The Abiding Tide to try to get them to carry his company's line of bath and body products. "As far as I can tell, he's not social. If I had his phone and laptop, I could turn up something more conclusive."

"He has a connection to The Eye." Jordan chimed in from his position next to Brandy. "There was graffiti at the scene. We'll eventually find out what it is."

Jed Kinsley crossed the aisle and plopped into the seat next to Liam. At 6'2, Jed was only two inches taller than Liam, but his powerhouse build made him seem much larger. Just like many of the agents Liam knew, Jed considered himself a Dom, though he didn't really talk about it much. "It could be a copycat. The Eye isn't exactly shy about broadcasting their tags, and this one was hidden inside a cave." He leaned over to look at Liam's laptop. "Let's look at the parking tickets. They'll tell us where he's been, and we can start to construct a timeline."

Liam had already thought of that. "The tickets are more than three years old, and they're from Los Angeles. They're not going to tell us anything of recent relevance."

Jed shrugged. "Let's do it anyway. We may find something that helps us figure out what happened or helps us piece together clues. Was he a random victim, was he a target, or was he part of their organization?"

It had to be done, but it was the kind of bullshit work that Liam hated. Yeah, it was thorough detective work, but it was unlikely to lead anywhere productive. He rubbed his sore shoulder and tapped in the commands to call up the data Jed requested.

"How's your shoulder?" Jordan's smirk blared through his tone. "Didn't Dustin tell you to switch sides?"

He had, but Liam had been too caught up in the experience to remember. "Yeah. I forgot."

Without looking up from the police history Liam had pulled up, Jed lifted an interested brow. "Sounds like you're practicing with a flogger?"

"Yeah. I'm not bad." He didn't want to brag, but Layla had been fairly pleased with his performance. Before Jordan or someone else could make some kind of snarky comment, Liam changed the subject back to the investigation. "It's weird that he doesn't have social media accounts. He's in sales, which is all about contacts. You'd think he'd be all over the place, Instagramming pictures of shampoo in hotel bathrooms."

Brandy tapped her fingernail on the table separating her from Avery. She brushed back a stray hair that had fallen from her ponytail. "So you're saying that he was probably in league with The Eye, and he pissed them off. We know they have no problem assassinating their own people."

Jordan nodded somberly. "And any witnesses. We had a witness, right? Is he or she in protective custody?"

"No," Avery answered. "Gertrude Martin is not. According to the report I have, she went on a tour of a vineyard and a hiking trip at a nearby park with a group of tourists today. We'll catch her tonight at the hotel."

"I guess it makes for a memorable vacation," Jed said. "Poor woman."

"She's drinking wine and hiking." Liam's sympathy soured. "She doesn't seem that upset."

Jed considered that. "Or whoever she's with made her go to take her mind off what she found. That's what I would do."

Three hours later, Liam found himself stationed at the far end of The Abiding Tide's parking lot with Jordan at his side. Behind them, the path to the small cove was cordoned off with crime scene tape. To the north and east, trails disappeared into the woods. None of the evidence was ready for them to view. The autopsy wouldn't be done until the next day, and the lab results needed time to process. Even though they'd prioritized and rushed everything, tests still took time to yield results.

So they were stuck hanging out at The Abiding Tide, which wasn't a hotel. It was a bed-and-breakfast getaway destination, one of those cutesy places that offered cooking and art projects for their patrons. The place bustled with activity, especially now that the body of a guest had been found and the beach was off-limits. Low tide would be in two hours, so they had time to kill. Liam hoped they'd spend it talking to the single witness, but after her hike, she'd disappeared with a group of amateur birdwatchers. They'd missed her by a half hour.

"So much for slowing down in your old age." Liam squinted behind his sunglasses to mitigate some of the brightness of the sun glinting from the ocean.

Jordan took a moment to finish chewing the handful of sunflower seeds he'd stuffed into his mouth. "What do you mean?"

"This Gertrude Martin woman. This morning she explored a cave and found a body. Then she went for a strenuous hike through the redwoods—I looked up the trail the group was scheduled to go on—and now she's walking around with birdwatchers." Liam wasn't lazy, but he preferred his vacation time to include a lot of lounging around. "I have this image of a battle axe in my head, iron grey hair and steely eyes. She's probably one tough old broad. I bet she can kick ass and take names."

Mouth pursed thoughtfully, Jordan stared at him. "You didn't see the photo with her statement."

Liam hadn't looked at her statement. He'd focused on uncovering data related to the victim. Based on Jordan's reaction, Liam figured he was way off base. "She's young and hot? With a name like Gertrude? Are you kidding me?"

With a casual lift of his shoulder, Jordan shrugged. "About your age. Pretty enough."

Feeling sheepish, Liam pulled up Ms. Martin's file on his phone. The face staring back at him seemed pale under her tan, probably a reaction to finding a body where she hadn't expected one. Dark brown hair framed a classically beautiful, round face. Her arms hugged around her body, and sadness marked the lines of her mouth. She wasn't quite facing the camera. Since she wasn't looking at it either, Liam figured she hadn't known someone was snapping a file photo of her. "She's definitely not a battle axe, though that doesn't mean she won't become one eventually."

Jordan chuckled and tossed another handful of sunflower seeds into his mouth.

Since they had time to kill, Liam decided to broach a topic that had been on his mind a lot lately, and more so since his session with Layla that morning. "Hey, can I ask you something?"

"Shoot."

Jordan was a different kind of Dom than Malcolm or Dustin, but he was the one with whom Liam spent the most time. Despite his deadly appearance, he was also remarkably easy to talk to. "I think I might be...you know."

Jordan's jaw slowed its motion, and Liam could almost hear the wheels turning in Jordan's head. "No, I don't know. If you're thinking you might be gay, then all I can say is be who you are. Nobody here is going to judge you, though Avery might try to set you up with her brother."

Caught off guard, Liam could only laugh. He'd met Avery's brother. Like her, he was a tall blond with a pretty, feminine face. Liam couldn't remember ever having that kind of chemistry with another man, so he discarded the idea. "No, I like women too much to give them up. I meant I think I want to become a Dom."

This time, Jordan's chest convulsed with laughter.

"I'm serious."

"Dare, there's a difference between topping a bottom and dominating a submissive."

He had no experience in either realm. Well he supposed he had a tiny bit of experience topping, but he'd done that under strict supervision. "Which is?"

"Topping is temporary, and the entire scenario is laid out ahead of time and agreed to by both parties. Some people even script it. A dominant is a person who exerts control in a respectful, intelligent, and humble manner. He or she is a natural leader. They have a strong character, high ideals, and they adhere to a moral code that allows them and their submissive to flourish." Jordan gestured with his hands as he ticked off boxes on his checklist.

Liam considered himself a natural leader, and his moral code was fairly strict. "I like to be in control, but I need help with the details. I'm not all that humble, for starters. Would you be willing to mentor me?"

Jordan had experience as a mentor to fledgling Doms, so this request probably didn't take him by surprise. He thought for several long seconds. "I'm not sure about you, Dare. I like you as a person and as a friend, but you live too much inside your own head. Even as an agent, you sometimes forget that we're here to serve and protect people. I mean, here we are, on the lookout for our witness, and you didn't even look at her picture."

Those accusations were true, and Liam didn't bother to make excuses. He'd dropped the ball where their witness was concerned. Though he knew everything there was to know about the victim, it wasn't enough. "So, if you mentor me, I'll become a good Dom and a great agent."

"You make a good point." Jordan rubbed the back of his neck. After a few moments, he sighed. "I'll mentor you if you agree to my terms."

Terms and conditions apply. Every relationship contained fine print. "Sure."

"I'm going to give you things to do—tasks that involve research and reflection. I'll have you interview people in the lifestyle as well."

That didn't sound unreasonable.

"And you can't scene or have Dominant sex unless an experienced Dom is present."

Liam lifted both brows and lowered his mirrored sunglasses. He peered at Jordan. "You want to watch me have sex? I didn't peg you as the voyeur type."

"I'm not, and a scene doesn't have to involve sex. You scened with Layla this morning, and since you're still alive, sex wasn't involved."

Liam let his sunglasses and eyebrows drop back into place. "Oh. What if I meet a woman I want to have sex with?"

"Ease into it. I can be present at your negotiation to help you both navigate it, especially if she's new to the lifestyle." Jordan dug deep into his bag of sunflower seeds. "Or Amy can help out if your sub is uncomfortable facing down two Doms. She's a natural negotiator."

Amy didn't strike Liam as a natural negotiator. "Amy? Doesn't she just do what you tell her to do?"

At this, Jordan chuckled. "No. No submissive who is worthwhile is going to let anyone walk all over them. Amy and I negotiate all the time. Any orders you've heard me give to her wasn't negotiation—those were things we've already worked out."

"But when we left, you told her to clean the apartment. You told her to pick up the mess in every room and do a deep cleaning—washing walls and dry cleaning the drapes and everything. Even my mom won't clean my whole apartment like that. She'll pick up my mail and water my plants, maybe do some of my laundry or vacuum, but she won't be my Molly Maid." Liam briefly entertained an image of a faceless woman wearing a sexy outfit and dusting his TV stand, but it threatened to degenerate into primal sex fairly quickly.

"The mess is hers. She has a ton of stuff for her event planning business, and it's scattered in every open space in the apartment. Somehow, she managed to also get glitter all over the wall and drapes in the living room. I hate clutter, and she knows it. Her event is over, and we've agreed that when her event ended, she would do a deep cleaning of every room she took over. Plus she needs to pack that stuff up for the move. Our house will be ready in two weeks."

Amy's house had been destroyed by a bomb meant to kill her, and the whole structure had to be rebuilt. Since he was moving in, Jordan had included some upgrades in the plans, including more bedroom space to house an eventual family. Liam nodded because he understood that he'd heard the tail end of that conversation—a reminder to follow through on something already agreed upon.

Jordan pointed to a couple having a conversation at the picnic table near the parking lot. "Let's practice living in the present. Read them."

Liam dissected them for a few minutes. He noted the way they stood. She had her arms crossed, but she looked relaxed. The man did most of the talking, gesturing toward the ocean every few seconds. Then he finished, and she took a turn talking. He laughed at something, throwing his head back and slapping his palm on the top of the picnic table.

"They're not a couple," Liam said at last. "Friends, maybe, or they're related."

Jordan nodded. "What makes you say that?"

"She's not playing with her hair or smiling up at him. He's not trying to touch her. They're comfortable being in close proximity, and they know each other's conversational style. Neither interrupts the other, or they're used to being interrupted. He's a little clueless when it comes to personal space, though." That was really all he had.

"Good. I agree. Don't know if we're right, but we're probably close." Jordan's phone buzzed. He slid it from his pocket. "Avery found our witness. She returned from the south side."

They trudged through the parking lot to the front of the establishment to see Brandy and Avery approach a dark-haired woman. She wore jeans and a jacket, and she'd tied her hair back in a ponytail. Her brown eyes were wary, but they still managed to be warm and friendly. Something primal in him responded to her—from the grace of her posture to the way she tucked a stray strand of hair behind her ear. He wanted to touch her, even if it was a light tap on the back of her hand, and he wanted to listen to her talk. This unexpected and extreme reaction took Liam by surprise, but he schooled his features into the neutral expression demanded by his job. He studied her, noting the impatient way she scratched her forehead and grimaced as Brandy introduced herself.

As they came closer, the witness looked away from Brandy and spotted him. The frown wrinkling her chin deepened. He stopped next to Brandy and extended his hand. "Hi, Ms. Martin. I'm SSA Liam Adair, and this SSA Jordan Monaghan."

Her gaze sidled to Jordan briefly before returning to Liam. She looked him up and down. Electricity arced between them, and for a second, Liam felt like they were the only two people on the planet, but that feeling faded when she declined to shake his hand.

Brandy shot him a curious glance, something he wouldn't have noticed before Jordan's lesson on how to pay attention to subtle signals. She gestured to Jed, who had finally joined them. "And this is SSA Jed Kinsley. We really would like to ask you to run though what happened this morning for us."

Birdwatching had been a sedate experience, which Tru welcomed after the way her day had begun. Though she didn't know much about birds, the outing, led by a volunteer from the local Audubon chapter, had been interesting and informative. She'd definitely recommend it in her review.

Right now she was tired. Between the vineyard, the hike, and the birdwatching, she had no idea how many miles she'd trekked. By the time they'd emerged from the woods, she was ready for a hot meal and a soft bed. First she'd call Gram. Earlier she'd phoned to give an update on the situation, but Gram had been called away to deal with a guest-related emergency. Running a bed and breakfast was a lot of work, and Gram took pride in making sure the Northport Bed and Breakfast delivered a quality experience to every guest.

Now, when she'd stopped the worst of those gruesome images from popping up in her head, these agents wanted to press the refresh button. "I already gave a statement." She wanted to soak in the luxurious tub waiting in her room.

"We really need to go over your statement before too much time passes." Agent Lockmeyer looked like the kind of woman nobody fucked with. With whom nobody fucked. The writer in her head autocorrected the thought. "Give us a half hour."

Tru wasn't the kind of person who was going to deny law enforcement anything, but she didn't see why they couldn't wait an hour. She rubbed her temple against the third tremor of a hunger headache. "After dinner. I haven't eaten in hours, and I'm starving."

"Sure. Absolutely. We appreciate how difficult this must be for you."

Tru looked toward the two agents on her left. One was extra huge, impossibly tall and broad-shouldered. His shaggy, dark hair brushed his shoulders in what definitely wasn't a regulation FBI style. She dismissed him and concentrated on the man who had spoken. Though he wasn't as gigantic, he was decently tall and well-built. His hair was wavy brown and neatly trimmed, and his crystal blue eyes seemed to bore right through to her soul. She felt an instant connection, and she realized that he was familiar.

In her whole life, Tru had not disclosed to another person—not even Gram or Poppy—that she sometimes saw images of people before she met them or snippets of events before they happened. Besides, her precognition was unpredictable and the visions were always out of context. This man had appeared in several of her recent visions, but those had been like still photos without a background or a timestamp.

SSA Liam Adair followed up his statement with a smile, an effortless move even though she'd rejected his offer of a handshake. *Liam.* He had a sexy name to go with a sexy body that looked really good in a suit. If she kept looking at him with her jaw hanging open, he was going to think she was an idiot, so she swiveled her neck to the right, and the sight there hit her over the head just as hard.

This handsome man was also familiar, and his broad shoulders made her itch to run her hands over them and squeeze-test their hardness. This was another man from one of her visions. He had black hair and almond-shaped chocolate eyes. Goodness, she was hungry, and being between these sexy agents made her want more than just food. Or she was so tired that she could only think of food comparisons. Yeah, that sounded better than struck silly because two hot guys whose images had appeared in her visions were smiling at her. She closed her eyes to combat the effects of Mr. Almond Chocolate and Mr. Blue Eyes. She'd never expected both the men from her visions to show up at the same time.

She sought to put an end to this awkward and unexpectedly heated—at least on her side—interaction. "Great. Let's meet in the common room in one hour." Food and sleep—that's what she needed. Tru threw a last glance at her dream men before she hightailed her ass out of there. She rinsed off in the shower and brushed remnants of the forest from her hair, and then she called Poppy. Her best friend since fourth grade would help her sort out her feelings.

"Sup?" Poppy answered on the second ring. "Find another body?"

Tru recoiled. "No. Thank goodness. If I never see another dead guy with his head bashed in, it'll be too soon."

"Did you go on the vineyard tour and the trail hike?"

"Yeah. I went out with birdwatchers too. I'm already so tired. I hope I don't dream tonight." Part of the reason Tru had added the birdwatching to her itinerary was to ensure exhaustion so that she wouldn't have nightmares.

"Oh, sweetie, I wish I was there with you." Poppy let that bit of sympathy sink in before continuing. "Did you see any cool birds, like an eagle or a hawk?"

"No. Most of them were the begging kind, like seagulls and cormorants. I...um...A bunch of FBI agents showed up here to question me. Two of them are smoking hot."

"Really?" Poppy's tone became conspiratorial. "Did they flirt and make lewd suggestions, or did you make the first move?"

Heat rose in her cheeks and chest just thinking about them. They'd both been utterly professional. Agent Kinsley hadn't said a word. He'd simply smiled and nodded when his boss had introduced him. "None of the above. The one guy, I think he finds me attractive, but the other one didn't give off any obvious vibes."

Poppy made a raspberry noise in a show of support. "One at a time is enough, sister-friend. See if he has handcuffs. Maybe he'll need to strip search and interrogate you."

Tru sighed. "Poppy, he's here to question me about a dead guy I found. He's here with a whole team. I don't think any of that is in the cards."

"You can always dream about it," she said softly. "Those would be sweet dreams, my dear friend. I'm wishing you the sweetest of dreams tonight."

Poppy always knew what to say when Tru's mind went to dark and depressing places. When Tru went downstairs a few minutes later, she wore a clean pair of pants and a resigned smile. She found Agent Lockmeyer sitting at a table in the corner sipping from a tall glass. The rest of the agents were seated at the next table, an intimate foursome eating and conversing.

Lockmeyer rose when she came into the room. "Gertrude, I saved you a seat."

She grimaced at the name and the fact that she was expected to have dinner with the FBI. Under other circumstances, she wouldn't have minded, but the upcoming conversation would be designed to give her indigestion. "Please, call me Tru." Even her grandmother went by Trudy.

Agent Lockmeyer flashed a friendly smile. "Tru, then. That's a pretty nickname. I ordered for you. The kitchen was about to close, and the waiter said it was now or never. I hope you like chicken, and I got you a salad because they were out of soup."

Tru was not a picky eater. She appreciated any good food, and The Abiding Tide had a great chef. She sat across from the agent. "It's fine. Thank you." The server set a salad in front of her. Tru thanked her and dived into the mixture of greens, which was better than admitting she was the star of the freak show that five government agents were watching and that questions concerning her puzzling visions still swirled in her brain. Lunch had been hours earlier—a hasty sandwich and an energy bar inhaled during a break in the hike. "I don't want to answer questions right now, Agent Lockmeyer."

With a friendly sparkle to her green eyes, Lockmeyer laughed and stabbed at her salad. "Call me Brandy, and I hadn't planned to ask you anything until after dinner. That was the deal, right?"

Tru felt a little better after that reassurance, but she still didn't love the situation. Gathering strings of bravado, she glanced to the next table, noting that Liam Adair sat across the table on the far side. She had a great view of him. If he'd meant to hide, he'd chosen the wrong seat, even if it did put distance between them. The other female agent, Forsythe, sat next to him. The big guy, whose name she'd forgotten, sat on the same side as her. He of the Chocolate Almond Eyes sat between her and the big one with the dark, shaggy hair. The men were generally handsome, though in very different ways, and so were the women. Like on a TV show, this crew seemed to have been cast by someone partial to attractive people with danger simmering just below the surface. Of course, it could have been the standard-issue Fed suits or the way they all seemed aware of every action happening in the nearly deserted dining room.

She forced her gaze back to Lockmeyer. "And you thought we should have dinner together so that I don't get away? Where, exactly, do you think I could go? We're kind of in the middle of nowhere, and I don't have a car."

Brandy laughed, a husky, sexy sound that was nothing like Tru's usual snort-and-giggle montage. "It's nothing like that. I was curious about what it's like to be a travel writer. That sounds like an exciting career." Finished with her salad, she put her fork down and sipped her water while watching Tru expectantly.

Okay, so this woman wanted to set Tru at ease and gain her trust. This wasn't the first time an authority figure had tried this tactic, though in the past, it had always been doctors. They started off asking about your day, and then they ended up getting to the heart of the matter, which generally led to less-than-fun bouts of chemotherapy.

Resigned to playing the game, Tru shrugged. "Sometimes. I'm doing a series on coastal bed and breakfasts. I was supposed to be finished a couple weeks ago, but views and comments on my last post went viral, so we decided to extend the series."

"Viral?" Brandy glanced at Agent Adair who pulled out a tablet and started tapping away like he was playing Space Invaders and didn't know how to aim. "What was it about?"

Tru was tempted to tell her that it was about an amazing one-night stand with a stranger backstage at a dance club, but she opted for the truth. While she hadn't been read her rights, she figured that she probably shouldn't get X-rated with the FBI. "The last B&B I stayed at had a plumbing problem. They fixed it and patched the ceiling, but they didn't replace the rotten timbers. A guest filled up a bathtub, and it crashed through the floor into the room below, where I happened to be."

At the next table, Mr. Chocolate Almond lifted his brows. "You weren't hurt?"

Tru shook her head, and when she looked into those dark pools, she almost fell in. "I was on the other side of the room trying to finish writing my post so I could file it before I checked out the next morning. Let me tell you, I did not get it done in time. My editor wasn't too upset once I texted pictures of the damage. We promoted the hell out of it, and it ended up being our most popular post to date."

Most of the agents frowned. Tru felt like she'd committed some kind of faux pas, but she had no idea what she'd said that was so controversial. Liam looked up from his tablet, and their eyes met briefly. That sizzling thing happened again, but she might have been the only one aware of it. After all, she was also imagining the agent diagonally across from him as dessert.

Brandy sipped more water. "Did you send pictures of what you found this morning?"

She hadn't taken pictures of the body. "My blog attracts people looking for travel and adventure, not tragedy or that kind of sensationalism. Nobody was injured or killed when the bathtub crashed through the floor. I will eventually post something, maybe with some of the pictures I took outside of the cave, but it'll be tasteful. I didn't take pictures of the man, and besides, I'm sure his surviving family members wouldn't want the world to see him like that."

Brandy leaned closer, like a friend about to disclose a sensitive secret. "I'd ask that you refrain publishing anything about this case until we conclude our investigation."

Having been in journalism for a decade, Tru knew the request harbored an unspoken threat of a gag order. However she doubted there were grounds for getting one. With the casual lift and drop of her shoulders, Tru declined to commit either way. "What are you investigating? He probably slipped, and when the tide came in, it bashed his body on the rocks." That's the conclusion Gram had suggested, and it sounded entirely plausible.

Brandy exchanged a look with Agent Chocolate Almond. He made her crave chocolate cake with almond buttercream frosting—spread all over his chest so she could lick it away. Tru smiled at the man from her vision. "What does SSA stand for?"

"Supervisory Special Agent." He returned her smile, and his eyes sparkled. "Tru, there's more to the situation, and the details are confidential right now."

In her attempt to not think about the incident, she hadn't thought about why the FBI would send a team of five agents to investigate one death. She'd thought it was more wasteful government spending, but it looked like that wasn't the case.

The server brought six plates, and they fell silent while she placed chicken dinners in front of each person. She looked over the two tables. "Can I get you anything else right now?"

Everybody but Liam assured the woman that they were fine. He flashed a smile, and though it wasn't directed at her, Tru felt a tremor of desire pass through her core. "Can I get some ketchup?"

Agent Forsythe wrinkled her nose. "Dare, try the chicken before you smother it in condiments."

"I like ketchup." His smile never wavered, and it seemed to grow a flirty edge.

"Of course." The server returned his smile with one that morphed from friendly to genuine. "Anything else?"

Tru ignored the server and concentrated on eradicating the small stab of jealousy at their interaction. So what if he was a flirt?

Turning her attention to her dinner, she cut a bit of chicken and loaded her fork with rice. "So it's murder.

That's what I originally thought." She wished Gram had been right, but then she would be eating alone and composing the beginning of her next blog post in her head. Part of her didn't want to eat, but her stomach objected with a loud grumble, so she acquiesced.

They ate in silence for a few minutes. Tru concentrated on her food, but she could see the looks the agents exchanged with one another. There were raised eyebrows and head tilts as they had a silent conversation that seemed more appropriate for a Laurel and Hardy act. Finally they decided on something.

Agent Forsythe had been elected to continue the conversation. "What made you think it was murder?"

Had it been a feeling or something more? As Tru thought about it, nightmarish pictures flashed through her mind. At the other end of the next table, Agent Adair squirted a puddle of ketchup onto his plate. The body hadn't been bloody, but the ketchup imagery didn't help. She set her fork down. "I don't know."

"Sure you do," she pressed. "Take some more time to think about it."

This wasn't a conversation she'd wanted to have over dinner. "I don't want to think about it. I wanted to have dinner." Her reaction wasn't selfish. She hadn't refused to speak to them—and she'd spent a good hour going over it with several different police officers that morning. However, the topic didn't sit well in her stomach, and she was still hungry. Rising, she picked up her plate and glass.

"I'm going to another table. Please leave me alone for the next twenty minutes."

Re/Viewed   Michele Zurlo

Chapter Three

Liam watched Tru cross the spacious restaurant and settle at a table on the other side. She sat with her back to them. He wanted to go to her—somehow make her feel better—but he stayed put. The waitress stopped at Tru's table. They exchanged words, and the woman squeezed Tru's shoulder before disappearing back into the kitchen.

He regarded Jordan with a steady gaze. "I don't think she's involved with The Eye."

His buddy shook his head. "Agreed."

Avery stabbed food onto her fork. "Yeah, her tolerance for the topic is weak. I thought she was going to reintroduce us to her salad course."

"Still interested in why she thinks it was murder." Brandy shifted to face their table. "I read the statement she gave to the police, but it lacks some key details. Mostly they questioned her about why she was down there and how she discovered the body, which makes sense given the limited background they have on the case."

Liam turned to watch Tru. She'd hunkered down over her plate. "I should go over there."

"Better take the ketchup." Jed snorted to punctuate the quip. "Show her how fine dining is really done."

"She said to leave her alone," Brandy reminded him. "We don't need you upsetting her even more."

He looked to Jordan, his mentor, for his opinion. Jordan shoved a forkful of chicken and rice into his mouth, probably to buy time. Finally, he shrugged. "She'll either find you reassuring or annoying. There won't be a middle ground. Given the way she kept looking at you, I think she finds you attractive, so hope for the best but prepare for the worst."

With that helpful advice playing through his mind, he rose.

"Sit down, Agent Adair." Brandy's order, crisp and commanding, made him freeze in place.

"All of us at once is too many," Liam said. He had an insane urge to protect her from this unpleasantness. "Let me talk to her. I won't mention the case at all."

Brandy's expression soured. "Negative. Finish your dinner. Avery and I will talk to her when she's done eating. Women generally have an easier time opening up to other women."

Liam followed orders, though he wasn't happy about it. By the time he finished his meal, Tru had returned. She resumed the seat she'd abandoned. Her color was better, and the air of vulnerability had vanished. Liam was both sorry to see it go and pleased to see that she'd pulled herself together.

She folded her hands on the table. "Okay, Agent Lockmeyer. I'm ready to answer your questions."

Brandy pushed her plate aside. "There's a sign at the trailhead that warns people not to go down there alone. It's rocky, and the tide comes in rather quickly."

Tru nodded as Brandy took a breath, but she didn't rush to fill the silence. Liam thought about what she'd look like on her knees, patiently waiting for him to start a scene. Her gaze would be focused on a point not far in front of her, and she'd be hyperaware of her surroundings, like she was now, but she'd trust him to keep her safe.

"It was just after dawn, and you were alone. What possessed you to take that chance?"

A grin transformed Tru's face, banishing all trepidation. "It's what I do. Haven't you read my blog?"

Liam had looked at it. Interspersed with reviews for places she stayed were narratives of her many adventures. According to her latest post, she'd jumped from a hot-air balloon.

Brandy made an encouraging noise. "I haven't yet had the pleasure, so perhaps you can explain?"

"Writing reviews is a small part of what I do. Many of my posts are about my adventures. When I was just starting out, I didn't have sponsors or editors. It was just me writing about living life and trying new things. My goal was to try fifty-two new things each year, one for every week. Sometimes I did big things, like spelunking or swimming with sharks. Much of the time, I was limited by my budget, which meant I did free or inexpensive things. I've hiked, made jewelry, attempted a three-tiered cake, volunteered at fundraisers for cancer research or at convalescent homes—things like that. My blog documents my adventures."

She paused and looked across the room to the table where she'd eaten. The server had already cleared everything away.

"Thirsty?" Liam came around the table with his full glass in hand. He'd drunk the pop and ignored the water. "I didn't touch it."

Her fingers brushed his as she took the glass. "Thank you." Their eyes met again, and just like before, electricity jolted though him.

He liked hearing her voice. "You're welcome." One day they'd have a substantive conversation that didn't involve gratitude or questions about a murder. "A half million followers is quite a feat."

"Yeah." She drained a third of the glass. "When I got to twenty-five thousand, I signed a distribution deal with The Eclectic Traveler, and that really expanded my audience. They cover most of my travel expenses, though a lot of the places I stay give free lodging in exchange for an honest review. I'm fair, and if I feel like a place deserves fewer than three stars, I give them the option to not have the review published."

Liam hooked his ankle around a chair at the next table and scooted it closer to join Brandy and Tru. "That's generous. You said the website covers most of your travel expenses. Who pays for the other stuff?"

She warmed to the topic, and her reticence seemed to fall away. "A lot of what I do is free, like the hike and the bird watching today. If the company or owners invite me, then they usually give me a free pass. If I decide it's something I want to do, then I sometimes pay for it. The blog makes money, so it covers my salary and some expenses. Often when I contact a place and tell them I want to try something, they'll comp the excursion."

Her adventures, he knew, would be tax-deductible as business expenses, as they would be for the businesses that provided their services for free. Brandy shot him a look for co-opting the interview, but she sat back and let him continue. He noticed the golden flecks in Tru's dark brown eyes and how the sharp line of her nose was accented by her round face and eyes. "That sounds like an amazing life. Does it pay better than a government salary?"

She shrugged. "I don't know. It's not great, but when I'm home, I live with my grandmother, so I don't really have a lot of expenses."

Still, it kind of sounded like a dream job. "It must be wonderful to have the freedom to come and go whenever you desire."

The corners of her mouth turned down. It seemed he'd stumbled upon a sore subject instead of engaging in mild flirtation. "I don't, not completely. Each trip takes a lot of planning. There are phone calls, emails, lots of pieces to coordinate. My itinerary has to be approved by the editorial board. Though they're pretty supportive, sometimes they want me to focus on something else. I was supposed to be at home for another two weeks, but when the series on coastal B&B's turned out to be so popular, they cancelled my plans to visit Arizona and New Mexico in order to extend this tour for another month. I'm not complaining, but I had other plans. I was going to go in a hot air balloon over the desert."

Recalling her post about dead-air jumping, he chuckled. "You probably can still do that afterward."

"Maybe. The future is always a question mark. Tomorrow doesn't always exist. Right now is the only thing that's for certain."

He hadn't expected such cynicism from someone who seemed so full of life, but then again, she'd witnessed death only that morning. He touched her wrist, a light caress of his finger on her soft skin. "This morning was difficult for you."

"Yeah. I thought I'd meditate by the sea, get some great pictures, and see a tide pool before breakfast." Her gaze dropped to the tabletop. "I guess I did those things."

"Did you see anyone else this morning?"

She sucked on her lip, a move that distracted Liam from his line of questioning. While he contemplated being the one to suck on her lip, she arrived at an answer. "No. It was early."

"What about inside or in the parking lot?" Brandy sat forward. "Maybe there was someone else in the hall when you left your room?"

"No. It was quiet."

"The front desk?" He prompted her because sometimes witnesses overlooked people who were working.

"I didn't see anyone. I assume someone was on duty, but when I went by, nobody was there. It's not unusual for the night person to step away to deliver towels or take care of something away from the desk."

"This was your first night here?" Brandy asked. "Are you familiar with how this place operates?"

"No, but I grew up living at a B&B, so I'm pretty familiar with the way most of these places operate." She huffed as if offended. "Sometimes duty or nature calls you away from the desk. You just put up the sign that says you'll be right back, and you go."

He touched her wrist again, and some of her vinegar disappeared. A thrill of power raced through his veins at how she responded to him. "Tru, think back to how you discovered the body. What made you go inside the cave?"

"It was a cave. I like to explore places. I had a flashlight on my phone, and I didn't plan to go in very far."

Brandy, he knew, wanted to get at what made her look there. A small, inconsequential detail could be a big clue. She clucked sympathetically. "You found the body shoved in a crevice. Did you see something that made you take a closer look?"

Tru gulped another swig of water. "I didn't even see the body until I crouched down to look under where the cave made a kind of upside-down shelf. I, um, I thought it was tentacles from an octopus or something." Some color drained from her face, and she grimaced. "It wasn't."

He wanted to take her in his arms, but Brandy would rip his arms off if he accosted a witness like that. "Was there anything else? Every detail is important."

She looked from Brandy to him, and then she swept her gaze over Avery, Jordan, and Jed. "The graffiti. That's why you're here, isn't it? It was some kind of gang symbol." She clamped her hand over her mouth and closed her eyes. After inhaling and exhaling, she slid her hand down her face and clasped her hands in front of her chest. "Am I in danger? Is that why you're all surrounding me?"

Liam rushed to reassure her. "We have no reason to think you're in danger. You didn't see anything."

Jordan opened his mouth, most likely to disagree. He and Amy had been targeted by The Eye, but they'd seen things. Tru hadn't. His jaw snapped shut before he said anything.

Brandy backed him up. "You have nothing to worry about. We just needed to hear you tell your story. That's all." She took a card from her pocket and handed it to Tru. "If you think of anything else, no matter how small, call me immediately."

Taking the card, Tru asked, "Are we done here?"

"Yeah." Brandy stood and offered her hand. "Thank you. I know this wasn't pleasant, and we appreciate your cooperation."

Tru shook hands with Brandy Lockmeyer. She didn't entirely believe everything the Feds had said—or didn't say. They hadn't exactly answered her question about the gangs. Now that she thought about it, gangs didn't operate in remote places like this. They were more of a big city phenomenon, weren't they? So what options did that leave for this circumstance?

She bade the agents a good night, and then she went upstairs. The day had left her exhausted, and she was looking forward to crashing on the comfortable bed. In a tired trance, she donned comfortable pajamas.

As she made her way from the bathroom to the lavender-scented bed, an image of Agent Jed Kinsley appeared, his translucent image standing a few feet away. Hands on hips in a casual, relaxed manner, he gazed at something on the bed with a small smile curving his sensual lips. No other impressions or feelings tickled her intuition before the still image faded. If she weren't so tired, she might have spent time trying to figure out what was going on, but if experience told her anything, it screamed that obsessing over it was a useless endeavor. Because the image had appeared without context, she had no idea where he would be when this happened or who he would be with.

Climbing under the covers, she emptied her mind of all thoughts not related to getting comfortable. She turned out the light and curled up on her side in her favorite sleeping position. Suddenly her mind roared to life. Macabre images and random thoughts, none related to her vision, bombarded her brain, forcing it wide awake. Tru opened her eyes. She hated when her body was exhausted but her mind wouldn't shut up and go to sleep. Turning over, she tried settling on that side, but her brain refused to be placated.

As a last-ditch effort, she started at her toes and tried to relax her body from one end to the other. It worked until she got to her head, and the horror festival in her brain launched into an extended replay of the morning's events. This was why she hadn't wanted to answer questions tonight. It had taken her all day to get the images of that man's lifeless eyes and screaming mouth out of her mind. Answering those questions had brought it roaring back.

Throwing back the covers, she sat up and gripped her head in her hands. She was frustrated enough to cry, but she didn't want to indulge. Years ago, she'd cried enough for a lifetime. Between mourning the deaths of her parents in a car accident and engaging in bouts of self-pity when her cancer had been at its worst, she'd cried enough to fill Lake Michigan. Once she'd achieved remission that second time, she'd vowed not to spend another minute feeling sorry for herself or her circumstances. Life was finite, and she was going to seize every day of this decade. Since then, she'd faced every hurdle head-on. This would be no different. With a low growl, she slid shoes onto her feet and grabbed an unused towel.

As she headed down the stairs and out the back door, she encountered several guests, each of whom she greeted with a brief nod. The sun had set an hour ago, and most of those who had gathered to watch the spectacular show had headed inside. A few couples sat on blankets and snuggled one another, and another couple leaned against the railing that marked the edge of the cliff. The cadence of their low chatter blended into the crashing of the waves below.

Tru spread her towel on the ground and sat down with her legs crossed, ready to meditate. She'd face this mental and emotional unrest, beat it into docility, and then she'd be able to sleep. She closed her eyes and silently counted backward from ten. *Come on, inner peace. I don't have all night.*

"Hey, I thought you went to bed?" Agent Adair's voice jerked her from the brink of peace. She opened her eyes. In the soft glow of the dim outdoor lights, she watched him sit on the ground next to her. He was close enough for an intimate conversation, but far enough away so that things weren't awkward. He folded his long legs so that his position matched hers.

"I tried. My mind won't turn off."

He chuckled, a low laugh of commiseration. "I hate when that happens."

She didn't reply, but meditating with him sitting this close was out of the question. They stared over the fathomless expanse in silence. Seconds passed, and she felt the weight of each one press against the base of her skull.

Finally he spoke, his quiet tones bashing against the stress. "I remember the first time I saw the body of a victim of violent crime. His name was Donnie Laginess, and he'd been shot four times in the chest."

She winced. This was not her forte. She didn't even like movies or TV shows with violence. "If you're here to question me some more, please stop now. I don't want to talk about it."

"But it's preying on your mind and preventing you from sleeping. That first time, I threw up."

"So did I."

"You left that out of your statement." Amusement lightened his observation.

"But not anything else," she assure him. "So don't feel like we have to go over it all again."

"My point is that I couldn't get my mind off of it either. I had to make sense of it before I could fall asleep. That's probably where you are now."

She rolled her eyes, mostly because she didn't want to think about it. "What happened doesn't make sense.

Violence and murder don't make sense. There's already so much pain and suffering in the world, and there's absolutely no reason to add to the misery."

"You're right—it doesn't make sense. And that's often hard to accept."

"What are you, an agent by day and a shrink by night? Don't quit your day job." She hadn't meant to sound so harsh, but she'd been clear that she didn't want to discuss it, and he wouldn't shut up about it.

"I'm not a psychologist. That's Avery's area. Mine is computers. I read some of your blog posts. You're a great writer."

"Thanks." Her reply was automatic, but her plea was heartfelt. "Listen, I'm not in the mood for conversation. I came out here to meditate so that I could go to sleep. I really don't want to talk about anything that happened today. Aren't you ever off the clock?"

"I'm not working right now."

"Seems like you are."

"I saw you come out, and I figured you were still bothered by this morning. I meant to help. You can talk to me. I know what you're going through." He turned to face her. "Tru, you're not alone."

She stared at him. In the dimness, she couldn't quite make out his eye color, though she knew they were blue. Why on Earth would he care about her mental state? "Look, Agent Adair, I'm exhausted, and I have a headache starting. I'm not good for conversation, and I'm not in the mood to flirt with you."

"I hadn't planned to hit on you." He moved, but instead of going away, he shifted to sit behind her, and he stretched his legs along her sides. Normally she'd freak if a virtual stranger tried to take such liberties, but with him it felt different. She was seized by a primal need to have him closer. She didn't know if it came from the chemicals simmering between them or from the residual feelings her visions had left behind. She felt his fingertips slide along her shoulders and his thumb press on either side of her spine. "Tension headache?"

He'd found the exact spot that hurt the most. She groaned as he massaged circles into her tight neck muscles. "Yes."

"You're a rock." With a gentle, firm authority, he pulled her so that she leaned against his chest, but he kept working the knots in her neck. "Try to relax."

She'd been trying for the past hour. "I can't seem to."

"Lay your head back. I've got you."

Putting herself in his hands seemed like a good idea. She chased away the voice of doubt that kept saying that seeing him in a vision or two didn't make them friends. Closing her eyes, she breathed through the pain as he worked on a particularly vicious knot. "Agent Adair?"

"Call me Liam." His fingertips spread along the back of her head, massaging her scalp. "I'm off duty."

It seemed too intimate, not that the whole situation wasn't intimate. She avoided touching him by resting her hands on her stomach. "Why are you doing this?"

"I don't know." A short laugh rolled from him. "I'm not much of a people person, but for some reason, I want to take care of you. Just go with it."

His commanding tone, though soft, overrode any objection her brain might make. Some tension left her body, and she leaned against his chest. Solid against her back, it felt good—strong and reassuring. He pressed his fingers and thumbs into key spots, and with a groan, she closed her eyes.

He smelled good. That's the first thing she noticed. It was more than the fresh ocean breeze or the pine scent from having been outside. The aroma was spicy—with a hint of vanilla and something else she couldn't identify. The warmth of his skin penetrated through his dress shirt and her pajama top. It all combined to fill her senses and lull her into a relaxed state. She felt liquid, malleable. He stopped massaging and wrapped his arms around her middle. She snuggled into his embrace.

"Are you going to kiss me?" It seemed like the perfect circumstance under which a man would make a move. Though she was exhausted, she wouldn't stop him if he took some liberties.

"No." He rested his cheek against her head and inhaled deeply.

"But you want to."

"Yes, but you've had rough day, and the last thing you need is some guy trying to take advantage of you."

Normally she'd agree, but Liam made her want different things, even if it was just a one-night stand. The way he felt and his unique scent combined to awaken her libido. She shifted so that his shoulder cradled her head, and she looked up at him. "I'm on board with you taking advantage of me."

He gazed down at her, shadows darkening his irises. "I'm not, and you weren't ten minutes ago." He looked away, and then he lifted his face to the night sky. "Look over there, by the horizon. See that bright star?"

Reluctantly, she set aside her awakening needs and looked in the direction he'd indicated. "Yeah."

"That's Antares, the belly of the scorpion. Follow it west to that big star, and that's where the claws branch off." He pointed to lines of stars that resembled an arrow. "There's a little too much light to see every star, but if you follow Antares the other way, you'll see most of the tail. It curves away from the skyline."

She'd looked at the stars before, but she'd never learned the constellations. "Are you a Scorpio?"

"Capricorn." He twisted his body to face the southeast, and she twisted with him. "There. It kind of looks like a triangle. And you're a Leo, which just stopped showing last month."

"How do you know I'm a Leo?"

"I finally read your file."

She stiffened. How much of her life was in there? She didn't go around sharing her private business with people. Yeah, she blogged about her adventures, but there were certain things she never mentioned. "The FBI has a file on me?"

He stroked a caress down her arm. She was wearing long sleeves, but it did the trick. "It's just your statement from this morning, Brandy's report from questioning you, and contact information. Your birth date was part of it. Though I'm sure the government has a more complete file on you somewhere. I wouldn't put it past them to collect information on everybody and lock it away in a classified area."

She laughed at his unexpected cynicism. "You're part of the government."

"That's true, but I don't have access to a lot of stuff."

"Or proof that they're collecting information."

He shrugged. "That's a matter of time. I'm still trying to figure out how to hack the CIA without them finding out. So far, they've caught me every time."

She would never have guessed that he'd be a rule breaker. Craning her neck to look back at him, she settled back against his shoulder. "And you're not in prison?"

"Not as long as I stay with the FBI. Fuckers keep sending me bonuses for finding weak points in their security. It's a game we play." He looked down at her. "This isn't working."

"What?" Her brow furrowed. She had no idea what he was talking about.

"I really want to kiss you. I thought showing you the stars would distract me, but it's not working." He cupped her face, and his thumb caressed a path along her bottom lip. "You should go to bed."

If she did that, then she'd be up all night wondering what would have happened if she'd stayed. So she shifted to give him better access to her lips. "With you?"

He groaned as he gave into temptation. His lips skimmed hers, teasing with a light caress. He played for a few moments, and she enjoyed the way it felt to let him be in control. Years ago, she'd served a Master, but when things had threatened to become serious, she'd found a suitable woman and groomed her to become her replacement. When she'd walked away, she had no regrets. Her former Master had married that woman, and they were still together.

The soft glide of Liam's lips across her lips, chin, and cheeks lulled her into a peaceful place. "Tru, I like to be in charge." With that whispered admission, he deepened the kiss. His tongue tangled with hers, a quick duel that established his dominance as he drugged her senses. Unhurried, he explored her mouth and lips before drifting away to trail sucking kisses along the edge of her jaw.

She tangled a hand in his hair in a vain attempt to hold him close, and she twisted to press her body against his. He felt so good, and she longed to know what it felt like to slide her naked body over his equally bared skin.

He broke it off suddenly, violently, and she hoped he'd suggest they head to her room. He threw his head back and gulped air, and she was forced to release her hold on his hair.

"We should go inside." Her voice sounded heavy with pleasure, and her tone promised more. "Unless you want to finish this with an audience?"

His chuckle came out with more than a hint of regret. "We'd need a willing audience. Otherwise it's illegal. And bad manners." He got to his feet and pulled her with him. "Let's get you to bed." He snagged the towel and, with a hand perched lightly against her lower back, guided her to her room.

She slid the keycard through the scanner, opened the door, and stepped inside, but he didn't follow. "Aren't you coming?"

He shook his head. "You need to sleep, and I would be the biggest dick in the world—not in a good way—if I put my wants above your needs." He brushed a light kiss across her cheek. "Goodnight, Tru. I hope to see you in the morning."

She stared after him as he walked away, questions swirling in her head. Their encounter had seemed like a prelude to a first date, which was an unusual thing to have happen while traveling. And his admission slammed into her like a ten-ton truck—*I like to be in charge*. It had been a long time since she'd allowed herself to play around with a Dom.

As she drifted to sleep, Liam's kisses still tingled on her lips.

Chapter Four

Jed pulled back the sheets on the queen bed closest to the window. Jordan lounged in the other one, two pillows supporting him in his half reclined position. He laughed softly, and Jed ignored it. His friend was on the phone with his sub. In close quarters like this, privacy wasn't easy to come by. When they traveled, they rarely had a hotel room without at least one roommate.

The door opened, and Liam came inside. Jed nodded. "How was your walk?"

Liam engaged the internal locks for the room. "The stars are out. They always look spectacular over a dark ocean."

Jed had never been one for stargazing, but he didn't comment on Liam's interest in such a romantic topic. When he'd first worked with Liam, he'd been surprised to discover that the agent who often seemed like he preferred machines to people did, in fact, have a sensitive side.

"I'm taking the left side." Jed plumped a pillow and hopped onto the bed. Earlier they'd flipped coins for who had to share, and Jordan had won both tosses.

"That's fine." Liam hung his jacket in the closet and loosened his tie. "I'm going to jump in the shower."

Jordan tossed his phone onto the nightstand separating the beds. "Turn off the lights, okay? We're going to sleep."

"Sure thing." Liam gathered some clothes and hit the switches.

Once he closed the bathroom door, Jordan turned off the lamp on the table. "Alarm is set for five-thirty."

The search warrant for Braithwaite's apartment had come through, and Brandy had assigned that task to Jordan and Liam. They had to make their flight to Encino at six-thirty. Jed didn't envy them their task because it meant that tomorrow night, he had this room—and a bed—to himself. While he didn't mind sharing with someone curvaceous and soft, his fellow agents didn't quite fit the mold of what he considered the ideal bedmate.

Five-thirty came quickly, and Jed lingered in bed while Jordan and Liam downed caffeine and day-old Danishes. Liam's Danish had a red stain in the middle.

Jed squinted in the dim light. "Did you put ketchup on a fucking *Danish*?"

"It's strawberry jam." Thick with sleep, Liam's voice barely carried to Jed. "Even I have limits when it comes to ketchup." He washed it down with a swig of coffee.

"Careful. Those coffee packets are mass market from a warehouse club." Jordan slurped another sip as he teased Liam about another one of his crazy government conspiracies.

"I used my own coffee." Liam took another drink. "And I made it before you got to the coffee maker, so I won't have your tainted sludge staining mine. I pay into Social Security and Medicare. I'm not going to let the government slowly poison me into an early grave so they can save money."

The first time Jed had heard one of Liam's conspiracy theories, he hadn't taken his colleague seriously. Over time he'd come to realize that Liam was very serious about these matters, and that meant his fellow agents had a responsibility to tease him about it. In the semi-dark, Jed grinned. "I replaced your coffee with the stuff from a packet in the room."

"Hey, do me a favor?" Liam brushed a crumb from his pant leg onto the floor.

"Unlikely." Jed fully expected Liam to tell him to go fuck himself.

Liam plowed forward as if Jed had answered in the affirmative. "Check on Tru. She was really upset last night."

Jed had noticed. Some witnesses had a hard time recounting disturbing events, and Tru Martin was definitely one of them. Her distress had tugged at his heartstrings, which was pretty significant because Jed rarely had sympathy for people who weren't victims. Even then, he presented a strong, understanding shoulder to the survivors in order to gain their cooperation—much as Liam had done the night before during questioning.

Jed sat up. He was only fooling himself with the idea that he'd fall back to sleep once they left. "Why do you care? Unless she suddenly remembers witnessing the murder, we're finished with her."

With a moue of distaste, Jordan tossed the rest of his breakfast in the trash. Jed wasn't sure if Jordan was reacting to the coffee or the Danish. "He's stretching his fledgling dominant muscles, and so he feels responsible for her. Dare, time to go."

Liam, who they'd nicknamed 'Dare' because there was no place he wouldn't dare hack, balanced a paper cup of coffee and his half-finished Danish in one hand while he slung the strap for his bag over his shoulder. "She's in a vulnerable place, and she's here alone. I ran into her last night on my walk, and she was still upset. She couldn't sleep, and so I talked to her until she could fall asleep."

Jed couldn't resist that one. "Yeah, conversations with you often have that affect on people. It's better than a sleeping pill."

Jordan smiled at the joke, but he focused on the new information. "Did you get any new details?"

"She threw up when she saw the body." Liam dropped his cup in the trash and stuffed the rest of his Danish in his mouth.

They already knew she wasn't a murderer, and they'd all seen people lose it at a murder scene. Jed leaned forward. "Anything else?"

Liam shook his head, and he stared at Jed expectantly.

"I'll check on her."

The duo left to catch the flight that would take them to the victim's apartment. Jed closed his eyes and tried to will himself to sleep, but the nagging feeling in his gut said that the attempt would only make him tired. With a sigh, he threw back the covers. "Fuck it. I'll take a long, hot shower."

An hour later he stood in front of the mirror and double-checked his chin to make sure he hadn't missed a spot. He grinned as he ran his palm over his smooth cheeks. "Like a baby's butt. When you're good, you're good."

Yeah, he talked to himself. It sometimes got a bit awkward when he wasn't alone, and when anyone answered back, he always pretended that he'd meant the comment for their ears. He drizzled some coconut oil onto his fingertips, and then he massaged it into his scalp. This stuff kept his hair nice and soft, which the ladies liked, and it smelled good, which the ladies also liked. Jed didn't consider himself a player, but he wasn't a hermit either. Being well-groomed and well-dressed meant a lot to him. He didn't understand Jordan's love of the disheveled look or Liam's apparent lack of awareness for anything having to do with fashion or grooming.

But Jed—Jed always looked good. He admired his smooth skin, the tawny color a perfect mix of his Asian and African ancestry. He kept his dark, curly hair clipped at a respectable half inch, and the cut of his sideburns complemented the sharp slant of his cheekbones and his eyes. Just because he felt like it, he blew a kiss at his reflection. One day he'd meet a woman who would appreciate all the practice. She'd take one look at his luscious lips and fall into his arms. But what would she look like? She'd have to be on the tall side. Not only did he love long legs, but he liked women he could kiss without having to bend over. If Liam hadn't already staked out the territory, he wouldn't have minded spending some time using his charm on the lovely Tru Martin.

A knock at the door interrupted his musings, and a glance down reminded him that he hadn't yet dressed in anything beyond his boxers. "Just a minute," he called as he raced into the bedroom and grabbed a pair of pants. While Brandy or Avery wouldn't be offended if he answered in just his underwear, unless it was an emergency he preferred to be clothed.

The visitor knocked again just as he shrugged into a white shirt with subtle gray pinstripes. "I'm coming." He didn't have time to button his shirt, so he zipped his pants and ripped open the door.

Tru Martin stood on the other side of the threshold. She wore one of those tight, stretchy athletic shirts that covered everything but left nothing to the imagination. He could not help the fact that his eyes were drawn immediately to her breasts. Yeah, he was a breast man, through and through.

She didn't try to look around him, so she probably suspected he was alone. In fact her liquid brown eyes traveled up and down his body, an appreciative gleam lighting them to mocha. "Holy crap. It isn't even my birthday."

"What?"

With a small shake of her head, she said, "Hi, I'm looking for Liam?"

He fastened the bottom button on his shirt. "He's gone. He left a few hours ago to follow a new lead."

Her frown came with a side of agitation.

For some reason he found himself scrambling to fix the problem. "I can help you with anything you need, or I can pass on a message."

Once again, she looked him up and down, her eyes traveling over his exposed flesh like a light caress. Then she took a step forward, and he noticed how wonderfully tall she was. She lifted onto her tiptoes, and he realized how easy it would be to kiss her. As she veered off to the side, he inhaled. She smelled fresh, minty with a hint of citrus.

He felt the scratch of her teeth along the shell of his ear, and a shiver of anticipation ran through him. If he had to name one place where a woman could touch him to wrap him around her finger, it would be his ear.

"That kiss last night knocked my socks off." The sensual whisper tickled across his consciousness and his brain short-circuited. "When I woke up this morning, I was craving another." She skimmed her lips over his cheek, and when she came to his mouth, she massaged her kiss into his lips. Slow and sweet, it overloaded his synapses.

Normally he'd take control. He'd take her in his arms, deepen the kiss, press her against the wall—something to unequivocally let her know that he was in control. But he wasn't exactly sure of her endgame.

She pulled away and dropped down to stand on flat feet. Eyes wide with shock, she stared at him for several long seconds. "Nevermind. No message."

And just like that, he remembered it wasn't his kiss that had knocked her socks off. It had been Dare's. An ounce of jealousy churned in his veins before it hit him anew that

Liam had dibs on her. He'd taken over Brandy's interview, insinuating himself right next to Tru so that he could ask the questions. In this situation, he was in the wrong. Well, maybe not so much. He'd merely offered to relay a message. She'd been the one to instigate the kiss.

Before he could think of anything to say, she walked away. He watched her go, a little sorry that he hadn't been the one to run into her last night. Who would have thought she'd be such a firecracker?

He finished dressing slowly, and by the time he went down to breakfast, Brandy and Avery were already in the dining room, drinking coffee and reading from tablets. He sat in the empty chair next to Avery. "Coroner's report?"

"No." Brandy closed her eyes as she took another sip. "This coffee is fantastic."

"And Liam isn't here to warn us away from the beans or the water." Avery smiled. "We're reading Ms. Martin's blog. She's a tad bit on the crazy side."

Jed had looked over some of the posts. She mostly talked about her experiences staying in different hotels and inns. Of course, he hadn't spent all that much time researching her. Like Liam, he'd been focused on the victim and his possible connection to The Eye. He thought about the fact that she'd kissed him as part of her message to Liam. "Crazy?"

"Yeah." Avery slid her tablet to him. "She went skydiving—jumped right out of a hot air balloon—the week before last, and she wants to try base jumping next."

He looked at the photo with the post. It showed the view from the balloon probably taken just before she jumped. Scanning the text, he saw that she'd loved the experience. "You think she's wrapped up with The Eye because she's a thrill seeker?"

Brandy shook her head. "This backs up her story about walking on the beach alone just a few hours before high tide was supposed to come in. She's the kind of person who doesn't factor in risk when deciding on a course of action."

The object of their conversation came into the dining room and selected a seat on the other side of the room. He watched her, wondering what she had planned for the day. The tight clothing suggested a physical activity, and the naughty side of his brain had several ideas for what activity he would like to propose. Of course, she wouldn't need clothes for that. Jed did his best to bottle up the attraction he felt toward their vibrant witness.

"Okay, so she's not a suspect. Dare said he talked to her last night, and that she admitted to tossing her cookies when she discovered the body." He turned over his mug and motioned to the waiter for coffee.

A small frown creased Brandy's brow. "We can't confirm that. The tide would have washed it away."

"Yep. Any of our other warrants come through?" They'd put in for several, mostly in southern California where Dare and Monaghan were headed.

"Not yet, but the owner of this place has finally agreed to let us see the registry." Avery took her tablet back, tapped and swiped at the screen. "So that's what we're doing today. It'll be fun."

This was the side of investigating that never made the headlines—the hours spent poring over documents to comb for clues. Jed sighed. "At least the weather is nice. We can take the books outside, sit at a table overlooking the ocean, and dream about better times."

Across the room, Tru smiled as she chatted with the waiter. They exchanged a few words, and when he left, Tru opened a notebook and started writing. Watching her hand fly across the page, Jed wondered if she was writing about the kiss. It had been so very sweet and unexpectedly sensual. Did the unexpectedness of it influence the sweetness factor? Or had her hesitant determination made her seem appropriately submissive—and that's what had appealed to his dominant side? So many questions, and almost no time to explore for answers. Plus, there was the whole Liam factor.

"Jed?" Brandy looked from him to Tru and back again. "*Et tu?*"

Was he the type of man who went after the woman in which one of his partners had declared his interest? Nope. He'd never encroach on a buddy's territory. Except—was she really his territory? Rather than discuss it with Brandy or Avery, he decided to play ignorant. "What are you talking about?"

"She's very pretty." Avery snorted. "But she also seems very confident. I didn't think you liked confident women."

That got his attention. "I love confident women. It's a very attractive quality. Just because someone is submissive doesn't mean they lack for confidence. Those things are completely different areas of a personality."

"I've profiled a lot of submissive personalities, Jed. Most of them lack confidence. They tend to be needy." She stirred sugar into her coffee that a waitress had just freshened.

He couldn't disagree with her because he'd noticed the same phenomenon. "It's challenging to find a submissive who isn't needy, but it's not impossible. Look at Malcolm, Dustin, or Keith. They each have strong women who are okay with them spending a lot of time at work. Sure they encounter bumps in the road, but they work through them. A needy sub wouldn't be able to withstand the stress of a Dom who is frequently at work."

Brandy nodded. Though he wasn't sure whether the Chief engaged in any kind of BDSM, he knew she was very familiar with the lifestyle. With so many Doms under her command, she had to be. "Don't forget Jordan. His submissive is strong and confident."

Jed hadn't quite passed judgment on Amy. Sometimes she seemed fine, and other times she seemed a little too clingy. "Monaghan is always on the phone with her. He calls her at least three times a day when we're away from home, and he texts her as well. Maybe he's needy."

Brandy laughed, and Avery frowned as she considered his assertion.

"He's in love," Brandy said. "I think it's sweet the way he's always checking up on her. As long as it doesn't detract from his job, I'm okay with it."

"Actually, it's probably good that he keeps in contact." Avery's frown disappeared. "Checking in lets him know that she's okay, and it lets him concentrate on the investigation the rest of the time. It's better than working with someone whose head is always in the clouds."

He heard the censure. His attention had wandered during their conversation. "We were finished discussing the investigation. We have no new information, and we won't have anything until later. Hopefully Jordan and Dare will be able to find something at the vic's house, and we have no idea what the autopsy will reveal."

The waitress stopped at their table. "Sir, will you be having breakfast this morning? We're featuring blueberry pancakes with your choice of bacon or sausage. We also have a selection of breakfast pastries."

"Pancakes—syrup, no blueberries, and sausage sound great. Can I get some wheat toast?" When the waitress left, Jed stood. "Excuse me. I'll be right back." He didn't feel the need to clarify where he meant to go, especially because he didn't need to hear whatever comments either of his fellow agents might make.

Lines from a song ran through Tru's head. She didn't know them all, but she wasn't one to let that bother her. She embraced it, singing along silently and filling in her own lyrics for those she couldn't recall. It was all background noise anyway, something to keep her mind from wandering while she recorded a few impressions of the food, wait staff, and the atmosphere in the dining room.

The chair next to her, the one in the periphery of her vision because she was turned toward her notebook, moved. Surprised, she glanced up to see Agent Jed Kinsley sit down. He smiled widely, and his dark eyes sparkled. "I wanted to apologize to you."

Why in the world would he have a reason to apologize? She stared at his handsome face, searching it for signs he was actually sorry for something. "Why?"

"For Agent Adair. You expected to see him this morning, and he wasn't there." He folded his hands on the table, and she noted the power in them.

Tru didn't quite know what to think of this apology. "He's investigating a murder. He couldn't have known when he said he'd see me in the morning that he'd be called away suddenly."

"Yeah, he could."

Tru didn't know whether she should continue to be perturbed with Liam or not. Their meeting was coincidental, and in a few days she would be gone. Despite the visions, it's not like she'd expected it to be the start of something beautiful. She hadn't hoped for anything more than a night or two together. She wasn't really a long-term kind of person anyway. And then there was the matter of her visions starring this tall, dark, and handsome drink of water. Having a vision was one thing. Knowing what they meant or how they fit together was a completely different thing, and often nothing was clear until after it happened.

With Agent Kinsley watching her expectantly, she shrugged away her thoughts. "It's not a big deal, and you don't owe me an apology for someone else's behavior."

"He kissed you, and then he left." Agent Kinsley set his hand over hers, and she liked the way it felt. Strong and firm, it communicated dominance and comfort. "You were angry when you found out."

She understood his implication—that she'd kissed him because she had been angry at Liam. Maybe she had been, but one kiss with this sexy agent had solved that problem. "A little, but then I got over it. I'm not one of those people who hold grudges or obsesses over inconsequential things. He knocked my socks off last night, and you did it this morning. It must be an FBI thing. Do they give you kissing lessons at Quantico?"

He laughed, a warm, rich sound that raced through her system and implanted in her core. "That's classified."

"Meaning that if you tell me, you'll have to handcuff me to your bed and make me forget?" Tru didn't have much use for a filter, and she liked to flirt with handsome men whose kisses made her knees wobbly.

He laughed again, mischief dancing through his irises. "I prefer rope or leather cuffs. Less bruising."

Lord help her. He was either kinky or dominant, perhaps both, and he was flirting back. Combined with his physical attractiveness and the way he kissed, he could have her on her knees in no time—and she wasn't in the habit of kneeling for just anybody. She pressed her thighs together to shut her pussy up. "That's sensible."

He pointed, indicating her outfit. "Where are you off to today?"

"They have bicycle paths around here. I'm going to explore, see what I find." She hoped it didn't sound like she was trolling for more bodies—because she wasn't. If she never saw another murdered body, it would be too soon. From his nod, she gathered that he hadn't gone down that path of thought. "Are you busy? You could come along. It'll only be a few hours."

"Sorry." He appeared genuinely regretful. "I have to work. Otherwise I'd join you. It sounds like fun."

The waitress set a plate in front of Tru. Pancakes heaped with fresh blueberries in a blueberry sauce created a visual feast, and the scent of fresh blueberries whet her appetite. She picked up her fork and dug in. "Thanks."

Agent Kinsley stood. "That looks so good, and I see that my food is ready as well. Enjoy your bike ride."

She waved because her mouth was full, and she watched him walk away, enjoying the view until he made it back to the table he shared with his fellow agents. She liked him. He had an intangible quality that piqued her interest. If she thought about it, she could probably pin down exactly what it was, but she didn't want to spoil with needless logic the pleasant feeling that lingered after their brief chat.

Intangible. It meant indefinite or unclear to the mind. The word itself disappeared after being thought or uttered, impossible to capture or hold. Tru liked to think that intangibles weren't meant to be confined or imprisoned— only appreciated and wondered at. She could enjoy appreciating and wondering about Agent Kinsley and his sexy, well-muscled chest. And she knew better than to try to capture her visions or force them to happen before their time.

The path she chose for the ride was a twenty mile trail that followed the ocean and wended through mostly inhabited areas. The coastline here was in no way rural, and as she rode, she composed lines for her blog. She'd include information about the beautiful scenery, the joggers, in-line skaters, speed walkers, and those out for a stroll. Every now and again, she came across vendors with their wares spread on carts. She could buy anything from a new purse to fresh fruit. On the way back, she stopped at a fruit stand blooming with cherries. Cherries always reminded her of home, and their season was coming to a close. Impulsively she purchased a bunch of cherries and four Red Delicious apples.

She didn't hold out long. Less than a mile later, she stopped and parked her bike off the path. She perched on an outcropping overlooking the ocean and dug into the cherries. At home, she and Poppy, her best friend, always had contests to see who could spit the seeds farthest. It annoyed the hell out of Gram, who maintained that spitting wasn't a ladylike pastime. Then she would lament that Tru had never been very ladylike. Once she and Poppy had convinced Gram to join in, and they found the woman could out-spit them all.

As she tried for maximum distance, Tru wondered if Liam or Agent Kinsley—he hadn't invited her to call him by his first name—could be persuaded to take part in her game. Liam probably would. If he liked to hack the CIA, then he definitely wasn't one who was all about rules and propriety. She had no idea about Agent Kinsley. He'd seemed relaxed and laid back, but then he'd apologized for Liam leaving the way he did. Unless he'd used it as an excuse to talk to her?

Her lips tingled in remembrance of that last kiss, and she wondered what it would feel like if he actively participated next time. Of course, there probably wouldn't be a next time, and her visions had never hinted that he would kiss her—only that he would stare at something, possibly a bed that she might or might not be in.

She made it back to The Abiding Tide before lunch, and she found the three agents camped out at one of the picnic tables in the fenced yard overlooking the cliff. They still wore suits, though in deference to the warming of the day, they'd each removed their jackets. They looked out of place, and that anomaly drew her inner moth to their collective flames.

Tru stopped inside to grab bottles of ice cold water, and then she beelined for the FBI table. She set water in front of each agent, and then she plopped the bags of cherries and apples in the center. "Presents," she announced. "Picked yesterday, according to the farmer."

Agent Lockmeyer looked up, a tired smile curving her lips. "I love cherries. Thank you." She reached into the bag and took a handful before passing it to Agent Forsythe.

The blonde agent snagged some and set the bag back in the center of the table. "Thanks."

A bit perturbed that they hadn't offered any to Agent Kinsley, Tru sat on the bench next to him and offered cherries.

He grimaced. "I don't like fruit."

Nobody had ever uttered such a sentiment to her before. Sure, people often disliked a certain fruit, but there was always something else they liked. And who didn't like apples? Shock must have shown in her face because he scrambled for cover.

"Of course, these might be tart." He took one and popped it into his mouth.

"It has a pit," she warned. If he choked, it would be an excuse to put her arms around him, but it wouldn't be the right kind of fun. It wouldn't lead to a second kiss.

He chewed carefully, and when he spit out the pit, he did it into a napkin which he wadded up and set on the table. He regarded her with a tight smile. "Not bad."

She laughed at his bad attempt to cover his distaste. "You hated it."

He twisted the cap to the water. "I appreciate the water. It's hot as sin out here."

"Yes, well there's no law against wearing shorts or T-shirts." She looked at Jed. "I wouldn't publish pictures on my blog, not even if you turned out to have sexy legs. Your secret would be safe with me."

"I'd appreciate it if you didn't mention any of this on your blog," Agent Lockmeyer returned. "But I know you will. Tragedy and sensation sell well.

Tru couldn't argue with that logic. She hadn't yet told her editor about the incident because she knew Julia would press her for an immediate story. She shrugged to let Agent Lockmeyer know it was out of her control. "I can give you another three days at the most." If Julia found out through other sources, then she'd insist on an early report.

Lockmeyer sighed, tilting her head in acceptance. "Well, I guess I can't ask for more."

She could, but she wouldn't get anything. Tru's gaze fell to the surface of the table, and she noticed a digital photograph on Agent Kinsley's tablet. "I know that guy."

He closed the cover, blocking her view of the information on the page. "Of course you do. You're the one who discovered his body."

The body of the person she'd discovered had been misshapen and bloated. He had barely appeared human. The picture on the tablet reminded her of someone else. She frowned. "That doesn't look like the man I found. No—I know him from somewhere else."

Agent Forsythe nodded. "Perhaps you saw him around here? He was a guest here until three nights ago."

"I've only been here two nights." Tru struggled to remember where she'd seen the face before. The trouble with constant travel was that after a time, the faces of the people she saw blended together. She held her hand out to Agent Kinsley. "Can I see the picture again?"

He glanced toward Agent Lockmeyer before flipping the cover open and unlocking the screen. Then he enlarged the picture so that no other information was visible. Only then did he hand it over. "Maybe you saw him as you were checking in and he was checking out?"

Tru studied the face of a man in his fifties, with graying hair and a receding hairline. His eyes were brown, and his eyebrows needed a trim. His long face was neither attractive nor ugly. He was very nondescript. Nothing clicked, but something definitely nagged. Finally she handed the tablet back. "I don't think so. He's not someone I've seen since I've been here. I think I've had a conversation with him, but I don't remember what, where, or when. Sorry. If I remember where I've seen him, I'll let you know." She kept notes about most of the interactions she had because she wanted her posts to be accurate. Later tonight, she'd look through her notebook to see if anything jogged her memory.

Agent Kinsley studied her face, his honey-brown eyes searching every inch. She didn't know what he was looking for, but something in the strength of his expression tapped into her submissive side, and she found herself powerless to move. She wondered if he liked what he saw, or if he was thinking about the brief kiss they'd shared. That kiss was definitely on her mind.

After a long time—too long, considering that Agents Lockmeyer and Forsythe were stuck watching them—Tru finally shifted her gaze. "I need to grab a bite before I head out for my kayaking excursion."

Agent Kinsley's face lit. "I've always wanted to go kayaking on the ocean. I've seen videos of people out there watching harbor seals or exploring caves. It looked so cool."

His enthusiasm was contagious. Tru smiled. "It'll be my first time on the ocean, but I've kayaked plenty in Lake Michigan. I'd invite you, but it looks like you're working."

Agent Lockmeyer jumped in. "We've got this covered. Jed, why don't you go? I'm sure Ms. Martin would love the company."

He looked at her, a question echoing in his eyes.

Did she want him to tag along? She wouldn't have asked if she didn't, so she offered an easy grin. "I'll call and make the arrangements. Be ready in an hour."

Chapter Five

Agent Kinsley eyed the kayak doubtfully, and Tru silently echoed the sentiment. When she'd called to make arrangements for him to join the kayaking excursion, she hadn't envisioned that they'd upgrade (downgrade?) her to a tandem kayak.

"We can do this." She hoped she sounded more confident than she felt.

He scratched just underneath his short sideburn. "You're sure they don't have two single kayaks available?"

They did not. She'd already tried to wheel and deal a second kayak into the equation, but they were sold out. "This is the only way we're both getting out there."

"I don't have to go." He glanced at her. "This was your thing. I didn't mean to screw it up for you."

"You didn't screw it up." She squeezed his arm, taking the opportunity to feel up his biceps. "It's an adventure. We'll figure it out. It can't be that bad."

He chuckled as he shook his head. "I've heard these referred to as divorce boats."

"Well it's a good thing we're not married. If we go into it with a positive attitude and a sense of humor, we'll have a great time. Even if we never get anywhere." She donned her life vest. "Come on, Agent K. You're up for this challenge."

"We could get lost at sea."

"Nah. We're with a group. The worst thing that could happen is they tie a tow rope to us and we get a free ride back to shore." She held out the second life jacket. "I promise not to divorce you over this."

He zipped into his jacket. "In that case, you should probably call me Jed."

"Jed, do you want to paddle or steer? I'm not bragging, but I kayak all the time. I'm quite good at steering." She didn't know his skill level, but she had the sense that he liked to be in control, and not just because he'd mentioned that he liked to use restraints. If she let him have control of the choice, then hopefully he'd make one based on kayaking ability and not hubris. Of course, she'd never steered a double kayak, but how different could it be from canoeing?

He nodded. "Then you should probably be in back. I'll set the rhythm and supply the muscle. You handle course correction."

It seemed a lot like sex. She preferred her partner to be in charge, but she wasn't shy about offering helpful advice like *harder*, *spank me*, and *pull my hair*.

They got in and workers from the company supplying the kayak launched them from the beach. She waited until he started paddling, and she matched his strokes. Steering didn't prove challenging, and they easily fell in line with the rest of the group. The day was beautiful, bright with just enough cloud cover so that there wasn't too much glare from the water. The group stayed parallel to the coastline, and they traveled south.

"Tell me a little bit about yourself, Jed." It was more than a conversation starter. She really wanted to know more about this man who rocked her world with a passive kiss and kept appearing in her visions. They were close enough to have an intimate conversation, but because sound traveled really well over water, it probably wouldn't be private.

"What do you want to know?"

"Where are you from?"

"Michigan, same as you, though I live in the Detroit area."

That meant seeing him would entail a four-hour drive—not that he'd indicated an interest in that direction. "Does your family live nearby?"

"Nope. I grew up in Cincinnati. When I graduated from Quantico, they placed me in the Detroit field office. My family is all down in Cinci." He peered over his shoulder. "What about you?"

"My grandmother is my only family, and she's in Northport. That's my home base. When I'm not traveling, I'm there with her."

"But you travel a lot?"

"Yeah. You?" The fact that he'd turned the conversation around so that he controlled the questions wasn't lost on her.

"A bit. More, now that I'm on a task force." He paused in paddling. "Are those dolphins?"

He pointed toward the horizon, and she squinted to see what had caught his eye. Several other kayakers pointed as well, and it took her a few seconds before she realized what she thought were swells were actually a pod of dolphins racing around. Suddenly one launched into the air. She gasped at the beauty and grace.

"Good eye." She would have thought their tour guide would be the first to spot anything.

Tom, the tour guide, piped in with words of caution. "Federal law requires that we stay one hundred feet away from marine animals. Stay where you are, and just watch. They often come closer to check us out."

Several tourists had brought binoculars, and they used those to get a closer look. Tru hadn't thought to bring a pair, so she enjoyed the sight from a distance. The dolphins raced along, dancing on the waves and jumping into the air, until they vanished from sight. Tru was sorry to see them go and even sorrier that they hadn't taken an interest in their party.

"If I could come back as anything, it would be a dolphin." She sighed wistfully. "To be wild and free, part of a pod society that accepted you for who you are, and still travel with loved ones—that would be the perfect kind of life."

"Or not." Jed grinned. "I admire them for the graceful creatures they are and because they can stay awake for five days straight without needing catch-up sleep, but they're also ruthless hunters and rapists. Males have been known to starve females who won't have sex with them and marauding groups of teenage males routinely gang rape females."

This must be a pitfall to hanging out with an officer of the law. Lawyers and social workers were probably just as bad. She glared in return, though her vexation was lost on the back of his head. "I did not need to know that, Jed. Sometimes ignorance is bliss. And how do you know it's not some version of dolphin kink? Some humans enjoy group sex—the kind of ménage where multiple men are focused on one woman, and lots of people like some version of dominance and submission."

At this, he shook his head. "People enjoy consensual group sex. They like consensual dominance and submission, where negotiation happens, and preferences and limits are agreed upon. When the female dolphin tries to leave, the males get aggressive and start slapping her around. That's just wrong."

"It is," she agreed. "It's probably too much to expect a wild creature to have human morality, though they seem to have picked up on the horrible side of human behavior. That's sad. I hope whales are nicer to each other."

"I haven't heard anything to the contrary."

"Okay." She'd changed her mind about dolphins. Yeah, they were all kinds of cute, but that lost steam in light of recent information. She'd evolved on the issue. "Then I'd come back as a whale and squirt you with my blowhole."

He turned, twisting his whole body. "Careful, now. It almost sounds like you're coming on to me."

She'd meant to joke, not flirt, but she had no problem shifting gears. After all, her brain kept imagining what it would be like to experience the one-sided kiss from two sides. "I hope I have better pickup lines than that. Like—apart from being sexy, what do you do for a living? Or, if being sexy was a crime, you'd be guilty as charged. Let's go with the second one because I bet you have handcuffs stashed somewhere."

Humor made his eyes sparkle. "I do, but if we were to use them, you'd be the one wearing them."

"Because I'm sexy or because that's your kink?"

"Both." His cocky smile left her unable to respond. She merely gaped at him, and his smile faltered. "Too much?"

Bondage was the second item on her list of favorite kinks, right under exhibitionism. Of course, it was more socially acceptable to find someone to tie her up than to find people who liked to watch. "Not at all. I'll safeword if you cross a line."

His luscious lips parted ever so slightly, and his gaze seemed to penetrate all the way to her soul. "You're in the lifestyle?"

"In and out. It's not a requirement, but it's a nice bonus to have in a play partner."

She hadn't played with a Dom since she'd asked Alex to release her almost three years ago. After four years of serving him, he'd become very attached to her, and he'd begun showing signs of wanting to take their relationship to the next level. Tru had decided a long time ago that she wasn't marriage material, and though she'd loved serving Alex, nothing about their arrangement had made her want more. It had been fun and fulfilling. She didn't regret the time she'd spent with him, but she hadn't wanted to make it permanent. And so she'd introduced him to her friend Jewell, and the two of them were now happily married. Tru stayed in touch with the couple mainly through social media, occasional phone calls, and sporadic visits.

Satisfied with her response, Jed turned to face the front of the kayak. They followed the guide along the shore, taking in the wondrous vision of nature juxtaposed with stretches of too much human interference. Tru loved living in northern Michigan where human presence was concentrated in a few areas but was, for the most part, absent.

About an hour later, they stopped at a beach that had vendors who sold all sorts of trinkets and processed food items. Tru turned up her nose at the idea of a hot dog and slushie. She peered down the short stretch of beach, noting where the terrain became rocky at the base of the cliffs.

"Are you hungry?" Jed dropped his life vest into the kayak. His light blue shirt sported huge wet spots wherever the vest hadn't provided cover from the splashes and swells. He pulled it over his head and spread it on the kayak so that the sun could work its magic.

Tru let herself bask in the vision of male beauty on display. Generous muscles defined his shoulders, neck, and torso. The sunlight glinting from his dark skin only made him more inviting. Her fingertips itched to trace paths along his ripples and bulges, but she kept her impulses under wraps. It would not do to feel up the FBI agent on a public beach. He probably wouldn't like that. Or maybe he would, and he'd return the favor.

"Tru?"

She jerked her attention from her impromptu fantasy. "What?"

He chuckled. "It's still not your birthday."

Snorting, she rolled her eyes and unlatched her life jacket. The shirt she'd worn was made from the same material as a wetsuit, so it was only wet on the outside. "I'm tempted to celebrate anyway." With the amount of eye candy he had thrown at her today, it might as well be a special occasion. She couldn't remember the last time she'd been so entranced by the sight of a man without a shirt.

"How about I buy you something cold to drink?" He laughed along with the offer, so she figured he wasn't telling her to cool off.

She eyeballed the offerings. Though she'd brought water, it was now warm. "Water is fine."

"Do you want something to eat?"

"Nothing from there. I have some granola, which I'm more than willing to share if you'd like to avoid the gross and unnatural additives in those foods." She slung a waterproof bag over her shoulder. "I'd offer you some fruit, but I know you don't like it."

He scrunched his nose and curled his upper lip. Even distaste looked good on him. "I'm not into health food. I love tacos too much."

Tacos could be very healthy, especially when they were packed with beans and other vegetables. From his reaction, she figured he was all about hamburger and "cheese product." Whatever. Her life philosophy included living her life the way she wanted and not judging others on their life choices. If Jed wanted to eschew healthy dining options, that was his prerogative.

"I'll get you some water." He jogged off toward one of the vendors.

"You guys are doing really well in the tandem kayak."

Tru turned to find the tour guide standing behind her. The man wasn't much older than her, and his tan attested to a life spent pursuing outdoor adventures. Though she'd met him in person for the first time today, she'd corresponded with him several times in the past month in order to set up the excursion. She grinned. "Hi, Tom. Yeah, we're doing okay. We're not married, so no divorce is imminent."

He chuckled. "From what you've told me about your experience on the water, I figured that even if he did nothing, you'd be fine. And if he gets out of line, you can always whack him in the head accidentally."

Hitting one another with the paddles was a real hazard in a two-person kayak because they were situated so closely together. She didn't laugh at his attempt to joke because she didn't find it funny. "Oh, I wouldn't do that. I'd run the risk of being arrested for assaulting an officer."

"Federal agent." Jed's correction came from over her shoulder. "It's a stiffer penalty."

If he were going to issue a stiff penalty, she'd gladly do the time. With that naughty thought firmly locked down in the part of her brain that knew not to let it loose, she turned her smile on Jed. "Right. Because you're so delicate once you're not local law enforcement anymore."

He handed her a bottle of water, and she could tell he was swallowing several comebacks that probably weren't appropriate. As she downed half the bottle, she wondered what kind of retort was running through his head.

For his part, Jed unwrapped half of a taco and studied Tom. "This is a pretty cool trip. How long have you been running these tours?"

Tom adjusted his fisherman's hat and assumed the wide-legged stance of a man about to shoot the breeze with another dude. "About twenty years. I started as an assistant part time in high school, and now I own the company."

Jed ate his taco in two huge bites. "That's awesome. You're your own boss. Living the dream."

Tru watched the duo make small talk, and she noticed that Jed surreptitiously positioned himself between her and Tom. She watched his alpha move with more than a little amusement. She ate granola and finished her water, and then she went in search of a recycling bin. When she returned to the beach where she'd left Jed with Tom, she found them discussing the pros and cons of interacting with the public.

"I wish you could arrest people for being assholes," Tom said. "I hate when I see people chasing pods or whales or whatever. Coast Guard almost never issues anything but a warning."

She had no interest in the conversation. When Jed looked over to acknowledge that she was back, she pointed down the beach toward where it became rocky. "I'm going to explore. We're here for another half hour, right?"

"Yeah." Tom lifted his chin. "Be careful over there, and don't climb anything."

"Aye aye, captain." She threw a mock salute and turned away.

Jed started forward with her. "I'll go with you."

"You don't have to." If he wanted to continue to socialize with Tom, she had no problem exploring by herself.

"I want to."

"Afraid I'll get lost?" The coastline curved around and out of sight, but it was fairly narrow. If someone had a horrid sense of direction, then it was conceivable that they could get lost. Luckily Tru had an awesome internal compass.

"Nope. You seem like the kind of woman who can take care of herself." His lips moved like he was going to say more, but he stopped himself.

"I'm sensing there's more to that statement."

"I guess I'm a little old fashioned. I don't think you should have to take care of yourself. As long as I'm around, I'll look out for you." He put out a hand to help her over a string of large, rocky outcroppings.

She let him hold her upper arm to provide additional stability. "It's the Dom in you. You see a woman who you think is submissive, and you just can't help yourself."

As they were on the other side of the hazard, he slowly released his hold. "You're not submissive?"

"Oh, I am. I've been a beta Domme before, but I identify primarily as submissive." When she'd belonged to Alex, they'd frequently brought in a third party for group play. Their play partners varied. Sometimes Alex proposed them, and other times Tru had brought offerings to Alex for approval. She knew his taste well, which was why she'd been so successful in setting him up with Jewell. At the time, she'd loved to watch him have sex with other women. Actually, she wouldn't have cared if he'd wanted to have sex with men, but Alex was firmly heterosexual. It was a pity because Tru had met some men who would have loved to kneel before Alex.

"Beta Domme? That explains why you rushed to defend the idea of ménage situations." The ground was littered with rocks, and he grabbed her elbow. "I hope you don't think I run around treating women like they're fragile or that they can't fend for themselves. I am a feminist."

She laughed, not because he proclaimed himself in favor of treating people equally without regard for gender, but because he seemed so concerned about not appearing sexist while he steadfastly held onto her to keep her from slipping or falling or something. "I know you don't. You didn't do anything for me until you found out I was a sub, and I haven't seen you treat your fellow agents as anything but equals. Well, you defer to Agent Lockmeyer, but she's your boss, so that's expected."

They came to a place where the cliff face jutted out into the sea. It was a natural barrier, and there was no way they were getting around it without climbing or swimming. The fact that Tom had told her not to climb it made Tru itch to find handholds and crevices. She wouldn't go all the way up, but she could get a few feet off the ground. Tru studied the rock and contemplated the consequences of breaking a rule while she was with a federal agent. Really she was soaking in the strength radiating from Jed while trying to ignore the fact that he looked like a male model out for a photo shoot on the beach.

"You're not climbing that." Jed parked a hand on her lower back. His tone brooked no argument, and she couldn't keep from leaning closer.

"I know. I didn't bring my gear."

"You have rock climbing gear?"

"I have spelunking gear, which isn't the quite the same thing." She wandered closer to the water, and he followed. "It's all packed away because I haven't gone in ages. I kind of miss it." She stopped at the shore just short of the leading edge of the surf. They looked out over the water in silence, but Tru wasn't one to waste an opportunity. They were alone, and he was subtly topping her. She had a puzzling vision, they had chemistry, and she yearned to see if it was going to lead anywhere. "Are you going to kiss me?"

"No." He didn't pretend to be unaware of the growing tension between them. "You've got a thing for Dare, and he's my partner."

Tru had heard another agent refer to Liam by that nickname. "I don't have a thing for Liam." She could have developed a thing for him, but he'd kissed her and left without so much as a farewell.

"You came by the room looking for him first thing this morning." He didn't remove his hand from her back. His fingers spread wider, and he ran a caress along her lower back and waist. The signals he sent were at direct odds with his verbal protest. "You were upset with him for leaving. That's why you kissed me."

Yeah, she'd been upset, but those feelings had disappeared. "Maybe that was true at first, but once I kissed you, I forgot about him."

"That's why you changed your mind about me delivering a message?"

"That, and the fact that I'll never see him again, so it really didn't matter." She turned to face him. Inches separated them, but she didn't push to close the gap. For the first time in years, she felt the need to submit to someone, at least for the duration of a kiss. "I bought the cherries and apples for you. That was before I knew you didn't like fruit. Next time I'll pick up tacos. And I got you a seat on this trip. I had to beg and obliquely threaten to get Tom to agree to letting you come."

He slid one arm around her waist and pulled her to him. Then he cupped the back of her head in his palm, tilting her face to his. "You begged?" The heat of his breath washed over her lips, a promise of things to come.

"A little."

He teased her earlobe with his thumb. "I would love to hear you beg."

All sense of structure evaporated from her knees, and she leaned her body against his to make up for the lack. He supplied her with the strength she needed. She lowered her gaze, focusing it on his lips. "Please kiss me."

It was enough. He closed his lips over hers and slipped his tongue into her mouth. The kiss filled her senses. The sound of the ocean and the waves echoing from the sheer face of the rocky cliff ceased to exist. In its place, the roar of passion mingled with her racing pulse to transport her to a world where only Jed existed. She didn't know how long the kiss lasted, but when he at last drew away and pressed her cheek to his chest, she had forgotten where she was. Safe inside the circle of his arms, location no longer mattered.

The Abiding Tide/Day 2
Tom's Ocean Kayaking Adventures Tour..................4
Friendliness/helpfulness of staff...............5
Sights and sounds.......................Beautiful
Kiss with a Dominant Federal agent............Toe Curling

Chapter Six

Angelo Braithwaite's two-bedroom apartment wasn't occupied, but it was far from empty. Three agents from the local FBI office had joined Jordan and Liam in their search through Braithwaite's belongings, jamming the small space to capacity.

Liam picked up a picture of Braithwaite with a much younger woman. He wore a suit, and she wore a white wedding dress. "His daughter?"

Jordan grimaced. "Given the way he's holding her, it looks like he's the groom, or he wishes he was."

Braithwaite's file indicated that he had divorced his wife fifteen years earlier, and there was no mention of a second marriage. Liam unlatched the back of the frame to search for anything that might be hidden inside. "I'm going to need to do another records search. He's listed as single and divorced. There's a record of him having a daughter, but she's single as well."

One of the local agents, Raina Longstaff, came over to them. "There's a framed wedding certificate on the wall in the second bedroom, which looks like it's a combination office and storage room."

"Let's run it." Finding nothing in the photo frame, Liam put it back on the mantle. "Something smells funny in the state of Denmark."

"Rotten," Agent Longstaff said. "The quote is about something being rotten in the state of Denmark."

Liam knew the real quote. He'd read his fair share of the Bard. He added Agent Longstaff to the long list of people who didn't understand his sense of humor. He went into the second bedroom to inspect the marriage certificate. It didn't take him long to notice that it wasn't notarized or that the signature of the County Clerk was very similar to Braithwaite's. "Run a records search. Check the signature."

Agent Longstaff bagged the certificate for transport as possible evidence. "The place is full of women's stuff—clothes, shoes, shampoo. A woman definitely lives here, or Braithwaite likes to wear women's things." With that, she exited the room, leaving Liam alone to go through the rest of the items.

Jordan visited a little later. "The apartment is rented in Braithwaite's name, but the landlord says he lived here with his wife whose name, he thinks, is Sarah. She's not listed on the lease."

This turn of events presented a puzzle that Liam needed to talk through. "It's Zarah Johnson. Her name is on the marriage certificate. I wonder if she knows the marriage isn't legally recognized?"

Jordan frowned. "It's conceivable that she thinks they're married. Let's go with that assumption. Why hasn't she reported him as a missing person?"

Liam let his gaze roam the messy room while they talked. "Perhaps she ran because she witnessed his death? They might have been traveling together. Maybe whoever murdered Braithwaite also murdered his wife? Or maybe she killed him and ran off? Has Brandy checked the hotel records yet to see if he was alone?"

Jordan drummed his fingertips on his thigh. "She's doing that right now. I'll call her to see if he was there with a companion and if they checked out together."

Liam nodded. He went to the desk and pulled out the chair. It was time to start going through Braithwaite's papers. It would be awesome if these things were digital, but they'd found no computer or laptop in the place. He was on the lookout for cash transactions or assets that had been suddenly acquired. "If not, see if they checked out electronically. Lots of places don't require people to check out in person anymore, but there should still be some kind of record."

Jordan punched numbers into his phone. "I'm going to put a BOLO on Zarah Johnson or Zarah Braithwaite."

While Jordan called in the alert, Liam extracted a pile of papers from the desk drawer and began going through them. He liked to get an idea of what he was dealing with before categorizing and cross-referencing the details. Given the amount of paper in the office, he had hours of work ahead of him. Sometimes being a data analysis genius meant long stretches that lacked excitement. Like tonight. He'd much rather be back at the bed-and-breakfast with the rest of his team. That way when he took a break, he could go outside and hope to run into Tru. Nothing had really started between them, but there had been definite sparks. He'd like to pursue the matter to see if those sparks could ignite anything bigger, maybe even long-lasting or—dare he dream?—permanent.

Jordan came to him sometime later. Liam looked up to find his mentor watching quietly.

"What's up?"

"They're finished with the search. Everything has been boxed up and shipped to evidence. We need to process this room and catalog the evidence you want to take with you. The rest of the team is giving the apartment a final look-through."

Liam had sorted the papers into piles of items he thought might be relevant and those he knew were inconsequential. The inconsequential pile was very tiny, as he never knew what would prove to be important. "Okay. I've been making a list and taking pictures."

He and Jordan worked quietly side-by-side. The day had been long, and they were both tired. As he sorted the last stack of papers, he came to a receipt from a BDSM-themed inn called Zangari's Fetish Inn. Liam had only heard of it in passing, but he was aware of its existence. He paused uncertainly.

"Problem?" Jordan noticed Liam's hesitation. "Did you find something significant?"

"I don't know. Was there kink equipment anywhere in the house?"

Jordan shook his head. "Nothing except some silk scarves that might have been used for bondage. From their condition, I doubt it. They all seemed new, and they didn't have any wrinkles that indicate they'd been tied in knots."

"There's a receipt from Zangari's Fetish Inn."

"Maybe he sold them some bath products? They probably have a spa somewhere on site, so that could net some larger profits." Jordan studied the receipt. "It's not very specific, but that's to be expected. Not many people want a line item about a spanking vacation for their records. We'll check it out, see where it leads."

Liam's mind raced with a hundred questions, but he concentrated on ones that had nothing to do with the case. "Do you think Tru is a submissive?"

Jordan didn't pretend to be lost. "I don't know. The best way to be sure is to ask her. If she is, she'll tell you. If not, maybe she's open to trying. Since you're new to the lifestyle, it might be good to hook up with someone else who is also new. You can make mistakes and grow together."

What if she wasn't new? She'd shown subtle signs like the dropping of her gaze and letting him take the lead. Of course those could be signs of natural submission. They could also be signs that she was experienced and that submission had become second nature because she'd been trained. Was there truly a way to recognize the distinction through behavioral observation—his weakest quality?

Liam recognized that he needed to get out of his head before it exploded. "I'll call her when we're finished up here. Has anyone questioned the neighbors about Zarah Johnson's whereabouts?"

"I went with Agent Longstaff. It's always good to have a local agent along for the questioning."

Liam thought that Agent Longstaff seemed a little green, and he couldn't see where she'd be an asset. However Jordan didn't seem to be joking. "What happened?"

"Nothing much. We found a nosy neighbor on the first floor who didn't know anything, but who had plenty to say about the age difference. She used the term 'gold-digger.' Given that Braithwaite didn't seem to have any assets, I don't know how the term applies." Jordan clenched his teeth together. "Just because one person is younger than the other doesn't mean they're after money."

Being younger than his girlfriend, Jordan was sometimes touchy about the issue. Personally Liam didn't think it was a big deal or a large age difference. Nobody would have thought twice about a man six years older than his lover, but people sure judged when it was the other way around. Still he couldn't let this opportunity slide. "Maybe she was looking for a father figure who was good in bed?"

Jordan glared, but Liam only laughed.

"You're taking this too personally. I found performance-enhancing drugs in the medicine cabinet. Angelo's wood had pharmaceutical assistance." It occurred to Liam that Jordan might have discounted a witness's observations for personal reasons. "Are you sure she wasn't a gold-digger? To someone with nothing, a two-bedroom apartment in a good area is golden, and California is not a cheap place to live."

While Jordan looked like he didn't rule it out, he didn't seem to love that theory either. "We need to find her.

Neighbors haven't seen either of them in over a week, and their car isn't in the parking lot here or at The Abiding Tide. She may be dead or on the run. We won't know until we find her."

He finished bagging and labeling the papers he wanted to study later. All electronics were missing, so if Braithwaite had a laptop it was probably in his car, with whomever had murdered him, or destroyed. On the way out, they encountered Agent Longstaff standing in the door to the bathroom and holding up a single red stone.

"Is that a ruby?" Liam wasn't an expert on gems, but he'd done some research after Avery had floated a diamond smuggling theory during their brainstorming session last week. Even more terrible than the conditions in the illegal diamond trade, the Pigeon's Blood rubies were mined by slave labor in Myanmar to support the military junta that controlled parts of the country. These were the most expensive gems per carat in the world.

Agent Longstaff sighed. "Uncut. I bet it doesn't have a KPCS number. It pains me that something this beautiful is going to spend the next hundred years gathering dust in an FBI evidence locker." She carefully placed it into a plastic evidence bag. "It was in the medicine cabinet tucked away in a bottle of store brand ibuprofen."

"That sheds a different light on trafficking illegal gems and drugs." Liam peered over Agent Longstaff's shoulder and into the bathroom. "Is that all you found?"

"So far. We weren't looking for gems, just anything that could indicate a connection with The Eye, most of which we expected to be on Braithwaite's missing laptop." She flashed a tired grin. "Gentlemen, we're in for a long night. I'll send someone on a coffee run."

Re/Viewed   Michele Zurlo

Chapter Seven

"I met someone." Tru folded the clothes she'd carelessly tossed onto a chair. She couldn't remember the last time she'd straightened up a hotel room with the expectation that she'd soon entertain a man in it.

"I know. You told me that yesterday." Poppy's voice came over the speaker on Tru's cell phone, strategically located on the table next to the chair.

She'd mentioned Liam and being questioned by the FBI. "Different guy. But that guy was a good kisser. I couldn't sleep last night, so I went outside. He was there. We talked. We kissed. This morning he was gone, and I spent the afternoon with this new guy."

Poppy laughed. "Geez, Tru. When it rains, it pours. I guess your drought is over."

"Temporarily, at least. I'm only here for two more nights." That didn't mean the FBI would stay for another two days, but at least she'd have tonight with Jed. "Anyway, his name is Jed, and he's also an FBI agent."

"I'm sensing a pattern. This is weird. You've never had a type before." Static interrupted whatever Poppy said next. Northport didn't have many cell towers.

Tru waited for the static to clear. "I like strong, dominant men. Apparently lots of them work for the FBI."

"The next time you have a chance to go clubbing, you should find a place near a field office." Poppy sighed. "And take me. I love small town life, but the problem with living in the same small town where I grew up is that I know everybody already. No matter what he looks like now, it's hard to get excited about a guy you've seen wet his pants in fourth grade."

"Ah, the Darren Gabton debacle. You're right. He's going to have to leave Northport to find a wife." Tru shook her head in remembrance. "Did he ask you out?"

"He did. I thought about it, but after I imagined what our kids would look like, I thought about him walking around with those wet pants, telling everyone that the drinking fountain had spit on him even though he smelled like urine. I couldn't do it." Poppy's laugh held a tinge of regret. "Tell me about this FBI agent who has swept you off your feet, and I'll tell you about the guy who tripped and fell into a curio cabinet full of carnival glass this morning."

Small towns were full of dull moments, but Poppy managed to attract her fair share of drama. Tru chatted with her best friend for fifteen more minutes before hanging up. She needed to shower the smell of sunscreen and ocean from her skin.

The knock on her door came promptly at seven. She threw it open to find Jed smiling widely. He wore a suit with a white shirt and no tie. He'd left the top two buttons open, but the shirt didn't gape enough to do more than tease. He was as sexy in a suit as he was wearing wet cargo shorts and beach shoes.

While she'd checked him out, he'd been doing the same with her. She'd chosen a simple, patterned dress that fell to her knees. The neckline plunged to show a generous amount of cleavage, and the three-quarter sleeves were split from elbow to shoulder. "You look beautiful."

"Thanks." She leaned close and tilted her face up for a kiss. "I left off the cherry lip gloss."

He laughed and pulled her against him. "I appreciate your thoughtfulness, though if there was a way to get me to like cherries, your lips being that flavor might do the trick." He kissed her gently, another teaser that made an implicit promise for later. "How was the rest of your afternoon?"

"I napped." The bike ride and the kayaking excursion had left her exhausted. She'd slept solidly for almost two hours. "And then I took a shower. It was very uneventful. How was your afternoon?"

"Not as restful as yours. Do you have your key? I reserved a table for us downstairs, and I've already ordered dinner." He waited while she locked her door, and then he offered his arm. It had been a long time since a man had treated her with such respect. This is what she missed about being with someone who practiced the art of respectful Dominance.

She walked down the stairs on his arm. Just like on the beach, she didn't need him to steady her, but the fact of him being there made her feel the power of her femininity. He pulled out her chair and made sure she was comfortable before assuming the seat across the table.

The salad course came before either of them could utter a word.

"I'm starved." He stabbed a cherry tomato and popped it into his mouth.

"You like vegetables?" This could be a fluke. When she thought back to last night, she couldn't remember what he'd eaten. She couldn't even remember what she'd eaten. The only clear memory about the food was when the agents had teased Liam about liking ketchup on everything.

"Love them." He grinned. "It's just fruit I'm not crazy about, though technically a tomato is a fruit."

She let the tomato as fruit/veggie thing go. It didn't matter. "That's a relief. I was getting worried about your health." Not that it was any of her business. She wasn't in a position to nag him for the lack of fruit in his diet, and she had no plans to gain the right. It was time to change the subject. "How was work?"

"Investigations are ninety-nine percent research and one percent action. Brandy and Avery brought me up to speed on what they'd found while I was out with you." He flashed a devilish grin that let her know he had no regrets about ditching his duties for a few hours. "It would be helpful if you could remember when and where you saw Angelo Braithwaite alive."

She hadn't yet looked through her notebook. "I'll look tomorrow to see if I mentioned him in my notes, but his name isn't familiar. I'm going to have to look for a description."

He loaded lettuce and cucumber onto his fork. "How about you look tonight?"

She finished chewing and swallowing before donning her flirtiest frown. "I thought we'd be too busy doing other things tonight."

"Such as?" That teasing smile was back, and his voice had deepened.

"Dinner, for one."

"Dinner will only take so long."

"A glass of wine, a moonlit walk. I'm not picky, but I do like a bit of romance on a date, especially if I plan to get lucky."

He motioned to the server, who brought forth a bottle of wine and two glasses. Once she left, Jed lifted his glass. "I wasn't sure if this was going to be more than dinner. There's no pressure, Tru. I don't want you to make a hasty decision that you may regret later."

The only thing she'd regret would be not taking this as far as it would go. "I'm not saying we should scene. We don't know each other well enough for that. But that doesn't mean we can't have fun. It isn't often that I meet an attractive Dom who is great in a tandem kayak."

He laughed. "That's what sealed the deal?"

"It was the kiss, though the kayaking was definitely a bonus." Rhythm and stamina would come in handy later. Finished with the salad, she put down her fork. Dessert wouldn't be for a while, so she changed the topic again. "You must meet all kinds of people in your line of work. What has been your weirdest case so far?"

"I once had to chase down a guy dressed in a clown suit who was wanted for embezzlement in three states. He was wearing these really long shoes, and he kept jumping into the air every few steps to keep from tripping. He only got as far as he did because I couldn't stop laughing, and that slowed me down. After I arrested him, he kept bopping his fake nose against the window of the car to make it squeak. He annoyed the hell out of Dustin, who was my partner at the time, and he mimed that he was sobbing when Dustin took away the nose."

Tru snort-and-giggled at the image of the clown leaping every few steps. "I used to be afraid of clowns, but one time when I was in the hospital, one visited. All the kids loved him because he made us laugh." After that, she'd let go of her fear. She'd let go of a lot of fears that year.

"What were you in the hospital for?" The main course had arrived, and he cut into his broasted chicken.

She didn't like to talk about being in the hospital, and she wondered what had possessed her to mention it at all. In the past, she'd always couched it to make any reference sound like she'd been visiting someone else. At least she hadn't specified that she'd been in the children's oncology ward. She scrambled to cover her tracks. "I'd been sick."

He chuckled. "Obviously. But you're over it now."

"Yes." Twelve years of remission meant it was unlikely to recur again, though it wasn't impossible. That's why she lived each day to the fullest and greeted each new experience with enthusiasm. Unbidden, an image of the bathtub crashing through the floor of that B&B came to mind, and she remembered where she'd seen Angelo Braithwaite before. She grabbed Jed's hand. "I think Braithwaite was at The Captain's Nest when I was there last month. I was in the common room writing my review. It was after midnight, and this man started a conversation with me. That's when the bathtub crashed through the floor. It wasn't his room, but he was there, hanging out in the common room after midnight."

"Do you remember what you talked about?"

"I had a headache, and he said he had insomnia. I wanted to finish my article before going upstairs to take something. You know, staring at a computer screen doesn't help a headache to go away. Anyway, he was going to go to the kitchen to get some warm milk." Bits and pieces came back to her. "He was there with his wife. She was younger, one of those California blondes that all have the same nose job and collagen lips." It occurred to her that maybe the woman hadn't been all that much younger, but she honestly couldn't recall enough to judge. Maybe she'd just had a really good facelift. "I didn't meet her. After the accident, they herded us all to our rooms. It was chaos. Most people packed up and left. I mean, I wasn't going to sleep well or shower after that happened."

Jed nodded, and she noted the change in his demeanor. Now he was all business. "Did he mention anything about where he was going or where he'd been? Did he talk about his job? Did you see him talk with anyone at all while you were there?"

That was a lot of questions at once. "He talked with his wife and some of the other guests. I didn't really pay attention to him. He wasn't very interesting. I only mentioned him on my blog because he was there when the tub fell through, but I didn't know his name, so I called him Insomniac Guy. I'm sorry, but that was the only time I talked to him, and I never had a conversation with his wife."

"How did you now she was his wife?"

Tru shrugged. "Body language. They seemed really into each other, so maybe I made an assumption. He might have mentioned having a wife, but I don't remember. I'm sorry I can't be more helpful. I didn't know that someone was going to murder him. He seemed harmless and forgettable."

Jed stood. "I'll be right back. I need to grab Brandy. She's going to want to ask you some questions."

At this point, Tru was wishing she'd kept her mouth shut. Not only had her date been interrupted, but she was about to be asked another barrage of questions to which she didn't know the answers. She'd told Jed everything she knew. With a sigh, she finished her broasted chicken. No sense in letting it get cold.

Jed was quiet as he walked her back to her room. Agent Lockmeyer's questioning had gone on longer than Tru thought necessary, and she'd asked the same questions in a multitude of ways. If there was an opening as the head of the redundancy department, Brandy Lockmeyer would be a shoo-in. Of course Liam's questioning technique had been very similar. This is where her tax dollars went. Well, there and to finance tax breaks for the wealthy.

"This must rate a place on your list of top ten worst dates." Jed's smile betrayed his regret.

They stopped in front of her door, and Tru pivoted to face him. "You'd have to vomit on me in order to come close to making that list."

"Good to know." The way his forehead wrinkled let her know that she'd gone in an unexpected direction. Good. She liked to keep him guessing. He took her hand in his and kissed it. "I'm sorry."

She shrugged. "No need to apologize. Your penchant for catching criminals is part of your charm."

"Yeah, but I'd planned to flirt a lot so that you'd be putty in my hands by now. Maybe tomorrow night you'll give me another chance? What do you say—will you risk having dinner with me again?" He followed the request with a flagrant grin that probably netted him a lot of second chances.

Tru wasn't immune. The way he held her hand, his soft grip not hiding a strength that could hold her down the way she liked and not let her get free, turned her into the aforementioned butter. No sweet talk required. Actually she preferred dirty talk, graphic and unapologetic. She flicked her hair over her shoulder and tilted her head as she looked up at him. "Can I let you know tomorrow morning? I don't like to commit to a second date until the first one is over."

It took a minute for him to process her oblique invitation. Desire kindled in his dark eyes, and he wrapped his free arm around her waist. "Do you want to come back to my room?"

She fished her room key from her purse. "Mine is closer."

He took the key and unlocked the door. "We'll need to talk first."

An insistence on conversation was a sign of a good Dom, but that wasn't going to turn Tru into a pushover. She had too much experience to agree to much when she'd only known a man for a day. She entered the room and let him lock it behind them. "I'm okay with a little kink, like hair pulling and spanking during sex, but I won't consent to bondage or impact play."

He threw her key on the small table where she'd set her laptop and notebook. "Fair enough. I can't turn off the dominant part of me, but I agree that it's best not to engage in some of the aspects of kink where you have to establish an advanced degree of trust first."

They were on the same page. "I'm okay with being held down, and I'm more than okay with you being in charge." Her knees trembled a little. It had been several years since she'd let someone do any of those things to her. The nomadic nature of her lifestyle ruled out relationships with the vast majority of people, and she liked it that way.

"Call yellow if I do something to which you object. Call red at any time if you want to stop."

"Sure." She liked that he'd brought up the safeword system. In covering the bases, he made her feel protected.

His eyes hardened, and if it was possible, they liquefied as well. Without moving, he'd bound her in place using only the intensity of his expression. "Take off your clothes slowly. Keep your eyes on me while you undress."

Given the warmth of the evening, she wasn't wearing much under the dress. Reasoning that he might like the way her legs looked in the three-inch heels, she opted to follow his orders to the letter. She scrunched her skirt in her hand, pulling it up by inches while she watched his very handsome face. He hid nothing of his reaction, openly appreciating the single thigh she revealed.

When she had the hem in her hand, she lifted the whole skirt. In anticipation of the evening, she'd worn a powder blue lacy thong that matched her dress. Jed sucked in a breath when he caught sight of that scrap of material. She continued lifting slowly until the dress blocked her sight, and then she ripped it off the rest of the way. Not wanting to drop it on the floor, she tossed it to the single occasional chair.

Wearing heels and matching lingerie, she waited for a moment as his gazed moved over her, the promise of a caress to come. She unhooked her bra and shed that next. Her breasts weren't anything spectacular, a handful at the most, yet his gaze lingered, burning so hot that her nipples pebbled.

Lastly she stepped out of the thong. Now when she faced him, she assumed the standing presentation pose of a good submissive—arms hanging at her sides and legs spread shoulder-width apart. He hadn't earned the right to ask her to kneel, and she liked that he didn't seem inclined to insist on rights that were not his.

He looked at her for the longest time, drinking in her features and establishing that everything would happen on his timetable. Tru felt herself hovering on the edge of submissive headspace. It was unlikely that she would sink further or give herself over tonight, but she'd missed being this close to submissive bliss.

He came nearer, and she tilted her head to adjust to the different angle. His gaze remained primarily on her body, though he flicked it up every once in a while to check on her. He touched her ribs lightly, the pressure of his fingertips barely registering. She thought he might try to cup her breast next, but his caress dropped to her waist. He walked around her, tracing his fingertips over her skin.

When he was behind her, he stopped. She felt his palms press to her back, and his caress moved upward, over her shoulders and down her arms. She felt his lips on her nape. Just as he'd touched her, his kisses moved over her flesh with an almost unbearable lack of pressure.

At last his teeth scraped the shell of her ear. "You're so fucking beautiful. I'm going to make you come several times tonight. I ask only that you thank me after each orgasm."

Given his tone, he wasn't asking. Tru shivered because of the things his teeth and lips were doing to her neck. "I will."

He gripped her neck and part of her jaw, tilting her head back so that he could ravage her mouth with a penetrating kiss. She moaned and leaned her back against his strong, broad chest. Passion exploded, and he turned her to face him. While he plundered between her lips, his hands roamed her body, touching every inch with equal fervor.

Tru slid her hands under his jacket and pushed it off his shoulders. He temporarily paused his exploration of her body to shed the material, and then he removed his holster and set it on the dresser next to the television before returning to her. Now that she could touch it, she wanted to bare his magnificent chest. She attacked the buttons, fumbling to undo them without impeding his access to her body. Just as she finished the last one, he gripped her hair hard and yanked, breaking the endless kiss.

"Condoms," he said. "I need to run to my room to get them."

She'd thought ahead. "There's a box in the nightstand. I took a gamble and got extra large. You seemed to be packing quite a package this afternoon. I was hoping it wasn't your gun."

He picked her up and tossed her onto the bed, and he landed on top, bouncing her deeper into the mattress. Pressing his pelvis into her stomach, he said, "It wasn't a gun."

Through the fabric of his pants, she caressed his cock. Yeah, she'd picked up the right size. She purred in anticipation. "I guess you're just happy to see me."

He closed his hands around her wrists and pinned them to the bed. "Don't get ahead of yourself, princess."

Her pussy, which had been moist before, was wet now. She temporarily forgot to breathe.

He dipped his head and laved his tongue over her nipple, teasing it to a sharp peak before giving the same treatment to the other one. This one, he sucked between his luscious lips, stretching it until she cried out. Back and forth he went, torturing her nipples as she writhed. He held her in place with his hands on her wrists and the weight of his pelvis against hers. Every now and then, when her squeaks and yelps became too loud, he would leave off and kiss her lips. But those kisses never lasted too long, and he always returned to her nipples, which were now as sore as if he'd used clamps.

She bucked, and he let go of one wrist to press down on her hip. Tru tried to thread her fingers through his hair to yank him away from her abused breasts, but his hair was too short to provide a handhold. He trapped that wrist again, and now he pinned both wrists over her head with one hand. He gazed into her eyes, his brown irises dark with passion and a rush of power. If she called yellow, he would stop, but she didn't want to do that. She wanted to know that he wouldn't be swayed by her fight, that he'd make sure his will prevailed. With a knowing grin, he planted a brief kiss on her lips and returned to the torture of her nipples. She stopped fighting and surrendered to his mastery. All of a sudden, her body stiffened as an unexpected climax washed through her. Stunned, Tru couldn't cry out.

He released her nipple with a loud pop and smacked his lips. "You have sweet tits, princess. They're so responsive."

She struggled for words. Her head screamed them, but her vocal cords didn't recall how to function. Soon the aftereffects of the orgasm waned, and she remembered his one request. "Thank you."

He knelt up and scooted back. Standing next to the bed, he gazed down at her. "I love that you left your shoes on. Nothing begs to be fucked like a woman wearing only high heels." He watched her closely, and she wondered if he was looking to see how his choice of words affected her. "Bend your knees and spread your legs. Show me that wet pussy."

She did as he asked, baring herself so that he could see everything. He shed his shirt the rest of the way and unbuckled his belt. The thin strip of leather slid from the loops, and she wondered if he was any good at impact play. In talented hands, that belt could make her beg him to fuck her.

But it was too soon for that. He tossed it onto the chair with the rest of their clothes, and his pants followed. Soon he stood before her naked. He paused to let her look. His glorious chest—the one that had stolen her breath only that morning—rippled with muscles that glistened in the lamplight. She drank in the sight of his narrow hips and long legs. Muscle corded his every inch, which she noted as her gaze locked onto his thick cock jutting from a nest of curls. Lord, he was magnificent. She took a mental picture because she knew she'd be envisioning Jed in this position the next time she masturbated. "Fuck me," she implored. "Fuck me hard."

In response, he leaned down and dragged a single finger through her wetness. He stroked her from hole to clit, stopping every few passes to circle the swollen bundle of nerves. She quivered and thrust her hips until he lifted his finger away.

"Put your hands above your head and keep them there, and refrain from moving at all."

With that order, she knew that he would have preferred to tie her up. She would like that as well, but not until she knew him better. Bondage was serious business, and she hadn't known him long enough to trust him. For the first time with a lover, she was sad that they wouldn't be together long enough to get to that level.

Obediently she lifted her hands and gripped the edge of the bed. He smiled his praise, and then he bent over and closed his lips over her clit. He sucked it gently at first, light pulls that felt good. But soon the pressure increased, and pleasant shards of pain traveled to her core. She struggled not to writhe or fuck her pussy against his mouth.

"Oh, Jed. Yes. That hurts just the right amount."

He slid two fingers into her vagina and curved them in a search for her sweet spot. He fucked her with his fingers while he sucked her clit. Tru felt her body become lighter and longer, a prelude to an orgasm.

Jed released her clit and withdrew his fingers. "Where are the condoms, princess? I need to be inside this sweet pussy right now."

She pointed to the nightstand, which was closer to her than to him. She was more than willing to get them, but he'd told her not to move.

He came around the bed. She heard the drawer scrape open, followed by the sounds of him messing with the box. "You're doing a great job staying still, princess. Right now, I want you to move so that your head is on the pillow, but I want you to keep your body in the same pose. You can grip the pillow or brace your hands on the headboard."

Tru scooted around. Once she was how he wanted, he settled between her legs and positioned the head of his cock at her entrance. Her entire body trembled in anticipation, and her clit throbbed to the same rhythm as her sore nipples. He kissed her, slowly and languorously, as if this lazy kiss was the whole point of the evening.

When he ended the kiss, he eased his thickness into her body. Degrees of bliss manifested in his expression, as did determination. "You feel so fucking good, Tru. I'm glad you like it rough, but remember to use your safeword if I get too rough."

His cock filled her, and it felt wonderful. Shocks of pleasure ran through her body even though he hadn't really done anything. "I will." Fat chance. There was almost no chance that he'd get too rough. Her pussy luxuriated in rough play, and he'd concentrated most of the torture on her breasts.

"Brace yourself, princess. For this, you're allowed to move, as long as you keep your hands above your head." With that, he withdrew almost all the way. Her pussy protested the loss, but it rejoiced when he slammed into her. Now she knew why he'd warned her to brace herself. She switched from holding onto the pillow to pressing the flat of her palm against the headboard. If he fucked this hard the whole time, he was going to bang her head into the headboard.

He lost no time. Bracing his weight on his forearms, he fucked her with wild abandon. With the restriction on movement lifted, she tilted her hips to meet his thrusts. He growled, a feral sound that matched the primal rhythm he set. She wanted to participate more, but he fucked her so fast that she couldn't keep up. With a desperate cry, she wrapped her legs around his waist and held on for dear life. She was the submissive in this. She was the vessel receiving the pleasure and pain he dished out, and she felt herself surrender even though she'd thought it wouldn't be possible. Her pleasure no longer mattered. It was an afterthought, a nice byproduct, but it was no longer the goal. She wanted to serve him, to deliver pleasure to him. She sobbed with this need, and the second climax washed over her.

No longer able to stay locked around his waist, her legs fell open. "Thank you," she whispered, half-wondering if it was lost in the roar of their heartbeats.

"More," he said. "I want you to come again." He slowed, varying his pace and the force of his thrusts. He slid a hand under her ass and squeezed. He rubbed and scratched, and then he hiked her right leg up. He hooked it over his shoulder, and then he did the same thing with her other leg. This changed the angle of his thrusts and exposed her ass. He smacked her lightly.

Tru blinked, surprised that he'd remembered. "Harder," she said. "I don't bruise easily, and it's okay to leave a handprint."

The next one stung, though it wasn't hard enough to leave a mark. He smacked her ass as he fucked her, and that combined with the feeling of helplessness from being pinned down, completely at his mercy. It didn't take long for her to climax again. This one was larger, and she felt her pussy contract around his cock.

Jed's eyes rolled back into his head. With a loud moan, he came hard. He collapsed on top of her, his body heaving with the force of his orgasm. She slid her legs from his shoulders and wrapped him in her embrace. They lay there, in a tangle of limbs, while their bodies cooled.

She knew when he regained awareness because he rolled them so that he cradled her in his arms, and he used a tissue to dispose of the condom. She may have drifted off for a little while because she awoke to him kissing her cheeks, eyelids, and temples. "That was amazing, Tru. You're a very well-behaved submissive."

She preened under his praise, but she brushed it off before it could penetrate too far. "You caught me on a good day."

"How's your ass?"

"Fine." She traced her fingertip down his chest, over his hip, and down his thigh until she couldn't reach anymore. Then she reversed direction. "My nipples and pussy are a little sore, but nothing that would prohibit round two."

He shifted under her caresses. "You keep touching me like that, and round two is going to come sooner than you think."

She kissed a path along his collarbone and closed her hand around his semi-hard cock. "I'll get you ready."

He kissed her, the long, lingering kind that bought him recovery time and robbed her of every thought. When it ended, he touched her hair gently, and that granite look was back in his eyes. "Use your mouth."

Challenge accepted. She sat up and prepared to position herself between his legs, but he grabbed her arm.

"Kneel right here." He patted the place next to his hip. "Keep your ass in the air and your knees apart."

She did as he said, and she responded when he adjusted her position so that he could reach her pussy. She wrapped her hand around the base of his cock and licked his crown.

He pushed her hair out of the way. "I want to watch that gorgeous mouth suck my dick."

She made a sound of acquiescence that vibrated around his cock and made him suck in a breath. Pleased at his reaction, she set to work coaxing him from half mast to full sail. It wasn't long before she felt his fingers caressing the tender parts of her pussy. This was such an alpha male move—reminding her that she belonged to him, at least for the night, while she carried out his orders.

She did her best to ignore the fingers circling her clit and penetrating deep into her pussy while she found her submissive headspace and concentrated on her task. She was doing well when she felt his touch at her back entrance. It had been so many years since anyone had dared to explore that area that it jarred her concentration.

"Have you ever been fucked here?"

She paused in her ministrations—he was almost there—to answer. "Yes, but not in a long time."

"Did you like it?"

She'd loved it, but that wasn't on the table tonight. That was a gift she reserved for a Master or a Sir. The act was one of deep submission, not one for casual, slightly kinky sex. "In a way."

He got the message, and his caress disappeared.

Without further discussion, she resumed giving him head. This time, she fondled his sac, and his cock finished lengthening. Now she sucked his cock in earnest, taking him as far into her mouth as she could.

He tugged at her hair, pulling her away. "I'm not going to come in your mouth tonight. Put a condom on me, princess. You're going riding."

She ripped open a second foil wrapper and rolled the clear, tight sheath over his long, thick cock. Her pussy pulsed, anticipating a repeat performance. She positioned herself over him, and he lined his cock up with her entrance. If she had any plans of controlling this, he disabused her of the notion. Once his tip was in, he gripped her hips and pulled her down.

"I want to see you play with your clit as you fuck me, princess." He bucked his pelvis to get her going.

Tru knew this performance was for his pleasure, just as her striptease had been. She closed her eyes and rocked her hips.

"Open your eyes. Look at me."

She did, and she watched shades of wonder pass over his features as she masturbated on his cock. He played as he studied her, lightly rolling her sore nipples between his thumb and forefinger until she whimpered. Then he squeezed sharply.

"You would look lovely in a pair of clover clamps." He clamped his hands on her hips and took control of the rhythm. "With a single chain connecting them together." He lifted her several inches and fucked her at an impossibly fast rate. "Weights that would swing as I pounded into you, and you'd cry out, not sure whether you were doing so out of pleasure or pain."

It sounded like a lovely, impossible dream. She said nothing because it wasn't a negotiation. He was fantasizing, and she liked his fantasy.

Suddenly he lifted her off him. In a flash, he positioned her on her elbows and knees, and he knelt behind her. He entered her pussy as if he owned it, sliding in and staking his claim. Then he grabbed a handful of her hair and slapped her ass. He fucked her with quick, shallow strokes. "Touch your clit, princess. I want to hear you come one more time."

With the electricity that raced through her body from the hair pulling and the excitement from the sharp slaps he delivered to her ass, she didn't need to touch her clit. By the time her trembling hand got there, her pussy had gone into convulsions. She cried out, the sound going on and on, drawn out by his relentless thrusts. Just when she thought she was going to die from pleasure overload, he buried himself deep and shouted his climax.

The Abiding Tide/Day 2—*Draft*
Bike riding on an oceanside trail............4
Kayaking excursion...............................5
Dinner with a hot FBI agent..................2*

Dessert with a hot FBI agent...................5
*C'mon now—he interrogated me about the case.

Chapter Eight

An annoying chirp noise, like the sound a smoke detector makes when the battery has run low, roused him from a deep sleep. The bed was unfamiliar, as was the woman with her naked back and bottom plastered to his right side. Traveling this much, he sometimes lost track of reality, but not this time. The woman sound asleep next to him wasn't someone he'd soon forget. Tru Martin was an amazing woman—beautiful, bold, intelligent, submissive, and she had a great sense of humor. If he played his cards right, he might be able to keep seeing her even after he left The Abiding Tide.

The chirping noise happened again, and he realized it was the alarm on his phone. Time to get up. Brandy would be expecting him to be ready for a full day of investigating, especially since she'd essentially given him half a day off yesterday. She'd expected him to find out if Tru knew anything more than what she'd said to Liam, and he'd come through in an unexpected way. He knew that Brandy and Avery had spent the evening following up on the new lead. If Tru hadn't asked him into her room last night, he would have joined his fellow agents and burned as much midnight oil as it took to track down every aspect of the lead.

He rolled from bed carefully so that he didn't disturb Tru. Using the bright glow of light outlining the curtains, he made his way to the chair where he'd draped his clothes, and he dug in his inside jacket pocket for the phone. Just as he pulled it from the pocket, it chirped again.

Tru shifted, lifted her head, and looked toward the sound. "Is that yours?" Judging from the slur in her voice, she wasn't quite awake.

"Yeah." He kept his volume low. "I have to go to work. You can go back to sleep. We're still on for dinner?"

She rested her head back on the pillow. "Okay. Have a good day."

He dressed and exited the room, making sure the automatic locks engaged before returning to his room for a quick shower and a change of clothes. Twenty minutes later, he held a hasty sandwich made from toast, bacon, and scrambled eggs in one hand and a travel cup of coffee in the other. Avery had snagged the front seat and Brandy drove, so he didn't have a cup holder for his coffee that would make it easier to eat breakfast on the go.

"The coroner's report is ready. She said cause of death was blunt force trauma to the back of the head." Avery's voice drifted to the backseat as she read through the report that had been uploaded sometime that morning. "The other injuries were post-mortem."

"Was it murder?" Jed would have liked to read the report for himself, but there was no way Avery was going to give him the tablet until she was finished reading it first.

"Inconclusive. He could have slipped and fell, hit his head on a rock. The water washed away any evidence that might have been there. Time of death is Sunday night between eleven and one." Avery fell silent as she read more.

"Looks like your girlfriend is in the clear," Brandy said. "She didn't check in until Monday night."

As he had plans along those lines, he didn't dispute her labeling of Tru. "It also means that when his wife checked out, she knew he was missing, and she failed to report it." Their investigation yesterday had turned up the fact that Zarah Braithwaite—not Johnson—had checked out of the room just before eight in the morning.

"Jordan called last night." Brandy sipped her coffee and swerved to avoid a small furry lump that darted into the road. "He said they found a Pigeon's Blood ruby, and that led their search in a different direction. They also found four unmarked diamonds."

"Unmarked?" He wasn't all that familiar with precious gems, but he had done enough research to know that Pigeon's Blood rubies, the rarest and most expensive gems in the world, were verboten because the mines were controlled by the military junta in Myanmar. That kind of scum perpetrated all sorts of human rights violations on the local populations of the areas they controlled.

"Gems that have gone through the KPCS have serial numbers laser inscribed on them. It's how you know they're legitimate." She took a corner without slowing down enough. Jed and Avery were thrown the other way, but they were used to Brandy's driving, and they took steps to counterbalance. Jed believed that in another life, Brandy had been a racecar driver. If she wanted, there was still time in this incarnation to take up the sport.

"So there's no way to tell where the diamonds originated?" Jed made sure they were on a straight stretch of road before taking a swig of coffee.

"Nope."

"I suspect Africa," Avery said. "Most conflict diamonds come from central or western Africa. And geeks at Quantico recently found connections between The Eye and the Democratic Republic of Congo."

Jed wondered how it happened that Quantico knew something before they did. After all, they were the team specifically assigned to bring down The Eye. "Yeah? What's their source?"

"The drive that Malcolm and Keith found two years ago when they were investigating the murder of Scott Yataines." Avery sniffed disdainfully, or because she had allergies. "Former Chief Lawrence sent it to them when he was trying to keep us from finding out too much about The Eye, and now they won't send it back. They say it has information on other cases and national threats."

If Dare were here, he'd insist on being allowed to hack the central FBI database, and Brandy would veto the suggestion. Jed suppressed the urge to petition in Dare's absence. Maybe it would help quell a little bit of guilt over having slept with the woman his friend found attractive. He reasoned through it, reminding himself that not only had Dare left without a word to Tru, the woman in question had also dismissed any claim Liam might have tried to make. Tru knew what she wanted, and she wasn't the kind of woman to change her mind on a whim. If she'd made promises to Liam, she wouldn't have asked Jed to kiss her that first time.

They made it to Sacramento in record time, and Jed flashed his badge as he followed Brandy and Avery into the medical wing of the FBI field office there. Viewing the body wasn't his favorite part of investigative work, but he donned the required coverings and followed the coroner, Doctor Decet, into the room full of bodies. She was one of those small women who was full of too much energy. He listened while she went over the various injuries on the body, and as he looked at Angelo Braithwaite's face again, he was forced to admit that Tru was right. With his head bashed in, swollen and misshapen, the man no longer resembled the photograph on his file.

"It was definitely murder." Doctor Decet pointed at the back of what used to be Braithwaite's skull. "My best theory is that someone hit him with a stone implement. Given the angle of impact, I estimate their height at about 5'3 or 5'4. Mr. Braithwaite was 5'9, and in reasonably good shape. I don't think he saw the attack coming. There are no defensive wounds. I found no hesitation marks and evidence of at least sixteen peri-mortem blows around the head and neck."

Avery pointed to the massive contusions covering Braithwaite's exposed body. "Rage is the only thing that could make someone continue to beat a dead body."

Doctor Decet shrugged. "Those don't have the same shape as the instrument that delivered the death blow, and they're post-mortem. I'd say they came from being bashed around on the rocks and in the cave where he was found—like a tennis ball in a clothes dryer."

That matched theories the team had already discussed. Jed surveyed the body, looking for anything the coroner might have missed.

"Oh, one other thing." Doctor Decet motioned to Jed. "Help me turn him over."

Jed didn't relish the idea, but he did it anyway. The doctor was a petite woman. He looked around, wondering if she had equipment to help her move the bodies around when she was alone, but he didn't find anything.

She pointed out marks on Braithwaite's heels and the back of his calves. "He was dragged. These are scratches, and I found some particles of sand and rock embedded deep inside. Maybe his shorter assailant hid the body in the cave."

Brandy again indicated the massive, purpled patches covering Braithwaite's body. "You're sure these are all post-mortem?"

Doctor Decet's eyes lit up as she was swept away in the excitement that came with putting clues together on a case. "Yes." She leaned closer to Brandy. "Do you have a suspect?"

"Not yet." Brandy smiled regretfully. They did have a person of interest—Zarah Braithwaite needed to be found. Even if they had a suspect, they wouldn't share that information with anyone outside their team. "We're still gathering evidence."

"Was he married? It's always the husband."

"He had a wife," Avery supplied.

Doctor Decet nodded, and her excitement turned sage. "Wives are notoriously vindictive. Was he cheating?"

Jed pressed his lips together to keep from laughing at the doctor's enthusiasm. She obviously watched a lot of police and medical dramas. "That's all we know. Thank you for your help, Doctor Decet." He handed her a card. "I know that you're still waiting on some tests. Please call when those results come in."

She took the card, and some of the wind went out of her sails as she realized she wasn't going to be invited to join the team. "Oh. Okay. Sure."

Doctor Decet shook hands with Brandy and Avery, and when it was his turn, Jed dialed up his natural charm. "You've been tremendously helpful. Remember to call if anything comes up." He held her hand a second longer than necessary, and she responded with a brighter smile and the return of her energetic aura. A little goodwill went a long way.

"I will."

Liam finished reading the coroner's report on the plane. Their search of Angelo Braithwaite's apartment had turned up a marriage where the paperwork hadn't been properly processed, and so it was invalid, five stolen precious gems, and one irate daughter. Angela Braithwaite did not like her step-mother, a woman merely five years older, and she had flung a multitude of accusations at the woman. According to Angela, Zarah had been homeless when she'd met Angelo. Within a month, she'd convinced the older man to marry her. Six months later, Angelo had left the security of his desk job for the uncertainty of living off commission because his wife wanted to travel.

"Jed came up with a lead." Jordan interrupted Liam's thoughts. "It seems Ms. Martin recalls running into the Braithwaites at another inn. Brandy, Avery, and Jed are there now, questioning the owner and the night clerk."

Liam made a thoughtful noise. That wasn't exactly the direction in which Brandy had been thinking when she'd asserted that Tru knew more than she had told them. However, her instincts had been correct since they'd gleaned another lead from Tru. "I wonder why she didn't make the connection earlier?"

"She saw a photo of Braithwaite alive. Avery said it took Ms. Martin all day to remember where she'd seen Braithwaite. She didn't connect it to the body she'd found at all." Jordan checked the time. "I need to call Amy. She has an event tonight, so we won't get to talk unless I call now."

Though he knew that Jordan had already texted Amy several times today, Liam didn't say anything. Maybe one day he'd understand this obsessive need some men had to communicate with their girlfriends. Right now it just seemed like Jordan was pussy whipped. Liam watched Jordan relocate to the far corner of this section of the plane, a soft smile curving his mouth as he listened to the woman on the other end.

Then again, maybe the bastard was lucky. For as long as Liam could remember, women had been a disposable commodity. They were sexy and soft, but even when he'd been in a relationship, Liam had found that he rarely thought of a woman unless she was right next to him. He'd been dumped for not calling and not caring, and he hadn't particularly mourned any of those losses. But Tru was different. She'd been on his mind since they'd met. A part of Liam awoke—one that fixated on a single woman in a way that had never happened before—and it buzzed with anticipation. In a few hours he'd be back at The Abiding Tide, and he'd have another chance to get to know Tru. Memories of that last kiss tingled on his lips and tongue. Maybe she'd be amenable to having dinner with him? He could take her away from the inn so that they could have some time alone. As much as he loved his FBI family, if they were around, they'd eventually interrupt the date.

The day had flown by. The Abiding Tide had staged a cooking class where they made crème brulee French toast. Guests had laughed and chatted, and Tru had managed to garner a few great quotes to use in her article. It amazed her how flattered people were when she asked for permission to use their words. The B&B was a great place, and she planned to give it a stellar review. Of course she'd have to mention the tragedy and the appearance of the FBI, but she would be sure to emphasize the friendly atmosphere, dozens of activities, and the quality of the rooms. By the time evening rolled around, she had banked three articles for her series. One detailed her grotesque find, the second one highlighted the hiking and birdwatching, and the third focused on the bike tour and kayaking. Jed figured prominently in that one, though she had given him a pseudonym. She'd mention that to him tonight because she didn't want it to be a surprise. Their fling might end tomorrow when she checked out, but she wanted to go out on a positive note.

Jed hadn't specified the time they would meet for dinner, and they had not exchanged phone numbers, so she couldn't call or text to ask him. She took a glass of Prosecco to the deck that overlooked the ocean. The best thing about this trip was that the B&B's she'd booked were all on the ocean. Growing up in Northport, she had a preference for being close to water. Lake Michigan had always been a stone's throw away. The Pacific was vastly larger, though from her vantage point, they seemed remarkably similar. The difference lay in the scent. Lake Michigan smelled fresh and sandy, and the Pacific tinged the air with a briny taste that lingered on her tongue.

Strong hands enveloped her shoulders, and she recognized Jed's touch. Pleasure radiated from the warmth of his palms. Happiness lighting her from the inside, she turned to see his handsome face and the sexy smile curling his kissable lips. "Hey. How was your day?"

He kissed her cheek. "Better now. Were you waiting long?"

Honestly she had no idea how long she'd been waiting. Tru excelled at solitude, and though she was often alone, she was rarely lonely. She'd passed the time by composing bits of her next article in her head and in luxuriating in the simplicity of just being alive. She set her wine glass on the railing and threaded her fingers through his. "You're worth the wait."

"Glad to hear it." He leaned down, intent on stealing a kiss.

"You'll also be glad to hear that you didn't make my top ten list."

His intention arrested, he paused inches from her lips. "I didn't?"

"Nope. Last night did not rate a place on my top ten list of worst dates. Your finesse and stamina definitely saved the night."

A low chuckle vibrated from his chest, and he resumed his quest for a kiss. His lips had barely grazed hers when they were interrupted.

"Seriously? This is how you keep an eye on her?"

Tru looked over to see Liam standing two feet away, hands on hips, and waves of anger emanating from his tight expression. She hadn't expected to see him ever again. Her jaw dropped, and she jerked away from Jed's kiss. "Liam?"

"I see you do remember me." He came closer and directed the entirety of his ire at Jed. Rage simmered below the surface, giving her a first glimpse at just how powerful he could be. She'd known he was strong, and she'd suspected he was dominant, but she hadn't realized that he had a dangerous edge. "I asked you to watch her, to be there for her, not to make a move on her." His fists clenched and flexed, thick tendons clamoring to make contact with Jed's face.

Though it looked like they were evenly matched, Jed didn't appear concerned about the physical threat Liam posed. He released one of her hands in order to face Liam, but he kept hold of her other one. "You left. You didn't bother to tell her you were going, and the two times you've called, you haven't asked about her. We both assumed you'd moved on."

"Well, I didn't."

Shocked that Liam thought he had a claim, Tru didn't know what to make of his jealousy. She'd liked him, but he'd left, exiting her life without saying goodbye. Whatever the issue and her role in it, she didn't want to see them come to blows. "Liam, it was one kiss, not a promise or commitment. I mean, you said you'd see me for breakfast, and when I stopped by your room, I found out that you'd gone."

"And that's when Jed moved in. He sensed a weakness, and he took advantage of it." His blue eyes flashed like a storm in the night.

"Hold up." Jed put up a cautioning hand. "That's not how it happened. I told her that you were gone, and later we went kayaking together. We hit it off, and the rest is history. You know the saying—once you have black, you never go back."

Liam's lips became a slash, the lightning of his internal storm. "You're half Asian, asshole, a quarter white, and only a quarter black. That saying is stupid for a lot of reasons, and not just because it's on the list of crap you say."

Tru had wondered about the ingredients of Jed's multiracial makeup, but she hadn't asked because she felt it wasn't her business unless he wanted to tell her. Right now she had other concerns. Jed dropped her hand and took a step toward Liam. Sliding between them, she parked one hand on Liam's chest and the other on Jed's. "Gentlemen, let's not hurl insults. Really, there's nothing to get upset about."

"He moved in on my territory." Liam's lip curled, a sexy growl that made her want to rub her body against his. Damn, but these were two very attractive men—and dominant to boot. She imagined what it would be like to be sandwiched between their naked bodies, and a tingling began at the apex of her thighs.

Shaking the thought away, Tru forced herself to focus on the real problem. She narrowed her eyes in Liam's direction. "I'm not your territory."

"Yeah, she's mine." Jed's chest puffed out, pushing against her palm.

Tru hated to burst his bubble, but it had to be done. "I'm not yours either."

He tore his glare from Liam and turned it on her. "What?"

It took a supreme act of will not to step back or lower her gaze. "Tonight is my last night here, and then I'm moving on to my next job. You're almost finished here as well, and who knows where your investigation will take you next? It's a fling, Jed. Neither of you has a claim to me."

That seemed to take the wind out of both their sails, and though each man relaxed, neither backed off. They studied one another, and Tru had no idea what either of them was thinking.

"You're friends, right?"

Silence greeted her question. After a time, Liam managed a curt nod, though his steady gaze remained glued to Jed.

"And you work together? You're a team?"

This time she didn't have to wait as long for a reply. Without seeming to move, Jed answered. "Yes."

"Then maybe you should look at this as an opportunity to work together in a different way." The need to keep them apart had passed. She slid her palms down each man's chest as she let her hands drop away. "I'm game if you are."

Both men's gazes snapped to her face, surprise and shock mingling in their expressions. Now she had their full attention, and she lobbed a flirty half grin into the mix.

Liam's shock wore off, and he frowned. "Are you suggesting group sex?"

"Yes. Sharing is so much better than fighting. And really, your friendship with Jed is the more important thing here. It'll be there long after I'm gone." This was the first time she had to negotiate this kind of deal. In the past, Alex had taken care of it. Even when she'd suggested a third party, she'd merely brought them to him for a meeting, and he'd handled the details. She hoped she didn't blow it.

Jed looked from her to the door that led to the dining room. "How about we discuss it over dinner? This is too big of a decision to make on an empty stomach, and I don't know if you get delusional when you have low blood sugar and a glass of wine in you."

Chapter Nine

Liam followed Tru and Jed into the dining room, noting the perturbed expression on Tru's face. While he understood that she hadn't liked the way Jed had phrased his reservation, he shared Jed's cautious attitude. Yeah, he liked Tru. He liked her a lot. He'd wanted to spend an evening with her, talking and getting to know one another. If it ended with the two of them alone in her room, then that would be an unexpected bonus. This proposition wasn't one he'd anticipated, and his mind raced with possible scenarios, actions and consequences. He couldn't foresee a related outcome that led to plans to see one another again.

Jed pulled out a chair for Tru, seating her with her back to the wall. If they flanked her at the small, rectangular table, then she would have no easy path for a quick exit. Liam was down with that plan. Jed sat to her left, and he took the seat on her right.

Tru nailed Jed with a sour slant to her mouth. "I'm not delusional, and this is your big decision to make. I've done this before, where it seems you have not. Would you prefer to discuss it without me? Because there will be incidental touching. With three people in one bed, you can't avoid it."

Not sure where he stood on the idea of incidental touching, Liam leaped on the next most obvious conclusion. He leaned closer to Tru. "Have you done this with just men, or have you had threesomes with women?"

"Since I lean mostly toward hetero, there's always a man involved, but I have played with women before.

Usually I'm a beta Domme in that case. Sometimes not. I've subbed for female Dommes before." She placed her hand on his arm. "I shouldn't assume you're a Dom just because you told me that you like to be in charge. Are you?"

He glanced at Jed quickly, wondering if he should claim the title. Jordan had explicitly told him not to go around calling himself a Dom. Liam settled on the truth. "I'm in training."

Her face lit. "Oh, then this will be good for you. You'll get to see a Dom in action, and you'll learn so much." She squeezed his arm, perhaps a little harder than necessary.

Jed's brows lifted. "I guess that means I get to go first. Watch and learn, buddy. You'll see how a real man pleasures a beautiful woman."

Thunder crackled behind Tru's light brown eyes. "Don't do that. Ground rules: No bragging or boasting. No being critical or putting each other down. This isn't a competition—it's a fun-for-all. There is no room for jealousy or pettiness. You will need to work together. You will need to talk to each other and solve issues that arise."

He was tempted to laugh at her use of 'arise,' but he held his immature sense of humor in check. He looked at Jed, analyzing his reaction. With a slight lift of his shoulders and a nod, Jed let him know that he was in. Liam nodded in agreement. "Okay, we're in." He faced Tru. "But you won't be a beta Domme. You're the submissive."

She clasped her hands over her heart. "Oh, this is going to be so much fun. Let's eat, gentlemen. We're going to need energy."

By the time the meal ended, Liam's brain buzzed with terms like safeword and double penetration. Tru had nixed the idea of them both having her at the same time. She'd felt it wasn't prudent to give it a try their first time in a ménage situation.

"I'm going upstairs to freshen up. Wait fifteen minutes, and then come to my room." She pressed a kiss to his cheek and another to Jed's, and then she disappeared from the dining room.

Liam regarded Jed curiously. "Are you sure about this?"

Jed lifted one shoulder in an entirely noncommittal gesture. "I'm always open to trying new things. Besides, if we'd turned her down, then this would be the last of her we'd see. I like her, Liam. She's special. Unusual. She's fun to be with, and she loves adventure and exploration."

Having spent far less time with her, Liam didn't know her as well, but he could see glimmers of those attributes. However he wasn't going to let that keep him from a woman he found attractive and intriguing. "I like her too. Just know that I intend to pursue her afterward. I'll share her for a night, and then I'd like you to step aside."

Jed laughed, a mirthless chuckle. "No go, buddy. Not only would I not step aside, but she's made her position clear. We're either going to have to pursue her together or not at all."

Liam tapped his fingertips on the table as he considered whether he'd be willing to share a woman. Honestly he didn't know. The idea was wholly outside his experience. "I guess tonight will be a litmus test."

Jordan plopped down in the seat Tru had vacated. "Brandy and Avery filled me in on what's been going on while we were gone. It's good to see that you two aren't beating the shit out of each other."

So far Jordan had been a good mentor. He'd made Liam do some thinking, talking, writing, and research in his quest to find out what kind of Dom he wanted to be. Jordan answered all of Liam's questions without judgment, so Liam didn't feel the need to hold back now. "Have you ever had a threesome with a woman? Two Doms and a sub?"

"I have not." Jordan didn't appear surprised. "But I know people who are in poly relationships. It's difficult to sustain. Communication is the key to any successful relationship, but with three people, it's exponentially more complicated. Is that what you've proposed to Ms. Martin?"

"It was her idea." Jed sipped a glass of water that had remained untouched throughout the meal. "Apparently she has experience with threesomes."

Jordan turned a troubled frown in Liam's direction. "Don't do anything you're not comfortable doing. My advice is to just dominate her. Don't engage in kink at this point."

"She won't let us." Jed outlined Tru's hard limits for tonight's tryst. "Basically she only consented to being dominated."

"I like that she's cautious." Liam didn't see a problem with tonight's parameters. "Relatively speaking."

"And experienced." Jordan leaned back and crossed his arms in a deceptively relaxed pose. "Which brings up the question of how you're going to balance power. Jed is experienced, and you are not."

Coming from anyone else, Liam would have felt like it was a critical statement. The truth of it wouldn't matter. But coming from Jordan, it forced him to think about the implications. Did this put him in a beta Dom position? That option didn't appeal to him.

Jed chucked him on the shoulder. "I got your back, buddy. Do what comes naturally, and I'll let you know if you cross a line. Tru has safewords, so she'll let you know as well."

In the field Liam had no doubt that Jed had his back, and this wouldn't be any different. They were a team. He looked at his phone to check the time. "It's been twelve minutes."

Five minutes later, he and Jed faced the door to Tru's room. Jed mumbled a reminder. "Remember—safewords are for Doms too. It's always better to call a time-out than to continue when you know something isn't working. A submissive will respect a Dom who is concerned for her safety and pleasure."

He also knew he could ask for her color, which was the D/s equivalent of a status update. Without responding, he knocked. The door opened immediately, and he wondered if she'd been standing behind the door, listening for them. She'd changed into a loose T-shirt and sweat pants, and though she wore it well, he didn't consider it the sexiest attire. Her dress at dinner had clung to her body and highlighted the swell of her breasts. The thin, decorative scarf accent had been held in place around her neck by a silver clip that reminded him of handcuffs.

"Gentlemen, I'd wondered if you'd changed your minds." She pushed the door wider and stepped back to let them pass.

Liam entered first. He stopped in front of her, cradled her head in one hand, and kissed her the way he had two nights ago. The same passion sparked to life, and the kiss deepened. When he finally released her, she looked a little dazed, and she wore a soft smile.

She didn't get time to recover because Jed claimed her for the next kiss. He held her the same way Liam had, but he parked his free hand on Tru's ass and lifted her against him. Seeing Jed's hand on her ass, a proprietary move that elicited a small squeak of pleasure from Tru, sent fire racing through Liam's system. In the past, he'd watched people have sex, and he'd found it hot and arousing. Now that a woman he liked was involved, it only increased his desire.

Tearing his gaze from the erotic sight, he closed and locked the door. The click seemed to jolt awareness into Jed, and he ended the kiss. Jed smiled at Tru. "We didn't change our minds, princess. But I have to ask if you're still on board. Your outfit says that you've resigned yourself to a night on the sofa watching a movie."

She looked down, her frown communicating that she didn't share his opinion. "These sweats look great on me."

"They do, but they don't scream 'take me, I'm yours.' I'm just saying that if you changed your mind, you need to let us know." Jed ran his fingertips up and down her spine. It could have been a soothing gesture, or he might have been feeling for a bra.

She giggled and pushed him away. Jed took a step back, but he made it look like it had been his idea. Liam had the feeling that she was up to something. She looked from Jed to Liam. "Take me, I'm yours and yours."

Liam started forward. If Jed wanted to participate, then he'd better jump in.

"Wait." Jed circled his finger in the air. "Strip. Put on a show for us."

Just like that, her flippant attitude fell away. Like a shroud, submission enveloped her body and subdued her soul. Her gaze dropped, and he recognized the mistake he'd almost made. She wasn't a pushover, but when she submitted, she did it all the way. He also recognized the skillful way Jed had assumed control of the situation. It was a signal—originating from him instead of her—that the scene had begun.

Jed sat at the foot of the bed, and Liam joined him. They faced Tru expectantly, and she didn't disappoint. With a push, her sweats whished down her legs to pool at her feet. She kicked them away as she whipped her shirt off over her head. Beneath the clothes meant for lounging, she wore a black teddy and thigh-high stockings. The lacy teddy had two pieces, so a strip of her sexy midriff separated the upper part from the thong on the lower half.

"Damn." The word whooshed from Liam. She was breathtaking.

A shy smile curved Tru's lips. "I'm glad you like it. I would have answered the door wearing this, but with my luck, it'd be the concierge."

Liam wasn't sure he wanted to continue the striptease. His dick was already hardening, and she looked so sexy in that outfit. It would be a shame to let it go to waste. She parked one foot between them and rolled the stocking down to reveal legs that looked great with or without lingerie. Liam noticed Jed's fingers flex, and he knew his buddy was also grappling with the urge to not let her finish.

She repeated the move with her other leg, but this time Liam was treated to a prime view of her pink pussy already glistening with juices. The striptease turned her on as much as it did them. Turning her back to them, she hooked two thumbs under the waist of her thong, and she bent over as she slid it down her legs. He shifted, ready to pounce like a panther in heat. As she unbent, she kept her legs spread shoulder-width apart. When she was fully erect, she tossed her hair and looked over her shoulder at them, openly enjoying their reaction.

She grinned playfully, and then she tossed her thong into Liam's lap. Next time, he was going to insist on a lap dance.

Her lacy top was the last to go. Crossing her arms over her chest, she held it up for the space of two heartbeats, and then she let it drop. Once it was gone, she stopped performing and stood before them in a classic submissive stance.

Two steps away, she waited. Liam rose, and her breath hitched. He closed the distance, and though she didn't move, the tension in the air thickened. Wordlessly he threaded his fingers through her hair at her nape and pulled lightly. She exhaled, the slightest hint of a moan hiding behind the sound, and followed his unspoken order to tilt her head back. Her gaze lifted as well, and it fastened on his lips. Too greedy to make her wait, he feasted on her lips, massaging his against hers until he couldn't deny his need for more. Then he plunged his tongue into her mouth. She melted against him, and he felt the tentative weight of her hands traveling up his chest to rest on his shoulders. With every inch, she asked permission and begged for the right. Power suffused his limbs. He tightened his grip on her hair and bit her lip.

She mewed, a sound halfway between pleasure and pain, and he broke away. Jed took his place, and he showered her face with kisses. Liam stood back and concentrated on breathing. If he lost control and let the power go to his head, then he would no longer be thinking of her, and it was his responsibility to make sure she enjoyed the experience.

Jed's kisses ventured lower, concentrating on her neck and shoulders. He nipped the tender flesh there, leaving behind a string of tiny pink marks. Tru opened her eyes and looked over Jed to Liam. She gazed at him, passion lightening her eyes to golden brown and inviting him closer.

He moved to stand behind her, and he peppered her exposed shoulder with tender kisses. She leaned against his chest, and Jed trailed lower, sucking kisses across her abdomen and hips. Liam could guess Jed's intention, so he wrapped an arm around her waist and angled her head back to kiss him again. He'd keep himself under control this time. As he kissed her, he cupped one breast and teased the nipple to a stiff point.

Jed lifted one of her legs and slung it over his shoulder. He licked her pussy, his tongue flicking over her clit, and then he closed his lips around the magic nub. Tru's body jerked, and Liam tightened his hold. He kissed her again, gagging her with his tongue and swallowing her moans. She fumbled, grabbing at his forearms, shoulders, and hair, but never settling on one place. He pinched her nipple, rolling it cruelly between his thumb and forefinger, and she settled on pulling his hair with one hand and digging her nails into his forearm. Her body bowed and stiffened, and she cried out in his mouth. He finally stopped the endless kiss. She slumped against him, panting and trembling.

Jed sat back on his heels and licked his fingers. "Princess, if fruit tasted like this, I'd eat it every day."

Her attempt at a laugh bordered on pathetic. "Thank you," she squeaked out.

Liam didn't recall ever seeing Jed eat fruit, not that he paid much attention to things like that. He drew a finger through her wetness and sucked it from his finger. "Mmm. I could go for some of that." He scooped her up in his arms and set her on the bed. She would look so good tied down, but she'd barred bondage. He wrapped a hand around each of her ankles and wrenched her legs apart. She lay there, with her legs spread and her hands positioned limply over her abdomen, and watched him.

He shucked his shirt, and her lips parted. She drank him in, staring with open appreciation at his chiseled chest. Long hours practicing Tae Kwan Do had produced this body, and he was proud of it.

"She's a chest woman." Jed's observation interrupted his musings. "That first morning, I had just gotten out of the shower when she knocked. I swear she stared for a full minute before saying anything."

A blush bloomed on Tru's neck and chest. "It's still not my birthday."

Jed unbuttoned his shirt, a slow striptease that held Tru's attention. While she was distracted, Liam lowered his torso to the bed and licked her glistening pussy. Her entire body jerked, and she cried out when he got to her clit.

"It's sensitive, Liam." Her tone implored him to be gentle, but a devilish streak warned him not to listen. The female body was an amazing machine. She was going to come again.

He used his shoulder and arm to hold her hips still, and he dived into his work. She wiggled at first, but gradually she accepted that he wasn't going to let her take control. Soon she tilted her hips to give him better access, and she started making noises that sounded like a cross between a yelp and a moan. When he glanced up, he found that Jed was torturing her nipples. He alternated sucking viciously with pinching and rolling.

"Yes, please," she breathed. "Oh, yes. Please don't stop."

Liam tasted her again, and he didn't stop until she cried out and a fresh wave of cream gushed from her vagina. The score was 1-1, and he passed the ball to Jed. Liam perched on the edge of the bed and watched Jed slide until he lay next to her. He turned her onto her side, and he pressed her body to his. Their kiss had an unexpected tenderness, and Tru's hands were suddenly in motion. She undid Jed's pants in seconds, and then she used her feet to help kick them the rest of the way off his legs.

Jed motioned to the bedside table. "Dare, can you grab a condom for me?"

Liam took out several condoms, and he threw one to his buddy.

Jed turned Tru around so that her ass was against his dick, and then he tilted her to put about a foot between his chest and her back. He lifted her top leg and put it over his, and then he slid a pillow under her head. This position exposed her body to Liam's view and still allowed Jed the access he wanted. He slid his gloved cock into Tru's pussy.

"Touch yourself, princess." Jed's tone made it clear that he'd issued an order. "Show Liam how much you want this."

As Jed fucked her, he continued to pinch and fondle her breasts. She arched into his touch, and she stimulated her clit by circling it with one finger. The entire time, her gaze remained fixed on Liam, and he realized that she enjoyed performing for him as much as he liked to watch her being fucked.

All of a sudden, a loud crack rent the air, and Liam realized that Jed had smacked Tru's ass. Again and again, he hit her cheek, and each time his hand came into contact with her reddened ass, she cried out in ecstasy. It didn't take long for her to climax. Her body seemed to spasm as she moaned so loudly that Liam covered her mouth with his hand.

Jed held her against him, stroking her hair until her sobs of pleasure subsided. He pressed a kiss to her temple. "You're not finished, princess. Liam is going to make you pass out."

Liam wanted to fuck her mouth first. Those luscious, kiss-swollen lips begged to taste his dick.

She nodded and stroked a caress down Jed's cheek. "Thank you."

Liam narrowed his eyes. "Why does she keep thanking you?"

"I told her to thank me for every orgasm I give her."

He'd given her an orgasm. "Why doesn't she thank me?"

Tru struggled to her hands and knees, and then she crawled to him. "You didn't tell me to. Is that what you want, Liam? Thank you for the orgasm. I very much enjoyed it, and I'd love to return the favor."

Something about having her on her hands and knees made his dick jerk. He unbuttoned his pants and lowered them to expose his cock. "Open your mouth."

With a gleeful smile, she obeyed. He traced the purpled tip on her lips before dipping it inside her hot mouth. He let her lick and suck long enough to get it wet, and then he surged forward to fuck her mouth in earnest. Behind her, Jed stirred. He mimed for Liam to pull her hair. Liam grabbed a handful of her thick tresses, and every time he withdrew, he pulled her head back. She moaned, the vibrations traveling through his cock.

Jed knelt up and rained rhythmic spanks over both of her ass cheeks. It occurred to Liam that a flogger would work very well for this situation, but neither of them had brought one and Tru had forbidden toys. Maybe next time she'd consent to bondage and some light flogging.

The combination of hair pulling and spanking did wonders for Tru. Moans and cries sounded in the back of her throat, and the feeling devastated Liam's quest for control. He surged forward, burying his cock as far as she could take, and he came in her mouth.

Chapter Ten

The same chirping that woke her the prior morning called in her dreams, forcing her to the surface. Though she was technically awake, full consciousness returned slowly. A body curved against her back, and another supported her from the front, preventing her from turning completely on her stomach. Enough dim light filtered around the edges of the room's curtains for her to identify Liam in front of her and Jed plastered to her backside. Queen beds were not made to sleep three adults. If she hadn't passed out after that last orgasm, she would have suggested that her two lovers would be more comfortable in their own beds.

The chirping came again, and she tapped Jed's shoulder. He grunted and rolled to his back. Tru eased from under the covers and padded to the bathroom. Though her ass had recovered from the sporadic spankings that both Jed and Liam had delivered, her pussy was still sore. If she hadn't vowed never to take a bath at another hotel, she would have soaked in Epsom salts. If she was still desperate tonight, she might break her oath and indulge in a soak.

Last night had been amazing. Though she'd played with ménage before, each time Alex had been in charge. The second man or woman had either been a submissive, or they'd understood that Alex was ultimately in charge. With Liam and Jed, she didn't get that feeling. They were both in charge, and though they'd worked together very well, they'd each taken what they wanted. It had been heaven. If she were to ever serve a Master again, there would need to be two, and they'd have to share her.

When she emerged from the shower, she heard the sounds of Liam and Jed conversing in hushed tones. That meant they were either talking about work or about her. Wrapped in a towel, she breezed out of the bathroom and threw a smile at her gentlemen, both of whom were dressed and seated on opposite corners at the foot of the bed. "Good morning. I hope you slept well."

Liam stretched his neck, probably seeking to crack it. "Like the dead. You wore me out."

She kissed the top of his head, but she evaded him when he tried to snake an arm around her to keep her there. "I have to pack up and finish my article. Checkout is in two hours."

Jed frowned, so she kissed his head too. "Do you have time to talk about last night?"

She stepped into a pair of cotton, serviceable underwear. Nothing about them invited a man to stay another night. She slid into yoga pants, suitable for a day spent traveling, and then she grabbed a shirt and bra. Those she took into the bathroom to put on. "A little. What's wrong?" Brush-offs were best handled from a distance, especially with Doms. This one-night stand was officially at the top of her Best Of list, and she didn't want to end it with platitudes or false promises to keep in touch.

"You mean, besides the fact that you're avoiding us?" Liam's voice barreled through the door and into the bathroom. She couldn't tell if he was irritated, amused, or both.

She emerged, fully dressed and squeezing the water from her hair into a towel. "I'm not avoiding you. I have a lot to get done this morning."

Jed folded his arms and regarded her stoically. "We want to see you again."

This was unexpected. The transitory nature of their meeting was an established fact. She looked from Jed to Liam. The corner of Liam's mouth turned up in a mirthless smile. "It's true."

She picked up her hairbrush and attacked any knots that lacked the sense to leave when she'd applied conditioner. "I travel a lot for work, and so do you. Even when we're both home, there are still about three hundred miles between us. I appreciate the sentiment—I had an unforgettable time last night too—but it was a single night experience. Besides, you can't improve perfection."

Liam got to his feet, and the firmness of his gaze let her know that the conversation wasn't over. "Let's get breakfast. We'd like to spend a little more time with you—unless you're completely against the idea."

She wasn't against the idea, but she wasn't in favor of it either. Between their attitudes and her visions—which hadn't yet occurred—she was worried that she might find herself heading down that long, winding desert road called Relationship. Something like that didn't fit into her plans. Having a significant other or others wasn't on her bucket list. Still she found herself following Liam and Jed downstairs.

They arrived at the dining room to find it transformed. A long table lined with chafing dishes and ice-filled bowls awaited morning diners. Tru clapped her hands over her mouth and nose in prayer position. They had a waffle bar. Tru didn't know if the chef had read her blog to discover her not-so-secret love of the waffle bar concept, but in any event, this definitely tipped the review scales to a full five stars instead of the four-and-a-half she'd been considering. This setup took her back to her childhood, when her dad used to help run Gram's bed-and-breakfast. Every Sunday morning, he'd put out a waffle bar. Gram had hated it, but Tru had loved it, and her memories of it were inexorably tied to her memories of her father.

Jed put an arm around her shoulders. "Princess? Are you okay?"

"It's a waffle bar."

Liam studied her curiously. "Waffle bars make you cry? It's not that bad, and the food here is pretty good, so I don't think there's anything to cry about."

She wiped a tear away and sniffed. That had been unexpected. She chalked it up to post-scene emotionality. With a Master at her side, she didn't have to worry about the light levels of subdrop she usually experienced, but in this situation, there was no way she wanted them to have to deal with the aftereffects. She could hold it together until she left The Abiding Tide. "I love waffle bars."

Liam and Jed exchanged a look over her head. Though she noticed their bafflement, she ignored it. Jed hugged her closer. "Let's get a table."

Tru led them to a large round table in the hope that other patrons would join them and dilute the conversation. The moment they sat down, a server brought three plates and took their drink order. Tru waited impatiently for her to leave, and then she leaped from her chair. Liam caught up to her at the waffle bar. She loaded a single waffle on her plate and went for the fresh blueberries.

"You really like waffles." Liam stacked three waffles on his plate and surveyed the selection of homemade fruit syrups.

"I love waffle bars," she corrected as she placed two plump blueberries in every other square on her waffle. In the blank ones, she carefully arranged a raspberry-blackberry combination. When she caught Liam studying her plate, she defended her choices. "It's an art."

"I see that."

She drizzled a light maple syrup over it all, and then she added whipped cream. On the way back, she noted that Jed hadn't made it to the waffle bar. He'd been waylaid by the rest of his FBI team. With more than a little relief, she found that his entire team had claimed the rest of the seats at the large round table.

She and Liam sat down, and Jed looked over their plates. He hadn't been sold on the waffle bar idea. She grinned. "You don't have to put fruit on your waffle. There are no rules at a waffle bar. They have bacon. You could put bacon on your waffle, smother the whole thing with syrup, and eat it like a sandwich. It's a heart attack waiting to happen, but you're young and in good shape. I think you can chance it."

The worry lines didn't ease from Jed's face, but Agents Forsythe and Monaghan dragged him from his seat and forced him to face a spread that included a vast amount of locally grown fruit.

Two seats away, Agent Lockmeyer quietly scooted a stack of papers closer. Tru hadn't noticed them before, and she couldn't help that she glanced at them now. Unfortunately a name jumped out at her—Zangari's Fetish Inn. It wasn't too far from where they were. Tru wondered if the murder victim had been a patron or if they were looking into her history.

She cut a perfect square containing two blueberries and threw caution to the wind. "What is your interest in Zangari's?"

"It's part of our investigation." Lockmeyer set the stack of papers on her other side, as far away from Tru as she could get them, and she turned the top sheet upside down.

Tru frowned. "Why?"

Liam touched her arm. "We can't discuss an open case."

She scowled. "Are you investigating me?"

"No. Why? Have you been to Zangari's?" His face remained neutral, but she picked up on the curiosity rooted in his personal interest.

She'd helped Alex convert the old house his grandmother had left him into a BDSM-themed inn, and when she'd served him, she'd visited him there every few weekends for almost three years. However Liam didn't need to know that. "Yes. My friends own it."

Liam looked to Agent Lockmeyer for guidance, and the woman folded her hands on the table and leaned forward. The boss was in. "Ms. Martin, can I call you Tru?"

Tru thought she'd already given permission, but she nodded anyway, and she went on high alert. When an authority figure asked for rights to treat you with familiarity, they inevitably wanted something they didn't think you'd easily give.

"Great. Tru, I wonder if you could help us with something?"

"Of course, Agent Lockmeyer. If it'll help you catch this criminal, I'm in."

"Call me Brandy."

Uh-oh. This was getting serious.

"Tru, we've reached a delicate point in our inquiry. We need to conduct part of our investigation at Zangari's, but the concierge claims they're booked solid. I know that all hotels keep a room or two open for emergencies. Do you think you could persuade your friends to let us book a room?" Brandy leaned back to let the server set down a plate filled with half a grapefruit. It looked like SSA Lockmeyer wasn't a waffle woman.

Tru shook her head. "They're booked months in advance. It's not like a regular inn where anyone can book a room. Alex is very particular about who can stay there, and he sells the bulk of his rooms like a time share. The same couple might commit to visiting four times a year, and they'll get the same room each time, but they have to commit to specific dates upfront."

As a business model, it worked for Alex and his wife, Jewell. It was the best way he'd developed to make sure the Dom/mes were reputable and the subs were genuine. He made it clear that he didn't run a sex club, just a place for those in the lifestyle to vacation without having to hide who they were.

Brandy frowned at Tru's response, but she directed it at her grapefruit. "What if they have a cancellation?"

"His cancellation policy is unforgiving." Leave it to a Dom to punish people for not following the rules. Tru had cautioned against it because she thought it might sour people toward the inn, but so far it had rarely been the case. "And people almost never cancel. Most patrons spend months looking forward to their time at Zangari's. Alex runs regular seminars, classes, and demonstrations. It's an unforgettable experience."

Jed returned as she finished speaking. He set his plate—waffles and bacon in a syrup bath—at the empty place next to her and sat down. "What's unforgettable?"

"Zangari's. I was just explaining to Brandy that there was no way you'd be able to book a room there. But there are other places nearby where you can stay. Alex would be more than willing to answer any questions you have, and if need be, he'll make his staff available to you." Tru didn't see the big deal, and the chances of the entire team being BDSM practitioners was slim to none. They wouldn't all want to stay there.

At this, Agent Monaghan—she may as well call him by his name—Jordan grimaced. "Here's the thing—we need to have a two-pronged approach, with one part being undercover. That's why we need to register as guests."

Tru didn't like that these agents were targeting her friends. She scowled. "Alex and Jewell run an above-board establishment. As far as I know, no murders have happened there. What, exactly, are you looking for?"

"We can't disclose that," Brandy said. "But hundreds of lives and national security are at stake."

Tru had suspected this investigation wasn't about one murder. The FBI only took an interest when there were larger implications. She sighed. "I could vouch for you. It might work, but then again, it might not. Alex is picky about who he lets stay. Doms have to be vetted, and if he thinks you hired the sub, like she's an escort or professional, he'll throw you both out. Who is going?"

Jordan pointed to Agent Forsythe. "Avery and I will pose as a couple."

Tru looked from him to the pretty agent, and she didn't buy it for a second, and not because he was at least ten years younger. "You have zero chemistry. Alex wouldn't even let you check in."

"He wouldn't know," Agent Forsythe—Avery—argued. "We've worked together for years. We can pull it off."

"I buy him as a Dom, but you're not at all submissive." Tru shook her head. "Alex is great at reading people. He'll sniff you out, and then he'll call me because I vouched for you, and I'll have to tell him what I know. Can't I just tell him? He'll keep it a secret." As she considered the validity of Alex keeping a secret, she rethought her assertion. He'd tell Jewell because he told her everything, and Jewell was a gossip. Tru loved Jewell, but there was no denying her friend's propensity for spreading the word.

"No. It's imperative that no one know we're there or what we're doing." Brandy set her jaw firmly, ruling out any argument Tru might make. She took a bite of grapefruit, and the table fell silent as the agents frowned while eating.

This was not the breakfast Tru had imagined. She hated goodbyes. She'd anticipated explaining how their lives had intersected for a brief, orgasmic time, and now it was time to go their separate ways. Free from the fog of morning-after bliss, they'd see reason, and then they'd part on good terms. She planned to cherish this memory, and she hoped they'd do the same. Eating breakfast with a herd of agents, all wearing the same pinched expression, had not been on her radar.

She quietly finished her waffle, and then she went back for seconds. This time she targeted sliced strawberries, banana coins, and the walnut syrup. A glance back at the table showed that the agents had begun sharing their various thoughts. Should she return or find another table? It was obvious that they needed to discuss the case and that they couldn't do it in front of her. On the other hand, Alex was one of her best friends. He'd always been there when she needed anything—a shoulder, a friend, or even a Master. She owed it to him to make sure the FBI didn't muck up his business.

Conversation dropped off when she returned. She glanced around, noting how gazes fastened on food instead of meeting hers. "What now?"

Liam set his napkin on the table next to his plate. "We were wondering what you had planned for the rest of this month?"

Okay, it seemed like they'd abandoned the topic of Zangari's and now Liam and Jed were back to looking for a way into her life. Truthfully, a casual relationship wouldn't be too bad. They were both fantastic lovers, and maybe they could work up to including bondage and impact play. It could be cool to meet up with two hot Doms in random locations around the country for trysts, and their lifestyles precluded the possibility that things could get serious. She didn't do serious.

"I have two bed-and-breakfasts booked for reviews. I'm staying four days at one and three at the other. Then I'm back home for the last week of September. Why?"

Liam exchanged a communicative glance with Jed before answering. "Instead of going home, how about you pull strings to book you, me, and Jed into Zangari's?"

Not certain she'd heard him correctly, her brain replayed his request over and over, searching for the part she'd misheard.

"It'll be fun." Jed set his hand lightly on her shoulder. "And you're under no obligation to actually sleep with us. You'd just pretend to be our sub while we're there."

Alex would know if they were pretending. While he wouldn't think twice about the lack of romance—because he knew her so well—he'd notice that they lacked a rhythm that came from familiarity. She pointed out the most obvious hole first. "Alex will figure out that Liam is a beginner."

"So?" Jed shrugged away her concern. "Everybody starts somewhere."

True. She'd started with Alex. Okay, next obstacle. "We have no established protocols. It could get awkward really quickly."

"She has a point," Jordan said. "The three of you will need time to practice. I propose they stay with you while you're at the next two bed-and-breakfasts so that you can learn to work together."

That would mean seven days and nights with these two. Oh, the dirty and naughty possibilities that ran through her mind made her pussy wet. From the heat traveling up her cheeks, she figured that she might also be blushing.

"They'd have to meet up with her at the second place." Brandy had finished her grapefruit, and now she sipped orange juice. The woman sure liked her citrus. "We have a lot of work to do before we get into Zangari's." She stood and smiled down at Tru. "Tru, please let me know when you've made the arrangements. I'll need to get you registered as a consultant, and we'll set you up with an expense account to pay for the time there. If you could book at least five days that include the last Tuesday of the month, that would be preferable." With a toss of her head, she signaled to her team that breakfast was over. Jordan and Avery followed her from the room.

Liam and Jed rose as well. Jed tucked a strand of hair behind her ear. "We have to go too, princess, but we'll check in with you in about an hour. We'll have a contract and contact information."

Liam looked like he wanted to give her a hug, but he refrained. "Remember, this is all an act. It's for show. Neither Jed nor I expect anything except your cooperation in keeping up the subterfuge."

It looked like Liam and Jed were walking back their earlier press. Though they were technically getting what they wanted, it was business, not pleasure. Somehow his platitude wasn't as reassuring as he meant it to be, but then again, she hadn't exactly been giving out signals that indicated she wanted to see either of them after today. She hadn't technically consented to working with the FBI at all.

The Abiding Tide/Day 3—Draft of overall review
Amenities..5
Food..5
Activities..4
Available excursions....................5
Being forced to eat another meal with FBI agents....................1*
*Only because the food was delicious

Chapter Eleven

Amy handed over a bottle of beer, sans lid, and set a coaster on the side table next to Liam. "Thank you."

"You're welcome." She tossed a saucy smile, and then she crossed to the sofa, knelt down and offered the other beer to Jordan.

His buddy waited several seconds, drinking in the sight of his submissive on her knees with her gaze lowered. Then he accepted the brew. "Come sit by me, babe." He patted the place next to him. "We're not talking business."

She bounced up, excitement bubbling from some place deep and genuine, and took her place at his side. Jordan put one arm around her, and she snuggled against him, a radiant smile lighting her face. Liam wondered if there would ever come a day when Tru would want to be with him like that. The thought of her on her knees, offering his morning coffee, made him have to cover his sigh with an exhale.

This was a rare day off. Liam had spent the morning with his mother. She loved the retirement community to which she'd moved, and it eased his conscience about not being there as often as he should. The community had kept her so busy that she hadn't dropped by Liam's apartment to clean it or reorganize his things. This was progress.

"Have you thought about what you want from a submissive?" Jordan sipped his beer and stroked Amy's hair.

Liam wanted the exact image in front of his face, but he didn't want Tru to call him Daddy. Sir or Master would be fine. But beneath the surface of Amy's actions and reactions lay complete trust and deep affection. That's what he really wanted. How she showed her affection and devotion mattered less. Liam shook his head. "I want Tru."

"What do you want from her?"

"Everything." He knew Jordan would make him elaborate, so he continued even though he wasn't one-hundred percent sure about what he was saying. "I want her to smile when she sees me because it totally made her day. I want her to think of me when I'm gone. And…And…I want her to want to serve me. The more I've learned about protocol, the more it appeals to me."

"You want her to like you." Amy traced lazy patterns on Jordan's jean-clad thigh. "She might serve you, but she can't fall in love with you if she doesn't like you. When you let your guard down and let people get to know you, they generally like you."

Jordan kissed Amy's forehead. "Dare is a lot like you, babe. He can be blunt, and since he spends a lot of time in his head, he doesn't always recognize other people's boundaries, but he means well."

Liam had only come to know Amy since Jordan had become his mentor, so he couldn't say he knew her very well, but he liked her so far. Then he thought of Jed, and he wondered how this was going to work. Sure, they'd partnered well for a great ménage experience, but what did that mean for the other twenty-three hours and fifteen minutes of the day?

He sipped the beer, enjoying the icy liquid as it slid down his throat. "How is she going to serve two Doms? What does that look like?"

Jordan pursed his lips thoughtfully. "That's a great question."

Amy's busy fingers moved to play with Jordan's shoulder-length black hair. "You'll have to be careful that you don't give her conflicting orders or punish her for carrying out a task the other gave her when you want her to do something for you. It's important to set her up for success, or she'll leave."

Liam had heard that Amy gave great advice. Perhaps he ought to tap her for insight into submissives. "Jed and I have talked a little about this. He isn't concerned."

"He's a smooth talker. I remember once when we stopped to pick up coffee, he ran into three women he'd been juggling who turned out to be friends. They were not happy, but somehow he came out of it with plans to take two of them out at the same time. The third one held out for a solo date." Jordan chuckled. "You're not that suave."

He also didn't think that Tru would buy Jed's bullshit lines. In that way Liam had an advantage. He didn't have any lines.

"You need to designate alone time with her." Jordan continued. "Jed's going to need that as well. That way you'll both get to know her."

Liam didn't know if Jed was interested in having more than a fling with Tru. At the end of this, no matter what Jed decided, he wanted to continue to see Tru. He beat tracks through his hair with his fingers. "I think I'd be jealous, knowing that they're together when I'm not there."

"But if you don't, then she'll never get to know what you're like when it's just the two of you." Amy stopped playing with Jordan's hair and nailed Liam with a steady gaze. "Women don't fall in love with two men at once. They fall in love with both of them separately."

Jordan parked his hand on Amy's ass and squeezed. "Babe, you'd better not be thinking of falling in love with someone else."

She giggled. "You're more than enough man for me."

"What if she falls in love with Jed and not me? As you've been saying, he's the smooth talker." This was a legitimate fear. Women swooned in the presence of Jed's movie star good looks and powerful, charismatic personality.

"Then she isn't good enough for you." Amy went back to playing with Jordan's hair. She reminded Liam of a kitten or a kid, which made sense with what he knew about their dynamic. Liam didn't understand it, but he wasn't about to judge. It worked for them, and that was the end of the story.

"What if she decides she wants us both?" Liam fussed with his hair some more, a nervous habit that he only controlled when he was at work.

"Isn't that what you want?" Jordan finished his beer and set the bottle on the coaster Amy had provided.

Liam had to admit that he liked aspects of sharing a woman. The sex had been phenomenal, and when she'd become stubborn and contrary, the other Dom had stepped in to defuse the situation. There were upsides, for sure. But there were downsides as well. Then again, there were downsides to every relationship. Was this a deal breaker? No. Before he could respond, his phone went off. Jordan's went off barely a second later.

"That's work." Liam set his beer on the coaster. He'd barely touched it. He and Jordan checked their messages. He found a text from Brandy, ordering them all to the Detroit field office.

Amy was already digging in the front hall closet. She handed a jacket and holster to Jordan, and she gave Liam his jacket. "Be safe."

Jordan donned his holster and jacket, and then he snatched Amy to him for an open-mouthed kiss. "I love you, babe."

"I love you too, Daddy. Text me later if you can't call."

They took Liam's car for the forty minute drive, and Liam did a lot of thinking about what he wanted from his relationship with Tru. He and Jed were due to leave in a few hours to meet her at the bed-and-breakfast where they'd spend the next three days working out as many kinks as they could. Of course sex wouldn't be part of the equation. Tru would be a consultant. She wasn't there because she wanted to be with him or Jed. She was there to help stop an organization that murdered people and threatened the security of her nation. He would have to use this opportunity to make her like him. Borrowing a little of Amy's faith in him, he tried to envision a future in which Tru belonged to him, but he failed.

"Have you told her that you like her?" Jordan broke through Liam's pessimistic internal tirade.

"I told her that I want to see her again. Well, Jed did, and I confirmed it." Traffic on I-94 was backed up at the US 23 interchange, which did not surprise Liam. If it didn't clear quickly, they'd strap the siren onto the dashboard and use government authority to barrel through. "She was against the idea."

"She didn't seem so against the idea when she agreed to go undercover as your submissive." Jordan opened the glove box and took out the siren. "Brandy said to be there in thirty minutes."

Liam opened the windows to let the shrill noise escape. Ten minutes later, they were in the open, and he turned off the sound. "I guess we'll see. I have the next six or so days to win her over. If Amy's right, and I have the ability to grow on a person, then I hope it's enough time."

"Just be open and honest. She knows you're new to the lifestyle, and she'll forgive a lot."

"If she doesn't?" Did Liam worry about fucking up? Yes.

"Then she's not worth it. People mess up in relationships. It's human nature. The way you deal with it reveals character." Jordan's phone rang, and he answered. "Monaghan. Yes, Chief." He checked the roads and their location. "Twenty minutes. Got it."

Liam kept his eyes the road as he weaved through slow-moving cars that wouldn't get out of the left lane. "What did she say?"

"Everybody else is already there. Use the siren." Jordan turned the sound back on, and Liam rolled the windows down again. Now people in the left lane cleared the way, and they cruised downtown without an issue.

Liam and Jordan rushed to Brandy's new office. After taking down the head of the Detroit field office who was also the head of The Eye's Detroit arm, she'd been offered many positions, including Miguel Lawrence's old job. Brandy hadn't wanted to run the entire Detroit branch of the FBI. Instead she'd jumped at the chance to head this task force, and that job came with an upgrade to a ginormous office. Jordan and he took their places at the short conference table.

Brandy breezed into the room, looking as if she hadn't bothered to spend her day off outside the McNamara Building. "You're all here. Great. Let's get started." She set a stack of papers in front of each of them. "I didn't have time to have it bound, so you'll have to make do with loose copies."

Liam preferred loose copies. It enabled him to reorder things and compare photographs. He opened the folder to find a list of robberies. Each had been committed in the past three days, and they all involved petty amounts. One consisted of the theft of a dozen candy bars and a rack of sunglasses. Yes—they'd taken the rack too.

"I don't get it." Avery flipped through her stack of reports. "They have nothing to do with The Eye. Why are we seeing these?"

Brandy set a stack of photographs on the edge of the table and, with a dramatic push, scattered them down the center. "Because every place that has been robbed is one

I've visited in the last six weeks. Each incident was reported to local PD. There may be others where thefts occurred, but they didn't report it for whatever reason."

"They might not have noticed." Jed examined a photograph.

Liam picked up several that had landed near him. Each featured Brandy in the center, unaware that she was being photographed. The mystery photographer had captured the image using a telephoto lens—otherwise Brandy would have noticed someone snapping pictures of her. Some of the photos showed her clearly, but most featured partially obstructed views. "Every place you went was robbed?"

"I don't know yet. That's what you're going to be doing. Flip to the last two pages. That's a list of every place I've visited since we've been back from California. Avery and Jordan, take the first page. Jed and Liam, take the second. Visit every place I've been. Double check the police reports, if there are any, and see if anything has been stolen from the places that didn't report a robbery."

Liam studied the reports, matching them with photos. "Where did the photos come from?"

"They appeared on my desk this morning. Forensics found nothing—no fingerprints, fibers, DNA, or anything that would help us narrow down the source of the envelope or photo paper. There's no post mark, so it wasn't mailed, though it's stamped by our internal routing system." She clenched her fists at her sides. "I ran surveillance tapes at each location and found nothing. I already have a team working on finding out how this got into the building in the first place."

A very important step was missing from this equation. "But how did you link them to the thefts? It looks like a stalker."

"Right now, it is a stalker." Brandy closed her eyes and exhaled a steadying breath. "Several of the stolen items have been left on my porch over the past few days. I thought it was weird, so I came in this morning to do some digging. I had bagged the items, and I planned to run them through forensics. But when I saw the pictures on my desk, I ran the places through the system and came up with these hits."

Avery scowled. "Why didn't you call us this morning?"

Liam knew why. They'd worked for two weeks straight without having time off, and she'd given them a few days to recuperate and see their loved ones.

"I wanted to be sure," Brandy said. "I'm sure. You have your assignments."

Avery and Jordan sorted through the pictures, grabbing the ones that corresponded with their cases. Jed snagged the ones that went with the cases Liam and he had been assigned, and they sorted the unassociated ones into a third pile.

Liam stood. "I'll call Tru to let her know that she can cancel the reservation at Zangari's."

"No." Brandy had been helping sort. She nailed him with a determined glare. "This fucker is not going to derail our investigation. Just tell her that you'll be a day or two late. You and Jed will do as much as you can, and then

Avery, Jordan, and I will handle the rest. I've tapped Keith Rossetti and Lexee Hardy for help as well."

Liam had worked with both Keith and Lexee before, and he trusted them to go balls-out on this. However one of their own was being targeted. He wanted to bring the bastard down.

But as much as Liam hated the idea of leaving when his friend and colleague was in danger, he knew that Brandy was right—they couldn't let this stop them from doing their job. This may very well be related. If anything, it underscored that they were onto something.

Re/Viewed   Michele Zurlo

Chapter Twelve

Tru held her phone in her hand, staring at the dark, sleeping screen so hard that she jumped when it rang. Her heart raced, but it calmed when Poppy's name showed on the screen. "Hey."

"Have your knights in shining armor showed yet?"

Tru sighed. "No. They're only two days late, so I haven't given up hope yet. Worst case scenario, I'm in for a weekend visit with Alex and Jewell. It's been almost a year since I've seen them."

Poppy gave a disgusted snort. "If they showed up now, I'd piss on their armor with them inside and hope it rusts shut."

Wrinkling her nose at the imagery, Tru said, "I don't think they're into that kind of stuff. Besides, I've been having fun without them."

Put-In Inn was everything its webpage said it was. The charming, seaside bed-and-breakfast had the obligatory nautical theme, and since it was located at the heart of the harbor, the ocean was very accessible. The inn kept several boats in the nearby marina, and they also rented out their single yacht in 3-hour increments. Additionally they offered classes in sailboarding, surfing, and cooking the catch of the day—which they purchased from local fishermen. Fisherpersons. People who fish. Tru made a mental note to look up the gender-neutral term for fishermen.

About a mile down the road—walking or biking distance—was a narrow strip of sand that the locals called a beach. It was good for the usual beach activities, and the inn provided picnic lunches to patrons who wanted to spend the day at the beach.

It would have been the perfect place to meet up with Liam and Jed, but the bastards hadn't shown up yet, and she was due to leave the next day. "They're working a case. They call every day to check in." They'd called one time each day together, putting her on speaker so she could hear them both, and then each of them called her separately as well. Since they hadn't intruded on each other's calls, she figured they'd designated times. Tru was impressed by how well they worked together.

Poppy, though, was less impressed. "They don't seem all that reliable."

They weren't. Their jobs made them unreliable in their personal lives, which was fine as long as they never established expectations to the contrary, which they hadn't. "They're making the world a safer place. It doesn't matter anyway. It's not like we're dating. I'm just helping them with their cover."

"I'm not stupid." A loud clanging crash came through the phone. "Son of a bitch." Poppy moved the phone so that her next words were muffled, but Tru heard them anyway. "Motherfucker, get out of my store. If I catch you in here one more time, I'll hang you from the roof by your dick!"

The threat didn't shock Tru, but the fact that Poppy had hurled it at an apparent customer did. "Poppy? Is everything okay?"

Muffled noises and the sound of something scraping against the phone greeted her question. After a minute, the sound of shop bells tinkled. "I'm back. Stupid twat waffle has been in here every day this week, and he's knocked something down each time. I'm going to beat the shit out of him if he comes back."

"Yes, and dangle him from the roof by his winkie."

Poppy laughed. "That might be too good for him. Where were we? Oh—I'm not stupid. You like these guys."

She did like Jed and Liam. "Yeah, but they said I didn't have to have sex with them for the undercover part. They've moved on."

"Don't pull this crap with me, Gertrude Hazel Martin. I've known you forever, and I know what you're doing. You're running away from two guys just because you like them. You're chicken shit when it comes to relationships."

Though Poppy wasn't wrong, Tru opted to obfuscate. "You just said I should pee on their armor and hope it rusts shut with them inside it."

"I was kidding. Solidarity, sister. You're upset, so I'm upset for you. I just happen to be the kind of brat who would make them pay for making me wait, whereas you're the kind of passive-aggressive person who'll say it's all right, but inside, you've written them off as not worth your time. In essence, you're pushing them out of your life."

Arguing wouldn't get her anywhere, but that was never a reason to give up. "They're not in my life."

"I think you should tell them that you want sex to be part of the deal. You're smart. You'll think up some good reasons, create a great supporting argument, bat your long eyelashes at them, and they'll be eating out of your pussy in no time."

Tru laughed. "Maybe I'll tell them that I'm open to negotiating different limits."

"You do that." Poppy's voice dropped to a whisper. "It'll be just like those ménage romances you love to read."

"You love them too."

"And?"

"And don't make it sound like I'm the only perv in this conversation."

Both women laughed, and then Poppy launched into a narrative about the idiot she'd thrown out of the store.

Tru had spent the morning at the beach. She'd swum in the frigid ocean, waded in the cold shallows, and walked along the shore until the beach became too rocky for her bare feet. When Poppy had called, she'd been lounging on a towel, soaking up the warmth of the sun. Once she finished chatting with her best friend, she packed up her things and slung her huge bag over one shoulder.

The path to the inn ran along the road. Tru would have preferred it to follow the water, but nobody had asked her when they'd planned out the path. "People should consult me on things," she mumbled. "I have great ideas." Tomorrow, for example, she'd booked a slot at a base jumping place. Not long after she'd gone for her first dive, she'd stumbled across more extreme sports. She'd been on the fence about whether she should train to base jump or go bungee jumping, but when she'd research both options, she'd found lots of problems associated with bungee jumping—like blindness, for one. Base jumping, by comparison, seemed positively safe. And so she'd begun working toward this goal. It had taken years for her to accumulate the training she needed, and now it was time to check base jumping off her bucket list.

She started down the road to find her path blocked by two attractive men wearing shorts, tropical-print cotton shirts, and sandals.

"Hey there, princess." Jed took off his sunglasses and held out his arms. "Did you miss me?"

She had missed him, but she wasn't going to run into his arms. Yeah, she was passive-aggressive all right. Poppy had nailed that one.

"Hi, Tru." Liam leaned closer and kissed her cheek. "Can I carry your bag?" As he was already sliding the strap from her shoulder, his question was more of an order.

Some of her residual anger disappeared. It wasn't their fault they'd been detained. She handed over the bag. "Did your investigation go okay?"

Jed smooched her other cheek. "Investigation? We're mere office workers. I'm in human resources, and Liam is the head of I.T."

They hadn't divulged the details of the cover story, so she had avoided telling Alex anything other than she'd met two Doms and she wanted to bring them to Zangari's. Alex, no doubt, was under the impression that she was looking for his opinion on her Doms. Tru wasn't sure whether she wanted his two cents or not. Alex was her friend, and he would keep her best interest in mind. But he wouldn't sugarcoat anything, and he wouldn't hold back if he had something to say that she didn't care to hear.

Since neither of them chimed in to answer her question, she figured they couldn't discuss the case—which meant it was an active investigation. She was learning. "Well, I hope everybody is okay."

"They're fine." Liam looked over his left shoulder at the small parking strip for the beach. "The bus won't be here for another hour."

She scoffed. "The inn is only a mile away. We can walk. That is, if you're up to the physical exertion." She motioned to the bag. "If it's too heavy, I can carry that."

Liam looked at Jed. "I say we institute mandatory spanking for when she gets snarky."

Jed considered the idea, but then he rejected it. "She'd like it too much for it to be a punishment."

"True. We'll have to come up with something else."

Though she liked the idea that they wanted to set rules and levy punishment, Tru held up one hand. "Hold on, there, gentlemen. You're getting ahead of yourselves. There's not a 'no snark' rule. You're not the fun police."

They exchanged a glance and a shrug.

Giving it up, the guys turned, and the three of them began walking along the path to the inn. Jed's hand landed on the small of her back. "We met at a B&B you were reviewing about six months ago, and we've been seeing each other casually ever since."

Alex had required that information when she'd called. "Two months. Alex would never believe that I'd see someone for six months and not tell him or Jewell." Actually, Alex would be hard pressed to believe that she'd keep someone in her life for that amount of time. He'd been shocked to hear that she had steady men at all.

"Two months. Okay, we can do that."

She turned to Liam. "This Saturday is public sex night." While Alex didn't operate a sex club, he did designate two days each year to celebrate voyeurs and exhibitionists.

"We won't be participating." Jed issued the dictate in a firm tone, his voice dropping so low that it ran rampant over her libido.

Tru seized this opportunity. Poppy was going to be so proud. She hooked an arm through Liam's and the other through Jed's. Now she was being escorted by her gentlemen, even though she'd started it. "Let's table that idea for now. I have something else I'd like to propose." She looked to make sure each one was open to listening before continuing. Liam glanced down, one eyebrow lifted, and Jed inclined his head in her direction. "You said you wanted to see me again." Okay, she continued a little bit, and then she had to pause so that she could chase down her fleeing courage.

"Yeah." Liam agreed, and the strength of his tone helped corral her nerve.

"I think we should take this weekend to examine if a casual relationship might work. I mean, it wouldn't be serious, but maybe while we're pretending, we can see if we actually want to do it again. Or not. We might decide this won't work. So we should keep it casual. Friendly. Because you're partners, and I'd hate to cause a rift or ill will or something." Now she was rambling, so she stopped talking.

Jed put a hand over hers where she held his arm. "Are you sure? You didn't seem all that jazzed about the idea when we brought it up before."

She was sure as hell not sure, but she wanted to be. "Yeah. It'll be fun, right? I mean, who doesn't dream about being the meat in a hot guy sandwich? Well, besides lesbians, but straight women and the gays, we're all about that kind of lunch."

"Are you hungry?" The smile playing around Liam's lips betrayed his struggle to keep from laughing. "It's past lunch time, but your bag is a little heavy, so I'm wondering if you brought lunch but didn't eat it."

As a matter of fact, she had eaten a very fine lunch. "That's because I ordered for three. You guys were supposed to be here over an hour ago."

"Sorry. Our plane was delayed. I texted you." Liam stopped and set the bag down. "What's in here? We skipped lunch, and we came looking for you the moment we got to the inn."

She hadn't noticed a text from Liam, but she let it go. Sometimes when she was traveling, texts came through hours—even days—later. Tru looked around. The path back to the inn was nothing more than a wide shoulder for the highway. "Are you going to eat it on the side of the road?"

"Sure." Jed dug into the picnic hamper in the bottom of the bag. "Don't worry—we'll save room for a sandwich later."

"Is that an answer, or plans for a mid-afternoon snack?" When deciding on plans, Tru preferred clarity. She wasn't sure if he was craving tacos, flirting or if he was finally responding to her invitation. "You don't have to say yes just to keep my cooperation. Either way, I won't let you down. Brandy said this criminal organization represented a new kind of global crime syndicate. Or something like that." Those hadn't been her exact words, but that's what Tru, with her expertise honed by crime television shows, had taken from the conversation. "I'm all for ridding the world of murderers and other kinds of jerks."

Liam unwrapped a sub sandwich and took a huge bite. He paused in chewing to smile enigmatically. Jed did the same. She'd opened herself to them—something she didn't generally do, and they were being other kinds of jerks. Seething, Tru rolled her eyes and stalked off in the direction of the inn. The world could stand to be rid of this variety of shenanigans.

Before she was able to take two steps, Jed grabbed her arm and halted her progress. He swallowed before saying anything. "Don't ever walk away from us. When you're upset or frustrated, tell us you've had enough. We will tease you. We're both kind of bastards that way, and we don't always know when to stop teasing, but if you tell us, we'll stop."

That quelled her ire somewhat. Tru folded her arms. "I'd like an answer."

"Yes." Jed released his hold on her arm. "We'd like to give it a try. Casual is a good way to start."

They'd have to pretend it was more meaningful than that, but as long as they'd established clear boundaries upfront, then Tru was fine with the situation. She threw her arms around Jed and reeled Liam in for the hug. Liam tried to both hug her and avoid contact with Jed, which made for an awkward embrace.

Tru growled, the exact same sound her childhood dog had made when she used to try to hug him when he wanted to sleep. It indicated annoyance, not an imminent threat. "Incidental touching is a real thing. Get used to it."

Liam acquiesced, and the trio hugged on the side of the road.

Tru shouldered the bag back to Put-In Inn while her gentlemen finished their subs and dug back into the bag for cookies. When they were nearly to the inn, some logistical questions came to mind.

"Due to you guys being two days late, we missed being able to ease into this. I think we need to dive in, full throttle. It might lead to more use of safewords, but we can't look like we're that new as an item." Tru didn't care to take emotional risks, but this was more of a physical one, and she didn't have an issue with those.

Jed threaded his fingers through hers and held her hand. "That's not ideal, but I agree that it's necessary. You can start by calling me Sir, and you can call Liam, 'White Knight.'"

She wasn't sure whether he was joking or serious.

Liam snorted. "You're part Irish, motherfucker. If she's calling me that, then she's calling you Brown Sugar."

Sensing a fight, she sought common ground. "What would you like to be called, Liam? I'm okay with calling you both Sir."

He shrugged. "Let's go with that, though White Knight could grow on me."

"I'm not sure I could say that without laughing." If she used it enough, though, it could grow on her as well.

"That's the point." Jed laughed, a devious sound that wended pleasantly through her system. "I'd love to see you bust up every time he gave you an order."

"You're naughty." Tru laughed with him because his joy was contagious. She put her hand in Liam's, and he squeezed, communicating that he wasn't upset. On impulse, she lifted his hand to her lips and kissed it.

They made it to the inn. Jed opened the door, and she went through first. Miss Steffi, the owner, greeted them. She was a stout lady, strong and barrel-shaped, and she looked like she'd be at home standing at the stern of a large sailing vessel.

Miss Steffi smiled, her face lighting with genuine warmth. "Ms. Martin, I see your guests found you. That's wonderful. Will they be joining us tonight?"

Tru had committed to playing an organized game with other guests at the inn. "Yes, Miss Steffi. They don't like to leave my side."

Miss Steffi looked from where she held Jed's hand to where she held Liam's, and she absorbed the new information without judgment. "I see. Well that'll make for an interesting game. Ms. Martin, Mr. Kinsley, and Mr. Adair,

I'll see you after dinner. Eight o'clock sharp in the large gathering room."

Jed inclined his head and a smile quirked his lips, flirting even with the ancient inn owner. "It'll be our pleasure, Miss Steffi."

Miss Steffi held out a hand. "I'll take your picnic hamper to the kitchen, unless you'd prefer to leave it in the hall outside your room?"

Tru lifted the hamper out of the bag and handed it over. "Thank you, Miss Steffi."

Liam waited until they were in her room before asking about the commitment. "What game?"

"A murder mystery party. It should be right up your alley." Tru set her bag on the floor. "I'm going to shower the saltwater off my skin, and then we can talk."

While Dare threw his travel bag on the single, king-sized bed and riffled through the contents, Jed took a closer look at the items in the room. Tru had wanted to dive in, and in Jed's mind, that meant bondage, nipple clamps, and impact play. The honorable thing would be to clarify her consent before beginning any of that kind of play. Of course, surprising her with it might be fun as well. He could imagine her shocked expression, and if he listened hard enough, possibly a screech of protest. Though he was a fan of some kinds of screeches, the protesting kind didn't make the list.

"Are you looking for the dossier?" He checked the bed frame as he inquired as to what Liam sought. The frame wasn't suitable for bondage. He'd need to tie one wrist and thread the rope under the mattress, which he didn't care to do. If she pulled hard enough, she'd lift the edges of the mattress. That was too much control in the hands of a submissive.

"Yeah. Are you looking for good places to attach your ropes?" Finding the hidden item, Liam set it on the nightstand. Then he zipped his bag and threw it on the floor.

"There aren't any." Jed shelved his plans. A BDSM-themed bed-and-breakfast had to provide beds with numerous eyehooks. "I can bind her wrists and ankles to each other, which will cut down on her movement. We'll have to take turns holding her down while the other one flogs her. On the plus side, with two of us doing the work, it'll be a lot less tiring."

"Sure." Dare drummed his fingers against his thigh. "Did you see the clothes she took into the bathroom?"

Jed hadn't been looking. "No, why?"

"I don't want her fully dressed unless she's leaving the room. Lingerie is okay, but shirts and pants are not." Dare glanced around. With a frown, he opened a dresser drawer. "She unpacked. How cute is that?"

Jed didn't see the significance. He'd also noticed that she'd hung dresses in the closet. "Lots of people unpack in hotel rooms if they're staying a few days."

"She's not one for fancy underwear." Dare picked up a stack of panties. "We're going to need to stop off at a fetish store on our way. I've already looked up several."

Though Jed could appreciate a woman in satin and lace, he didn't need fancy trappings to stimulate his baser instincts. Tru had an amazing body, soft and curvy, yet strong and responsive. The sight of her wearing nothing was enough. He held out a hand to take the underthings that Dare had selected. "I'll take them in and swap them with the clothes she picked."

With a self-satisfied grin, Dare handed over the white bra and panties.

Jed went into the bathroom without knocking, a risky proposition when they hadn't established norms.

"Hello?" Tru's voice and a good amount of steam came from behind the shower curtain.

Jed threw the lingerie on the counter before sliding back the curtain. "Hello." He drank in the visual of her luscious perfection. She had curves that didn't quit, and he wanted to travel every inch.

She wore the surprised expression he'd expected, but without a glimmer of protest in her eyes. "Sir?"

Oh, sweet lord. That title, an unwavering show of respect from a woman who knew exactly what it entailed, topped off the fuel tank to his libido. He reached into the shower, grasped a handful of hair, and pulled her to him for a kiss that made the steam roiling around them seem cold by comparison. She gripped his shirt, but she didn't press her wet body against his dry one. He was about to order her to turn around and bend over when he remembered that he hadn't brought a condom. Reluctantly he released her.

She stepped back so that the warm spray sluiced down her body, and faced him with a heaving chest. "You missed me already?"

"Something like that." He indulged in another slow perusal of her assets before sliding the curtain closed. "I set something on the counter for you to wear."

The water sounds changed as she moved to direct the spray to different parts of her body. "Okay."

"We haven't discussed the issue of clothes."

Her laugh tinkled along waves of steam. "We haven't discussed a lot of things. It's okay to take on the issues as they come up. I think it's within the purview of my Sir to sometimes pick out my clothes as long as they're appropriate to the occasion. If either of you tried to do that every day, then we'd have issues."

"Fair enough." He returned to the room to find Dare setting out a box of condoms.

Dare glanced up. "You're wet. You weren't in there that long."

"I peeked in the shower and stole a kiss." Jed gestured to the condoms. "You want to scene right now?"

"Not a scene." Dare peeled off the coverlet, rolled it up, and tossed it onto the floor next to the dresser. "But I'd like to exercise the right to fuck her whenever I want that she gave me on the way here. Later, we might have time for a scene. I brought some new toys that I'd like to try out on her."

Jed chuckled at Dare's thoughtful, analytical approach. "Women like romance, man. What you're proposing isn't the least bit romantic."

A frown wrinkled Dare's brow. "Right now, romance wouldn't seem authentic. In case you haven't noticed, she's not one of those women with stars in her eyes. For her to believe the romance, she has to trust the intention. We haven't earned her trust yet."

The sound of water ceased, and they both looked toward the door to the bathroom even though they knew it would take some time for her to engage in her post-shower ritual. After a moment, Dare resumed to setting up. It was now clear to Jed why Dare was still single.

Jed had planned to talk to her, folding in a lot of flirting and touching—foreplay. That way when he suggested bondage and sex, she would feel amenable to the ideas. He feared that Dare was going to ruin it for the both of them, but he'd promised Jordan that he'd let Dare exercise his fledgling Dom muscles. If things went sideways, he'd mediate the conflict. At least Tru was open to overlooking the pitfalls of the trial-and-error method. He perched on one of the two occasional chairs set up on either side of a small, round table that contained information on activities offered in the area.

Tru came out of the bathroom wearing the white bra and panties that Dare had selected. They were plain, but she didn't need special clothing to make her attractive. Her damp hair hung loose over her shoulders. She stopped several steps into the room and looked to Jed. Jed motioned to Dare, and she directed her attention there.

"You went through my things?"

"Yeah." There was no trace of apology in Dare's response.

This was an interesting turn of events. In the past Jed had always been solely responsible for dealing with his sub. Now he sat back and watched as Dare took the lead. He'd known that he would have to do this, and he hadn't looked forward to it. However something about this seemed natural, albeit new and unfamiliar. The seeds of jealousy that he'd been keeping locked in a small, iron box failed to thrive on this.

And it had nothing to do with the fact that she'd challenged Dare when she'd been ready to accept Jed taking this kind of liberty.

Tru crossed her arms over her breasts, and her eyebrows formed V-shaped slashes above her flashing brown eyes. "We need to establish some boundaries right now."

Dare met her ire with unimpressed stoicism. "Like?"

"My laptop and phone are off limits. I don't even want you to answer if it's ringing and I'm indisposed. Let it go to voice mail."

Dare took one step closer, and his powerful stance seemed to tower over her even though she was only a few inches shorter. "Is that all?"

Tru's gaze dropped. "My stuff is password protected, but you said you were a hacker."

His thumb traced a light caress along her eyebrow, coaxing it to return to its unvexed position. "Off limits, unless I have a warrant or probable cause."

"And my permission, Sir." Her arms fell to her sides as she shifted from upset woman to Dare's sub.

Jed knew Dare wouldn't debate the law with her, just as he knew that Dare would hack her laptop or phone if he had a good reason. Dare wasn't the kind of agent who always waited for the warrant unless it was connected to a prosecutable case. Brandy had issued more than one reprimand to Agent Adair.

In lieu of revealing that damning bit of truth, Dare cupped her face with one hand and leaned down. He kissed her, his lips moving slowly and lulling her deeper into submission. His hand stroked down her throat and over her breasts. Down her body they traveled, until he came to the apex of her thighs. He pressed his palm to her mound and stroked his fingers against the white cotton.

With an almost vicious intensity, he ripped his lips from hers. "That's one very wet cunt, sub."

Tru kept her hands at her sides, though Jed recognized her fight to keep from touching Dare. "Yes, Sir."

Dare bypassed the panties and sunk two fingers into her pussy, forcing Tru to her tiptoes. "So hot and ready to be fucked."

"Yes, Sir." Tru panted and swayed toward Dare.

He caught her so that her face rested against his neck, and he slowly worked his fingers in and out of her pussy. "You like this, honey?"

Tru answered with a vigorous nod, and if Jed wasn't mistaken, she was biting Dare through his shirt.

For a brief second Dare closed his eyes and surrendered to the ecstasy. The he withdrew his fingers and held her close. "Undress and go lay on the bed, legs spread and knees up." As Tru scrambled to obey, Dare looked to Jed. "Want to tie her wrists?"

Did he? Hell, yes. Various images of Tru bound to his bed had appeared in his dreams and fantasies since that first kiss. He glanced at Tru, seeing if she had an opinion on the issue, and he found that in addition to positioning herself according to Dare's instructions, she'd lifted both hands over her head.

Years of training kept him from leaping at the opportunity he wouldn't have thought to create. He knelt on the bed and looked her in the eyes. "Princess? Let's establish safewords. The normal stoplight system applies, but I want you to choose one word that is uniquely yours."

Tru pursed her lips as she thought. "Methotrexate."

Jed had no idea what that was, but it was sufficiently outside anything one might utter during the throes of passion. "That works. What's your color right now?"

"Green, Sir."

He backed away to get his ropes, and he found Dare frowning at them both. Dare gestured to Tru. "It's not a scene."

"Doesn't matter." Jed set his travel bag on the bed and unzipped it. They'd been forced to travel on a commercial jet, so he'd only brought the equipment he could fit into his one bag. "It's a Dom's job to see to his sub's physical and emotional health and wellbeing no matter the situation."

Wheels turned behind Dare's eyes. "The stoplight system is always in effect?"

"Yes." Jed found the length of rope for which he'd been searching. He'd packed two, but he needed the shorter one in this case. "And when she calls yellow or red, whatever is going on stops immediately."

Dare accepted the rule with a brief nod. "I'm going to fuck her. I don't mind if you tie her hands while I do it."

Tru listened and watched as her Doms conversed. She'd never been with a beginner before, and she kind of appreciated that Jed was there to explain the nuances because it would blow the mood if she had to do it. The fact that they talked without including her also turned her on. Right now she was an object there for their pleasure. Her thoughts, feelings, and wants didn't matter. She wondered if Liam would forbid her from coming. Alex used to deny her all the time. It might take a little practice, but she could hold off if ordered not to have an orgasm.

Liam shucked his shirt and pants, and he donned a condom. Tru indulged in an unabashed study of his brand of masculine perfection. He and Jed were built very differently. Though they were both tall, Liam had a slimmer build with longer lines and a surprising amount of muscle. Jed, on the other hand, had broad shoulders and muscles bulky enough so that his clothes didn't hide a thing. With regard to penises, she was reluctant to compare. Jed's cock was longer, but Liam's was thicker. Both had no problem bringing her to orgasm, and that's all that mattered.

Liam settled between her legs, entering her swiftly. Her pussy had begun weeping the moment she realized that Jed had replaced her outfit with a bra and panties. The move had been a signal that they'd taken her seriously when she said they should dive right into a D/s relationship, albeit a fake one.

Liam's gaze roamed her face, watching the tiniest nuances of her reaction. Did she like being used by her Sir? Yes. And not having the pressure of a 'real' relationship left her free to enjoy the physicality of submission. Being under him, pinned by his order into a position of his choosing, and providing a vessel for his pleasure—this experience was the reason being a submissive appealed to her so much.

"I want to please you, Sir." She spoke low, loath to distract him. He hadn't forbade her from speaking, and she wanted to tell him that she heartily approved of his actions. "I want to make you climax."

As if this was the permission for which he'd been waiting, he set a vigorous pace, rotating his hips as he thrust forward to give a little twist at the end. He not only hit her sweet spot, but he did it in such a way that her toes curled and her back arched. Every time he surged forward, she lost a little more control. Her knees shook so hard that she couldn't hold them up anymore. They fell to the side, opening to take him deeper, and he took advantage of the opportunity.

He mastered her by degrees, riding her body up that cliff and demanding her submission so that she couldn't notice her location. She couldn't mark the exact moment she lost control. She had a fleeting moment of clarity when she realized that her body writhed and bucked under his, sometimes thwarting his ability to keep the rhythm. She wanted to touch him, to rake her nails along his back and arms—any way to relieve the tension building in her core—but she couldn't move her arms. "Sir," she cried. "Oh, yes, Sir."

Tiny explosions dotted behind her eyelids, melding into one huge blast that left her a liquefied and trembling mess. Through the haze of pleasure enveloping her senses, she was aware of Jed replacing Liam between her legs. He thrust into her, his cock pushing through the swollen and throbbing tissues of her vagina.

He moaned, a short cry that barely penetrated her consciousness. "You feel so good, princess. You're going to come again."

Was he crazy? Her pussy had taken quite enough. Even though she was sopping wet and Jed's cock had an easy time entering, it verged on too much stimulation. She thrashed her head and tried to tug her arms down, but the restraints kept her from moving them. "It's too much, Sir."

"No, gorgeous, it's not. You can handle it." He set a steady pace, fucking her to a different rhythm, one that her body struggled to accept.

She wanted to protest again, but her words were already slurred and hard to form. Tru tossed her head, a token protest, but Jed had no mercy to give. He fucked her, varying the pace and the depth of his thrusts until he found one that made her thrash and cry out.

Jed whispered things in her ear, naughty phrases that her brain couldn't quite process but whose meaning would be clear in any language. She stopped thrashing and turned toward the strong, soothing sound of his voice. The moment she surrendered to him like this, waves washed over her. Gentle at first, they licked at her nerve endings, sending ripples of pleasure over her body. They spread to her shoulders, up her arms, and tingled in her fingertips. The next wave came stronger, and the third had even more power. After that, they came too quickly to count, and they all blended together, multiplying until they sucked her under and held her captive to such intense bliss.

She became aware of herself some time later. Warm bodies pressed to her on either side, comforting her with their heat and presence. Hands stroked along her arms, sides, and back. The slight weight of a sheet caressed her hip and leg. Lips pressed a kiss to the back of her neck, sending shivers down her spine. A tiny moan escaped.

"I think she likes that." Jed's voice came from in front of her.

"Yeah. She has a sensitive neck." Liam's reply came from behind her. He brushed his lips over her responsive skin, and she couldn't help the kittenish mew.

"Welcome back, princess." Jed kissed her forehead.

She opened her eyes to see him gazing at her, self-satisfaction evident in the way his lips curled into a smile. "Hi."

He kissed her again, this time on her temple. "Did you have a good nap?"

Tru tried to peer over his shoulder to see the digital clock, but he was very broad-shouldered, and she was too weak to lift herself very high. "How long was I asleep?"

"About a half hour." Liam's breath tickled her neck, and she felt herself waiting for another kiss there.

She pressed her ass against his thigh, seeking more of his touch. "Is it time for round two?"

Jed chuckled. "It's time to go over our cover stories. You don't strike me as a natural liar, so it'll take some studying for you to remember important details for our covers."

She brought her hands up, but her wrists were still bound, so she couldn't rest her hands on his chest. "Why am I still tied up?"

"Because I like you that way." Jed's grin dared her to argue. "Now let's get our facts and details straight."

Tru frowned. "But Alex and Jewell know me already. I'm not the one who's undercover."

"You'll need to know our cover identities." Liam finally bestowed the kiss on her neck for which she'd yearned. "A good sub will know things about her Doms, and a good Dom will know things about his sub."

She'd already told Alex some things about Liam and Jed. She hadn't said much because she didn't know them all that well. It would be difficult to argue with his logic, though she was tempted. Quelling the urge, she opted to cooperate. "True."

Liam twisted away, and when he came back, he had one of those Federal-issue file folders with the FBI seal embossed on the cover. "Favorite color: Blue."

She rolled, and they scooted to allow her to lay on her back. "Everybody's favorite color is blue."

Liam regarded her with a wry twist to his lips. "Actually most people don't have a favorite color. The majority of people have a range of colors they prefer."

"I like rainbows." Tru had an appreciation for every color. After her parents had died, she'd designated a special memory for each color of the rainbow. Even though she mostly remembered her parents from pictures, she had been able to hang onto those specific memories. "When I was little, Gram painted one on the wall of my bedroom. She even put glitter in the paint so that it sparkled."

Liam's gentle smile was aimed at her, but his eyes showed a mind miles away.

She touched his face. "It's okay to like rainbows and glitter. It won't impact my opinion of your masculinity."

His eyes focused on her. "We really need to get through these items."

Jed took the file from Liam and tossed it on the floor. "Liam and I live in Denver."

"Okay. I can remember that. Why did you move to Denver?"

"Work." Jed propped himself up on one elbow. "We both moved there for jobs at the same company. I moved from Ohio, and Liam moved from Michigan. If you get those details wrong, it's okay. We can always cover it with an argument about how you don't listen well and need discipline. A D/s cover can be an asset."

Having conversations about what a person did for a living was definitely first-date material—or something discovered when hot FBI agents showed up to interview you about a murder you'd stumbled upon. She sighed. "It sounds boring. What does this company do?"

"They advise people on investments, which is boring." Jed traced a finger along her collarbone. "People aren't supposed to want to probe deeper."

"Not unless they want to diversify their portfolio. Tell that to the wrong person, and you'll be stuck discussing stock options for hours." Tru sometimes disliked telling people that she was a writer. They were either unimpressed or they had tons of ideas for her—with plans to split the profit should she ever use any of those ideas.

"Jed can hold his own." Liam had propped himself up so that they both towered over her. "He used to investigate white collar crime."

She fingered a strand of Liam's wild, dark hair. "And you can handle a tech conversation because you like to hack the CIA in your spare time."

"You told her that?" Jed's entire body stiffened. "Brandy's going to kill you one day, my friend, and nobody will find the body."

"It's not that big of a deal." Liam shrugged it off, but his body language told another story, and Tru realized that not only had Liam told the truth the night they'd looked at the stars, but he didn't normally run around bragging about his hacking abilities.

She rushed to reassure them both. "I won't say anything. Really, I'm not a gossip. I listen more than I talk. Let's discuss your kinks because that'll definitely come up."

Jed pursed his lips, and his attention was back to her. "Basic history—I'm the middle of three boys. My parents are retired and living in Florida with all the other retirees. My older brother lives in Colorado, which is a great reason for me to have accepted a job there, and my younger brother is in grad school at the University of Wisconsin."

Tru blinked. She wondered how much of that was true, but she deemed it wise not to ask. The last thing she needed was to get real life mixed up with the cover story. "Got it."

Liam went next. "I'm an only child. My mother died when I was younger, and after several years in the foster system, I was adopted by my current mom. She recently moved into a condo in a complex that caters to retirees, and I visit her every day when I'm home."

Except that Gram would rather die than retire and Tru had never been in the foster system, Liam's cover story was too close to her own history. She wondered what, exactly, was in the file the FBI had on her. "Do I have a cover story?"

"Nothing other than what you already know." Jed smoothed a thumb over her chin. "What's the frown for?"

"Your stories are each so simple. Real life isn't like that." Tru knew she was being a pain. Everyone had a story that could be simplified if only the emotion and meaning were removed.

"Simple is best for now. We'll add layers as we get to know one another."

Once again, he was right. It made sense that he'd know what he was doing. After all—this is what he did for a living. "We should really talk about kinks. I know you like bondage, and that Liam has a voyeuristic streak, but I should know more than that about you."

"And we should know more about you." Liam shifted, stretching his neck and repositioning his shoulder so that it was centered over his elbow. "You're from Northport, and you live with your grandmother, for whom you were named. What else?"

She didn't want to share anything else, but she knew that Alex wouldn't buy the relationship if they didn't at least know the basics. She exhaled. "My parents died in a car accident when I was almost seven, and my Gram raised me after that. She runs a bed-and-breakfast in Northport, so that's where I learned the business. My best friend is Poppy Elliston, and we talk on the phone nearly every single day no matter where we are. I went to college after high school, though I did not finish, and I've always wanted to have a job where I could travel and experience the world." She said nothing of the visions that occasionally appeared to her because that was also something she'd never told Alex about.

They both looked like they had a million questions buzzing on the tips of their tongues, but they endured the stinging rather than let them fly free, and Tru appreciated their restraint. She didn't want to tell them anything else.

This was enough. Alex would buy that she would keep things from them because he knew that it took a tremendous effort before she would let anyone get close to her.

Jed rolled his lips in as he thought. "Nipple torture is my main kink. I'm a sadist when it comes to that, but I'm not really into flogging or impact play for purposes of pain. I like to use it to induce subspace, but that's all."

Tru considered what he meant by nipple torture because the label covered a host of options, some of which she liked and some that were hard limits. "I'm not into edge play. No knives, needles, or cutting. I can handle all sorts of clamps, though."

He circled one fingertip over her nipple, bringing it to a point. "Suction, nipple and breast bondage, and the use of a crop?"

She hadn't done any of that before, but as they didn't violate her hard limits, she nodded. "That sounds okay, though the nipple bondage isn't something I've done before. I'll use my safeword if I need to."

"You'd better. There will be consequences for failure to use your safeword. You won't like that spanking. I guarantee it."

Liam frowned. "I've heard about that—how spanking can be a punishment or reward depending on the circumstances. It'll be interesting to see it in action."

Tru laughed. "You're looking for me to misbehave?"

His frown morphed into a grin. "I'm sure that's just a matter of time. You're willful and kind of bratty."

She liked his smile. "Yeah, but I'm also the kind of sub who would remember to buy ketchup at the bulk food store because you like it on everything. I'd even let you lick it off me if that turned you on."

Jed snorted. "Liam would never willingly eat anything from a bulk food store. He thinks the government spikes it with mind control drugs designed to make us docile and suggestible."

"It's a great distribution mechanism." Liam's skin grew ruddy, and Tru couldn't tell if he was angry, embarrassed, or a little of both.

She lifted her bound hands and cupped his cheek the best she could. "You're a conspiracy theorist? Like you believe in Bigfoot?"

His lips thinned. "The existence of a squatch or other cryptids has not been disproven."

"Or proven," Jed interjected. "Please don't get him started."

Tru eyed Jed dispassionately. "The existence of many cryptids has been proven—the giant squid, coelacanth, and the Komodo dragon, just to name a few. 'There are more things in heaven and earth, Horatio, than are dreamt of in your philosophy.' We have not explored every inch of this planet. Bigfoot could be hiding anywhere."

Jed rolled his eyes. "How can they survive in the hostile environments left alone by humans?"

Tru had no idea because she hadn't spent much time thinking about the issue, but Liam apparently had. He snorted. "They have evolved to thrive in cold, hostile, mountainous, and forested regions. That's how they've survived this long, and that's how they elude capture."

"I would be against capture," Tru said. "They should be left free."

"Great. I'm in bed with two crazy people."

Sensing that he was feeling left out, Tru switched to caressing Jed's cheek. "You're in bed with two dreamers, and the great part about that is your access to our limitless imaginations. We could pretend you're squatch men, and I'm the only female in the area—and I'm in heat. Or I could be running from you, and you have to catch me first. It might be kind of like this afternoon, only I won't be as compliant."

His cock stirred against her leg, so she figured that he liked her imagination.

"I like compliance," Liam announced. "That's the part of D/s that appeals to me the most. It turned me on how you wore the clothes we picked out and followed orders and got on the bed." He pulled her knee up and draped her leg over his. "Touch yourself. I want to watch you masturbate."

She hadn't expected that. Following orders turned her on as much as it turned him on to give them. She was rarely contrary. Jed pulled her other leg up and over his hip, and Liam kicked the sheet away.

With nothing more than pleasing her Sirs on her mind, she lowered her bound hands and slid two fingers through her juices.

The Put-In Inn
Amenities............................5

Food..4.5
Activities..5
Available excursions......................5
Sandwiches..................Mindblowing

Chapter Thirteen

"Billy Ray, I do declare, you are not good at following instructions. I pay you good money to keep yourself down in the holler and out of my beautifully coiffed hair." Tru batted her false eyelashes and fanned herself.

Though her acting was so far over the top that half the room covered their mouths to keep from chuckling, Jed didn't find it difficult to stay in character. He didn't like the idea of Tru—no matter what role she was playing—telling him to stay away. He scowled and strove to keep speaking in the passable Southern accent he'd practiced at Quantico when they'd considered stationing him in Louisiana. "Now, Tulip, don't get your panties in a twist. You invited me to the party."

She huffed and shifted in her seat to give him her back. "Billy Ray, I would never invite you to a party where my fiancé is the guest of honor."

With a growl, Jed grabbed Tru by the forearms and hauled her against him. He didn't like the jealousy boiling in his veins, but he couldn't deny that it lent a realistic air to his acting. "You're my wife, darlin', and don't you ever forget it."

Dare stood, drained his drink, and intervened. "Mr. Sticks, I'm going to have to insist that you unhand my bride-to-be."

Tru glanced over, a hint of reprimand behind her fake outrage. Dare was not getting into the spirit of the murder mystery party Miss Steffi, the owner of Put-In Inn, had arranged. His portrayal of Rich Richerson, a wealthy suitor for Tulip's hand, was stunningly lackluster. Tru whispered, "Say it like you mean it."

"He doesn't mean it." Another guest, a woman whose role caused people to call her Anita Plum, made the comment to her real-life husband, but she spoke loud enough for everyone to hear. Anita wore a layer of makeup that would require excavation to find her actual face, and her husband had bathed in cologne. "The three of them are sharing a room—with one bed."

Before either he or Liam could defend her honor, Tru's attention snapped to the woman. Her upper lip curled in a high-class sneer. "Sounds like someone is jealous."

Anita scoffed. "I don't believe in that kind of lifestyle."

Tru's eyes narrowed, and Jed made sure he had a good hold on her arms. The last thing he needed was to see Tru use this woman as her portable punching bag. "You mean, you don't *approve*. Belief requires either proof or faith, and since we're right here, you have proof. I highly doubt you'd be so critical if you worshipped us, therefore you should say that you don't *approve* of our lifestyle. Not that it matters. Your bigoted, close-minded opinion doesn't mean Jack shit to us." Through it all, Tru's tone remained modulated, and she didn't once stumble in keeping her Southern accent.

She faced Jed and planted a firm kiss on his lips. Then she did the same with Dare. As the other players picked their jaws up from the floor, Tru preened with pride. Jed released her arms, and she made a show of fanning herself, as if kissing them had ignited a fire she was powerless to extinguish. "I have never been able to resist a pair of handsome men who know how to handle a woman."

Some people laughed nervously, while others continued to stare. Dare didn't seem to notice. He slung his arm around Tru's shoulders. "Thanks for unhanding my future wife. Come now, Tulip. You're overwrought because your father was just murdered in the study, probably by Ms. Plum and the candlesticks she stole and is hiding in that big bag she hauls everywhere."

"He was shot." Yet another guest, the male half of the only Asian couple taking part in the game, interjected. Blake Wu, a bona fide crime scene investigator when he wasn't playing the part of the unclaimed bastard son of the deceased, cleared his throat. "Not bludgeoned."

Dare pointed and winked. "Right. So not killed with the candlesticks. She just stole them because they're silver, and the price of silver has been steadily on the rise."

If Jed hadn't known Dare for as many years as he had, he would have bought him in the role of I.T. specialist for an investment firm attempting to have a weekend getaway with his girlfriend and her other boyfriend. It was clear to Jed which role Dare was actually playing.

His part over for now, Jed resumed his seat on the ottoman across from where Dare and Tru parked themselves. Dare held Tru's hand, a move that would have worked in either role and served to stir jealousy in both Jed and Billy Ray. Ever since witnessing Dare and Tru discover things they had in common—like a crazy belief in Bigfoot—that seed of jealousy had blossomed, and Jed had struggled with the feeling that he didn't belong with Tru.

She'd met Dare first. She'd liked him first. She'd kissed him first. It was only when she'd thought Dare was out of the picture that she'd set her sights on him. Maybe when this was all over, he ought to step aside and let them pursue a future together?

Playing a role where she rejected him in favor of Dare had to be fate's way of warning him that it wouldn't work out. After all, how many people did he know who had made a ménage relationship work? Zero.

The impromptu play continued around him. He followed along in the booklet, but his part was mostly over. He was the abandoned first husband who refused to divorce the heiress whose father had been murdered. Like every other player, he had a motive for the murder. However it seemed as if the other players were uncomfortable bringing him into the conversation. He couldn't tell if it was due to the fact that his skin was a different color or because he was the third cookie in an ice cream sandwich. How, exactly, did someone fit that monstrosity in their mouth?

He looked up to see Tru watching him, a frown creasing her chin and marring her gorgeous forehead. He smiled, but the troubled expression didn't disappear. "Billy Ray." She spoke softly and in Tulip's accent. "I know father invited you here to sign the divorce papers. I heard you in his study before the party started, but like the delicate flower I am, I fled rather than confront you."

He didn't know where the glimmer of hope came from, but he seized on it. "You don't want a divorce?"

The concern melted away, and she grinned devilishly. "Oh, I do want the divorce. I can't have my full inheritance unless I marry Rich. If you sign the papers, I'll give you fifty thousand—for your trouble."

Jed snorted and tried to pretend that the green-eyed monster wasn't barking in his ear at her casual dismissal of his presence in her life. His character was supposed to be an ex-con who wanted his wife back—or he wanted to keep blackmailing her. "I'll never let you go, Tulip darlin'. As I told your father, 'til death do us part. You're mine forever."

Her dark eyes gleamed with excitement. "And he threatened to have you framed for a crime that would send you away forever. That's why you killed him."

Jed had looked ahead in his booklet, so he knew that he wasn't the murderer, but he was determined to keep up the act because he could see how much fun Tru was having. Truthfully it was kind of exciting to solve a fake murder for once. Pride was at stake, but no actual crime had been committed.

He fixed Tru with a hard stare, and she responded by softening and lowering her gaze. "Do you really think I'd kill your father? I know how much he meant to you."

Tru—Tulip—dabbed at the corner of her eye. "There's no telling what you'll do for money. After all, you went to prison for grand theft auto after you stole those expensive sports cars."

Dare looked at her. "You can't name an expensive sports car?"

"I can name expensive jewelry, shoes, and handbags." She batted her false eyelashes, and the right ones got tangled together. She tried to unweave them, but the top one fell off and dangled from the bottom one. Jed and Dare both laughed, and Dare helped disentangle the mess.

"I can't stand this." Anita jumped to her feet and hauled her stinky husband up. "This is disgraceful."

Their hostess and the owner of the inn, Miss Steffi, tried to make peace. "People in love are not disgraceful, and let he who is without sin cast the first stone. Glass houses and all that."

"My house is normal." Anita turned a livid shade of red and exited the room. Her husband, who hadn't said a word the entire time, followed her.

Blake Wu sneezed. "Her perfume was driving my asthma crazy."

"That was her husband." Blake's wife, Nguyen, waved the final fumes away. "I want to know if Tulip is going to get divorced or not. At this point, I kind of don't care who killed the old coot."

"That man didn't deserve to die. He was a father, a husband, a son, and a brother. He was a friend and business partner. Everybody here loved him." Then Tru tossed her head and flung her hair over one shoulder. "Besides, Tulip sees no reason to choose one man. She's the greedy kind who wants it all, and she'll have it all, whether or not her father approves."

Jed wasn't sure if Tru was still in character because she'd responded in her regular, Midwestern accent. Her declaration, cheesy as it was, served to remind him why he was really here. Someone had been murdered, and he had to catch the culprit, bring down an international crime syndicate, and explore the dynamics of a casual D/s ménage relationship that may or may not lead to something more.

He winked at Tru. "Tulip, honey, I'll be your piece on the side. For a price."

The next morning, Jed woke to the ringing of a phone. He opened his eyes, blinking away sleep in the semi-dark room. Next to him Dare rolled out of bed and grabbed for his pants. Jed assumed he would put them on, but he merely fumbled in the pocket. The ringing grew louder as he fished out his phone.

"Adair." Dare's voice, thick with sleep, croaked in the silence.

Jed had sat up, stretching and yawning, and listened to Dare's end of the conversation. Though they'd come across the country to complete their assignment, they were both concerned about Brandy's stalker. Following that trail had turned up nothing conclusive. They had a few grainy images of a suspect, but it would take time for the FBI digital recovery algorithms to refine the image so they could make out some facial features. Results weren't guaranteed. They could just as easily find themselves back on Square One if the images weren't fixable.

"Yeah. She's straight on the story. We're driving up there today, so we'll drill her on the details to make sure she knows what's what." Dare shoved a leg into his pants and paused.

Jed and Dare had decided not to share details about themselves that conflicted with their cover identities so that Tru wouldn't get her facts confused. Jed grabbed fresh clothes. "Ask if there's anything new on the stalker."

Dare glanced up. "No news."

Agents Lexee Hardy and Keith Rossetti had been assigned to follow Brandy to see if anyone was following her, and Dare's lack of news meant they'd found nothing as well. Scowling, Jed disappeared into the bathroom for a quick shower.

As the hot spray washed over his skin, he woke up fully, and he realized that Tru hadn't been in the room. That put a quick end to his shower. He rinsed away the Inn's body wash, threw a towel around his waist, and poked his head into the bedroom. "Dare?"

Dare tossed his phone on the table and finished donning pants. "Yeah?"

"Where's Tru?"

Glancing around, Dare frowned. "Geez. I'm so used to sleeping in a bed with you that I didn't notice our woman was gone. That's pathetic." He picked up a pad of paper near his phone, and his gaze flew over the writing. "She left a note. It says she's in the dining room working on her review."

Knowing she was working mollified Jed, and he went back into the bathroom to shave.

"I'm going downstairs." Dare yelled through the door, and a second later, the door to their room closed, leaving Jed alone. He knew that Dare was going to find Tru. The two of them would have breakfast together, bonding over talk of Bigfoot and government conspiracies. Jed swallowed the stab of jealousy and concentrated on getting a close shave.

Three hours later, he found himself in the middle of nowhere. No, that wasn't exactly true. Though the road had been steadily climbing, mountains rose on both sides. He followed the highway that Tru had insisted would take them to their destination, a frown furrowing his brow and chin. "This isn't near the ocean. We're heading east. The ocean is west."

Tru giggled and rubbed her palms together as she looked out the windshield. "We might be taking a small detour."

They didn't have time for a detour. Jed shot her a hostile glance. "Tru, what's going on?"

"There." She pointed to a small, dirt road that disappeared behind boulders and trees. "Turn left."

Jed had the feeling he shouldn't, but he did anyway. If nothing else, it was a place to stop off and check his GPS for a route to get them back on track. "Where are you taking us?"

"I made this appointment before you extended my trip. It took years to set this up, and I'm not missing it for anything. Don't worry—it won't take long. We'll be at Zangari's by dinnertime." She pointed out the next turn.

The sandy road opened to a parking lot. Jed read the sign on the small building at the end of the parking lot: Hang Gliding, Balloon Rides, and Zip Lines. The building was large enough to house an office with a small gift shop occupying space along one wall. Behind it, a metal roof loomed just higher than the treetops. That must be where the equipment was kept.

Dare cleared his throat. "Tru, are you going hang gliding?"

Jed remembered from her blog that she'd jumped out of balloons. "You're not jumping out of a balloon today."

She grinned. "No, I'm not. I'm going base jumping."

Before either of them could tie her to the seat, she leapt from the car and bounded toward the welcome building.

The full weight of what she'd declared sunk into Jed's head. "That's not legal." Base jumping was illegal in most places due to the inherent dangers associated with the extreme sport.

Dare nodded. "She's lucky you work in human resources and I work in I.T. Otherwise we'd be forced to stop her and shut down this place."

The deeper point—that they couldn't blow their cover in order to stop Tru from following through—sucked. Jed cut the engine and pulled the latch to open the car door. "I'm going to blister her ass tonight."

"Sounds like a plan." Dare alighted from the back seat.

They caught up with her in the lobby. Jed slipped his arm around her shoulders and pulled her close. "Princess, this can't be above board."

She leaned into his embrace and turned her face so that he felt her breath on his neck. "Colt is one of the best. He has an international reputation, and he's the one who insisted I have two hundred skydives and at least ten dead-air jumps before he'd agree to let me do this."

The back door opened, and a medium-height man with short blond dreadlocks and a skater-boy vibe entered. He grinned at the trio, but he held his hand out to Tru. "Tru, it's great to finally meet you in person. Elvis has told me so much about you."

She stepped forward to shake his hand. "Likewise. I'm so excited for this. I want to introduce you to Jed and Liam. They're going to watch."

Colt shook hands with Dare. "Hey, man. It's good you came along. She'll be calmer with friends waiting for her."

When Jed's turn came, he made sure his grip was extra firm. "I trust that you'll take special care of my woman?"

An understanding passed between him and Colt, and the other man nodded. "Sure thing. She'll be fine."

After he released Colt's hand, he caught Tru's frown, but he ignored it. If he had his way, she wouldn't be jumping at all. It was far too dangerous, and he saw no reason for her to risk her life for this. However he needed her cooperation in order for this operation to have a chance for success, and pissing her off now wouldn't lead to her continued goodwill.

Colt gestured for them to follow him out the back door. Tru walked next to him, listening to Colt rattle off instructions and safety procedures, while Jed and Dare brought up the rear. Colt led them into the large structure with the metal roof. The inside was like a garage. Baskets and deflated balloons occupied the central area, while hang gliding equipment lined two walls. Jed saw no sign of zip lines.

"I packed your chute myself." Colt picked up a pile of fabric and handed it to Tru. "Changing rooms are behind you. Put this on over your clothes. You know the drill."

Tru took the pile of what must have been a nylon suit, and she disappeared in the direction of the changing rooms.

Colt faced Jed and Dare. "You want to watch from the jump point or the landing area?"

Dare gestured to the changing room. "You're just going to let her jump? A woman you've never before met and about whom you know nothing?"

The skater-man's tanned skin turned ruddy. "We've been emailing and video chatting for a couple of years. She's been training for this for over a decade. She's more than ready."

There was so much he didn't know about Tru. Somehow he'd thought her posts about skydiving or dead-air jumping had been fictitious. It looked like they weren't. Had she brought them along to prove to them that she was comfortable in dangerous situations? Because it didn't help her case. Jed had every intention of shielding her from anything that could get dicey, and shit like this just riled his protective instincts.

He wanted to haul Tru out of the dressing room and back to the car, but he settled for clapping Dare on the back. "We'll wait at the landing point."

Tru came out then, wearing a black nylon bodysuit with hooks and straps all over the place. She spread her arms. The suit made her look like a flying squirrel, which Jed thought apropos because Tru was a little nuts. Her brown eyes sparkled with excitement, and she nearly skipped back to the men waiting for her return. "This is going to be amazing."

"Yeah, it is. Let's go over the procedure and safety protocols, and then I'll take you to the jump point." Colt crooked a finger at a man who was tinkering with an air compressor. "Cody, take these dudes to the valley."

Tru kissed Jed on the cheek. "I'll see you at the bottom." Then she kissed Dare the same way. "If I give you my phone, will you take pictures? Just swipe up from this corner to open the camera app."

Dare accepted her phone and slipped it into his back pocket, watching Tru with a firm gaze and lips pressed together. "This is crazy."

She grinned. "I know, but we all need some crazy in our lives."

A few minutes later, Dare and Jed squeezed into the extended cab of a heavy duty truck, both glancing back doubtfully at the huge garage they'd just left.

Cody, still in his dirty overalls, chuckled. "Is she your girl?"

Dare and Jed exchanged a look. "Yes." They answered in unison.

Cody frowned, and Jed could almost see the gears turning behind his eyes. "Both of ya?"

"Yes."

Now Cody nodded knowingly. "Adrenaline junkies. They definitely make their own rules."

Dare scowled. "I should have forbidden her from doing this."

It was Jed's turn to chuckle, the pathetic kind that screamed about futility and shit like that. "You honestly think that would have worked?"

"No, but it couldn't hurt to try. At least it would be something."

Jed didn't agree. "It would absolutely hurt to try. If you overstep your authority, it could backfire in the worst way." He meant that it would cause Tru to run in the other direction, but he wasn't sure if Dare took it that way.

His buddy nodded. "Yeah. It could ruin our plans for the weekend."

The sheer side of the cliff fell away, and the valley below was dotted with trees. Scrub and a few determined evergreens clung to life through the cracks in the rocky mountainside, reminding Tru a little of herself. The view was breathtaking, and she took some time to memorize the sights, the tittering of birds and the rush of faraway traffic, and the sharp scent of evergreens. Later when she wrote about today's adventure, she'd recreate it for her readers.

Colt pointed to a series of bright red flags in a narrow clearing. "There's your landing strip. Once you pull your chute, steer yourself in that direction. The wind is on our side. You should get a nice glide after the free fall."

She took a deep breath to steady the exhilaration rushing through her veins. "I should get a seven count out of this, right?" Seven seconds didn't seem like much, but when you were falling through the air down the side of a mountain, it was enough time to relive an entire lifetime and several seasons of a favorite TV show.

Colt nodded. "You can probably get nine or ten, but for your first jump, aim for seven." He pointed to her wrist where she wore her altimeter. "I've set it for 250 feet. It will give you a warning vibration at 350. Let the pilot chute go when you feel that first buzzing, that'll ensure that the chute's open when you reach 250. If you haven't deployed by 250, that thing," again he motioned to her wrist, "is going to shake the hell out of your arm. Listen to it. If you decide to pull early, that's okay too."

Many people reacted to their first jump with terror and deployed their chutes sooner than necessary. Tru had seen it happen with skydivers many times, but she'd never been tempted to pull it too early. If anything, she held out for as long as she could. For that reason, she'd long ago stopped telling Gram about her jumps. Poppy knew about them, but she'd never seen one because she didn't have the heart of a daredevil and was deathly afraid of heights. Poppy freaked out when she had to climb a ladder to reach the top shelf in her parents' antique store. As long as her understanding of Tru's extreme sport was entirely secondhand, Poppy was willing to remain positive and be supportive.

She took a running leap off the edge of the cliff and stretched her wings, and the moment she did, a vision appeared. She saw Liam and Jed on the porch of Northport Bed and Breakfast, the place where Gram had raised her. Both men smiled as they greeted Gram. Jed tried to shake her hand, but Gram pulled him closer for a maternal hug. She did the same with Liam. Tru felt someone tugging on her arm. The vision faded, and because it wasn't like one of those Hollywood moments when time stops or the vision happens in an instant, Tru shook away the cottony feeling. The ground rose quickly, zooming at her with incredible speed. She had no idea how many seconds had passed since she'd jumped, and so she fumbled for the pilot chute on her pack. Her parachute deployed without a problem, jerking her to a slower speed.

Still, the ground approached faster than she was accustomed to, and she knew she'd pulled her chute late. As happened whenever she faced death, a heavy peace settled in her core. She watched the ground longingly, but her better sense must have been on autopilot because she steered her glide to follow the wind. She'd miss the mark in the second field, but she'd land better if she changed her trajectory. She pulled hard on the handles, and lifted her legs to delay impact. At the last possible second, she straightened out, and the hard, uneven valley floor met her feet. She'd intended to run out the momentum, but the hit was too hard for her to do more than stumble a few steps.

This landing wasn't going to be the smooth, easy one she'd pictured when she'd thought about how impressive this would be for Jed and Liam to see.

Thinking quickly, she tucked her knees into her chest and rolled with the forward force. The lines of the parachute tangled around her body, an inexpert natural bondage. There was no way she was going to come out of this without a few bruises. Thankfully she stopped after a few yards.

Heart beating erratically, she sat up. Never before had a vision interrupted her thrill-seeking, and the experience left her trembling. She heard voices, and she looked up to see Liam and Jed running toward her. They came at her much faster than Cody, Colt's partner who was supposed to meet her at the bottom and give her a ride back to base. She blinked, and she wondered if their haste was fueled by concern or if the FBI required agents to meet certain running speed guidelines, and these two were used to moving quickly.

Liam reached her first. He looked at her face, and then he ran his hands down her arms and over her ribs. "Are you hurt? Lay down. Let me check your legs."

The lines had twisted around her legs and arms in such a way that she wasn't going to straighten out without untangling first. She grinned at Liam and Jed, who'd made it over a shade after Liam had spoken. "I'm fine." She tried to shake off some of the lines so that she could stand, but the muscles in her legs and arms were too tremulous, and they didn't quite cooperate.

Jed put a hand on her shoulder, stopping her from trying again. "Give it a few minutes. You're in shock."

She'd never reacted like this to a jump before—even when she'd botched the landing. Afterward she'd always been excited, filled with indescribable energy and joy. This time she felt as if she'd come close to tasting death. It was more like the eighth round of chemo and less like the way her first skydiving experience had made her feel—vital and alive.

"I'm fine," she said, but this time she heard the tremors strangling her voice. She looked at Jed, and another vision appeared. This one superimposed a ghostly image over his corporeal one. Blood dripped from cuts just above his eyebrows, near his hairline, and on his strong jaw. His clothing was damp, stained with dirt and blood, and torn, and his pallor frightened her. From a distance, she heard Liam calling her name, and so she looked at him to find the vision continuing.

If Jed's condition was bad, Liam's was worse. Slumped against a dark, rocky wall, he held a broken arm close to his chest as he struggled to sit up straighter. Blood flowed from a cut in his lip, the bright substance standing out in sharp relief to the grayish cast of Liam's pain-twisted face.

This was the first vision in a long time that scared her. The last one had been when she was seven, and she'd seen her parents lying dead in the wreckage of a mangled car. She'd refused to go with them that day, and she'd begged them not to go either. They'd left their obstinate daughter with Gram and drove off. Gram had held her as she'd cried great sobs that hurt her chest, and she'd assured her that everything would be all right. That's the last time Tru had seen her parents alive.

Later that night, Gram had held her tightly, sharing grief, and she'd asked Tru how she knew that the accident was imminent.

"Tru!" Liam's shout and a swift shake dissolved the disturbing vision.

She blinked at him. "I'm fine."

"You're pale and shaking. You're not fine."

"It's the adrenaline." Cody had joined them, and Tru hadn't noticed. "It'll wear off in a few minutes. You had us a little on edge, Tru, waiting eleven seconds to pull your chute. Luckily you kept your head." He set to work untangling the lines from her limbs. Jed and Liam pitched in, and soon she was free.

She tried once again to get up. This time Jed and Liam helped her to her feet. They flanked her, each holding her by an arm. Her legs weren't nearly as liquid, though she felt a little like a newborn fawn. "Really, I'm fine."

"Color's looking better." Cody helped her off with the empty pack, and he began rolling the used chute for transport back to base.

She drew a finger along Jed's forehead where the worst cut had been. Then she ran her other hand down Liam's forearm. Even though she knew the events in the vision hadn't happened, she needed to make sure they were okay. Seeing them injured had freaked her out far more than base jumping ever could. For that reason alone, she was very docile as they walked her to the truck and loaded her in the backseat of the extended cab. She didn't protest when they peeled off her jump suit in the middle of the hangar. In a fog, she thanked Colt for the experience, and she numbly allowed Jed and Liam to load her back into the car.

Twenty miles of road disappeared under the wheels before Tru shook off the worst effects of the vision. It hadn't happened yet, and she still had a shot of preventing it from coming true. She unlatched her seat belt and scooted so that she was nearly in the front seat and between them.

Jed glanced over and frowned, but he kept his attention on the road. Liam scowled. "There's no end to the chances you'll take with your life, is there?"

Tru lifted her eyebrows to let him know that his vehemence was misplaced. As far as she was concerned, she was living on borrowed time, and that was no reason to be extra careful. "The jump was fine. Colt has a great reputation, and he's done this hundreds of times."

"Someone died there two years ago." Liam's scowl showed no sign of letting up.

Tru knew about that. "That guy didn't jump with Colt. He also didn't have the kind of experience I do with skydiving and dead-air jumping."

"You waited eleven seconds to pull your chute. I counted." Jed growled this at her, though he didn't look in her direction. "And Liam filmed it."

She hadn't meant to. Truthfully she'd like a redo on the jump. Her vision had robbed her of the best part of it—the freefall. Her body had oriented itself without her conscious input, and she'd really only been mentally present for the last part. As she'd jumped hundreds of times with a parachute, remembering only that part was very disappointing.

"It worked out." She set a placating hand on Jed's arm, and the firm feel of his flesh reassured her that he was okay. No way in hell she was going to tell him about her visions. That would not make him feel better about watching her fall from a high cliff and botch the landing. "I know what I'm doing."

"It didn't look like it." Liam shifted his body, putting his face inches from hers. "It looked like you wanted us to film you committing suicide."

She scoffed at that. Though she'd sometimes wanted to die, she would never take her own life. If those visions hadn't come to her at a most inopportune time, her landing would have been perfect. "I pulled my chute late, and I took a tumble. But I'm fine. A few bruises, that's all."

His blue eyes darkened, and they might have zapped her with lightning. "You could have told us what you had planned."

She hadn't wanted to give them the opportunity to talk her out of it. They were very bright and logical men. They could have appealed to her rational side—she had one—or even strongly objected. It would have given her pause, and she would have rethought the timing of the event in question. Maybe she wouldn't have done it today. Maybe she would have called Colt to reschedule for after her time was up with these two intriguing, sexy Doms who were willing to share her.

"I know we couldn't have stopped you by ordering you not to do it." Jed pressed his lips together. "But we could have discussed it. We could have been better prepared to watch the woman we both like hurl herself off the side of a mountain."

Tru sniffed at his dramatic description. "Even though I've been working toward this for years, you would have tried to talk me out of it. You both have hero complexes."

"We know next to nothing about base jumping. Neither of us were Airborne." Liam's hiss washed over her, banishing the battered image of him that haunted her mind. "We didn't know what to expect. We knew something was wrong when Cody started mumbling for you to pull the rip cord, and there was nothing we could do to help you. We had to watch you come in too fast and hit too hard. It sucked, Tru."

She grinned. "Hero complex."

Liam jerked his head back and nailed Jed with a steely glare. "Pull over."

Alone on a deserted stretch of highway, Jed braked hard. Tru braced her hands on the backs of their seats to keep from being pitched forward. As the car came to a halt on the shoulder, she scooted back into her seat. "I don't need saving. If you recall, I'm here so that I can help you solve a murder and potentially save other people."

Liam opened his door and got out. A second later, he joined her in the back seat. She moved over to make room.

His lanky frame filled more than just the area he took up. He dominated the small space, and she was hyperaware of exactly how pissed he was.

He rested an arm along the top of the seat and leaned closer. "Since last night, you've been trying to control everything outside of the bedroom. We let you take the lead in choosing our activities because you were working. You had a review to write. But today you don't. You used the fact that you know this area better to steer us off course so that you could indulge in a dangerous, illegal activity."

To her knowledge, base jumping wasn't illegal. It was just impossible for anyone to get insurance to cover the activity, so businesses that had featured jumps were forced to stop. Her jump had been off the books—an arrangement between friends—but not illegal. "It's not against the law to base jump."

Thunder from his stormy blue eyes hit her square in the chest. "The only place in the United States where it is legal to base jump all year without a permit is in Twin Falls, Idaho on a bridge over the Snake River. Five people have died there. Do not argue the law with me, *Princess*. You'll always lose." Without moving, he managed to loom even closer. "I won't tolerate manipulation, Tru, and I will punish you for this."

It had been far too long since she'd been under the control of a Dom. Even then, Alex hadn't forbidden her from doing any of the extreme sports she wanted to try. He'd been with her for many skydives, and he was the one who'd suggested that she should try spelunking. She drew back at the idea he would punish her. Was she guilty of the crime of manipulation and topping from the bottom? Yes. Docility was not in her DNA, and she'd never promised not to push and challenge their authority. A Dom had to earn her submission; it wasn't something she gave away for the fun of it. "We didn't negotiate a punishment for topping from the bottom."

"We're taking it as it comes, remember?" He motioned to her jeans. "Pull down your pants and lay over my lap."

Jed watched from the driver's seat, an experienced Dom watching the interaction of a newly minted Dom with their submissive. Tru appealed to his experience. "Jed, don't you think this is a little much? I mean, it's not like we've established protocols or rules that I broke."

His remote expression didn't change. "Liam, be sure to cup your hand, and it's okay to spank her upper thighs too. She has enough meat on her bones to handle it. Thank God."

She looked from Jed to Liam, and she realized that she'd pushed them too far. They were willing to go along with her zany ideas, but topping from the bottom was a hard limit for them. Tru had to admit that she wouldn't like it if they manipulated her either.

As she unzipped her jeans, she wondered something. "If I hadn't delayed opening my chute, would you still be angry with me?"

"Yes." Jed answered, no hesitation in his voice. "Liam wanted to spank you before you jumped."

Liam slid to the center of the seat, and Tru arranged her bare ass over his legs. He wasted no time. "This is for topping from the bottom." He slapped her ass hard, no doubt leaving a handprint where it stung. Then he did it twice more. "This is for manipulation, which is just as bad as an outright lie." He spanked her three more times, stinging her tender flesh with the force of his displeasure. "This is because you broke the law and you put your life in danger." He followed that up with three more swats. "And this is so you remember not to do it again." Four more rounded out the punishment.

Her ass smarted. Though she loved a good spanking, this wasn't the kind that made her pussy damp with anticipation. The car door at her feet opened, and she felt herself lifted. Liam slid toward her head and out that door, and Jed took Liam's place.

"Double the Doms, double the punishment, Princess." He caressed her stinging skin, and she exhaled a hiss through her teeth. "I hadn't even realized that you were topping from the bottom, but that's exactly what you've done. For that, and for trying to get me to intervene in your punishment, you get five more." He delivered those quickly, and although he was larger and more muscular than Liam, he didn't hit as hard—though it was definitely hard enough.

When he finished, he sat her up and cradled her in his lap. She hadn't cried during the punishment—it hadn't hurt all that much—but now a single tear fell from her eye. "I'm sorry," she whispered. "You're right. I was being manipulative and topping from the bottom. And I shouldn't have been so blatant about trying to get you to talk Liam out of punishing me."

Jed's dark brows came together, forming a severe wing over his chocolate eyes. "Blatant? You shouldn't have tried at all. I will never interfere with his right to punish you, just as he won't interfere with mine."

She'd already noted how well they worked together. She lowered her gaze. "Sorry, Sir."

Jed kissed her forehead and got out of the car to return to the driver's seat.

Though it wasn't comfortable, she leaned forward to peer into the front seat where Liam had gone. "I'm sorry, Sir. It won't happen again."

Liam nodded, accepting her apology. "You won't go base jumping again?"

Tru wiggled back into her jeans. "I didn't say that. I'd never rule out a chance to base jump. Next time I'll stick the landing."

Base Jumping at Colt's Place
Professionalism of staff..5
Friendliness of staff..5
Punishment for topping from the bottom.........Effective

She left the last category off the final post, but she did include a portion of the video Liam had taken.

Chapter Fourteen

Zangari's Fetish Inn had been a quaint seaside rooming house at the turn of the Nineteenth century. It had catered to those who'd come long distances to work in the fishing industry. Over the years it had passed through many hands, and in the 70's, Alex's grandparents had overhauled it and turned it into a vacation house for their eleven children and their extended family. It had witnessed birthday parties, midnight bonfires with marshmallows perfectly browned or scorched beyond saving, romantic proposals, three break-ins, epic arguments, whispered secrets, stolen kisses, four births, and six deaths. Echoes of love and laughter were still sometimes carried on the wind.

It had eventually fallen into disrepair, and when it had come to Alex, he'd remodeled it yet again—this time with an eye for opening a retreat for those in the D/s lifestyle.

The trees surrounding the remotely placed Inn, mostly Leyland cypress and madrone with the odd birch or maple mixed in for color, cleared. Zangari's was a long, two-story building with white clapboard siding. Two other buildings on the property, neither of which had been there the last time Tru had visited, were situated farther down the path. Behind the inn, land fell away, and cloudless, early evening blue sky—like Liam's eyes—filled the endless expanse. Though closer spaces were open, Jed found a parking place at the far end of the lot. He and Liam got out of the car, and the two of them studied their surroundings.

Tru felt at home here. Not only had she helped Alex with the design, but she'd discovered and explored her submissive and lightly masochistic sides under its considerable roof. Only when Alex had developed romantic feelings for her had she fled. Over the past few years, she hadn't been back nearly as much as she would have liked. The two new buildings puzzled her. One of them looked suspiciously like a house, and the other looked like it could hold more rooms, but she didn't understand why Alex hadn't simply expanded the main structure if he wanted to expand. But the house—Jewell had been hinting at wanting a domicile separate from the inn for at least two years.

It looked like her friend had successfully lobbied for her dream home. Tru exited the back seat and stood stiffly next to the car. Her butt was sore. It had been a long time since her bottom had experienced lingering soreness.

She bent over, stretching to touch her toes. It helped her legs and lower back, but not her ass. When she stood up, Jed caged her in his arms, trapping her between his body and the car. He kissed her, lightly grazing his lips across hers before deepening it. She gripped his shirt and lost herself in the sweet bliss. Jed pressed her back, lifting her leg so that he could better grind his pelvis against her pussy area. She moaned, and he trailed sucking kisses down her neck and across her shoulder.

"Are you guys going to get the suitcases, or are you going to have sex in the parking lot?"

Jed tapered off the kissing. She emerged from her sugar high to find Liam returning to the car. "Where did you go?"

Liam gestured to a bin diagonally across the lot. "I threw out the trash from lunch."

Tru felt bad that she hadn't helped clean out the car. She looked to Jed. "We should get the bags."

Jed leaned in. It looked like he was going to kiss her neck again, but he whispered. "He was filming the plates of all the cars in the lot so we can run them later. Don't feel bad, Princess. We were the distraction."

The trunk of the car opened, and Liam hauled out four suitcases and two garment bags. Most of the luggage belonged to Tru, who had been traveling for weeks. Tru slipped under Jed's arm. "I'll feel bad if Liam carries all these suitcases by himself."

She tried to take her two pieces of luggage, but Jed and Liam each took one from her. She knew better than to argue the point. Instead she took the two garment bags. One contained dresses, and the other belonged to the guys. She guessed at two FBI-issued black suits. Slinging the bags over her shoulder, she hurried across the parking lot so she could open the door for her men.

Before she was close enough to reach the handle, the door burst open. A petite woman streaked down the walkway, shrieking. "Tru—I can't believe you're really here."

Knowing Jewell's penchant for enthusiastic greetings, Tru stopped walking and braced herself for impact. When Jewell hugged, she expected the other person to bear the brunt of the force. It was a petite person thing, maybe.

One step from Tru, Jewell leaped, limbs spread like an octopus torpedo, and landed with too much force. Tru tumbled backward, her feet tripping over suitcases, and that did nothing to help her regain her balance. Holding loosely onto both Jewell and the garment bags, Tru teetered backward, and hands and a strong body halted her fall. With Jewell wrapped around her, she shot Liam a grateful smile as he set her back on her feet.

"Jewell, honey, it looks like Tru is carrying a few too many things. How about we get you down from there?"

Tru peered over Jewell's shoulder to see Alex striding toward them, his long legs easily eating up the distance. Impossibly tall and thin, he reminded Tru of a clay figure she'd made for art class in middle school. The thing had been too skinny in the center to support the weight of the top half, and her person kept bending over. She'd fixed it repeatedly, but when it had come out of the kiln in that position, she'd given up. Gram had remained positive, though. When Tru had brought it home from school, Gram had said the guy had obviously seen something interesting on the ground. Part of her expected Alex to keel over like that, but he was in the habit of remaining upright.

Alex lifted Jewell, who reluctantly released her hold on Tru, and then he hugged Tru with one arm. "Welcome back, sunshine. It's been a while."

It had been a while. She motioned to the two newer buildings. "When did that happen?"

Jewell squirmed because Alex hadn't yet put her down. "We broke ground two summers ago, and they finished up this past fall."

"If I put you down, you can't jump on Tru again. Nice hugs only." Alex's rolling baritone had a firm edge, and Tru laughed. Jewell was a handful, and Alex loved always having his hands full.

"Fine."

He set her on the walkway, and she hugged Tru again, this time without almost knocking her on her ass.

Alex held his hand out to Jed. "I'm Alex Zangari, and this is my wife, Jewell."

"Jed King." Jed shook Alex's hand. "This is my buddy, Liam Adams."

Tru hadn't known they were going to use code names. She frowned, and Jewell's endless hug provided cover as Alex greeted Liam.

Finally Jewell let go. "You can't stay away for two years next time."

"It's only been a year." As she said it, Tru looked at the new structures. She hadn't seen anything being built there the last time she'd visited. Had it really been two years since she'd been to see this couple? "Sorry. I guess I didn't realize."

"We came to visit you in Northport last Christmas, and we met up in Seattle the summer before." Alex always seemed to know what to say to make her feel better. That had been one of the things she'd always liked about him. "You've seen us, just not here."

Liam cleared his throat, and Tru automatically set her hand on his arm. "This is quite a place you have here. I'm wondering what the inside looks like. Particularly, I'm wondering about a bathroom."

Chuckling, Alex took the garment bags from Tru. "Of course. You've been driving all day. Let's get you settled. You have a couple of options. The guest rooms were fully booked, so Jewell and I thought you could stay with us in our house. We have a fantastic guest room, and you'd still have access to the Inn. The only drawback is that it has a queen bed."

Tru caught the looks that passed between Liam and Jed. The size of the bed was only a minor inconvenience. "Alex, we wanted to stay in the Inn. We kind of want to be in the thick of things. Your house is a little far away from the action. Are you sure you have nothing?"

He glanced at Jewell. She rolled her lips together and sighed. "We have one room, but it's a staff room, not a guest room."

Sometimes Alex employed staff members who needed a place to live, and so he kept several rooms for that purpose. They were plain, not decorated to cater to a particular fetish, but they contained everything a normal hotel room would have. Tru smiled. "Thanks. We'll take it."

Jewell stuck her lip out in a pout, and then she turned the power of her large brown eyes on Liam and Jed. "But you'll have dinner with us tonight at the house, right? I'm making Tru's favorite—glazed salmon with cheesy biscuits and corn-on-the-cob. For dessert, I made strawberry sorbet."

"Sure." Jed responded with a flirty smile. "We're looking forward to getting to know Tru's friends better."

Alex inclined his head toward the door. "Let me show you to your room so you can get settled."

They followed Alex into the lobby, a long room that accommodated a common room at one end and a reception area at the other. Decorated in a blue-and-white nautical theme, this room was stunningly vanilla. Wicker sofas and chairs with thick cushions were placed invitingly around a large stone fireplace that was flanked by floor-to-ceiling bookcases. Tru and Alex had gone a few rounds arguing about the flavor of the room, and eventually Tru had won. Not everyone wanted to hang out with fetish décor all over the place. The only indication that this room belonged in a fetish inn was the proliferation of pillows stacked for use on the floor, and even that could be open to interpretation.

Well, that used to be the only indication. Since she'd last been there, they'd added a huge, iron ship's wheel. It had a padded section down the middle, and places to restrain arms and legs along the spokes. The base allowed for the wheel to be flat or upright. Tru stared, not sure whether she was upset that he'd changed the way the room was decorated or happy that Jewell was so firmly established as a manager of Zangari's Fetish Inn.

"Like it?" Jewell appeared at her elbow, a bundle of energy bouncing on her toes. "I wanted to keep with the nautical theme, and this fit so well."

"Yeah, it's...I never would have thought of a bondage wheel."

Jewell leaned closer, not that she had ever been someone who recognized the boundaries of personal space. A few earrings—Jewell had at least four holes in each ear—scraped Tru's neck. "Master likes to put me up there and torture me while the guests watch, play games, or just ignore me."

That seemed like something Alex would do. He'd always liked to put on a show. Tru looked at Liam, watching him and Jed converse with Alex as they formally registered as guests, and she wondered if he'd like to see her on a bondage wheel.

Liam signed a paper, and as he lifted his gaze, he caught her staring. His blue eyes seemed to sparkle with a special level of cockiness and maybe residual satisfaction from having spanked her that afternoon. Heat traveled up Tru's neck as she thought about the reasons he'd given for spanking her. Mostly it boiled down to the fact that he hadn't liked being surprised by seeing her do something dangerous. Her temporary Sir definitely had a hero complex, and there was no way she wasn't going to continue to tease him about it.

Alex led them down a hallway that also led to the kitchen, storage, and utility rooms. Though it was nice enough, in keeping with the rest of the inn, it lacked the cozy ambiance of the part where guests were allowed. It had been a long time since Tru had seen the staff rooms, and she'd forgotten how austere they were—white walls with no paintings, pictures or wallpaper borders; plain, wood veneer tables paired with serviceable chairs; and a queen bed that was nothing more than a mattress on a metal frame. At least it had a mini fridge and a microwave under the sink, which was in the bedroom part instead of the bathroom.

"It's not much." Alex glanced around, a frown marring his forehead. "If you change your mind, the offer to stay with us is always open."

Liam parked his rolling suitcase next to the bed and set hers next to his. Her bag had wheels as well, but he'd chosen to carry it. He took in the bed, small for three people, the short sofa, and the small window overlooking the parking lot, and nodded. "This'll do."

Jed added his bags to the train and agreed with Liam. "We'll be fine. Liam can take the sofa, while Tru and I get the bed."

Liam snorted. "Not a snowball's chance, buddy."

Not about to let them disagree over this issue, Tru pursed her lips. "Can we get a portable bed?"

Alex looked to Liam and Jed because they were the Doms, and so Tru wasn't in a position to make that kind of decision. "No children are allowed here, so we don't have roll-away beds. I have what amounts to a bedroll and a sleeping bag."

Jed waved away the offer. "Thanks, but we'll all be in that bed. Neither of us likes to let Tru get too far away at night."

Alex nodded, a knowing gleam in his eyes. Jewell threw her arms around Tru for a brief hug, and then she stood on her tiptoes to kiss Jed and Liam's cheeks. "We'll see you for dinner in one hour. Don't be too late."

Once they were gone, Jed and Liam searched the room. They removed the drawers from the dresser and felt under tables. Tru watched, fascinated by their actions. What did they think they'd find in a seldom-used staff room? It's not like the bad guys knew they were onto them, much less that they'd show up at an Inn that was sold out a year in advance.

Satisfied that the room was safe, the men shared a silent exchange, and then Liam came over to her. He cupped her cheek in a gentle caress. She thought he might kiss her, but he only ran his gaze over her features. Then his lips parted, and he spoke, his voice soft and low. "What's wrong?"

"Nothing." She answered reflexively, a lifetime of denying there was ever a problem that couldn't be fixed with a powerful drug.

"When you took us on that guided detour and put your life in danger, you said that you'd made the appointment weeks ago. But it seems to me that you were trying to delay coming here."

Speculation. That's what he was doing. Speculation was a word that Tru had always liked. It evoked feelings of the hope that came with guessing at the unknown. Even the pattern of soft-hard-soft syllables hinted at adventure. Right now, Liam was speculating that she had wanted to avoid coming to Zangari's, and he was right, though his lens for the term probably had nothing to do with hope and other positive feelings.

Tru looked away, trying to escape his probing gaze while not overtly rejecting his touch. "I just didn't want to miss my chance to jump. I live for those jumps—the danger and excitement make me feel so alive."

"That's not what he's talking about." Jed crowded next to them, arms crossed to demand an answer. "You weren't half as happy to see your friends as they were to see you. If anything, you were tolerating Jewell's attempts to show affection."

Tru had never been very demonstrative. Jewell's constant need for physical contact was one of the reasons she knew the diminutive submissive would be great for a Dom like Alex who liked those high-maintenance types. However she didn't think that Liam or Jed would be so in tune with her that they'd notice her reticence. She held Jed's gaze for several seconds before switching to do the same with Liam. "I'm nervous, okay? I don't want to say anything I'm not supposed to say to them. I'm not sure what parts of the things you've told me are cover and which parts are real."

Liam drew a caress across her cheekbone. "It's mostly real. We told you not to worry about making mistakes. We can cover you. Trust us to make it work."

She did trust them. "And then there's the fact that it finally hit me that you two would be under a microscope. I know you're used to scrutinizing, but you're probably not used to being scrutinized."

Scrutiny—there was a scrunched-up word she found unappealing. It was crinkly and hard, completely judgmental. She hadn't held up too well under the scrutiny of her two Doms.

Liam's hand slid down her neck and across her shoulder before slipping away to hang at his side. "Don't worry about us. We'll be fine."

"Princess, our cover is that we're two Doms visiting a fetish vacation destination with our new submissive. It's strong because it's close to the truth. The only people who might possibly suspect us are the bad guys, and that suspicious behavior will help us catch them." Jed kissed her forehead.

Had they lost their minds? Tru didn't doubt their professional abilities. "No, I was talking about Alex and Jewell. I've never brought anyone here before. This dinner is a ruse. They're going to have the two of you under a microscope to see if they think you're good enough for me."

Thoughts creasing his chin and the space between his eyebrows, Liam took a step back. "She kissed us both on the cheek before she left the room."

That wasn't a big deal. "She kisses everybody—babies, puppies, an alligator once—basically anyone who will let her. It used to drive Alex nuts, but he's learned to accept that she's one of those gushy, affectionate people."

Jed chuckled. "She's giving us the benefit of the doubt. Tru, they're your friends. They want to like us because you've chosen us. We're not nervous, and you shouldn't be either."

Telling someone not to be nervous wasn't a great way to soothe their anxiety, but Tru wanted to end the conversation. "If it's okay with you, I'd like to unpack and freshen up before dinner."

"Sure," Liam said, stepping out of her way. "As long as you're naked."

Poised to brush past Liam, Tru froze. She gaped at Liam, asking wordlessly if he was serious. Not even Alex had ever ordered her to get naked unless it was a scene. Nothing in Liam's demeanor indicated that he was kidding, so she reluctantly undressed.

Neither Liam nor Jed watched. As soon as she started to comply, they grabbed their suitcases and threw them on the foot of the bed. Liam riffled through the stack of clothes inside while Jed just reached into the zippered pocket on top and extracted a zip top, plastic bag with a toothbrush and toothpaste inside.

They didn't ignore her as she unpacked her things, but they both went about their business quietly. Jed's cell phone rang, and he went into the bathroom to take the call. Liam fired up his laptop and started tapping on the keys.

Tru decided to unpack their things as well. She preferred to move into a hotel room rather than live out of travel bags. "Is your porn addiction that bad?"

Liam glanced up with a grin. "It's not as bad as my addiction to the Squatch Cam."

This idea intrigued her. While she didn't discount the idea that there were creatures on this planet that humans hadn't discovered, she doubted they'd get video evidence of a Sasquatch. It seemed like a Squatch Cam would capture footage of trees and bears. "Is that what I think it is?"

"Twenty-four hours of surveillance on areas where Squatch sightings have been reported? Yes. But that's not what I'm doing right now. When we checked in, I noticed that all the records are computerized."

It took Tru a second, but she realized what he meant. "You're hacking Alex's books? That's an invasion of privacy."

"Oh, please. He's networked, which means the CIA and shadow organizations like the State Policy Network have already looked." Liam's gaze roved over the data onscreen, so he didn't notice Tru's growing ire.

"Stop it. Alex doesn't deserve to be treated this way. He's a good man—honest and honorable."

He must have heard the catch in her voice that betrayed her anger because he finally looked at her. "If I thought there was anything here, I'd get a warrant. Nothing I find is permissible in court, and none of it is actionable. I'm just making sure he's in the clear."

That did nothing to soothe her rising fury. "I didn't bring you here to spy on Alex's business. He's poured his heart and soul into making Zangari's a successful, lifestyle-friendly vacation spot."

Jed came out of the bathroom and tossed his phone on the bed. "Thanks for unpacking our stuff."

Unwilling to throw in the towel in her staring contest with Liam, Tru nodded curtly.

Liam closed his laptop and crossed the room to where she was standing, hands on hips and steam puffing from her nostrils. "I see that you didn't learn your lesson this afternoon."

He'd not only been upset with her for the risk she'd taken and the time she'd cost, but for topping from the bottom. She put a hand on his chest to protest his assertion and stop him from getting even closer. "I'm not topping from the bottom. I'm sticking up for my friend. It's called loyalty."

"Yeah. I like that about you." He wrapped a hand around her wrist and gently pushed her hand down. "I like your feistiness too. I'd love some trust, maybe the benefit of the doubt?"

"The benefit of the doubt?" She echoed him in an attempt to understand what he meant.

"This is my job, Tru. I can't step around your sense of misplaced outrage unless I lie to you. Is that what you want?"

She wasn't sure whether she wanted him to tell her the truth. Certainly they wouldn't be arguing if he hadn't told her that he was hacking Alex's system. "Perhaps you should keep some things to yourself." It was the best compromise. "I don't need to know everything about your investigation."

"I agree." Jed perched on the edge of the bed. "She should be on a need-to-know basis."

Liam nodded. "I felt she needed to know I was ruling out Alex and Jewell—her friends—as suspects. I thought it'd make her less anxious at dinner to know we weren't targeting them for the investigation."

"That's reasonable. Tru?" Jed's expectant expression prompted her to answer.

The way he phrased it sounded rational. It cast her reaction in a different light, one that wasn't standing on a foundation of altruism and loyalty. She faced Liam. "I'm sorry. I overreacted."

A hard emotion glittered in his eyes, darkening his irises to the color of a storm on the ocean. He grasped her chin with his thumb and forefinger. Though it looked harsh, his tender touch said something else entirely. The contradictory sensations and the look on his face stole her breath. She felt herself surrendering to his gentle dominance.

"The next few days won't be easy. It's imperative that you trust me to both do my job and to be your Dominant. I understand the implications, Tru. I will take care of you. I will see to your needs—not necessarily your wants—but your needs. And I will bring down this murderer."

Something intangible passed between them, the next step of what he'd begun the night they'd watched the stars together. Tru lowered her gaze and fought the urge to sink to her knees. She wanted to kneel before this man, to honor what he wanted to be to her, but she couldn't. Too much was at stake, and so he had to be content with this level of submission. "I understand, Sir."

"Great. Now go freshen up. Jed and I will pick out your outfit for dinner."

Chapter Fifteen

The bathroom door closed, and Jed turned to Dare. He'd been surprised to see Dare and Tru arguing, and he'd been even more surprised to see how well Dare had handled the situation. "You're really coming into your own."

Dare shrugged. "I'm just doing what feels right. I can't believe how liberating it is to just be who I am."

"I feel you." Jed knew exactly what Dare was talking about. The first time a woman had submitted to him, he'd felt a rush of power unlike anything he'd experienced. "It's natural for a sub to push back, especially one with backbone. If she doesn't make you work for her submission, it's not the real thing. You took her in hand and showed her that she could rely on your authority and dominance."

Opening the third drawer in the chest of drawers, Dare extracted a neatly folded stack of clothing. "She definitely keeps us on our toes. I'm glad you came in when you did. Otherwise I think we might not have had such an amiable resolution. You worked your magic, and she calmed right down."

Jed hadn't done much. Both Dare and Tru were reasonable people, though lately he'd been noticing a volatile side to Dare's temperament. He'd also noticed that Tru's carefree, fun-loving attitude came and went with the tide. This woman had depth, the kind he could spend years exploring. "She's stubborn, and that requires a little finesse."

Since that night when Dare and Tru had bonded over cryptids, Jed had sometimes felt like a third wheel. Tonight he'd been the one to take her from upset to contrite with one simple question, something Dare hadn't managed with his explanation. It made him feel more like his old self, suave and confident. He still had a chance to get the girl. Jed looked at the stack of clothing Dare was sorting through to find it consisted of intimate apparel—mostly teddies and half corsets.

He snagged a black corset that would push up and feature the tantalizing swells of her breasts. "She can wear this to dinner."

Dare shrugged, and he appeared relieved that someone else had made the choice. "Where was she hiding this at the last place?"

"Probably in one of her suitcases. I noticed that she didn't unpack everything, so she probably keeps the items she doesn't think she needs put away." This enigma of a woman had a practical side.

Dare's cell phone rang, and the familiar ring tone distracted them. "It's Brandy. She'll want to know what I found out. She thinks we've been here for a few hours already."

Neither of them wanted to tell Brandy that their asset had taken them for a dangerous detour. She'd pull the plug if she thought Tru was off her rocker. Jed didn't think Tru was crazy, but she definitely was an adrenaline junkie. Jed held up the corset. "I'll take this to Tru and keep her busy until you get off the phone."

"Adair." Dare shot him a nasty glare as he answered the phone.

He found Tru standing in front of the mirror with a towel wrapped around her torso. Her hair was up in a messy bun on top of her head, and she applied mascara with a steady hand. Once she finished, she smiled into the mirror at him as she replaced the cap. "Hello, handsome."

He held up the corset. "I want you to wear this."

Her smile stretched into something brilliant. "Let me guess—Liam's the snoop, and you're the hot delivery guy?"

Tugging at where she'd tucked the corner of the towel, he watched as it unraveled and fell away from her luscious, curvy body. "I'm your Dominant, Princess." He wrapped the corset around her ribs, and then he reached in front to adjust her breasts so they fit the cups. "And I want to see you in this."

She held still as he played with her nipples and kneaded her soft globes. All too soon, he heard her breath hitch. Yeah, he loved how responsive she was to his touch. She held the corset against her front while he took his time latching the little hooks in back that held the material together.

"Sir?"

Hearing his title roll from her tongue, the syllable soft and sibilant, gave him a thrill he'd felt very few times before. "Too tight, Princess?"

"No. It's perfect. It seems though, that you forgot a lower half to this outfit. While I don't mind wearing this when it's just the three of us or if we're in a public scene, I do mind dressing like this for dinner with friends."

Somehow that hadn't occurred to him. He chuckled and kissed the curve of her neck and let his hands wander over her exposed skin. "You can pick the rest of the outfit, preferably a skirt, though I don't want you wearing underwear."

"Of course not."

He ran a caress down her hips and squeezed her bottom, and she only pressed her hands to the counter to help her balance.

"Widen your stance."

Wordlessly she obeyed. For the time being, he avoided her offering and continued his slow, sensual exploration of her shower-soft skin. She closed her eyes and gave herself over to him, and that appeased the Dominant part of him that balked a little at sharing her with Dare. The scent of her arousal mixed with the lingering fog from her shower, and he slid two fingers into her pussy.

She moaned, a soft noise that didn't carry far. Perhaps she didn't want to bring Dare into this either.

"Keep quiet, Princess. Dare is on the phone with Brandy straightening out some of the issues you caused by making us get here late." The whole time he warned and admonished her, he pumped his fingers into her.

She opened her eyes halfway and met his gaze in the mirror. "Yes, Sir."

"This is one hot, wet pussy, Princess. Every time I pull my fingers out, it sucks them back in." He curved them to hit the roughness of her sweet spot and to also stimulate the swollen, responsive tissues outside her vagina. Her eyes rolled back, and she grabbed onto his thigh with a grip that would leave bruises. He liked that she was active and physically strong.

Soon enough she came, her pussy walls throbbing on his fingers, and he wrapped an arm around her waist as her legs and knees shook.

Before she could come down and thank him, he extracted his fingers from her pussy and circled the puckered hole she'd denied him before. Shocked and still riding the waves of her orgasm, she gaped at his reflection in the mirror.

"Soft limit?"

She struggled to control her voice. "Yes, Sir."

He inserted the tip of one finger that was still slick from her juices. "I'm going to push your limits tonight." He moved his finger, stretching the muscle she'd already relaxed. "We're going to take you at the same time—Dare in your pussy and me in your ass." He and Dare had discussed this on a theoretical basis, and he wasn't absolutely sure that Dare was on board. However he knew his friend would be up to trying if Tru agreed to it.

She looked away, heavy thoughts jerking her from the cloud of climactic endorphins.

Adding a second finger, he stretched her opening. "What do you think about that, Princess?"

She once again met his gaze. "It's been a really long time for me. I think you should try anal sex without something in my pussy first, Sir."

Jed nodded. With his free hand, he took a condom from his pocket. "Right now?" If she refused, he wouldn't push the issue. This was a soft limit for a reason, and while he knew general reasons for someone not wanting to do this, he didn't know her exact reason. "If you say no, I'll honor your wish."

At his assurance, the rest of her reticence dropped away. "Please go slow, at least to start with." She snagged a fresh towel from the shelf next to the sink, and then she bent over the counter with her legs spread. The towel was under her head.

Jed wanted to see her face, but he reasoned that this was probably the best position to acclimate her to the act. However the lube was in his bag. He picked up her wet towel from the floor and wiped his hand. "Stay like that. I'll be right back."

Dare was in the far corner, tapping away on his keyboard and talking into his phone. He waved Jed away, a silent signal that meant he needed to keep Tru away for longer—which is exactly what Jed had planned.

He returned to find her in the exact same position. Her face was turned toward the door, and she smiled to see him, but this one lacked her usual brash flirtation. He held up the lube to let her know the reason he'd left. He closed and locked the door. "Princess, stay quiet for this. Call yellow if I'm hurting you, and use your safeword if you need it. Remind me what it is."

"Methotrexate."

"Great. For this, you are allowed to masturbate. I'd prefer it if you had a climax too."

"I'll try, Sir."

He smeared lube on his fingers and rubbed it into her tight sphincter, and then he cleaned his hands in the sink before adding a little to the condom. Then he aimed his cockhead at the target—he'd been hard since he'd taken her towel—and pressed forward. She exhaled without being told. He watched her face for signs of distress as he worked his way deeper. Soon he was all the way inside. "How are you doing, Princess?"

"I'm fine, Sir. I do like anal. I just don't let it happen very often. Maybe once before."

He heard her unspoken admission, that she'd given him more than she typically gave to a sex partner or even a Dom. He stroked a soothing circle over her lower back. Last night he'd felt like a temporary addition to a couple that included Tru and Dare. Now that all went out the window, and he'd never felt closer to another human being in his life. Navigating this triad was going to be tricky, especially if Dare was dealing with the same kind of turmoil concerning their gorgeous, captivating submissive.

She reached between her legs and began playing with her clit, and he took that as his cue to get going. He started slow, withdrawing carefully and sinking back into her heat. The noises she made came faster, and he increased his pace. She felt so good, so fucking tight and hot. Her inferno fed his desire, and he needed more. Soon he was fucking her the way he wanted, and she buried her face in the towel and screamed. Jed surged forward once more and swallowed his cry.

At dinner, Liam found himself distracted by thoughts of the job. He had a list of current guests at Zangari's, and now he and Jed needed to find a way to narrow it down. He wanted to ask Tru if she knew any of the guests, but after her reaction to finding out that he had hacked into Alex's system, he didn't know if he should risk it. He needed to get Jed alone to ask his opinion, but ever since they'd had sex in the bathroom while he was on the phone with their boss, Jed had kept Tru close. First he'd helped her select a skirt to go with her corset, and then he'd held her hand or somehow touched her the rest of the time.

The five of them sat around Alex and Jewell's rectangular table, the dark walnut in sharp contrast to the pale yellow walls, and ate salmon. Whatever glaze Jewell had used tasted excellent. This dish didn't need ketchup.

"Liam?" Across the table, Tru watched him with a wrinkle of concern in her chin. "Is everything okay?"

"If you don't like salmon," Jewell said, "I can heat up something else. I have leftover stuffed pork chops from yesterday. Or I can get you something from the restaurant. Our chef can make a lot of different stuff on short notice."

He smiled at Jewell. "This is delicious. I was just lost in thought. I left a tricky problem on my desk."

"Leave work at work." Jed, who'd artfully slid into the seat next to Tru, laughed. "Enjoy your vacation." He squeezed Tru's thigh under the table, but the way he did it made it obvious what he was doing.

Liam turned his attention to Jewell. "So how did you and Tru meet?"

At the foot of the table, Jewell giggled. "Let's see. It was about four years ago, I think. I was at a rest stop in the middle of nowhere, New Mexico. It was super hot, like a hundred and ten, and I wanted to get inside, find some cold water and a bathroom, you know? Anyway, this trucker catcalls me. He says, 'Hey baby, it's ninety-eight-point-seven over here.' I keep walking, do my business, buy some snacks and an iced drink. I run into Tru in the bathroom, and we had a laugh about the asshole trucker dude because he used some other dumbass line on her. She made me feel better—he really had freaked me out."

Alex, seated at the head of the table, pressed his lips together. This was obviously a tale he'd heard before, and he'd probably come to terms with the fact that he couldn't drop kick that back-alley scum out of existence.

Meanwhile, Jewell continued. "I leave, heading back to my car. The jerk is still there, and he says, 'I want some stanky on my hang-down.' I'm scared, you know? I'm really scared because this guy is bigger than me and covered with tattoos—real scary."

Liam shot another glance at Alex. Though he had a lanky build, he was muscular and significantly bigger than Jewell. His arms sported sleeve tattoos. Those on his left arm came all the way up to his shoulder, and the art on his right arm was nearly that high.

Oblivious, Jewell plunged forward with her story. "Tru had come out right behind me. When that guy opened his mouth, she said, 'If you don't shut the fuck up, I'm going to break your jaw.' So, okay, I know she's like a heck of a lot taller than me, but Tru seems so nice and gentle, so I'm afraid for her too. Then the guy says, 'I'll break your jaw by shoving my dick in it, bitch.' I'm trying to grab Tru's hand and tell her to come on, but she's not having any of it."

Jewell giggled at this point, so Liam figured that Tru ended up with the last word.

Leaning forward as if to let them in on a big secret, she finished her anecdote. "Tru shakes me off and goes up to him—he's sitting on a picnic bench about ten feet away—and she slaps her hands over his ears. He wasn't expecting that, let me tell you, and I was thinking that we'd better run, but then he lets loose with this high-pitched scream and falls to the ground."

Regarding Tru with respectful surprise, Liam said, "You ruptured his eardrum?"

She shrugged. "We didn't stay to find out. We ran to her car, which was closer, and she drove me to the next city. I had a rental car that had broken down on the off ramp to the rest area, and I needed a tow."

Jewell piped in. "It was only twenty miles, but I knew we'd be friends forever. Then she introduced me to Alex, and now my life is perfect."

Liam had been under the impression that Tru knew Alex because she was friends with Jewell. He gestured to Alex. "How long have you known Tru?"

Alex finished swallowing his potatoes before responding. "About thirteen years. We met at a cancer survivor support group. Tru's cancer had just come back, and she was having a tough time. I stayed after to talk with her, and we've been good friends ever since."

Tru and Alex exchanged one of those looks that said they'd been through Hell and back together. This close friendship didn't push any jealousy buttons, but it definitely bothered Liam that she hadn't found an opportunity to mention surviving cancer—twice. Through this lens, her risk-taking took on new meaning. All this reading and research on personality and behavior that Jordan had been making him do flooded back into his brain. Six likely reasons for why she insisted on base jumping swirled through his mind—everything from chemo messing with her brain chemistry to her having an addiction to near-death-experiences. He exchanged a look with Jed, and he knew his partner had realized some of the same things.

"Cancer, huh?" Liam strove for a neutral tone. "How long have you been in remission?"

"Almost twenty years." Alex sipped his wine. "I was fifteen when I was diagnosed with leukemia, and once I beat it, I became a counselor for a teen group. Tru was co-counselor with me."

Liam wished Tru would have revealed all of this in private, but now that it was out in the open, he was compelled to ask follow-up questions. Call it a professional hazard. He loosed his interrogative skill on the woman he liked. "What about you, Tru? How old were you that first time around?"

She didn't look like she wanted to answer, but she did. "Nine the first time and nineteen the second time. Somehow or another, I didn't get it again at twenty-nine. But, hey, there's always thirty-nine, right?"

"Don't talk like that." Alex's brows drew together in a severe slash. "You're a survivor."

"Yeah," Jewell echoed. "You're going to die peacefully in your sleep of natural causes when you're ninety-three."

That seemed an awfully specific sentiment. Jed's short burst of laughter drew all eyes to him. "Ninety-three? Are you psychic?"

Liam sensed that Jed was going to work a way to make fun of him into the conversation. While he might believe that there were plenty of undocumented species out there, and that the government and big business were all up in people's private lives, he did not believe in extra-sensory abilities or sixth senses. The one psychic he'd worked with before at the Detroit field office hadn't been accurate about anything. Liam rushed to Jewell's defense. "She's being positive. Our Tru was very negative about her future prospects."

"I'm not psychic." Jewell giggled. "It would be so awesome if I was, though. Can you imagine being able to know what's going to happen? It might ruin the ending of a couple movies, but those are so predictable anyway."

Jed nodded thoughtfully. "I always thought it would be useful to be able to see the future."

"Forensic psychics see the past." Liam didn't put much stock in them. "Shawn Spencer used observation and clues to deduce what happened at a crime scene, and he extrapolated what people might do based on evidence."

"That's a TV show." Jed snorted. "Not real life."

"But plausible." Alex threw his support behind Liam. "More plausible than someone holding onto a scarf and saying they see the murderer—especially before it happens."

Tru didn't participate in the conversation. She merely listened while she ate, her expression tight and guarded. Liam wondered if she was still upset by the revelation that she'd beat cancer twice or if she didn't like the current topic of conversation. If she was open-minded about the existence of cryptids, then she was probably a believer in the sixth sense.

It was after nine by the time they returned to their servant-themed room. Tru sat in a chair and undid the straps binding her high heels to her ankles. Liam wanted to bind her in other ways. Restricting her movement made him feel powerful, but he wanted more than a physical show of submission. He needed to see it in her eyes, on her face, and in her posture.

She looked up when he came toward her, a soft, tired smile on her lips. "I had a nice time at dinner, Sir."

He lifted her up, took her seat, and put her on his lap. Jed perched on the foot of the bed across from them. Tru dropped her gaze, waiting for him to take the lead.

"Methotrexate is a chemotherapy drug." And she'd chosen it for her safeword. Taking a breath, he decided not to pussyfoot around the issue. "How come you never told us that you were a cancer survivor?"

She stared at a spot on the floor, her spine stiff. "I don't see that it's relevant."

He smoothed a hand up and down her spine. "Is that why you do dangerous things? Are you addicted to the rush, or do you feel that you're not worthy of being alive?"

Slowly she lifted her gaze, and when her eyes met his, he was shocked by the sadness haunting the depths of her brown pools. "When I got sick the second time, I thought for sure that I was going to die. The second time leukemia comes back, the chances of recovery suck. Gram had me make a bucket list. We're both realists, and neither of us saw a reason to pretend that I'd outlive her. She took me to swim with sharks and to see Australia. I dropped out of college because what was the point of continuing?" She swallowed and looked away.

Liam gave her time because he knew this wasn't easy for her to talk about, and he never stopped the soothing pattern he traced on either side of her spine. Jed reached out and caressed her cheek, and she leaned into his tender touch.

"It's going to come back again." She sighed. "Third time's the charm. So I travel. I see the world because I may never get another chance to do this again. My number could be up at any moment, so I'm not going to pass up any experience that appeals to me." Turning to him suddenly, she cupped his cheek. "Like you, Sir. You appeal to me. Submitting to you appeals to me. Giving myself to you appeals to me. I know it's just while we're here, but I'm not going to pass up the chance to live out my dream." She reached for Jed, and he gave her his hand. "You said you had plans for me tonight. Please don't let something that's so far in the past affect how you see me. I'm not fragile, and I'm not currently sick. I am your submissive, and I don't want that to change."

Liam loved the way she embraced life, though he disliked what it cost her to maintain that attitude. She hadn't answered his question—it was likely she didn't know the answer—and he realized that she'd never stopped checking the boxes on her bucket list. How many cancer survivors had this much trouble accepting the fact that they had survived? He needed to ask Avery if it was possible for someone who beat cancer to have survivor's guilt this badly.

He frowned at Jed because his buddy hadn't shared any plans with him. He didn't even expect to have sex because the day had been long, and they were all tired. "What plans?"

"Anal sex." Jed stood and pulled Tru to her feet. "We're going to have her at the same time."

They'd talked about double penetration, with Liam taking her pussy and Jed fucking her ass, but they hadn't finalized anything. The kinky idea appealed to Liam, though he wasn't one-hundred percent sure that he'd like it in reality. Incidental touching happened, as she'd teased them, but so far they'd kept it to a minimum.

Liam stood and traced a caress down the side of her face. "Are you sure about this? I thought this was a limit?"

"Soft limit." Her subdued tone washed over his Dom instinct. "I promise to use my safeword if I need to. Please, Sirs. I want to do this. I want to be between you, to have you push me to a new level—to know what it's like to have both of you claim me at the same time."

He kissed her, a sweet show of affection as he tried to communicate that she didn't have to live her life as if tomorrow would be her last day on Earth, but he wasn't sure if the message registered. And so he silently vowed to claim her, to strip her of control and drive her out of her negative headspace.

"I want to flog you." He sucked kisses down her neck, leaving pink marks in his wake.

"I saw a bondage frame in one of the playrooms we passed on our way back from dinner." Jed wore his problem-solving face. "It would be perfect for this situation because her front and back would be open."

Liam was sure those rooms had to be scheduled in advance.

Tru confirmed this. "It's signed out already, but I know Alex has one in his private dungeon that he'd let us use."

"He won't mind us using his private play space?" Jed lifted a brow. "I'm not sure I'd be so generous, especially if I planned to use it."

"They're not using it right now." She grasped Jed's hand. "Didn't you notice how Jewell kept shifting while we were eating? He's already had a session with her today, probably after she tackled me. I'll call and ask."

Asking to use another Dom's equipment was something the Dom should do. Liam swiped her cell phone out of her hand. "Alex? This is Liam. We're wondering if the bondage frame is free? No? Yeah, we'd love to use yours, if you don't mind. Great, thanks." He ended the call and set her phone on the table. "Let's go, Princess. It's time to earn your crown."

Jed had already grabbed the toy bag. He slung it over his shoulder. "That's my name for her."

Liam shrugged. If they were going to share her submission and her body, then they could share the cute nicknames. "Now it's ours." He parked his hand on the back of Tru's neck and guided her toward the exit.

Jewell answered the door wearing a luxurious robe, and she guided them to the basement. "Alex is in bed. He took a sleeping pill tonight, so don't worry about being too loud. I'll be up late because I'm on call at the Inn, so don't worry about me either. The room has been soundproofed, so any noises will be dampened anyway." She unlocked the door with a key on a string she wore around her neck. "Alex says it's okay to use the rope and floggers, just don't put them away when you're done so that I can clean them."

Inside Liam found the dungeon of his dreams, not that he'd started thinking about the type of dungeon he'd build if he had the space for one. This one, though, gave him definite ideas. The obligatory St. Andrew's cross was positioned against one wall, the black lacquered timber dominating that space. Behind it, many implements hung from hooks on the wall. Alex had installed the peg board typically found in workshops, and he'd organized his impact play toys neatly.

The dungeon also contained a padded spanking bench that looked like it could be modified to bind the sub in several different positions. Chains hung from the ceiling in a few places, attached to the semi-exposed rafters with massive O-rings. The bondage frame occupied a third wall, but it was the setup on the fourth wall that drew Liam's attention. The whole wall was tiled like a bathroom, and stainless steel restraints protruded from the wall at strategic intervals. Five feet in front of it, the floor was similarly treated, and it sloped toward two different drains. A hose was coiled near one side, and the other side had different detachable shower heads. Finally, a glass enclosure completed the motif.

"What's this for?" Liam considered the different kinks he'd studied, and none of them fit what he saw.

"It's a Houdini tank." Jewell smiled. "We like water play."

Liam didn't judge. If Alex liked to bind his submissive wife and squirt water at her, more power to them. The enclosure mystified him, though. It was only open at the top. "How do you get in there?"

She pointed to a stepladder. "Master ties me up, carries me up the steps, and lowers me in."

Jed tapped on the glass. "Plexi. How high does he fill it up?"

"All the way. He likes to put me in there when it's empty—he attaches weights to my ankles so I can't float—and he watches me struggle to keep my face above the water line." Her eyes softened and clouded over. "He won't give me the snorkel until I beg, and I like to see how long I can go without begging."

It didn't seem very sexy or sensual. Liam couldn't help but ask. "Then what?"

"Then he gives me a snorkel so I can breathe. Water calms me. It's incredible, to be in there, unable to move, and to see him out here, watching me, and to know that I can't get out unless he wants me out."

Liam was about to ask another question, but Tru's headshake caught the corner of his eye. "Okay. Well, thanks for letting us use your dungeon."

Jewell gestured to a door on the far side of the room. "There's the aftercare room. Feel free to use anything you want. I have creams and oils, blankets, towels, and I put a robe in there. I didn't know if you'd remember to bring one for Tru or not." She backed out of the room. "I'll be around if you need me. Just poke your head in the hall and holler. Like I said, Alex will be dead to the world in about ten minutes."

The door closed, and the three of them stared at the water tank in silence. Finally Jed cleared his throat. "Well, that's a new one."

"Yeah." Liam shook his head. "To each their own."

"Jewell loves water bondage." Tru spoke softly, hesitantly. "I've read that the pressure on the sprayers can be changed to feel like different floggers. But I don't think we should use any of that equipment without permission."

"And training." Jed crooked his finger at Tru. "I want you on your knees, Princess."

She went to him, her position submissive, but she didn't kneel. "Sir, that's a hard limit, remember?"

"Why?" Liam had a suspicion that she was trying to keep from submitting completely, which was unacceptable. She stared at the floor, and she showed no sign of answering. "Do you have an injury we should know about?"

"No, Sir."

"Then that's not a hard limit I'll honor." Liam gripped a handful of hair with the intention of forcing her to her knees, but Jed put a hand on his shoulder.

He regarded Liam with empathy in his brown eyes. "You can't disregard a hard limit. You can question it, and you can disagree with it, but you have no choice but to honor it."

"This is bullshit."

"I agree."

Tru looked from Jed to Liam. "I'm not ready to kneel before you, Sirs. It isn't personal. Please be patient. We're only together for a few days."

Liam vowed to get to the bottom of this. Her reticence had its roots in something deeper, and it was probably related to her post-cancer issues. Since he had his hand tangled in her hair, he pulled her to him and kissed her roughly. She yielded to the onslaught.

Once he released her, Jed did the same. His kiss controlled and possessed, and it communicated his displeasure. Tru melted in his arms, and when he finished, he pushed her into Liam's arms. They took turns, violently assaulting her with their ardor because they were going to have her submission whether she knelt or not. By the time they had enough, she stood between them, gasping for breath but begging no quarter.

Liam's ire fled, and he peppered her neck with gentle kisses as he untied the stays on her corset. Jed removed her skirt, and she was naked in no time.

The footings of the bondage frame were bolted to the floor, and the device was situated perpendicular to the wall. Jed grasped the crossbar and swung from it. The thing barely dipped under his weight. "Solid."

Liam joined him, and the contraption held them both. "Safe enough for Princess." They dropped to the floor, and he faced Jed. "Have you ever used one of these things before?"

Jed shook his head. "I've seen a demonstration, though."

"Sirs?" Tru stood before them, her head bowed in a show of submission. "I've used a bondage frame before, both as a sub and as an alpha sub or beta Domme. I can help."

While she talked, Liam studied the placement of O-rings. "Thanks, but we can figure it out. I brought a gag for you, Princess."

It took longer than he thought it would to get the rigging right. Jed had an idea of weaving her into the ropes like she was caught in a makeshift spiderweb, but Liam remembered Jordan's advice—keep it simple until he was ready for complicated. They ended up tying Tru's wrists and ankles to the frame so that she was spread out but still able to stand up.

They circled her, looking for weak points in the design or places where the rope might cut into her circulation. Liam had spent some time studying the issue, and he'd ended up wrapping the rope almost to her elbows so that it didn't dig in at one point when pressure was applied.

A sharp crack rent the air, and Tru yelped, reminding him that he hadn't yet gagged her. The ball gag he'd purchased with her in mind wasn't all that large, but it would muffle her screams. Power surged through his veins as he tightened the strap that held it in place. Bound and gagged, she was at their mercy. With the feeling of power came a profound peace that confirmed once and for all that he was right to pursue this path.

He and Jed touched her everywhere, gentle caresses turning rough as they prepared her for the torture they'd planned. This was something he and Jed had talked about at length while they'd been waiting to rejoin her. Communication between the two of them during the scene was of paramount importance. Jed pressed squishy, bright red foam balls into each of Tru's hands.

"Drop these if you need to safeword, Princess." At her nod, Jed continued. "We're going to blindfold you."

Liam fit the padded mask over her eyes. He'd tried it on himself, and he'd found that the thing let in no light. This was the moment he'd anticipated for weeks, ever since he'd briefly flogged Layla. This was different because Tru was *his* submissive, not a loan from a friend. He started on her back with a deerskin flogger. She relaxed into the rhythm quickly, and he knew the random jerks and muffled cries had to do with Jed who was playing with her nipples.

Soon he switched to something with more bite, a classic cat made from elk hide. Malcolm had used this one on him, and so he knew that it would hurt at first, but the sensations would soon blend together and take her to subspace. She cried out, a high, clear sound that penetrated the ball gag as if it weren't there. Liam looked to her hands to see if she'd dropped either ball, but she still had them squeezed tightly in her fists, so he kept going.

Jed stood in front of her, and Liam was grateful to have him there. It gave him more confidence to let loose and give her exactly what he wanted her to experience—and if he accidentally entered Dom space, Jed would get him out of it.

Tru's back was on fire, and the sensations moved to her ass and upper thighs. She couldn't remember the last time she'd been flogged like this. Alex had never been much of a sadist, but it didn't seem that Liam had that problem. Each lash fell forcefully on her backside, and his heavy-handed style didn't wane.

Dimly, she heard Jed tell Liam to switch hands, and the bite eased a little.

In front of her, distracting her from concentrating on the pain, Jed wrapped a rope twice around her left breast. He plumped her right one and bound it in a similar fashion. Blood pooled in her white globes, making them tingle with pain. Then he alternated flogging each boob. The tingling sting came from the restricted blood flow, and though the flogger didn't hurt, the impact of each blow sent delicious prickles that radiated in her pussy and her toes.

Behind her, Liam's unwavering enthusiasm picked up, and she figured that he'd switched back to his right hand. For a beginner, he'd sure discovered his inner sadist quickly. The pain was beginning to blur together, though, and the haze of light subspace clouded her thoughts.

Then a searing pain in her breasts cleared some of the fog away. Jed had freed her breasts, and now he didn't have to touch them to make her scream through the gag. Tears rained down her cheeks, and she was sure drool did as well since she'd forgotten to swallow the saliva a ball gag stimulated.

Sharp pinpricks of pain traveled up the underside of her arms and radiated over her ribs. Her body jerked as much as it could in this position, but the agony followed her wherever she moved. Suddenly her mind took flight, and the pain became a distant sensation that morphed to pleasure. Each pinprick was a caress, and each lick of the flogger was the pressure of a snuggle. Vaguely she was aware of her knees giving out.

When her mind remembered how to function, she found herself stomach down on the spanking bench, unrestrained, with her face resting on the pad meant for her chest. The ball gag was gone, and someone had cleaned her cheeks and chin, but the blindfold was still in place. Behind her, she felt a cock enter her pussy, and she didn't know whose it was. She waited for the feel of thighs against hers—Liam had more leg hair than Jed—but the sensation never came.

The puzzle helped her brain return to rational thought, and she realized the thing inside her pussy wasn't a cock. It was harder, and as the right term came to mind, the thing purred to life. She meant to gasp, but a soft sigh was the only sound she heard.

Her arms moved. One of her Sirs was positioning them behind her back. She had no energy to help or resist. When they didn't fall back down to her sides, she figured he must have tied together the ropes that were still wrapped around them. Next, they slid her completely onto the bench, and her head was no longer supported. She let it hang down because she didn't have the energy to lift it up.

The Sir behind her spread her legs wider and tied her ankles to the posts of the bench. He moved the vibrator, fucking her with long, slow strokes. Pleasure filled all the points pain had vacated, and she whimpered.

"You're going to climax, Princess." Liam's voice sounded near her ear, and she figured he was the one near her head. "You did beautifully tonight. You're so fucking gorgeous. With a room like this, I could torture you for hours. I'd flog you, bind you, fuck you, and force you to orgasm—whatever I wanted."

The idea of being at his mercy pushed her over the edge. Tru had never seriously entertained the idea of belonging to anyone before, and now a seed of hope, hidden in a dark corner of her heart so that sunlight would never find it, sprang to life. Too tired to stomp it down, she left it alone to deal with later. A climax washed through her insides, and she could only moan.

The vibrator vacated its place, and the ropes binding her wrists and ankles dropped away. Jed picked her up and carried her to the aftercare room, the solid wall of his bare chest providing more comfort than she had ever let herself feel before this. He set her on a soft bed, and then he peeled away the blindfold.

She prepared to squint and blink as she became used to the glare, but they'd dimmed the lights. She said nothing as they rubbed her down with a sweet smelling cream and wrapped her in a large, soft blanket.

Then Liam gathered her in his arms. "We're going to go back to our room, Princess."

She snuggled into his embrace and closed her eyes. This wasn't how she'd thought the night would end.

Chapter Sixteen

Tru woke to the feel of an erection pressed against her ass. She struggled to shake off the fog of sleep, but with a masculine body pressed to each side of her, it proved difficult. Hoping movement would help rouse her, she shifted.

"You keep doing that, I'm going to fuck you whether you're asleep or awake." The sleep-rough voice belonged to Liam.

Neither of them had climaxed last night, and she felt guilty about that. "Sir," she mumbled, "I'm awake enough."

He flopped onto his back and reached clumsily for something on the table. Someone had left the bathroom light on, though the door was mostly closed, so Tru rolled and lifted her head to see what he was after. That woke her fully.

Someone had put condoms on the bedside table. Liam snagged one, pushed the covers down his body, and rolled it on without opening his eyes. "Hop on."

She straddled him and grabbed the bottle of lubricant someone had also put on the table, and she rubbed it from clit to hole before she positioned his cock at her entrance. "I'm going to wake you up, Sir." She sank down slowly, luxuriating in the feel of his thickness penetrating her thirsty pussy. "I'm going to thank you for last night."

"It's still last night." Jed's rich baritone came from the darker side of the bed.

She looked over to see the scant light reflecting in his dark irises like candlelight and chocolate. "I seem to remember you promising to have me at the same time." She drew her hands up her thighs and across her stomach. Traveling higher, she lifted the tender round globes of her breasts, still sore from Jed's ministrations, and a whimper escaped.

"I seem to remember that as well." Jed pushed the covers down, and she realized that they'd both gone to bed as naked as her. By the time they'd made it back to the room, Tru had been sound asleep. She barely remembered them putting her in bed, and nothing afterward.

He got out of bed and went into the bathroom.

Tru focused on pleasuring Liam. She fingered her clit as she rocked her hips, giving him a show because she knew how much he liked to watch. He let her play for the space of three heartbeats, and then he pulled her down to take control with one demanding kiss. Tru melted in the face of his mastery. When it came to these two, she had no will to resist their demands or the way they watered the newly awakened seed in her heart.

He released her lips almost reluctantly, and a cocky smile tilted the corners of his mouth. "Get Jed ready, Princess."

Another set of hands, this time belonging to Jed, guided her face to the side. Jed held his semi-hard cock in one hand, and she opened her mouth. He let her lick and suck until his erection was full, and then he took over, fucking her mouth with shallow strokes. Beneath her, Liam moved her hips up and down without urgency.

Jed withdrew his cock and claimed her lips for a kiss that drugged her senses. When he ended it, he traced a finger along her bottom lip. "Remember to use your safeword if it's too much."

"Yes, Sir."

Beneath her, Liam spread his legs, which forced her to also spread wider. The bed dipped, and she realized that he'd made room for Jed. She felt his fingers at her back entrance, spreading lubricant, and she remembered how wonderful it had felt to have him take her this way earlier. However at the time there hadn't been a cock in her vagina. Things were going to be tight for sure.

She felt the gentle pressure of his cock on her sphincter, and she exhaled as he pressed forward. It felt good—so unbelievably good. She was full, trapped between the two men who made her feel so very alive. Her entire body trembled with pleasure and anticipation.

A hiss beneath her caused her eyes to fly open. Liam's blue eyes were wide with shock, and she realized that this was his first time as well.

He swore softly.

"Sir? Are you okay?" It hadn't occurred to her that he might find this uncomfortable. After all, she was the one with two dicks in her body.

"Fine." He exhaled hard, a sibilant sound that belied his assurance.

"Are you sure? You can safeword too." Somewhere in the press of bodies, she'd collapsed against his chest, and she felt the staccato rhythm of his heart thumping against hers.

He smacked her thigh, his sharp reprimand catching a welt from her flogging. She yelped.

"No topping from the bottom. I said I was fine, now drop it."

Tru knew when to shut up. Jed withdrew, and he surged forward as Liam withdrew. They experimented in search of a rhythm that worked for both of them, and Tru remained as still as she could while they played around.

Except that it was difficult to not move when her Sirs were doing wondrous things to her body. She moaned and whimpered, burying her face in Liam's neck and digging her nails into his arms and shoulders in her struggle.

Liam murmured halves of phrases meant to comfort her, but his eyes had taken on that dreamy half-mast look they got when he was close. Jed pitched forward, planting his hands on either side of Liam and sealing his front to her back. He grunted swear words and dirty talk into her other ear.

"Beautiful, you're doing great." Liam's assurance was slurred, but the meaning was there. "You feel so good."

"Your ass is so tight and hot, Princess. I could fuck it every fucking day."

So alike, yet so different. Her Sirs were perfect in every way. An orgasm washed over her, the kind that was hot and cold at the same time. It detonated in her pussy and traveled up her spine. She lost control, and her body bucked wildly. Dimly she realized that Liam had banded his arms around her, and that Jed had wrapped his hand in her hair and jerked her head back to stop her from bashing it into either him or Liam.

They kept fucking her. The orgasm stretched, and she heard a shrill scream before a hand clamped over her mouth. Wave after wave battered her until their shouts joined her never-ending, keening cry.

Orgasm. There was a word she loved. It was round and made the speaker's mouth pucker and hum, which her body was still doing.

Later, they both held her, raining soft kisses on her head, face, neck, and shoulders while their hands trailed soothing caresses down her body. Safe and secure between her Sirs, she fell back asleep.

"Tell me something I don't know about you." Tru followed her request with a flippant wink.

Jed's first inclination was to not answer. They were in the public dining room during the height of breakfast service, and he knew she wasn't after more information on his cover. A steady *scrape-scrape* came from across the table. Dare glanced up for a second, but he said nothing as he continued buttering his toast.

"Come on." Now her luscious lips turned down in a cute pout. "I told you stuff about me that I don't go around telling people."

"That you're a cancer survivor?" Jed needed clarification because he thought her preference for having two lovers was pretty much out in the open.

"Yes. That."

"You let us figure out the death wish thing on our own." The snarky statement slipped out. Jed wasn't okay with her dangerous pursuits, and the more time he spent as her Dominant, the less he felt inclined to indulge that particular interest. "By making us watch."

With the flick of her wrist and a sour moue, she waved away his concern. "I don't have a death wish. I just like extreme sports. Look, if you don't want to share, don't, okay?"

A server set a bottle of ketchup next to Dare. He shook it up and squirted some on his eggs and hash browns. "I like ketchup on my eggs. It's like a tomato veggie smoothie."

She pressed her lips together. "You're both assholes, you know that?"

Jed closed his hand over the fist she'd balled up on her lap. "Princess, this isn't the right place for that kind of conversation."

Tru rolled her eyes, and that's when he noticed they were tearing up.

"I'm adopted." Dare studied her expression, so Jed did too. She seemed to be on the border between Sarcasmland and Tearsville. At his admission, she veered toward Tearsville. "And you're having subdrop."

"I'm not—" She broke off. "Maybe I am. I'm sorry."

Jed pried open her fist and threaded his fingers through hers. "It's okay to drop. We're here for you, and we're not going anywhere."

"I was seven," Dare continued. "My birth mother became addicted to meth, and I ended up in the foster care system. I moved around to different homes for a couple years, and then I met my adoptive mother. She was a single mom too, but she didn't feel the need to escape into drugs. She's a great lady."

Tru's mouth opened and closed. "I'm sorry to hear that, but I'm glad you ended up with a new mom that you like. Have you ever tried to reconnect with your birth mother?"

Dare used his fork to scoop ketchup-covered eggs into his mouth. "She had her chance, and I've moved on. I have a mom who cares about me. That's all I need."

Tru's eyes glazed over for several seconds, like she was seeing something that wasn't there. Perhaps she was lost in memories of losing her parents at around the same age. Before long, she returned to them, and she stared down at her plate of half-eaten fruit and waffles. "If you happen to bump into her anywhere, you should be polite. It's not easy to get clean and put your life back together."

As a response, Dare scowled. Jed knew what Tru didn't—that Dare's birth mother had left him home alone without food for days on end. Social services got involved because he had been chronically truant from school, and they'd found him malnourished, living in an apartment that didn't have electricity or running water. He'd been through so many foster homes because he'd hoarded food and acted out at every single one of them.

Jed tried to smooth things over, but tears gushed down Tru's cheeks. She jumped up, mumbling, "I'm sorry," as she fled the room.

"I'll go after her." Jed threw his napkin on the table. "It's subdrop more than anything else."

Dare stared at his ketchup-stained eggs. "I do look her up from time to time. She's married and has four kids."

Jed put a hand on Dare's shoulder as he passed his buddy. "Joyce is an amazing mom. I'll make sure Tru knows you're not upset with her."

Dare aimlessly stabbed at his eggs, but he didn't reply.

He found Tru with her face buried in a pillow, sobs shaking her whole body. He gathered her into his arms and rocked her gently, making soothing *shhh* sounds. Five minutes passed, then ten. By the fifteen minute mark her sobs had calmed into occasional sniffles.

"Dare isn't upset with you."

"I know. He's upset with his birth mother, and he's going to be very mean to her when they meet—mean, like he's never been before. Maybe she deserves it, but he will feel very guilty about it for the rest of his life. He's not a mean person."

Jed chuckled. "Princess, don't worry about that. It isn't going to happen."

"They're going to meet up at a park with lots of people around." Tru slapped her palm over her mouth. "I need to stop talking. I have no idea what I'm saying. I'm sorry."

Thinking back to their conversation the night before and the way Tru had withdrawn from it, Jed leaned back to better see her face. "Tru? Can you see the future?"

She shook her head, but she refused to meet his gaze. "I'm just a little crazy with the subdrop. Give me some time. The insanity will fade."

He grasped her chin and forced her to look at him. "No lies, Princess, or you will be punished."

"No, I can't see the future." She held his gaze until her face scrunched up and she jerked away in time to sneeze. She slid off his lap and went for the tissue box. "I see images, snippets only, that flash through my mind once and then they're gone. They never repeat, and they don't come with a caption to help them make sense." She blew and wiped, and then she faced him. "Please don't tell Liam any of this. He already thinks I need therapy."

Turning the issue over in his mind, Jed didn't see where Dare needed to know about this until Tru told him herself. "Did you see Dare meeting his birth mother?"

"I see an image of her with some guy who's about her age, and three or four kids. Two are teenagers, and the other one is younger. I'm not sure about the fourth one. Maybe it's a friend. I don't know how they come to be in the same place. There are lots of people in the background, so maybe it's a public event or a park. I can't hear what he says, but the look on his face is hateful. She tries to speak, but he won't let her."

Jed ran a washcloth under cold water and pressed it to her eyes. "Hold that there for a bit." He guided her to the bed and made her sit down. Her vision fit with what Dare had just told him about his research. "What makes you think it's his birth mother in your vision?"

She shrugged. "I don't know."

"What makes you think he'll feel guilty afterward?"

"I would." She slid the cloth from her eyes and turned the full power of those deep brown pools on him. "Please don't say anything, okay? If I was in my right mind, I wouldn't have said anything in the first place. Can we forget about this conversation?"

He stroked her hair and kissed her forehead. "No, but I won't say anything to Dare. You can tell him yourself when you think the time is right. I think it's kind of cool that you have visions. Did you see me before we met?"

"Yeah. And Liam. That's why I knew the three of us would work together." She put the cloth back in place. The coolness would help the swelling around her eyes.

He wanted to ask more, like if she saw a future for them, but he held his tongue. If he had his way, it would happen. Instead he turned his thoughts to more practical matters. "What about the body you found? Did you have a vision to tell you where to look?"

"No. But I did have a vision that told me you were coming. When I saw Liam and you in the same place, it was a little shocking at first. I didn't know what to do with both of you—at first. Then I went with my gut, and here we are." She laughed a little, and he took that as a good sign.

"What about the murderer? Can you get a vision of him?"

She removed the cloth again and stared at him. "It's not like the movies. I can't control it, and I don't generally get helpful visions. They're mostly flashes of faces or things, and if there's any talking, the sound is turned off."

He wanted to discuss it further, but the door opened, and Dare came inside. He set two foil-wrapped plates on the dresser before sitting on the other side of Tru.

He stroked her back. "Princess, I'm sorry. You meant well. It's just that it took me a long time to stop hating the world. I have looked her up. It's why I got caught hacking into the CIA in the first place."

Jed eyed his friend skeptically. "Why would you think the CIA had information on her? You'd need the State database, not a Federal one."

Dare made an open-handed, circular gesture in the air as he thought. "I didn't know where to find information, and one of my conspiracy groups said that the CIA kept records like that. If I had done research, I would have just hacked into the State of Michigan, and then I wouldn't have been arrested or forced to work for the FBI in exchange for not serving time."

Tru cupped his cheek, turning his face to hers. "No, I'm sorry. I forgot that I get a little crazy the day after an intense scene. Last night was intense. And incredible. Thank you."

Dare must have moved on because he kissed Tru with possessive tenderness. "It's okay to want to get to know me better. I probably should have led with something more innocuous like the fact that I'm an only child or that my mom is seventy-five. That's unusual for a thirty-four-year-old man."

She giggled. "Gram is seventy-four, and she raised me. I bet Gram would get along well with your mom."

Jed felt a little left out, especially since he'd been the one to follow and comfort her, but as the day wore on, that feeling subsided. They took turns cuddling in bed with her and watching television, and after lunch, he took her for a romantic stroll along the shore while Dare worked in the room. They talked a lot, and he ended up telling her about his family. He didn't have a tragic story like Tru or Dare. His parents were racing through life at full speed, his younger brother was in law school, and his older brother was a wildlife researcher who traveled a lot. He amused her with tales of his childhood exploits.

She laughed a lot, and she shared similar stories that opened her life to him. By the time they climbed the steep path back to the Inn, he felt like he'd known her for years. This woman, he realized, was beautiful inside and out. Despite his best efforts to treat this as a fling—as per their agreement—he was falling for her. He held her hand as they walked because he couldn't stand the thought of not having physical contact.

They ran into Alex on the way back. He grinned to see them approach, and he broke away from the group of employees to whom he'd been speaking. "Jewell said you had quite a session last night."

Neither Jed nor Dare had said anything to Jewell except to thank her for the use of their dungeon. He wrinkled his brows. "She did?"

"Yeah. She said you had to carry Tru back to the room."

Tru leaned closer to Jed and squeezed his hand. "They did. I don't remember getting back to the room at all. Thanks for letting us play."

Alex nodded. "My pleasure. Hey, there's a new white water rafting outfit about an hour from here. Jewell wants to check it out tomorrow, but between my heart and back, I can't go with her."

"I'd love to go." Tru's eyes sparkled. "Sir, can we go?"

"We?" Jed wasn't sure if she was asking him along.

"You, Liam, me, and Jewell. It'll be fun."

Jed wondered what was wrong with Alex's heart that he couldn't go with his wife. The man was too young for heart disease. The back thing was easier to infer—active people often suffered from problems later in life. Out loud he shook his head. "Not this time, Princess. We have other plans for you tomorrow." And now he was going to have to think of an activity that would also let him stick around and do the kind of surveillance he needed to do. As it was, he'd planned to steer Tru toward the common room so they could engage other patrons in small talk. It would be fun for Tru, and he'd be firmly in investigation mode.

"I love rafting." Her bottom lip came out in a pretend pout that didn't last long. "However I'm looking forward to whatever you have in store for me, Sir."

Alex looked from Jed to Tru. "If you change your mind, let me know."

"We will." Without letting go of Jed's hand, she stepped forward and rose to her toes to kiss Alex's cheek. "Dinner tonight?"

"Sure." He peered over her head at Jed. "How about we hang out while the subs cook? I have a great single malt I was going to open tonight."

Tru turned the full power of her begging face on him, and he found himself consenting because it's what she wanted. Really he should be in the Inn's dining room so that he and Dare could work the room.

"Great." Alex smiled tightly, and Jed remembered that Tru had warned him that he was going to be under a microscope. It looked like he hadn't yet passed inspection. "I'll see you at five."

A couple approached, a man who exuded authority towed a shorter blonde woman, maybe late twenties. She was pretty in a plastic sort of way, and he might be called handsome. Jed recognized him as one of those poser Doms, the kind who cared about wielding power and not the person giving her submission. Instantly he disliked this guy, and instinctively he stepped between him and Tru.

"Zangari, this is a great place you have here."

Alex frowned. "Have we met?"

"No. I just checked in this afternoon. I'm Anton Schatz." He held his hand out for Alex to shake.

The owner of the Fetish Inn seemed to reluctantly oblige. Jed wanted to leave, to get Tru away from this unsafe Dom, but he couldn't ignore the warning buzzer emanating from his investigative instincts.

Alex, for his part, didn't seem to mind Jed sticking around. He motioned to Jed. "Anton Schatz, this is Jed King. He and his sub are guests here as well."

"Hey, did I hear you say that you had seats open on a white water rafting adventure tomorrow?" Anton Schatz smiled, but it was the kind that both twisted and ingratiated. "I'm always up for that kind of thrill ride."

The man's sub remained quiet and in the background, almost like she was afraid to draw attention to herself. Jed jutted his chin out to indicate her. "Does your sub also want to go?"

"Yeah, yeah. She's up for anything."

Jed didn't want to introduce his submissive to this piece of trash, but he needed Schatz to introduce his sub. She looked familiar, but Jed couldn't quite place her. He couldn't directly ask for an introduction without pissing off the supposed dominant, and he needed to know more about the guy before dismissing him outright as just a regular asshole instead of a criminal asshole.

Alex stepped in to save the day. "Anton, this is your first visit to Zangari's? Interesting. I didn't know we had any new residents scheduled this month."

Schatz motioned to his sub. "Sarah has been here before. She's a member."

Alex frowned, and Jed got the impression that he didn't approve of Schatz either. "New guests must be vetted, even if they're with a current member. I'm sorry, but—"

Tru put a hand on Alex's arm just above his elbow. He broke off and leaned down. Jed couldn't hear what she whispered, but when she stopped and stepped back behind him, Alex scratched his chin. "You can stay tonight, but you'll need to fill out some forms and consent to a background check."

Jed decided he liked Alex a lot. Not only was he a conscientious Dom, but he was going to get a history and consent for a background check.

"What about the rafting trip?" Schatz frowned.

Sarah touched Schatz's arm. "Master, we can go white water rafting if we want. It's an expedition outfitter, not one related to the Inn."

He nodded. "Okay. Yeah. Look into it."

Alex motioned for his concierge, Janean, to take Schatz to the front desk to fill out the appropriate forms.

Once the pair exited, Jed turned to Alex. "I changed my mind. We'll go rafting tomorrow. Don't worry about Jewell. We'll make sure she stays with us."

Alex frowned. "I'm not sure I'm going to let her go. That guy rubs me the wrong way." He stared at the door through which the couple had gone. "I'm going to help Janean."

Jed didn't blame the guy. He slung an arm around Tru's waist. "What did you say to Alex?"

"That all the hotels in the area are booked and that he should let them stay one night. Jed, that woman was Braithwaite's wife. I don't think she recognized me."

This proved Jed's instincts. She'd altered her appearance from the photos he'd seen of her. A new hair style and creative makeup skills did a lot to disguise a face. "What about the guy?"

She shook her head. "I've never seen him before, though that doesn't mean he wasn't there."

He kissed her briefly on the lips. "Alex was going to throw them out. That was quick thinking. I'm proud of you."

Her gaze dropped shyly, and a blush crept up her neck. "Thank you."

"Come on. Let's fill Dare in on what we did today."

Dinner didn't quite go the way Jed thought it might. The moment they arrived, Tru and Jewell disappeared into the kitchen, and Alex led Jed and Dare through the house to the back patio. It was private from the Inn, delineated by a tall cedar fence, and it overlooked the cliff, so nobody was going to come stumbling up from the beach to crash their private party.

Jed watched Alex sip the whiskey. "If you have a heart condition, should you be drinking that?"

"You sound like Jewell." He chuckled. "I indulge once in a while, four times a year, max."

Dare tilted his head and regarded Alex curiously. "Heart condition? What's wrong?"

"I did lots of drugs as a kid. It takes a toll on the old body. I have osteoporosis too." Alex savored another sip. "But I'm not dead, so there's that."

Jed realized that Alex's health issues were side effects of chemotherapy, and he kind of felt like an ass for questioning why a relatively young, active man had physical issues. He wondered if Tru had any as well. He already knew she'd been emotionally traumatized by it. Dare had shared some of his profiling theories, and Jed agreed that they needed to watch out for some of her wilder tendencies.

Jed raised his glass. "To survival."

Alex acknowledged his toast and took another sip. "Look, I'm not going to let Jewell go rafting with you guys tomorrow. Something about that Schatz guy doesn't sit right with me. It's not personal."

"I understand. He's definitely a shady character." Jed didn't want Tru going either, but he couldn't very well make her stay behind and maintain his cover.

"I can get tickets for another day." Alex rubbed the stubble on his chin. "If you want."

They needed to spend time with Schatz. And Zarah was either a captive or a criminal. He needed to figure out which.

"Thanks." Dare shook his head. "But they'll be okay. Jed can take care of himself, and Tru isn't a pushover. She'll box the ears of any guy who has it coming."

"You're not going?" Alex eyed Dare speculatively.

"It's not my thing. Jed and Tru like the water sports. I can't swim." Dare lied smoothly. He was a great swimmer, but he needed a reason to remain behind and search Schatz's room. "What made you let this guy stay if you don't like him? Zangari's Fetish Inn is known for being selective about its guests."

"I wasn't going to, but Tru said to let them stay one night. She rarely asks for anything, and this is the second time in a month she's asked me for a favor." Alex shook his head. "Nothing like falling in love to make a woman's heart go soft."

Jed wondered if Tru was developing tender feelings for either or both of them. He knew she wanted the murderer apprehended, but she hadn't seemed all that interested in doing it herself—which was good. He didn't want her in the thick of the action. Having her here was dangerous enough, but at least he knew that if the situation went to hell, he and Liam could put her under Alex's care and she'd be safe.

On the other side of the table, he caught Dare's eye, and he knew his buddy was also wondering if Tru had real feelings for them—and what it meant for the future.

Chapter Seventeen

Jed had been white water rafting once when he was twelve. On a family trip to Yellowstone, they'd passed a billboard advertising a two-hour adventure. His mother had turned to his father, eyes sparkling with excitement, and suggested they see if there was room on a rafting adventure. There had been no discussion because Mom had magic powers of persuasion, and Dad caved immediately—without consulting the three boys crammed in the back of the minivan amid suitcases, coolers, and random bags of stuff.

None of them had wanted to go rafting, but they knew better than to argue. It had been moderately fun. Jed wouldn't go so far as to admit to enjoying it because his brothers had loved it. As a middle child, it was his duty to be the holdout.

This time was different. He'd spent hours agonizing over whether to ask Schatz if he wanted to carpool. On one hand, he didn't want Tru exposed to the man more than necessary. On the other hand, it would be an uninterrupted hour where he had Schatz at his mercy, conversationally speaking. Just when he'd decided to bite the bullet and approach Schatz, the man in question sought him out and suggested they go together.

And so Jed found himself in the backseat of a Buick, holding Tru's hand and wishing he'd trained her in basic self-defense moves. The thrill-seeker in her would probably enjoy it. He vowed to begin lessons tonight once they returned to the inn.

"Jed, how did you get your sub to agree to be shared with another Dom?" Schatz tossed the question over his shoulder as he sped down the crowded highway, weaving between the slower-moving commuters.

Sticking as close to the truth as possible worked best when undercover with an inexperienced asset, so Jed chose an easy story that had a ring of truth. "We met her together at a work-related event. It was never in question that she would need to choose between us."

Tru peered at him, but she didn't comment on the inaccuracy. In fact she didn't comment at all. Jed noticed that Zarah Braithwaite didn't speak unless Schatz directed her to speak, and he wondered if Tru was quiet because she was nervous or because she thought Schatz would be impressed with Jed's Domly skill of making his submissive be quiet. Who the hell wanted to spend time with someone prohibited from having a conversation? Not Jed. He loved talking with Tru.

Schatz chuckled. "Good deal. I'm trying to get Sarah to agree to the same thing, but so far she hasn't caved."

Forcing a sub to do what they didn't want to do went against every fiber of who Jed was, and it eclipsed his urge to correct Schatz's mispronunciation of Zarah's name. "You can't force it. Tru has a connection with both Liam and me, but they're different connections. How did you and Sarah hook up?"

"A mutual friend introduced us. We have a lot in common, and when she begged to become my sub, I figured—what the hell? Why not?" He chuckled as he reached over and squeezed Zarah's leg. She didn't react except to smile softly in Schatz's direction. "I'm going to introduce her to a friend of mine soon, and maybe she'll change her mind about threesomes."

Jed didn't like this guy at all. He schooled his features to hide his gut reaction. "Incidental touching happens."

Tru pressed her lips together to keep from laughing.

They continued talking while the ladies looked out the window at the passing scenery. The ride lasted over an hour, but they made it to the outfitter in Maupin where Alex had tickets waiting for them. They loaded into a bus and ended up at Harpham Flats, which was the launch point for their half-day excursion.

The tour company packed them onto a raft with five other people and a guide. A family with children took the front two seats on the raft, sitting the smallest kid on the thwart, a structural support that ran between the sides of the raft, so Jed steered Tru to the rear left. Schatz and Braithwaite took the rear right. They set off, and their guide kept up a steady stream of chatter. He began by asking each of them their skill level and previous experience.

Tru, unsurprisingly, had rafted too many times to count, including class five rivers—the kind that required the highest level of skill—three times. She muttered this in reply to the guide as if this wasn't an accomplishment. No doubt she was on the hunt for a class six river, the kind where destruction of property was an assured outcome and death was likely to happen as well. The part they were to raft was mostly calm, a class two, but several stretches were considered class three (intermediate) or four (the kind intermediate rafters could handle skillfully if they had an expert guide.) Luckily they had an expert guide who practically lived on this stretch of the Deschutes.

The guide, Evan, was one of those tanned, athletic guys who tried to be every man's buddy and every woman's love interest. Perhaps because Tru was the closest woman, but probably because she was so freaking beautiful, Evan seemed to single out Tru more than any of the other adult women on the raft. He said things like—

Is this your first time on the Deschutes?

Have you rafted the Upper Gauley? That was a wicked ride. I bet you handled those sharp turns and steep drops like a champ. I'd love to see you handle some of the waves in the Lower Gauley.

What about Colorado? The Eagle River is wicked intense.

Dig in, people! Left side, paddle faster. Nice job, Tru. You have great form.

It wasn't her first time on the Deschutes; she hadn't been to the Gauley, but she said she'd check it out; and she'd rafted down the Eagle a few years ago. She agreed that it was intense. When Evan praised her technique for the third time, Tru finally looked at Jed and noticed that he was gritting his teeth to keep from knocking the guide from his perch on the rear of the raft.

A small smile, the kind that reassured and promised fidelity, curved her lips, and then she nodded in the direction of the couple he was supposed to be investigating. Schatz was paddling frantically, while Zarah seemed to be doing the minimum amount of work possible. She mostly looked like she was trying to avoid ruining her manicure. She'd spent some serious money on fake nails painted teal with flakes of glitter to make them sparkle in the sun. Jed squelched his caveman urge to punch Evan and focused on navigating the river.

By the time they stopped for lunch, Jed was ravenous. White water rafting wasn't easy, and the green-eyed monster riding his shoulder needed a break. He'd known Tru for less than a month, and already he'd spent most of his non-bedroom time with her battling jealousy. He wanted verbal assurances, but now wasn't the time to demand something she may not want to give.

He spread his life jacket in the sun, and Tru set hers next to his. She grabbed his hand and drew him closer.

"Hey, are you all right?"

The edges of her shirt and shorts were wet, as were his. He wrapped his other arm around her waist and pressed her body against his. "Unless you're the guide, a raft isn't a great place for conversation."

She traced his jaw with her fingertip. "And he wasn't very forthcoming with details in the car. It makes sense. If he did the...thing...then he's not going to come out and admit it. It's going to take time to earn his confidence. In the meanwhile, let's not waste our day together. It's been a while since I've had you to myself."

He wasn't looking for a confession, and today would be a success if Dare found something in Schatz's room while they were gone. Still it did some good to hear that Tru wanted to have time alone with him.

"How about we sit with them for lunch, and I'll see if I can get Zarah to open up?" She pressed a kiss to his cheek.

Jed didn't want her too involved, but Schatz didn't seem keen on his submissive getting chatty with another Dom. Reluctantly he nodded. Lunch was a grilled affair provided by the outfitter running the excursion. Jed chose chicken and veggies, as did Tru. She snagged a ladle full of cherries as well.

Schatz and Braithwaite disappeared behind the small building housing indoor outhouse-style bathrooms. Jed handed his plate to Tru. "Get us a place to sit, okay? I'll be back."

Without another word, he jogged toward the restrooms. Their raft had been one of the last ones in the water, and the majority of the rafters were settling down to lunch. He slowed as he approached the door to the facility, and he strolled past it as if his aim was to stretch his legs. Stopping several yards past the other side, he lifted his arms overhead and stretched. Trees lined the periphery of the park, and he scanned the tree line for evidence of Schatz and Braithwaite. In no time, he noticed they'd gone around to the back of the building.

Jed opted to go inside. The windows, high and rectangular, were propped open to aerate the room, and sound carried through them. He couldn't hear it all, but he made out enough to know that Anton Schatz was berating Zarah for not disclosing that it was a full day excursion. He'd been under the impression it was a half-day adventure. For her part, Zarah didn't seem to be taking his abuse, but her hissed responses were too high-pitched to carry very far.

As soon as Jed heard them come closer, he headed to the door. Waiting a few seconds meant he timed his exit to coincide with the couple as they went past the bathrooms. He glanced back toward the trees and pasted a welcoming grin on his face. "Hey! It's good to be back on land."

Schatz stared at him, but Zarah returned his smile. "It sure is. I can't believe we're not all soaked through. I always thought you were supposed to wear a wetsuit when white water rafting."

The river was relatively calm, with just a few patches that could be considered a class three, so Jed wasn't surprised. "I think we'll get wet this afternoon. I hear the class four portion is still ahead of us."

"Fantastic." Schatz's tone dripped sarcasm. "Can't wait. We'd better be back by four."

Jed grinned knowingly. "You're looking forward to public sex night?"

Dare and Jed had discussed their plans for this featured night at Zangari's Fetish Inn. Though Dare liked to watch, Jed didn't care to perform for a crowd. It was different when Dare watched—it enhanced the experience to have his friend and Tru's other love interest there. But with a crowd? Being an exhibitionist just didn't appeal to Jed. They'd agreed that if Tru wanted to participate, Dare would tie her up and make her have as many orgasms as he wanted to see, and then he'd bring her back to the room where they could have their way with her privately.

Schatz shrugged. "Maybe. We'll watch for a bit, anyway, but our room has some great décor that appeals to me more than a public performance."

They'd made it back to the picnic tables where Tru had saved a place for the foursome. Evan, the pesky guide, stood across from her, his foot perched on the bench as he openly flirted. He had that sparkle in his eye that players got when they thought they were going to score. Jed was well acquainted with the man's attitude and the way he stood over Tru because prior to Tru, he had been a master at the Love-Em-and-Leave-Em game.

Schatz and Zarah took off in the direction of the grill, and Jed sat next to his submissive. He wanted to kiss her on the lips, but she'd just taken a huge bite of chicken. "Miss me?"

Tru didn't seem to notice or hear him. She was smiling, and her eyes sparkled with joy, but she seemed to be frozen in time. Though her face was tipped up in Evan's direction, she seemed to be looking through him. Wondering what she was doing, Jed took his place next to her where she'd set his plate, but he directed his inquiring frown at her. "Tru?"

She blinked, and she seemed to shake herself out of her funk, but she didn't immediately reply because she had a mouth full of food. Instead she turned her brilliant smile on him, and suddenly the feelings of intense jealousy that dogged him made sense. He'd fallen for this woman, and he'd fallen hard. Logic couldn't explain when or why it had happened, and identifying the emotion did nothing to ease his heart.

She finished chewing and swallowed. "I saved you a seat."

"I see that. Are you okay?"

"Yeah, why?" She popped a cherry into her mouth.

Evan watched her lips with open fascination, even when she puckered them up to spit the seed into a napkin.

Obviously Evan didn't pick up on subtle hints, like the fact that her reaction to Jed indicated that they were a couple, so he opted for the direct approach. He gripped Tru's ponytail, turned her face to his, and staked his claim with a deep kiss even though he hated cherries. She melted into him, a kittenish moan purring from the back of her throat. When he let her go, she nestled her head against his shoulder in a lingering cuddle, and Evan had gone.

"That guy keeps flirting with you, and I may sucker punch him."

She laughed. "I can't imagine you sucker-punching anyone. You're too honest and noble for that kind of underhandedness."

Before today, Jed would have thought so as well. Now, he wasn't so sure. The words jumped to the tip of his tongue, and he shoved food into his mouth to keep them from leaping off. He couldn't come out and profess his undying love and devotion to a woman who viewed him as a vacation fling. It looked like he would be joining Dare on the love boat. They'd have to convince Tru that a permanent cruise would be worthwhile.

The two of them ate in silence until Schatz and Zarah Braithwaite joined them. Jed didn't know whether he should think of her by her last name—as he would a suspect—or her first name—as he would a victim, so he opted for both. Tru went with her plan, and she tried her best to engage Zarah Braithwaite in conversation.

"Have you been to Zangari's before?"

Zarah paused, her lips slightly parted, and she glanced at Schatz. "I've been here a few times before. You're new, right?"

"No. I'm friends with the owners, so I mostly come to visit them." Tru wiped her hands on her paper napkin. "This is my first time bringing anyone with me, though. I wanted my Sirs to meet Alex and Jewell. Are you from around here?"

With a polite smile, Zarah shook her head, but before she could speak, Schatz interrupted. "This is our vacation. We don't want to think about home. What do you guys think of the theme tonight? We sure lucked out. They only have an exhibitionist/voyeur night once a year. Are you guys watchers or performers?"

Tru had that faraway look again, her face frozen with an annoyed slant to her eyes. Jed worried that maybe she was having a seizure, but then he realized that she must be having a vision. He covered for her sudden imitation of a statue by chuckling. "Liam likes to watch for a little while, so we'll probably do a little of both."

"We're watchers," Schatz said. "So we'll probably watch, and then we'll head back to our room. Have I mentioned that we have a great room? It has one of those beds with a stockade in the footboard and a cage underneath. I prefer my subs caged when I'm not using them."

Jed may have played around a lot, but he'd never harbored a utilitarian view of submissives. Their service was a gift, one he cherished for a night or two before moving on. Though he understood that some subs craved that level of submission, and he didn't judge, he had the impression that Schatz wasn't the kind of Dom who cared about his submissives as people or cherished what they gave him. He hated assholes like that. These fake, wanna-be Doms gave real Doms a bad name.

Evan called them back to the raft, and as everyone got up to dispose of their paper plates, Tru stopped him with a hand on his arm.

"Are you okay?"

"Fine. Why?"

"Because you suddenly got all dark and brooding again."

He leaned down and kissed her neck, and then he whispered. "I hate that fuckwad."

"Well, you can't let him know that yet," she whispered back. She took his plate and piled it on top of hers. "I'll take care of these if you want to go grab our life jackets?"

Before she could take a step, he put a hand on her waist. "Did you have a couple of visions today?"

She froze, her eyes wide as she stared at him. It was different from earlier because she was mentally present. "How did you know?"

"You kind of get a far-off look and your expression freezes. You'll have to tell me about them later." He kissed her forehead and went to retrieve their life jackets.

The afternoon part of the trip wasn't bad. Much of the river was quiet, and the views were spectacular. After a longish rest period during which Evan chattered about what they were seeing, the history of the place, or fishing, they'd paddle furiously through rapids. Jed kept an eye on Schatz and Braithwaite, but he was mostly conscious of Tru. He wanted to reach out and touch her—just because he could. He wanted to take her in his arms and kiss her or say something that would make her laugh. But he didn't, and she spent a lot of time watching the suspects as well.

"Ladies and gentlemen, we're approaching the Wreck Rapids." Evan interrupted Jed's musings with his pronouncement. "This is a tricky bit of river, but I'm an awesome guide, so I'll get you through it with no problem. We need to enter this section backward, otherwise we'll get flipped."

Jed and Tru followed Evan's instructions, but the kids in the front couldn't seem to figure out when and how to paddle no matter how many times they were told. It didn't help that the parents gave advice opposite from what Evan was saying. This resulted in half the raft not paddling at all or paddling counter to what they needed.

"Brace yourself." Tru had a huge grin on her face as they entered the rapids sideways.

Jed heeded her warning, and he prepared to get wet. The first wave hit them hard. The kids screamed. One of them sounded afraid, but the others were of the excited variety. Evan called out commands, but if the family heard him, they ignored everything he said, and they shouted orders at the kids while not paddling at all. Similarly, Schatz shouted at the kids—mostly unkind things—and Zarah screamed in terror. Evan had lost control of his passengers, and the monster-sized paddles he used to steer the raft were no match for the water's might.

Tru propped her toes under the edge of the thwart. Jed figured she knew what she was doing—she was the only one not freaking out—and he mirrored her position. The raft was pummeled by waves and flung down the class four drop. The kids in front and their father were the first to go. The mother held on for another few seconds, but she ended up in the water too.

Behind them, Evan swore. Across the raft, Schatz swore. Next to him, Tru laughed as if she was having the time of her life. Jed had to admit that it was a fun ride.

Zarah pitched into the water at the bottom of the drop. When everything calmed down, the only people left in the raft with him were the woman he loved, a probable murderer, and a playboy guide. The raft came out of the rapids backward, and Jed looked to make sure everybody was all right. The entire ordeal had lasted perhaps ten seconds, and the rapids didn't look all that intimidating from this angle. He counted three kids and two parents, but he didn't see Zarah.

"She's clinging to the rock." Tru pointed to a place near the bank of the river.

"We're going to pick up the Golinas first, and then we'll get Mrs. Schatz." Evan instructed them to paddle upstream to where the family had come out of the rapids unscathed.

Jed pulled two of the kids into the raft while Tru helped the mother and the youngest kid. Evan helped the father in, and Schatz merely watched. Loading them took no time at all, and then they crossed to the other side to pick up Zarah. She clung to the rock and refused to get on the raft.

"I want to go home." She sobbed. This hadn't been a fun ride for her. "I don't want to go rafting anymore."

"Get in the fucking raft." Schatz eyed her with calm detachment.

If his sub had been traumatized by an experience, Jed wouldn't have responded so insensitively. She needed a strong shoulder, not cold commands.

"It's okay, Mrs. Schatz. The rest of the ride is pretty calm. That was the hardest part." Evan tried to provide encouragement, but Zarah wasn't listening. She shook her head and refused to look at them.

Jed noted her gulped breaths. He slid out of the raft and waded to her. "Sarah, it's okay. I'll help you get back in, and the rest of the trip is going to be like floating on a lazy river. We won't flip again." He spoke with calm authority, and he put his hand under her forearm, urging her to hold onto him.

After a moment, she transferred her hold from the rock to his neck. He held her gently and guided her back to the raft. Tru helped her on board, and Jed climbed in once she was safe in her seat.

Schatz glared at Zarah, but he said nothing. Tru also said nothing, but the look on her face was one of pride, awe, and deep affection. The heaviness in his heart and the last vestiges of jealousy fled. By the end of this investigation, she would be his.

The rooms were quiet, soundproofed. If Liam had been here to have a wild time with his submissive, he would have appreciated the care Zangari had put into crafting this haven for kinksters. Because his lookout had gone on a white water rafting adventure with the suspects, he cursed the foamy layers in the walls that absorbed sounds and the seals around the doors that kept noise to a minimum.

Schatz's room was messy, which suited Liam fine. Though he was careful about putting everything back where he found it, the slovenly environment meant that if he messed up, they were unlikely to notice.

He searched everywhere, especially inside the pill bottles he found cleverly hidden in the lining of Zarah Braithwaite's suitcase. Stumbling upon a cache of diamonds was unlikely. There was no way they'd leave those unguarded for a moment. However he was impressed by the amount and variety of pills Braithwaite had at her disposal, and none of them were in a legal prescription bottle. He took pictures of them just in case they became relevant later.

The search of the room turned up nothing. Liam sat on the lone chair in the room and stared at the frame of the bed—iron bars that formed a cage—and thought. If he were Schatz, he'd keep diamonds or incriminating documents with him. As he was going to get wet, anything of note would likely be found in the car.

Which would be left unattended in the parking lot of the expedition outfitter.

As the idea struck Liam, so did the notion that a cage could hold more than a submissive, and that there was no reason to lock an empty cage. He found a couple of hair pins in Zarah Braithwaite's haphazardly placed collection of personal care products, and he picked the lock. This lock wasn't designed for containing an unwilling prisoner, and it came open quickly. He crawled in, rolled to his back, and studied the underside of the bed.

The first thing that struck him was the lack of cobwebs underneath the bed. He knew the cleaning staff was well-paid and dedicated, but this was an area that many people wouldn't even think about, right?

He looked to the side, and he realized that he was wrong. As long as they weren't blindfolded, any sub locked in this cage would definitely notice cobwebs. The underside of the bed was a solid sheet of wood broken by wide slats that reinforced the expanse. He touched the surfaces, running his fingertips and palms over them to find anything that might indicate a hidey-hole.

Nothing. Nothing at all.

Just to be sure, he inspected the metal bars and pulled up the soft, plush rug that lined the floor. He found a nipple clamp and an earring, which he left there.

Exiting the room was almost harder than breaking into it had been. Liam peeked out through the peephole to see two couples standing a few feet down the hall conversing. He watched them laugh and talk for almost fifteen minutes before the coast was clear enough for him to leave.

It looked like he was going on a road trip.

Alex caught him as he crossed the lobby on his way to the staff wing. The tall, skinny guy had the sleeves of his dress shirt rolled up, and the juxtaposition of his tattoos with his professional style of dress struck Liam as kind of cool. This guy was living his dream as the owner of a fetish-themed destination inn, and he marked each year of life with a fresh tattoo to commemorate the fact that he'd lived it. Perhaps when he left the FBI, Liam would get a tattoo or ten. Maybe he wouldn't wait that long. What were they going to do—fire him?

Alex held a hand out in greeting. "Hey, how are you faring today?"

Liam shook his hand heartily, as if greeting someone he'd known for years. He could see why Tru had maintained a friendship with this man for so long. He was inherently friendly and welcoming. "Great. I was just out and about, checking out the public areas."

"Fair enough. Listen, what are you doing for lunch?"

Driving to the rafting outfitter was the next item on Liam's to-do list. "I was going to go for a drive, check out the area."

"After lunch. Jewell wanted to make sure you had something to keep you occupied today, but I managed to get her to leave you alone for the morning. I figured you were noodling on that work problem you've been thinking about for the past two days."

The "work problem" wasn't going to be solved in one morning. Their task force expected to spend months or years researching The Eye in order to take it down. They didn't want the murderers and thieves at the lower end of the organization—they wanted to take down the whole enchilada. Liam laughed sheepishly. "Guilty."

"Dedication is a great quality to have. Anyone who wants a future with Tru needs to be dedicated."

"To keeping her from killing herself with some crazy stunt?" Liam huffed at the memory of Tru jumping from that bridge. "She needs to be kept on a short leash. Did she tell you that she tricked us into letting her base jump on our way here?"

Alex lifted a brow. "You don't approve?"

"No. After she pulled that shit, she tried topping from the bottom and manipulating Jed to get him to intervene. I spanked her, and then Jed had a go." He couldn't go into the way she'd teased them about having a hero complex because that would be too hard to explain. Liam knew the man was judging him based on the way he talked about Tru. Jordan had impressed upon him that a good Dom doesn't shy away from punishing his sub when she needs to be punished.

Alex's expression was guarded. "How did she react to that?"

"I think she was mostly shocked, but she was definitely contrite. She hasn't tried to top from the bottom again."

Lips pressed together and arms crossed, Alex stared into the distance for several long moments. "I get that you need to keep her in line. She respects strength of character. But with the stunts..." He shook his head and nailed Liam with a fierce light in his eyes. "Her jumps are like my tattoos. They're milestones that commemorate the fact that she made it another month, season, or year. Think about that, and talk to her about it, before you decide it's a good idea to try to take that away."

It hadn't occurred to Liam that her stunts were anything but an attempt to test death to see if she'd keep up her winning streak. Yeah, they needed to talk about her extreme activities. Liam nodded. "Thanks. I appreciate your insight. I'll keep that in mind."

"Great. Can I tell Jewell to expect you for lunch?"

"Sorry. Thanks, but I have some errands to run as well. I'll grab lunch in town. Tell Jewell I said thanks." He took a step toward his room, but Alex stopped him again.

"One more thing?"

Liam turned back to Alex.

"She would like to request an hour alone with Tru, preferably tonight before the exhibitionist/voyeur event."

This was perfect. Tru would have some time with her friend while Liam and Jed debriefed each other on the case. "Yeah. Sure. No problem. It'll give Jed and me a chance to finalize the details of our scene tonight."

Ten minutes later, Jed was on his way to the rafting outfit. He called Brandy to update her on his search. "Hey, how is the investigation into your stalker going?"

Her exhale growled across the distance. "I have a picture from a security camera that doesn't coincide with a place I've been. It's not as grainy as some of the others. It's being analyzed now, and if that sucker is in our database, he'll be arrested as soon as we get a hit. If not, I'm going to track him down and tear off his testicles."

Liam laughed, more from surprise than amusement. "I'm glad you got something."

"Now for the more important question—do you have anything?"

He pictured her sitting at her desk, shooting aggravated looks at the computer as if that would make the system work faster. "Zarah Braithwaite is here with a man named Anton Schatz. They're white water rafting with Jed and Tru right now. I searched their room, and now I'm heading to where their car is parked."

"Is it a rental?"

Registered guests had to report their car's license plate number, and so Liam had Schatz's from when he'd hacked Zangari's system. He'd run the plate, and it had come back as not a rental. "It's registered to Angelo Braithwaite. Reasonable cause."

"Let me call for a warrant just in case. I'll call you back as soon as we have approval."

"I'll be there in an hour, so put a rush on it."

"There's no guaranteed half-hour-or-free delivery on this one."

Liam wished he hadn't called his boss because now he was stuck waiting on a fucking warrant. He stopped for lunch and ate it while sitting in the parking lot of the nearly deserted rafting company. A single young man occasionally showed himself in front of the window where people paid for their trip. Mostly he stayed hidden and probably asleep. Two hours went by, and Brandy didn't call, so he called Jordan.

"Hey, mentor. How are things?"

Jordan's voice sounded froggy, like he'd been asleep. "Shitty. We found one decent image of Lockmeyer's stalker, and I have some kind of virus. How are things in Oregon?"

"Great. I spent the morning crawling around the suspect's room and finding nothing but a broken nipple clamp."

Jordan may have tried to make a sympathetic sound, but he hacked up half a lung instead. "Sorry. Amy will be in here any minute, and she's going to make me get off the phone so she can feed me some chicken soup. I meant how are things going with Tru?"

"Good. Great." He thought about the deep connection he felt to her and the way she looked at him when she submitted. "We had an amazing scene, and then the next morning, she had subdrop. Is it wrong that I kind of liked it?"

"What part did you like?" This time Jordan sneezed. Liam did not want to be the man's phone. It was going to need some heavy duty disinfecting.

"That we could make her feel that way. That we'd affected her so much. And, if I'm being honest, I liked that she needed us to help her through it. She's so independent most of the time. She knows her mind, and I like that about her. But I liked that she couldn't do this alone." He hadn't loved seeing her so emotional, but he'd reveled in the surge of power that came from knowing he'd driven her to such a height that she needed him to cushion the fall. "Please tell me that this doesn't make me an asshole."

"It doesn't. Actually the fact that you want to be there for her is a good thing. It's your responsibility to make sure she has a safe place to fall apart. It builds trust and a bond, and you'll find that she'll surrender to you on a deeper level next time." Jordan coughed some more, and Amy's voice came through in the background. "Dare? I have to go. My little is going to nurse me back to health."

As he waited for news of the fucking warrant, Liam thought about the things both Alex and Jordan had said to him about his relationship with Tru. He felt a deep-seated need to take care of her, to see to her emotional needs as well as have her in his life permanently. Was this love? He honestly didn't know. The only person in his life that he could claim to love was his mother, the woman who had rescued him from loneliness and neglect and who had patiently navigated his maze of thorns and walls that had been constructed to protect a traumatized little boy.

He called his mother next. She picked up on the first ring. "Liam, I was just thinking about you."

"Hi, Mom. How are you?"

"Excellent. I have a date tonight."

He didn't want to hear about his septuagenarian mother dating, but he swallowed his misgivings. "Yeah? Anyone I know?"

"You will. Sanjaya and I have become quite close. When you get home, I want you to come to dinner. He grills a mean salmon." She laughed, the light sound making him a little homesick.

"It's a plan. You sound happy. I'm glad." Surprisingly, he wasn't lying. While Joyce Adair had always been one of those bright people who were in a perpetually good mood, she'd been alone long enough. Her husband had died before she'd adopted Liam, so he only knew of him from photos and old videos.

"That's a relief. I was nervous about telling you. In the past, you haven't exactly taken it well when I've gone on dates, so I mostly keep that side of my life from you. But now that you have a girlfriend, I felt like it was time."

Shocked, Liam sputtered. "I thought you didn't date because you didn't want to after you lost Bill? I didn't mean to keep you from being happy."

"Oh, sweetheart, you didn't." She rushed to reassure him. "After Bill died, you came into my life, and I devoted myself to you because you needed me. And I needed you.

But now you're an adult, and you're finally ready to spread your wings."

Wait. She'd said that she knew Liam had a girlfriend. "What makes you think I have a girlfriend?"

She laughed. "Oh, sweetie. A mother just knows. Tell me about her."

This is why he'd called. His mother knew his heart better than he did. "Her name is Tru Martin. She's a writer for a blog called The Eclectic Traveler. I met her a few weeks ago in California while I was working a case."

"It was fate." Joyce's grin came through the phone loud and clear. "I always told you that the universe has a plan for you."

Liam had grown up hearing his mother say things like that, but now he was starting to believe it. He relaxed against his seat and told her everything he could about Tru. He talked about her passion for life, her adventurous spirit, her childhood battle with leukemia, that she was raised by her grandmother, her singular beauty, and the fact that she agreed with him about cryptids and some of his conspiracy theories. He left out the kinky parts and the fact that she was working with him undercover.

When he stopped talking, Joyce clicked her tongue. "You're going to have to bring this young woman when you meet Sanjaya. I think the four of us will hit it off famously."

"Mom? There's more."

"Is she pregnant?"

"No." They'd been careful, using condoms each time. "It's…There's someone else."

Joyce was silent for ten shocked seconds before Liam realized she'd taken it the wrong way.

"I don't mean that I have two girlfriends. I mean that...You remember Jed Kinsley? You've met him a few times."

Her tone turned crisp. "Of course I remember your friends. I'm not senile. Yet."

Liam scrambled to explain. He knew she was seconds away from lecturing him on how age was a state of mind. "He's sort of dating her too. We both hit it off with her, and we're both seeing her. Together."

She was silent again, but not for long. "You're both seeing her?"

"Yes."

"Together?"

"Yes."

"Like a ménage situation?"

"Yes."

"Hmm."

He waited for her to let loose. Joyce Adair never kept her opinions to herself.

"Does he love her too?"

Liam stumbled. This is exactly why he'd called. "What makes you think I'm in love with her?"

"The way you talk about her, sweetie. You've never told me much about the women you've dated, and today you've talked about one woman nonstop for forty-five minutes, singing her praises until I was sure a chorus of angels was going to start with the backing vocals."

Liam still wasn't sure. "How do you know you're in love? How did Bill know he was in love with you?"

She laughed. "How often do you think about her?"

If he were to be honest? "Pretty much all the time."

"Just sexual thoughts?"

"MOM!"

"You're thirty-four. I'm sure you've had sexual thoughts for the past twenty years, though for the longest time I wasn't sure if you were having them about people or computers. If you haven't had sexual thoughts about a woman, then you would be having them about men. It's okay either way. Like if you also are in love with Jed. He's a nice man, and I think he's very handsome. I just want you to be happy."

He wasn't in love with Jed. It was strictly a friend thing. He sighed. "I think about being with her, just talking and hanging out. I'm trying to figure out how my job would work with hers. We both travel so much."

"Have you talked with her about that? What does Jed think? He travels with you."

Liam sighed. "It hasn't come up. I don't know if Jed is as serious as I am. I think he is. But then I don't know what Tru thinks, either."

"And you won't unless you either ask her or develop the ability to read minds. The first option is more likely." Joyce was quiet again, and he pictured her frowning all the way across the country. "Sweetie, talk to her. If she loves you half as much as you love her, then you'll find a way to make it work. A woman in love will meet you halfway."

He heard what she didn't say—that if Tru didn't have deep feelings for him, then she wouldn't bother to help find a solution to their logistics problem.

"Thanks, Mom. I'll call you in a few days and let you know how it went."

"Wait! Liam, are you on a case?"

"Yeah."

"And Tru is there with you?"

"Yeah."

"Well, it seems you're finding solutions already. I love you, and I'll see you soon."

He gave his love and plugged his phone into the charger. Brandy hadn't called, and the first rafters were paddling toward the dock. It was too late to check the trunk now, and he had to get out of the parking lot before Schatz realized something was going on.

Chapter Eighteen

Liam arrived back at the inn, freshened up, and found a comfortable chair in the sitting room with a view of the front door. He perused a sport fishing magazine while he waited for Tru and Jed. The words on the pages didn't register because his thoughts veered wildly from Tru to his investigation and back. Before long, Jewell approached. She knelt at his feet, her knees firmly together and her gaze respectfully lowered. He glanced around to see if perhaps Alex was standing behind him, but the only people there were a couple of guests discussing whether they wanted to have dinner at the inn or drive up the coast.

He peered at her curiously. Nobody had ever knelt for him before. "What are you doing?"

"You look upset. Would you like to talk about it?"

If Tru had done something like this, it would have barreled through the last of his doubt about his feelings for her. This woman was not his submissive, and while her gesture appealed to his Dominant nature, her reasoning eluded him. He'd be pissed if Tru knelt for another man. Jed was the only exception. "I think you'd better get up before Alex sees you."

"Alex knows exactly where I am and what I'm doing. I would never do something like this without his blessing. He agrees that you look upset. Do you miss Tru?" She lifted her gaze, blinking at him with empathy and innocence in the depths of her blue eyes.

"Yes, but she should be back soon. I was waiting for them." He tossed the magazine onto a table. "Why don't you pull up a chair? I'm not sure I'm comfortable with a sub who isn't mine kneeling like that."

"You're Tru's Sir, and I am her friend. If Alex was upset, and I wasn't around, I would want her to comfort him, and I know she'd want me to take care of you. Please tell me how I can help you."

He didn't get the sense that she was hitting on him or offering anything more than friendship, and that mitigated a lot of his discomfort. "I don't know. I'm new to the lifestyle. And polyamory. I'm not upset as much as I'm anxious for them to get back. It's been a while since I've had time alone with Tru." The last time he'd spent time alone with her had been when he'd shown her the stars. It seemed longer than just two weeks ago.

"Do you have a schedule to ensure that you both get time with her?" Jewell nestled her head against the side of his knee, offering comfort.

Liam rested his hand on her head, softly stroking her hair. It was blonde and downy, the exact opposite of Tru's dark brown, thick tresses. "No, but I know Jed expects me to take her tonight. The public sex thing is my kink, not his."

"If you don't mind me saying, it seems like you guys don't talk enough. Relationships are work, and yours is even more complex. Tru is reasonable most of the time."

He laughed, but before he could agree, the bell on the front door tinkled, calling his attention there. Zarah Braithwaite came through first. Her usually perfect hair and makeup were ruined, and her clothes were damp. Anton

Schatz followed close behind, his face set in a hard expression that managed to appear cynical and dangerous but not angry.

Tru came next, her face bright with laughter and darker from the sun. She turned to look over her shoulder, and Jed followed her inside, also laughing.

Jed saw Liam first. He inclined his head to indicate the direction Tru should look. She did, and she stopped short when she noticed Jewell on her knees with her head on his knee and Liam's hand stroking her hair.

Tru's momentary frown vanished, and she nodded to Jewell. "It looks like you had a productive day."

Jewell got up and threw her arms around Tru. "We were talking. He missed you."

Tru hugged her back, and she didn't look angry or upset. Liam got to his feet and waited for his turn at a hug.

"I'll see you at six." Jewell placed a chaste kiss on Tru's cheek and glided away.

Jed motioned toward the hall leading to their room. "Let's take this into the bedroom. I could use a shower."

He led the way. Tru slipped her hand into Liam's, and they followed Jed. He pulled her closer and kissed her cheek. "Are you upset about Jewell? I didn't ask her to do that."

"I know." Tru paused at the door to their room that Jed had opened. "Jewell is one of those big-hearted people who likes to take care of others. She was showing that she respects you. It's a big deal, Liam. It means she and Alex like you."

They went into the room, and Liam locked the door. "I passed inspection?"

"Looks like. Did you hang out with them today?" She peeled out of her shirt and shorts.

"No. I worked."

Jed selected fresh clothes and headed to the bathroom. "Wait until I shower, and then we can debrief."

"Tru is going to go visit Jewell in ten minutes. We can talk then."

Standing before him in a teal sports bra and matching cotton underwear, Tru pouted. "You don't have to wait for me to leave to talk about the case. It's not like I'm going to tell anyone anything."

In response, Jed closed the bathroom door. Liam faced Tru. "You know that parts of the case are confidential, so no pouting. Tell me about your day."

She stopped pouting and went to the sink where she attacked her hair with a brush. "It was fun. We rafted for about six hours, had barbecue chicken for lunch, and the family in the front of the raft couldn't follow directions. We entered a rapids sideways instead of backward, and a bunch of people got flipped out of the raft. Jed had to get out, get Zarah Braithwaite—poor thing was terrified—and carry her back to the raft. Her own Dom wouldn't help her. Asshole."

Liam leaned against the wall and watched her tie back her hair and wash her face.

"He's one of those jerks who has no feelings for his submissive. Alex was right to want to refuse to let him stay.

He has good instincts about people. I don't know why women stay with Doms—or anyone—who don't treat them with basic respect and kindness."

"Some people lack the self-esteem and self-respect it takes to leave abusive or unhealthy relationships. Maybe they're just sexually compatible?" He didn't believe that. You didn't go on a vacation with someone unless you want to spend quality time with that person.

Tru patted a towel on her face and snorted. "They don't belong here. This morning I talked Alex into letting them stay for the time being, but if he doesn't like their behavior tonight, he'll send them packing."

Liam didn't blame him. If this place was his pride and joy, he'd eject anyone who didn't meet his standards. He pulled Tru into his arms and kissed her tenderly. He held her lightly, but his lips staked an assured claim. She melted against his chest, and he felt the gentle glide of her palms moving up his arms and settling on his shoulders. When it ended, he tucked her head under his chin and held her for a moment.

"I missed you too, Sir."

"I thought we'd scene tonight."

He felt her grin grow. "Thank you, Sir."

Twenty minutes later, he kissed her goodbye at the door to the Zangaris' home, and he promised to return in an hour to pick her up. He came back to find Jed on their FBI-issued laptop encrypted for secure communication.

"Submitting a report?"

"Looking up Schatz."

"Already done." He took the laptop, typed in his logon information, and showed Jed the FBI file on Anton Schatz. The man was the son of a high-end real estate developer. Schatz had lived a privileged life until college when he'd run afoul of the law. His father had stayed with him through accusations of drugging college women and raping them, but he'd cut ties after Schatz had been accused of fraud.

Jed shook his head. "Rape is okay, but allegedly stealing from your father's corporation is not."

They talked for a while longer. Liam described his investigation, including the attempted search of Schatz's car, and Jed related what he'd overheard in the bathroom. He'd also managed to attach a tracking device to the underside of Schatz's passenger seat, so if they left suddenly, they wouldn't lose them until they ditched the car. In the middle of their talk, Liam tried to bring up the evolution of his feelings for Tru, but he couldn't seem to get the words out, and then Jed would mention something related to the case, which kept the topic firmly in that realm.

On the way to Alex and Jewell's house, Liam bit the bullet. "Tru is very special."

"I know."

They continued along in an awkward silence. Liam didn't know what to say next. Should he come out and tell Jed that he was in love with their submissive? What if Jed wasn't in love with her? What if he was?

"Remember when we said we wanted to get her to agree to keep seeing us after this trip?"

"Yep."

"What do you think the chances are that she'll say yes?"

Jed exhaled a sigh. "I'd like to believe our chances are good. She isn't treating us like we're a temporary diversion, the sexual equivalent of a base jump, which I think was her original intention."

They'd arrived at the front door, but Liam had one more question. "Are you still on board with sharing her?"

"Yes. I don't imagine it's going to be easy, but I think we can make it work. It's what she wants, and I want her to be happy."

Liam's sentiment ran along the same lines, which wasn't a ringing endorsement of their arrangement. They were sharing because she wanted it, not because they did.

Alex opened the door before they knocked. "I thought I heard someone out here. Come on in. The girls aren't quite finished."

Liam and Jed followed Alex to the kitchen, the source of some seriously scrumptious aromas. "What are they doing?"

"Talking. Jewell lost her cat last month, and she's still pretty broken up about it. Tru is the first person besides me that she's talked to about it. I imagine that she'll somehow manipulate Tru into flogging her into a cathartic release." Alex gestured to the stove. "Dinner should be ready soon."

Liam and Jed slid onto high stools on the other side of the U-shaped counter. Jed furrowed his brows. "Sorry to hear about your pet. I didn't know we'd been invited to dinner."

Alex shrugged. "I wasn't sure, but I made enough for everybody. It's spaghetti and meatballs. I don't cook much, but I make a killer marinara sauce, and my spicy meatballs are a family secret, so Jewell lets me take the lead on this."

Liam didn't care what they had for dinner, but he wanted to eat in the dining room to watch Schatz. He thought Jed would arrive at the same conclusion, but his buddy grinned. "It smells great. Thanks. I'm looking forward to it."

He wanted to kick some sense into Jed. Their primary concern was for the investigation, and it felt like they were abandoning their responsibility.

When Alex turned away to stir the sauce, Jed leaned closer. "They plan to take a nap, order room service, and stay in tonight."

Liam didn't trust the plans that criminals shared, and he couldn't believe that Jed did either. Then he remembered the tracker on the car. If they left, it would trigger a notice on Jed's cell phone. Liam relaxed and turned his attention to their host. "So, you're okay with Tru flogging Jewell?"

"Yeah. She's pretty good at it, though a little out of practice. As long as they don't have sex afterward, then it's all good." He dumped two boxes of spaghetti noodles into a vat of boiling water.

The image of Tru and Jewell going at it made Liam need to adjust his position. "You have to admit that it would be very hot to watch, though."

Jed chuckled. "Damn. I'm going to be thinking about that all night now."

Alex frowned. "Tru never told you that she used to top Jewell?"

"She said she'd been a beta Domme before, but she didn't say with whom." Jed's gaze sidled toward the door to the basement where the dungeon was located. He looked like he wanted to go down and watch.

Liam understood the urge, but he respected her privacy. Tru wouldn't have sex with anyone outside their dynamic. She had a loyal heart, and she was down there comforting a friend. He knew that Tru had introduced Jewell to Alex, so he directed a question at Zangari. "Did it cause problems in your friendship with Tru when you stole her sub?"

Alex focused on stirring the sauce. "I didn't steal Jewell. At first I thought Tru was just bringing Jewell around as a play partner. She's always liked threesomes, but usually I selected our third, even when she made suggestions. But then I realized that Tru wanted me to fall in love with Jewell so that I wouldn't be upset when she asked me to release her. Of course I was already head over feet for Jewell, so it didn't take me long to get over Tru, and now we're all just good friends again. So when she says that she introduced me to Jewell, it's the truth." He killed the flame on the burner. "Do one of you want to go get the ladies and tell them dinner's done?"

The erotic vision of two lovely, naked female submissives touching and kissing melted from Liam's brain when he realized that Alex had been the one watching them get it on. And participating. He'd most likely participated. Hell, Liam would have if he were in that position. Rage—anger and hurt mixed together—burned like a fire in his throat. She'd brought them to the home of her former Master, and she'd only told them that Alex and Jewell were friends. Friends—not former lovers. Friends—not former Master and submissive.

Jed jabbed him hard with his elbow. "Why don't you fetch Tru and Jewell?"

Liam glared at Jed, and then he realized his buddy was giving him a chance to walk it off and get his head back in the game. There were a lot of things he didn't know about Tru, and there were a lot of things she didn't know about him. However, she should have told them about Alex. That was need-to-know information. When you cared about someone, you didn't let them walk into a situation like this without knowing pertinent facts.

He opened the door to the dungeon to find Tru loosening the restraints holding Jewell to the St. Andrew's cross. She smiled, a huge, welcoming grin that blazed from the depths of her eyes and transformed her face from beautiful to radiant.

"Hello, Sir. Would you mind helping me untie Jewell?"

Wordlessly he unbuckled the last cuff binding Jewell to the cross. She slowly lowered her arms, and she faced Tru with a serene expression. "Thank you for this. It helps more than you can possibly know."

"Dinner is ready." Liam was furious with Tru, but he didn't want to rain on Jewell's parade, so he kept his ire from his tone.

This day was shaping up to be one of her five best. It was right up there with learning she was in remission—twice—and the day she'd met Poppy. No—this whole trip was incredible. She'd been right to take a chance on these two. They'd taken her to such great heights. She'd given more of herself to them than she'd ever given to anyone, and she didn't regret it one bit. They'd cherished her, loved her well, and then they'd patiently seen her through the worst subdrop she'd ever experienced. Normally she didn't let herself get too invested in a scene. She treated them as games, fun to be had for a little while. But it was different with Jed and Liam. *She* was different with Jed and Liam.

For the first time in her life, she wasn't terrified of falling in love. Jed and Liam made her want to take that chance. Given the way they looked at her, the way they touched her, and the way they took care of her, she felt secure in their intentions. After all, actions spoke louder than words.

Liam waited while she closed up the dungeon, and he escorted her upstairs to the kitchen where Alex and Jed had set up an informal dinner. The two of them were already eating, and Jewell was nowhere to be found.

Alex gestured to the stove. "It's self-serve tonight."

"Where's Jewell?"

Pointing to the ceiling, Alex swallowed his mouthful of food. "Upstairs. She was tired, so I sent her to bed. I'll heat up something for her later. She had a late lunch, and she's supposed to help me monitor exhibitionist/voyeur night this evening. A nap is just what she needs."

Tru put a hand on Liam's arm. "Would you like me to make you a plate?" She wanted to serve him. She wanted to honor him the way he deserved.

He snagged a plate from the stack on the counter. "Nah. I'm good." He heaped on noodles and meat sauce, and then he joined the other men.

She tried not to dwell on his refusal. Liam was used to fending for himself. She'd have to change that about him. He was new to being a Dominant, so he probably had some kind of feminist hangup about having her serve him. But that reasoning didn't sit right with her

When she sat down, she realized she had neglected to get a drink. "Alex, what do you have to drink?"

He pursed his lips as he thought. "Don't know. Water. Maybe cranberry juice? Jewell won't buy pop anymore because the doctor said I should lay off."

Tru laughed. It was just like Jewell to enforce healthy habits. She wanted to have Alex around for a long time. "I'll raid the fridge. Jed, Liam, can I get you something?"

"Water is fine." Liam twirled spaghetti on his fork.

"I have a beer." Jed lifted the bottle and took a sip.

She opted to have water as well, but as she filled the glasses, she frowned. Something was wrong. She knew that Jed wanted to talk to her alone so that she could tell him about the visions she'd experienced on the trip, but that didn't explain his suddenly subdued manner. He hadn't seemed to notice that she'd joined them until she asked him if he wanted a drink. Liam also seemed to be holding back. She wondered what they had talked about after she'd left. Was the case going badly?

Or maybe they felt they needed to be in the inn so that they could keep an eye on Anton Schatz and Sarah Braithwaite? Damn! Being here was taking them away from their investigation, and it was her fault. They hadn't wanted to join her friend for dinner, but they hadn't known how to get out of it without being rude.

They ate in silence. Alex watched them, and he shot her a couple of questioning glances, but she couldn't answer him without jeopardizing their investigation. As soon as her men finished eating, she jumped up. "We should probably get back so that we can get ready for tonight." She met the hundredth question in Alex's eyes. "We're super excited for it. Do you mind if we take off? Or I can stay behind and help you clean up while these two head back and get things ready."

Alex waved her off. "Go. I'm sure I'll see you around."

"Thanks for dinner." Jed pushed in his chair and waved.

"Yeah, you were right. You do make kickass meatballs. Thanks." Liam put a hand on Tru's lower back and steered her toward the front door.

They walked back in silence. Tru didn't stir the pot until they were safely ensconced in their room. "Sir? What's wrong?"

"Sir?" Liam whirled on her. Fire danced behind his brilliant blue eyes. Unfortunately it wasn't the kind that smoldered and made her panties wet. "That's convenient, isn't it?"

This was the first time she'd seen him this angry, and she wasn't sure why his ire was directed at her. She drew back. "I don't understand why you're mad at me." She looked to Jed for answers or support, but he merely crossed his arms and glared at her the same way Liam was. "You're both mad at me? This isn't fair. What the hell could I have possibly done?"

"How about taking us to a place owned by your ex-Master without mentioning that you two had a relationship?" Ten feet separated her from Liam, but the distinct force of his vehemence easily traveled the span.

She took a defensive step back. "I brought you here because you needed to come here. You asked me to bring you here."

"And you wouldn't have if you had a choice?" Jed's quiet question cut through her armor. She'd hurt them both.

"I—I don't know. Maybe. Not this quickly, but eventually." Would she really have brought them here? In a word—no. She wouldn't have given them a chance to make her fall for them. That had happened here.

"You're lying." Liam clenched his jaw and shook his head in disgust.

Yes, she was technically lying, but things were different now. It wasn't a lie now. "It's not a fair question."

"It's not fair to bring us here and throw your ex-lovers in our faces." Liam shook a finger at her. "Twice we walked into there to find out major things that should have come from you. The first time, we made excuses. It's a new relationship, it's not something you run around telling people."

Tru's defensiveness was morphing to outrage at their antagonism. "I've known you for two weeks, Liam. Two weeks where you were also working on an investigation. That doesn't leave a lot of time for heart-to-heart talks. And you don't get to throw my cancer in my face. I would have told you eventually, when the time was right. It's not information I trot out on the first few dates." Some people liked to wear shirts to proclaim their status as a survivor, but Tru was a private person. When she volunteered every year at the hospital that had become a second home through her years of treatment, she talked about it openly and freely. When she met a hunky guy, she didn't use that information as a pickup line.

He waved away her concern. "I'm not throwing that at you, just the fact that you don't tell us anything. I'm really pissed that you didn't bother to warn us that Alex was your Master. You said he was your friend. Just a friend."

"He is my friend." She hated that he was furious with her. Swallowing back the prick of tears, she plunged ahead. "He's been my friend for a long time. About six years ago, he introduced me to the lifestyle. I trained with him whenever I came for a visit, and when I realized he had feelings for me, I looked for ways to let him down gently. That's when I met Jewell, and I had a vision of them together." She clamped her mouth shut because she'd fucked up big time. Only Jed knew about her visions. Liam didn't believe in such things.

But she needn't have worried. He didn't seem to have caught it. He closed the distance, towering over her as only a Dominant could. "All the more reason to tell us. You warned us that we'd be judged. We thought you meant that your friends would be looking to make sure we treated you right, not measuring us against how they treated you when you were theirs."

Alex and Jewell weren't like that. Sure, Alex had been hurt at first, but he'd moved on quickly because he and Jewell were soul mates. Defiant, she lifted her chin. "I was never theirs, and I warned you about the most important thing. Yes, they care about me—as friends do. They want me to be with someone who makes me happy." She had more to say, but he cut her off.

"I'm not interested in your excuses or explanations. The fact of the matter is that YOU should have told us."

She agreed. Alex had no business shooting his mouth off. She moved closer to Liam, openly challenging his dominance. "You're right. It's my business, and I should have told you when or IF I thought you should know."

The flames turned to steel, and when he spoke, his soft voice was edged in jagged, sharpened glass. "Sure, Princess. Why tell us about your exes when it doesn't matter? After all, this is just temporary, right? Make believe? Once we're finished with the investigation, we'll go our separate ways. It'll be over. We'll leave here with a murderer and fond memories of a smoking hot good time."

He hadn't touched her, but she staggered back as if he'd slapped her. In a way, he had—twisting her words and throwing them at her after he'd made her fall in love with him.

He didn't wait for a response. He pushed past her and stormed out.

She looked to Jed for help, but she saw that she'd hurt him just as deeply. "Jed, I didn't mean for this to happen."

Misery broke the surface of his chocolate eyes. He looked at the floor rather than meet her gaze. "No, of course not. It was just supposed to be some fun on the side, right?"

"It started that way, but—"

"I'll go talk to him." Jed left before she could think of a way to explain reasonings that weren't clear or coherent in her head.

She sank down and sat on the foot of the bed, staring at nothing because she was too stunned to cry. Today had started so wonderfully, and it was ending so fucking badly.

Chapter Nineteen

The evening had cooled off in direct proportion to the rise in Jed's temper. He wasn't given to productive outbursts, and he was glad that Dare had taken the lead on that interrogation. Where Jed would have yelled and maybe punched a wall, Dare had been through enough therapy that he used his words no matter the circumstances. It made him a great field agent, though he knew his buddy would have preferred to sit in front of a computer all day long.

Jed found Dare sitting on a bench near the far end of the parking lot, staring over the cliff at the turbulent sea. In the distance, the sun touched the horizon, but it was mostly obscured by clouds and a thick fog that seemed to creep over the water.

He sat down next to the man who had, in some ways, become his closest friend.

"Don't tell me I was wrong to walk away. Maybe it's not what a Dom is supposed to do, but it's what I needed to do. I wasn't going to cool off if I stayed there." Still as granite and tense as a hostage negotiator, Dare didn't move.

"I walked away too." Jed ran a hand over his hair. The bumpy texture tended to help him calm down. Or maybe he just liked petting himself. "I don't think I've ever been so pissed at a woman before."

"I'm in love with her."

Jed had suspected as much. If neither of them had strong feelings for her, then they wouldn't have cared about any of the things she hadn't told them because they were inconsequential to the investigation. He shook his head. "It's going around."

"I know she's had other boyfriends, other Doms. She's trained, an experienced sub. That had to come from somewhere." Dare finally moved. He rubbed his palm on the thigh of his jeans.

"But it would have been nice if she told us that we were about to meet the man who introduced her to it all. We used his dungeon." Jed didn't want to think of her with another man who wasn't him or Dare. "Jealousy is a new emotion for me. I've been jealous of you, and now him. And her. Jeeze—can you imagine Tru going down on Jewell? Holy shit, that would be so fucking hot. At the same time, I don't think I could watch."

Dare's chuckle was bereft of all humor. "I know what you mean. I watch her with you, and I think I don't have a snowball's chance with her, and then I realized that you must be thinking the same thing when you see her with me. You know what we need? Time alone with her. You had today. I get tomorrow. We need to make that a regular thing."

"I agree that we need a schedule, but she should have some say in it. And you're getting her tonight. I won't do a public show."

"Oh." Dare sounded disappointed. "I thought afterward that we'd come back to you. She really liked when we had her at the same time."

Jed washed his hand over his eyes. "I hate to say it, but I think tonight we all need to sit down and talk. A scene isn't what we need. We need to be brutally honest, lay all our cards on the table, and so does she."

Sitting back, Dare looked like a man about to be led to his execution. "Do you think she'll do it? She was pretty clear about this being temporary."

"She said that we'd see where it goes. Well, it has gone in a serious direction. We have to make sure she understands that, even if she's not on the same page yet."

"I admire your optimism." Dare chuckled again, but this time it had an edge of humor to it. "I told my mom about all this."

Jed had no idea how to even begin to have a conversation like that with his parents. "What did she say?"

"She's happy for us, and she wants to meet Tru."

If he hadn't been looking over his shoulder at Dare, he wouldn't have caught the movement in the corner of his eye. Two figures, dark shadows against the darkening sky, darted between two cars. He shifted to face Dare, leaning in like things were about to get intimate.

Dare put a hand up. "Whoa, there. While this would also make my mom happy, I'm just not that into you."

"Shhh. Our suspects are sneaking around like thieves in the night. Man up. Pretend you love me." In the twilight, it probably looked like a romantic interlude, and that suited him just fine. It meant Schatz wouldn't know he'd been spotted. He put a hand on Dare's neck and leaned even closer.

"Where are they, hot stuff?" Dare stared into his eyes like a star-crossed lover.

"You talk too much." Just then, Zarah Braithwaite looked in their direction. Jed pressed his lips to Dare's. He wasn't nearly as soft and welcoming as Tru, and he sure didn't smell as good. He mostly smelled like spaghetti and meatballs.

Schatz and Braithwaite disappeared into the bushes, and Jed let Dare breathe.

"Dude, I don't know how Tru puts up with the way you kiss. You lack finesse, and you smell like beer."

"And you smell like Alex's spicy balls, but at least it's not ketchup." Jed sat back and openly stared at the place where the suspects had gone and willed his brain to make sense of what he'd witnessed. "This settles the question of whether Braithwaite is a hostage or a suspect. She led Schatz into the bushes."

"Let's see where they're going." Dare leaped to his feet. "Tru is going to have to wait."

They crept to the place where the suspects had slipped into the brush, and they followed on silent feet. The sun hadn't quite set, so there was still a little light for them to see where they were going. However there wasn't a path to follow, so they had to rely on their ears and intuition to tell them where Schatz and Braithwaite had gone. Branches of brush snagged at his shirt and scratched his arms and legs. If he'd known that a nature hike in the frigid, foggy night air was on the agenda for the evening, he'd have worn pants and long sleeves.

The sounds of someone moving through foliage ceased, and Jed stopped, holding up his fist to signal Dare. They stopped and listened. After the longest time, Dare tapped Jed's shoulder and shook his head. Just as Jed was about to suggest they continue with caution, they heard the sound of voices.

"The opening is somewhere around here." Carried on a soft ocean breeze, Zarah's words skimmed past their ears.

"You said you knew where it was." Schatz's deeper voice didn't need the help of the wind to travel.

"I do, but it's been forever since I was here. And Angelo didn't take me with him that time. I had followed him because he wasn't acting like himself." The sound of her voice moved away, and Jed followed it the best he could. Moments later, she laughed, a musical sound. "Didn't he go to meet you? Why don't you know where the hidden entrance is?"

"No, he didn't meet me. I told you that I'm new to this branch of the organization."

"What about the guy we're going to meet? He's your boss, right?"

Schatz made an aggravated noise. "You talk too much. Just find the cave entrance."

They were being loud enough to put Jed's mind at ease. Those two had no idea they'd been spotted or that two FBI agents were in hearing distance of their quiet conversation. Jed didn't know how long they crept through the tangle of high bushes and scrubby pines before they came to the edge of the continent.

The growth didn't fade or drop away. Instead, it tried to creep down the edge of the cliff, stubbornly clinging to life via crevices and clever roots. In the daytime, this camouflage wouldn't have fooled them, but darkness shrouded them. The sun had set, and they didn't have flashlights. The one on his cell phone would have lit up the place, but that would have also alerted Schatz and Braithwaite to their presence.

On the edge of the high cliff, Jed's foot slipped, but he didn't go far because Dare grabbed him. Heart racing, Jed threw a stoic nod of thanks over his shoulder at his buddy. This wasn't a fall anyone survived. The two of them carefully followed the edge of the cliff for a while longer, but the voices and sounds of Schatz and Braithwaite had disappeared.

Jed stopped and looked around. "We lost them."

Dare peered back the way they'd come. He used the flashlight app on his phone to shed some light on the issue, and they backtracked with Dare in the lead. The path they'd made was easy to see now, and they retraced their steps.

Before long, Dare pointed to a place where broken branches marked a possible path down the cliff face. He crouched down and pointed his flashlight to illuminate the evidence. Though it was difficult to see, a shelf came out about six feet down, and it looked as if there might be a cave or deep crevice leading into the rock.

"You think they went that way?" Jed hoped not. He wasn't keen to climb down the sheer face of a cliff without any equipment or even the right kind of shoes. He was wearing sandals—sexy, manly sandals.

"One way to find out." Dare slipped his phone in his pocket. "I'll go. You keep watch."

Jed hadn't brought his gun, and neither had Dare. "I think that's a bad idea. I can't cover you if they are down there. I say we find a good hiding spot and keep watch. They're going to have to come out eventually."

"But they're going to meet someone, probably to pick up illegal gems."

Yeah, they wanted to catch the bad guys, but Jed didn't see where that was going to happen tonight. "They're in a cave high above the ocean. It's more likely they're stashing something or retrieving something that's been stashed. Our best bet is surveillance. We'll catch them red-handed on the way out."

Dare didn't look sold on the idea. "We don't know they're down there."

Jed used the flashlight on his phone to search for clues—a scrap of clothing, a footprint, anything to indicate they'd been there. On the dirty floor of the rocky shelf, something metallic glinted. He focused his camera on it, set it for nighttime mode, and snapped a picture. "Broken fake fingernail. Braithwaite had teal, glittery polish on her nails."

They moved farther down the cliff and positioned themselves so that they could see the shelf with the broken nail. It wasn't a lot to go on, but it was something, and stumbling around in the dark was getting them nowhere.

Tru waited for an hour. At first she didn't move. Too stunned to think, she remained on her perch at the foot of the bed. The thoughts tumbling through her head were too random and incomplete to make sense. *Liam's quiet pain... Jed's face turned away... Giving...Taking... Submitting... Feeling... Gram... Alex... Poppy...Visions...*

Once the shock wore off, her brain sorted out the relevant details and began shouting at her—regrets and recriminations mostly. She hadn't meant for any of this to happen. Liam's parting shot had hit hard because nothing he'd said was wrong. This wasn't supposed to be serious. Like every relationship in which she'd ever engaged, it was supposed to have been temporary fun.

But it wasn't. Not anymore. She'd suggested seeing where this experiment led. At the time, she hadn't thought it would go anywhere serious, but it had—for all three of them.

She found no comfort in the fact that Liam was keeping in mind the terms of the deal, but she took heart from the fact that the terms made him upset. That meant he was at least invested in the relationship. She wasn't sure if his feelings ran as deeply as hers—but at least he had them.

And Jed did as well. He may not have been active in their "discussion," but he had been just as hurt as Liam. She hadn't meant to hurt them, and that pain weighed heavily on her heart. Perhaps they'd gone off to develop a plan for how to get Tru to fall for them? They had no way of knowing that she already had.

After all, what clues in her behavior could have led them to think anything had changed on her part? None. She hadn't changed a darn thing. They wanted her submission—her complete submission—but she hadn't given it. Oh, she'd given piecemeal parts, especially during sex, but she hadn't surrendered to them. Not once had she knelt for them. That had been a hard limit, even with Alex after that first time. Kneeling for a Dom was a deeply spiritual experience that had sent her reeling into the deepest levels of submission. That wasn't something she had ever wanted to give to another person.

It wasn't that she was afraid Liam or Jed would abuse or fail to cherish her submission; it was that she'd never before wanted to let anybody get that close to her. Yeah, she'd been having visions of Liam and Jed for a while, but that was no substitute for spending the time necessary to build a relationship. And yeah, she hadn't known them for that long, but it didn't seem to matter. She'd been close friends with Alex for seven years when she'd agreed to be his submissive, and that hadn't made her want to get on her knees and give him everything.

But this was different. She hadn't wanted it to be, but it was. And so she slid to the floor and knelt to wait for them to return. Her actions would speak when her words were not adequate.

She remained that way for twenty minutes—a test of endurance for anyone's knees—before she had to get up and move around. While she didn't have osteoporosis yet, the bones in her legs and knees weren't used to holding that kind of position. Sometimes sitting for long periods also caused soreness. It could have been a long-term side effect of chemo, or it could just be bad genetics. Tru chose not to think about it. She emptied her mind and tried the position again. And again. And yet again.

After two-and-a-half hours with no sign of Liam or Jed, she gave up. She knew they hadn't left because they weren't here for her. They were here for work, and they weren't going to give up until they caught their murderer. They had most likely caught sight of the suspects at the public event and stayed to watch. Tru knew that Anton Schatz and Zarah Braithwaite had said they wouldn't attend, but they'd probably changed their minds. Voyeur/Exhibitionist night may not have been their cup of tea, but it was one of those events that tended to draw people in whether they liked the brew or not.

She pictured Jed and Liam sipping beers and watching their suspects watch people have sex. If she wanted things to happen tonight, then she needed to go find them. In preparation, she selected the corset top and skirt that her Doms had chosen for her once before, and she spent some time making sure her hair and makeup were styled attractively.

The "shows" were confined to the event room, a place where regular demonstrations and classes were held. It had originally been a banquet hall when this place had been expanded in the 1940's as a summer camp.

Tru entered the room unnoticed. In several places, couples performed for the audience that had gathered, and that's where everybody's attention was focused. She passed a bound man being spanked, but she didn't notice any other details because she was focused on the onlookers. That's where she'd find her Sirs. Other stations showed various degrees of people engaged in foreplay or sex, and she searched among the audience for Liam and Jed. They had to be there somewhere. However, two circuits of the room proved her wrong. Tamping down a mixture of alarm and despair, she roamed the public areas of Zangari's Fetish Inn, but it was mostly deserted. Everybody was in the banquet hall, eating in the sight of people having kinky interludes.

She found herself in the deserted dining room. Dinner service had long ago ceased, and she wandered to the server station where she knew there was a bar. Zangari's didn't have a formal bar, but it did have a liquor license to serve drinks with dinner. Tru helped herself to a whiskey sour. Leaning against the stainless steel counter of the server station, she contemplated her next steps. Jed and Liam were nowhere around. In her search of the public areas, she'd spied their car still in the parking lot. They hadn't gone far without a car.

She worried that they might have come across some trouble. Nowhere in her wanderings had she come across Schatz or Braithwaite. What if the duo was in the midst of some other nefarious, illegal scheme and Jed and Liam had discovered them?

What if they were hurt or stranded somewhere, and they needed her help? Setting her glass down, she resolved to find them. First thing, she headed in the direction of the room Braithwaite and Schatz shared. If they were inside, then she'd know that Jed and Liam were hiding from her and not working on their investigation. She went through the dining room to the sitting room off the lobby because that was the easiest way to get to the room she sought. The moment she stepped through the threshold of the sitting room, the bell on the front door jingled. Jewell had introduced that signal for use when the front desk clerk had duties to complete that would take them away from the desk.

Tru crouched behind a sofa. She felt stupid, but if someone discovered her, she could always pretend to be adjusting the strap of her high-heeled sandals. From her vantage point in the sitting room, she saw a couple stroll through the lobby, holding hands and smiling the way lovers did. She was about to get up and continue on her mission when a noise from the kitchen startled her into staying put.

A dark head of hair poked out from the door that swung both ways. Anton Schatz looked around the room, but he didn't seem to notice Tru crouching in the sitting room behind the sofa in clear view of anyone on that side of the dining room. The lights in the dining room were off, but ambient light spilled in from the sitting room and from the lamps lining the patio outside.

Still, he didn't look in her direction as he crept from the kitchen. Zarah Braithwaite followed him. The pair exited the dining room through a side door and turned toward their room. Tru slowly got to her feet and tiptoed to the lobby. She followed the pair at a distance, and she was mildly disappointed to see them return to their room.

While raiding the kitchen at a bed-and-breakfast made the list of things normal people didn't do, it was an action Tru wouldn't put past either Anton or Zarah. Both were unsavory characters, and if they were hungry, they wouldn't let a closed kitchen stop them from eating. Scowling on behalf of Alex and Jewell, Tru went back to the kitchen to make sure they hadn't left a mess. She checked the counters, sink, refrigerator, and pantry. Nothing seemed amiss. At least they'd cleaned up after themselves.

That meant Liam and Jed were out there somewhere with the sole purpose of avoiding her. Still scowling, she returned to the server station and finished her drink. Then she made another. And another.

She'd lost count of her drinks when she noticed Alex standing at the entrance to the server station. "Hey. I thought you were supervising tonight."

"I was. It's over. The staff is cleaning and sanitizing, and someone pointed out to me that a guest was raiding the liquor supply." He set his hands on the decorative molding topping the short wall that separated the station from the dining room. "Tru, what's wrong?"

Tru had a high tolerance for alcohol. She had a high tolerance for just about any drug or amount of pain. Chemo and many rounds of bone-marrow aspirations did that for a person. Alex had a similar capacity. They'd spent many nights together drinking too much alcohol and not noticing. She lifted the bottle of whiskey. "Want me to pour you a drink?"

"I'll drink with you, but you're going to have to talk to me." He waited while she mixed a whiskey sour and handed it over. He held out a hand. "Let's sit down."

She took his hand and let him lead her to the nearest table. She set her drink down before sitting in the chair he pulled out for her. "What do you want to talk about?"

He assumed the chair next to her and sipped his drink. "You always pour a strong drink. This is why you can't be a bartender."

His short-sleeved shirt showed off his arms, and Tru noticed a tattoo that hadn't been there the last time. In fancy script, it said *Go confidently in the direction of your dreams*. That wasn't something Tru had ever done. She'd subverted her dreams into dares and dangerous sports. She traced a finger over the quote.

"Like that? Jewell found it for me. She wants kids."

Like Tru, Alex couldn't have kids. Chemo and radiation had messed with their reproductive parts. If Tru had been older, they would have banked her eggs for later use, but she had been too young that first time around. Tru nodded. "Four." She'd seen it in a vision.

Alex started. "She told you?" He shook his head. "We're not here to talk about my problems. We're here to talk about yours. Why are you sitting in a dimly lit room draining my liquor supply? Where are Liam and Jed?"

She shrugged. "We had a fight. They left."

His face darkened. "What the hell? They abandoned you?"

"No. The car is in the parking lot and their clothes are still in the room. Liam was mad, and Jed went after him. I hurt them, Alex. I didn't mean to, but I did. I shouldn't have come here with them." She sipped more of her drink, letting the sour heat and cold spread through her chest. "But then you wouldn't have let them have a room, and a murderer would go free. I couldn't let that happen." She faced Alex. "I never loved anybody before."

He nodded. "I know. I was shocked—happily shocked—when you wanted to bring them here, and so was Jewell. I mean, it's a big deal if you want me to meet someone you're dating. You have never introduced me to a boyfriend on purpose."

"I didn't know I loved them. I thought it was just a fling. It started that way, a couple nights of fun. It wasn't supposed to be more." She drained her glass, but when she rose to refill it, Alex stopped her with a firm hand on her arm.

"Let's wait a little while before you have more. You were telling me about falling in love for the first time."

She relaxed, and he released her arm. "They were mad because I didn't tell them about you, that you trained me. And about Jewell, how it started out as a threesome."

He washed a hand down his face. "Christ. I never thought you'd bring a Dom here without telling him everything. I'm sorry. I shouldn't have said anything. I thought I was just confirming what they already knew."

"Nope. I didn't tell them anything. It wasn't supposed to be serious."

"But it became serious anyway."

She fished an ice cube from the bottom of her glass and crunched it between her teeth. "I don't know how to do serious. What if they fall in love with me and I die?" She wasn't counting the days until her cancer returned, but she fully expected it to make a third and final appearance in her life. This time, she wouldn't be so successful in fighting it.

Alex shrugged. "So what if they do? What if you don't die, and you live happily ever after?"

Closing her eyes against the idea that falling in love with her would bring pain to Liam and Jed, she shook her head. "I'm not that lucky."

"It's not about luck. It's about living your life to the fullest. I'm not talking about jumping off a bridge. I'm talking about taking the chance that you might, in fact, have a future with two men who love you."

She didn't know if their feelings ran that deep. This was her greatest fear—falling in love. She was fine with falling from a plane, balloon, bridge, or cliff, but she was terrified of falling in love because she didn't think she could survive losing it. "I need another drink."

Alex got it for her. "This is your last one."

"Then make it a double." She might have slurred her words.

He chuckled. "So what did you say when they told you they were mad?"

She didn't remember saying much of anything. The alcohol was beginning to have an effect. Time stuttered, and when Alex set down her glass, she had a hard time getting her hand to it. All of a sudden, she realized she hadn't talked to Poppy in a couple of days. "I miss Poppy. I love her so much. She's my best friend. An' I love you too because you're my other best friend."

"You're wasted. Tell me what you said to Liam and Jed to make them leave."

He just assumed she'd shot off her mouth? Why? That wasn't how she operated. "Did I tell you that I found a dead body?"

Alex's eyes opened wider. "No. Where? When?"

"A little over a week ago. That's how I met them." She dropped her volume to a whisper. "They're FBI agents, cuz I found a murdered body. It was so horrible."

He sipped his drink, though not much disappeared from the glass. "Are they investigating the couple you asked me to let stay here?"

"Yep. They're murderers and prolly do other bad things. Don't know what, but it's the FBI, ya know? They don't do local murder stuff." Before she knew what was happening, the entire story poured forth. It was most likely disjointed and there was no way parts of it made sense.

Alex, in his patient way, listened to her talk and asked questions when she skipped over parts. By the time she finished talking, she found herself back in the room Alex had given her with no memory of how she'd come to be there. The ceiling spun, and she yearned for Liam and Jed to hold her until it stopped.

"I love them." She heard herself talking, but the sound seemed to come from someone else who might have been under water or at the other end of a long tunnel. "They're good men. Liam is kind of crazy like me. We're gonna find Bigfoot. It's gonna happen. Jed is so easy to talk to. I told him my secret that I didn't even tell you."

Alex was doing something by her feet. "What secret is that?"

"Nope. I'm not gonna tell you. Just Jed. He understands. Maybe Liam. Jed says that Liam will understand, but I don't know yet." She looked at the spinning ceiling. "Whattaya doin with my feet?"

"Taking off your shoes. I'm thinking you'll pass out after you tell me your secret."

She sat up suddenly and tried to figure out which image of Alex was the real one. "Four kids, Alex. Get ready because it's gonna happen soon."

The two images of Alex frowned. "You know I can't have kids."

"Adoption. I seen it." She closed her eyes and willed the memory of the vision forward. "The older two look Hispanic and the other two are mixed race. The littlest one is a pistol. She's running around in circles like a puppy, just laughing and laughing. Four kids. So there."

The spinning of the room exponentially increased, and the next time she was aware of anything, she was on her knees in front of a toilet. Alex pressed a cold cloth to her neck. "Think there's anything left?"

Her stomach still felt queasy, but at least the room had stopped spinning. "I wanted to kneel for them."

He shifted, adjusting his grip of her hair. "That's great. I'm sure you'll get a chance to do that soon." He flushed away evidence of her last bout of sick and helped her to the sink so she could rinse her mouth.

She did that, and then she burst into tears. "What if they never come back? Maybe I chased them away because I didn't want to love them."

"Nobody who loves you would leave you. Your relationship is less than two weeks old."

He was right. She followed him into the room and let him put her to bed. "What if they're dead?" Her eyes wouldn't stay open, but the nagging worry wouldn't leave. Her tears came faster. "What if the bad guys killed them? I don't want to lose them Alex. I never loved anybody before. I was afraid. I was stupid."

He hugged her and made soothing noises, and that's the last thing she remembered.

Chapter Twenty

Dawn broke, a glimmer of light through the trees that reminded Liam of how much it sucked to spend the night on surveillance duty on the edge of a cliff. Oh, wait—they didn't have cliffs like this in southeastern Michigan, and sitting in a dark van for days on end was not a fit comparison. He missed the creature comforts of his computer-filled office.

"I don't think they're coming out." Jed's voice was rusty from disuse.

"Or there's another exit." Liam peered over the edge once more. "We're going to need some gear. Flashlight. Map. I hope to fucking God there's a map of this cave system."

"You think it's a whole system?" Jed stood up and stretched.

"It fits with the geology of the area. I'd be surprised if there wasn't a network of caves and passageways." He sighed. "It was too much to hope they'd come out the way they went in."

Jed nodded. "Let's head back. We need to report in, refuel, find some helmets with the flashlight on the front. See if Tru is still speaking to either of us."

"She probably needs another spanking." Liam was thinking about the way she'd challenged him last night. If he didn't watch out, her insubordination was going to become a habit. "It seemed to work last time."

"The three of us need to sit down and talk." Jed yawned and shook his head, and he led the way back to the inn. "We need to know if she's willing to take the next step."

"A collar?" There were a number of "next steps" that could be taken from this point. A collar, even if it took the form of a necklace or ring, was the one that appealed to Liam the most.

"Or even just seeing us again. That would be forward progress." Jed chuckled. "Christ. I never thought I'd want to be in a serious relationship. I've never had this problem before. Usually I'm planning an exit strategy at this point. I mean, yeah, we threw around the idea of a casual relationship, but this isn't the same thing."

They trudged the rest of the way in silence. The room was quiet and dark when they entered. Liam turned on the bathroom light, and a glance at the bed showed Tru sound asleep. The noise from the sofa nearly had him reaching for his weapon, which would have been pointless because he'd left it in the room.

Alex sat up and threw off a blanket. "You're back. Great." He stood up, stretched, and scratched his stomach. "Damn, I hate sleeping on couches. They're too short to get comfortable."

Liam blinked. Part of him had not processed the fact that Alex had spent the night in his room.

"What are you doing here?" Jed parked his hands on his hips, somehow managing to come off as both friendly and menacing.

"Tru had a rough night. She drank most of my whiskey, but in the end, she gave most of it back. Of course it's no longer salable, so it's still a loss." He made a face, possibly at the memory of Tru vomiting up what she'd drunk. "She passed out at around three."

Liam glanced at her, asleep and oblivious. "So you stayed here with her?"

"Like I said, she was in rough shape. Listen, I'm going to say something because not only is this my home and my place of business, but Tru is one of my oldest friends. First, I don't like that you lied to me. If you needed to come here to catch a murderer, I would have found space for you, opened my records, and worked with you however you needed me to. I want nothing more than for my wife and guests to be safe here. I don't appreciate you using my friend in order to get in here to conduct a clandestine sting operation." He came closer and poked Liam in the chest. "She may appear strong, but she's hiding a very fragile side. You left her alone when she was most vulnerable, and that is not cool. If you want to be her Dom, you can't abandon her just because you had an argument. She's misguided, emotional, and unaccountably stubborn, but that doesn't mean you can't break her heart."

"We didn't break her heart." Jed sidled up to Alex, letting him know that if he wanted to go up against Liam, then he was also going to have to get through Jed. "She's not emotionally invested in this."

Alex, to his credit, didn't back down. He turned his steely stare to Jed. "She said you were smart, but from that statement, I'm thinking she's mistaken. She would not have brought you here—no matter the circumstances—if she wasn't emotionally invested. Most of the decisions Tru makes are based on emotion and intuition. Nobody would ever accuse her of being driven by logic."

Liam's heart thumped with joy. In her much too detailed, drunken confession, Tru had disclosed her feelings for them to her friend. Backing down a hair, Liam exhaled hard. "She told you who we are and why we're here?"

The abrupt change in subject threw Alex off for a second. The inn's owner scowled. "You should have told me that you were Federal agents."

Liam wasn't inclined to agree. "The fewer people who know about us, the better our chances of keeping our cover intact. If the suspects know who we are, they'll flee, and we don't have enough evidence to make an arrest."

Jed put a hand on Alex's shoulder. "However it's good to know you'll cooperate with our investigation. Are you aware of the cave system under this place?"

Alex didn't look surprised at the question. "Yeah. This place was built for bootlegging. There's a sealed entrance in the cellar. Is that where you were all night? You have to be careful down there. It's dark and dangerous, especially at high tide, and it's easy to get lost."

Jed's eyes lit. "You know your way around? Can you make a map?"

"My heart was never healthy enough for that kind of exertion, but Tru knows them pretty well. She learned spelunking down there."

Of course the woman who loved skydiving and base jumping would know how to rappel down cave walls.

However that solution didn't sit right with Liam. "I'd rather not take her when we don't know what we'll find. There has to be somebody else who can guide us."

"There is, but it would take at least a week to get him to come here. His granddaughter is getting married today—in Spain." Tru sat up, and she whispered as if the sound of her voice was physically painful. "Did you just now get back?"

"Yeah, Princess. We didn't mean to be out all night, but we followed Schatz and Braithwaite to a hidden opening to a cave. We waited for them to come out, but they didn't." Jed shot Liam a warning look.

Alex looked between the two of them. "They showed up at the Voyeur/Exhibitionist event at around ten-thirty. They stayed for a few minutes, and then they went back to their room."

"I saw them come out of the kitchen." Tru swayed and laid back down. "Don't know what time. Thought they were raiding for snacks, but if they were in the caves, they probably came up that way."

"I sealed that entrance years ago." Alex snagged a bottle of water from the mini-fridge and handed it to Tru. "Drink this slowly."

"Jewell and I were messing around in the cellar the summer before last, and we found out that the door you put up opened even when it looked like it was locked." Without opening her eyes, Tru sat up enough to sip water. "Can one of you get me something for this headache?"

"Messing around?" Liam wasn't inclined to give her aspirin until she'd eaten something. "What does that mean?"

"I have a hangover, Liam. I'm not in the mood to deal with your petty jealousies right now."

"You have to eat something first so it doesn't tear up your stomach." He crossed his arms and convinced himself to abandon that line of questioning. She was right—he needed to not get caught up in things that happened in her past. If she'd left them there, then he had no reason to drag them into the present.

"They were canning." Alex supplied an answer. "They'd picked tons of strawberries, tomatoes, blueberries, and I don't know what else. They spent a week in the kitchen, and we still have some preserves left." He headed toward the door. "I'll have the kitchen send breakfast to the room. I think the three of you have quite a conversation ahead."

The door closed behind him, and the three were silent for many long seconds. Finally Jed cleared his throat. "Tru, we need to talk. We were about to come back last night when I saw Schatz and Braithwaite skulking around. We had to follow them."

Her eyelids cracked open a minimal amount. "I'm just glad you're not dead. How about sending a text if it should happen again?"

Liam wasn't sure about the procedure here. Jordan probably would have texted Amy if she'd expected him home and he couldn't make it. Still, there might be a circumstance where he wouldn't be able to send a message without fear of ruining the operation. He settled on a compromise. "If we can, then we will."

"Thank you." Her eyes had closed again.

Liam slid an arm under her shoulders, perched on the edge of the bed, and leaned her against him. "Drink your water."

Moving incrementally, she lifted the bottle to her lips and tipped it up.

"Princess, we're in love with you."

Her eyes flew open and she spilled water down the front of her corset. The sheet absorbed most of the flow before Liam took control of the water bottle. She sat up, looking between him and Jed with bleary, bloodshot eyes. She was a beautiful mess.

He wasn't sure how he felt about Jed declaring something that should have come from him. When her gaze rested on him, Liam smiled gently. "I know it wasn't supposed to happen. I certainly wasn't looking for it, but Tru, I fell in love with you. I'm not sure when or how it happened, but it did. That's why I was so mad at you last night. I wanted to be as important to you as you are to me."

A tear fell from her right eye. More followed as her left eye got into the game.

Liam moved his leg so that Jed could sit next to her hip. Jed wiped her face with a tissue, and she turned those luminous, bloodshot brown eyes on him. "Princess, I'm sorry too. I've never been jealous before. It doesn't bring out the best in people. We're not expecting you to reciprocate, but we'd like to ask you to consider making this a permanent arrangement. You know—a serious relationship?"

She launched herself at Jed, somehow managing to throw her arms around both of them and bring them in for a tight hug. There was more incidental touching, but Liam noted it only because it had become a normal part of his life. She cried harder while he and Jed petted and attempted to soothe her.

"Tru, honey, what's wrong? Why are you crying?" Liam didn't like these tears because he didn't know what had caused them and he didn't know how to stop them.

"Because I love you too, and I didn't expect any of this either. I should have because I've been having visions of you two for years."

"Visons?" This was the second time she'd said something like this, and Liam was beginning to think she wasn't talking about fantasizing.

"Tru has visions." Jed mumbled into Tru's wild hair. "She sometimes sees images of the future."

Liam didn't know how to take that. Not long ago, he'd dismissed the psychics and their abilities in a conversation in which Tru had only marginally participated. He'd unwittingly shut her down and made her reticent to open up to him—but she'd opened up to Jed. He kissed her cheek. "That's a pretty cool superpower. Any clue as to when we're going to catch these scumbags?"

Tru eased her stranglehold and drew back. "It doesn't work like that. I don't control the visions that come to me."

He pushed her hair away from her face. "I'm sorry I made you feel like you couldn't tell me about this. I want you to know that I'll listen to whatever you have to say."

She nodded and sniffled. Her tears had subsided. "I'm new at this relationship thing. You're going to have to be patient with me."

Jed chuckled. "This is new for all of us, Princess. It's good that the trial-and-error method seems to work for us."

Her Sirs took turns showering while Tru choked down waffles and fruit. Normally she'd be over the moon about waffles for breakfast, but with a headache pounding out a rude rhythm behind her eyes, she was happy she managed to eat most of a waffle. After two ibuprofen capsules and a nap between Liam and Jed's warm bodies, she woke in the afternoon feeling much better.

While she showered, Liam and Jed took turns talking on the phone and typing on their official FBI laptop. They seemed to be planning something more than a jaunt through the caves, and they shipped her off to spend the day with Jewell and Alex to keep her out of the way, lest she should overhear some confidential information. Since her only role would be as their guide, they didn't feel she needed to be in on the plan. For her part, Tru raided the storage room in Alex and Jewell's lower level, searching for the spelunking gear they used to have. She couldn't see Jewell—the woman who still had every note someone had passed to her in high school—getting rid of it. Jewell was not only sentimental, but she firmly believed she'd use everything again one day.

"Do you have any idea where it might be?" Tru moved a stack of plastic containers labeled for Halloween.

Jewell crossed her arms. "This doesn't feel right."

Pausing, Tru looked back at her friend. "What doesn't?"

"You going down there. I don't like it."

The prospect of being here to catch the murderer or murderers in the midst of a crime gave Tru a little thrill. Though the experience hadn't been on her bucket list, she wasn't in the habit of letting that stop her from trying new things. "I think it'll be cool, and I'm excited to be part of taking down people who could so heartlessly murder a man and throw his body in the ocean. Sometimes when I close my eyes, I can still see his face with those lifeless eyes staring up at me. I want to replace that image with one of those two in handcuffs being shoved into the back of a police car."

"I still don't like it." Jewell's mouth twisted sourly, but she helped Tru move boxes and more plastic containers. "This is what you're after. There's gear for four. Maybe I should go with you."

Jewell had accompanied her several times when she'd explored the caves. She had some skills, certainly more than Liam or Jed. However Tru shook her head. "They wouldn't let you. They don't even want me to go, but they don't have a choice. I'm the only guide available. Plus Alex would just as soon tie you up at home to keep you safe."

She sighed. "You're right, of course, and I'm glad he would forbid me from going. Sometimes I wish I was as fearless as you, but I'm not. I'd be terrified the whole time."

Terror wasn't an emotion Tru accepted. So many terrible things had happened to her that she didn't acknowledge the idea that a horrible emotion could usurp control of her life. Except that it had. She'd let fear keep her from taking emotional chances. Jed and Liam had somehow slipped past her defenses, and now she realized how closed off she'd been. Well, no more. From this day forward, she would embrace and cherish the love she'd been so fortunate to find. She unpacked the helmets, knee pads, flashlights, and other equipment, checking them for signs of wear. "I'll do anything I can to help my Sirs."

Jewell giggled. "It's so refreshing to hear you call someone by title. Alex and I lamented that you'd ever find someone who could break through that wall around your heart, and now you have two very wonderful men."

Tru rolled her eyes. "Help me smuggle this stuff into my room."

"I have just the thing. Alex ordered a new spanking bench. We'll put it in that box, and then everyone will just think you're going to have a great time tonight."

The box was larger than expected, and the unwieldy size meant it took two of them to carry it across the large expanse of lawn to the inn. They made sure people saw them, and Tru found herself grinning as Zarah Braithwaite read the description on the side of the box.

"Have a fun night," she called after Tru and Jewell.

Tru laughed. "I'm sure I will."

Alex greeted them in the lobby, and he helped carry it down the hall by calling out helpful instructions. "Turn left. That's it. Just a little farther. Don't scuff the paint." Then he knocked on the door because their hands were full.

Liam answered. He frowned at the box. A line formed between his sexy, dark eyebrows. "What's that?"

Jewell clucked her tongue. "This room has no kinky equipment, so we found a spanking bench. If you move out of the way, we can bring it in."

Liam stepped aside, but the question didn't fade from his eyes. She and Jewell set the box on the floor on the far side of the room.

Jewell slapped Tru on the ass. "Master and I have things to do. You guys enjoy your present." And then she took Alex's hand and led him from the room. The door closed softly behind them, and the lock automatically engaged.

Jed examined the box. "Princess, I like this in theory, but we don't have time right now. I promise when this is over, we'll spend some quality time with you tied to a spanking bench."

"It's not a bench." Tru opened the box and drew out an oversuit, a one-piece coverall made from abrasion resistant material. "It's spelunking gear, but Jewell and I figured that we shouldn't advertise the fact that we're going into the caves. I saw Zarah Braithwaite on my way here, and she wished us a fun night."

With a thoughtful nod, Liam took out a pair of elbow pads. "Smart and sexy. I knew there was something I liked about you."

She preened under his compliment. "When is this going down?"

Jed laughed softly at her double entendre. "We're in a holding pattern until Schatz and Braithwaite make a move, which we hope isn't until after our team gets in place."

Liam scooted the laptop so that she could see the screen. "Alex put a surveillance camera tied into his closed-circuit system on both entrances to the cave as well as the door to their room. We'll know the minute they step foot inside."

Waiting sucked, and as the hours ticked by, the excitement wore off, and Tru found herself knocking out a couple of blog posts. She wrote about base jumping, white water rafting, and falling in love. If her blog was supposed to be an accounting of her exploits, falling in love was the most dangerous thing she'd tried yet. Of course she didn't disclose personal or professional information about Liam or Jed, but she couldn't refrain from confessing to her readers that she'd fallen for two men.

Liam stretched out on the bed next to where she was propped against the headboard. He waited for her to stop typing and glance over at him. "Remember the first time we met?"

That wasn't something she was likely to forget. "Yes."

"Did you know this was going to happen?"

She needed to be honest. "Yes. I mean, not at first, but I eventually put the pieces together."

"And when you met Jed—did you know you'd end up with him as well?"

"My visions aren't that specific. I knew I'd be with him, but I didn't know I'd be with him and you together. Hindsight definitely puts the visions into perspective."

He tucked his hands under his head. "The other day, you said that I should be nice to my birth mother. Right before that, your eyes kind of glazed over like you were lost in thought. Were you having a vision?"

At his reminder, the image of him peering hatefully at his birth mother resurfaced. "I saw the two of you together. Others were around. It was some kind of public place. She tried to talk to you, but you wouldn't listen."

He considered this for several moments. "That seems about right."

"The expression on your face was malevolent." She set aside her laptop and slid down to snuggle against his side. "I don't think you still hate her."

His arm came down, and he played with her hair. "No, I don't hate her, but I probably haven't forgiven her. I have no interest in hearing excuses for what she did to me."

Tru's heart went out to him. "I don't know what she was trying to say. It's just an image. But know that I'll be there for you, Sir."

He shifted, rolling to face her, and his kiss was full of slow-burning tenderness. Delicious feelings radiated from that point of contact, spreading through her body. Though he was a skilled kisser, the languorous feelings were equally the result of this newfound mutual closeness.

Knowing that they cared deeply for her and that she returned their feelings had changed everything for the better. She slid her fingers over his chest and down his abdomen. With a low, throaty moan, he pushed her onto her back and covered her body with his.

"We're on." Jed's pronouncement interrupted anything erotic that might have happened.

Liam rolled away, grabbing his holster from the table and putting it on before he was fully vertical. "Are they in the cave?" Liam had channeled the feed from Alex's camera into his laptop, so they had a real-time view of what was going on.

An image flashed in Tru's mind, a memory of a vision. She dropped to her knees near where Jed and Liam stood.

Jed touched her shoulder. "Princess, I love that you're kneeling for us, but right now we don't have the time to properly appreciate what you're giving."

"Sir, please." Bucking protocol, she grabbed his hand. "It's about a vision I've had. There's going to be a rockslide. If you dive to your right, you should avoid the worst of it." Next she took Liam's hand. "And Sir, after the chaos, stay put. It's better if I come to you."

Liam squeezed her hand, his way of letting her know that he believed her vision. "Where are you when all of this goes down?"

She shook her head. "Not hurt. Don't worry about me."

"Not hurt? Excellent. I knew leaving you behind would be a better option." Liam hauled her to her feet and crushed her to him.

"Sir, we've been over this. I know the cave system. You don't."

"She's got you there." Jed took her from Liam and kissed her hard on the lips. "Get into your gear. They've entered the tunnel. I don't want to give them too much of a head start."

Liam and Jed issued a series of commands, and before she knew it, the three of them, dressed in coveralls, kneepads, and helmets, were ready to enter the cave. They used the service entrance to get into the kitchen, and she found Alex waiting in the cellar. He nodded to Liam and Jed. "Bring her back safely."

She pressed a quick kiss to his cheek. "Tell Jewell that I'm going to want a snack when we get back."

"Will do." Alex gave her a brief hug, and then he slapped Liam on the back. "They have a six-minute head start."

Tru switched on her headlamp and went through the heavy metal door that wasn't supposed to open. The coolness hit her immediately, as did the stillness of the air. The moment the door to the cellar closed, the lack of light registered as well. Their headlamps were adequate enough to lead the way, but not bright enough to illuminate more than a few feet. Thoroughly in her element, Tru grinned. She led them down the only path that led from the cellar, widened years ago by nameless smugglers. They walked silently, Jed halting her progress several times to take the lead.

The part of the system with passable passages wasn't overly convoluted, but including the parts where crawling or squeezing through a narrow opening was required lent a whole new dimension to the available routes. She didn't think that Schatz or Braithwaite would take those routes when easier options were available, but she kept them in mind in case they came in handy.

When they came to a point that opened up to a sizeable room, Tru held up her fist as a signal for her Sirs to stop. She wasn't sure it was a real thing, but she'd seen it in enough movies and TV shows to be reasonably certain that they'd get the right message, which they did.

"The path opens up into a sort-of room with alcoves on either side." They'd been very silent, but if Schatz and Braithwaite had heard them following, this would be the perfect place for an ambush.

Liam nodded. "Stay here."

He and Jed disappeared around the bend. Tru knew they were clearing the room so that it would be safe for her to enter. It hit her for the first time that she was in a cave with murderers. Either Anton Schatz or Zarah Braithwaite—or both—had bludgeoned Angelo Braithwaite to death. It took a depraved mind to kill another human being on purpose. Though she very much enjoyed the danger associated with sports, she found that this kind of peril didn't give her the same thrill. In fact she was a little afraid.

Liam returned, the beam from his headlamp leading the way. "It's clear." He held out a hand, and he guided her to the familiar little room—which looked very different from the last time she'd been inside. The empty alcoves weren't so empty anymore. Someone had stacked boxes and boxes of supplies in them.

"What's in there?"

"Looks like heroin and guns." Liam's lips set in a grim line.

This was some serious shit. Tru swallowed her trepidation and took a step forward. "I've been thinking, and I know where the perfect spot is for a meeting with someone coming from below. Are you up for taking a parallel path to get there? It's hidden from most of the room, so they won't be able to see us. On the downside, it's about a fifty feet above them, so we most likely won't be able to hear them clearly."

Jed nodded. "Sounds like a plan."

Liam agreed.

"There will be crawling involved. If you have a problem with tight spaces, then this won't work for you." She'd been spelunking with someone who had a panic attack in a tight space. It hadn't been easy to calm him down and get him to a larger space, and that had been without the added pressure of catching a murderer.

"It's fine." Jed gestured for her to get moving.

They walked along for another ten minutes, the path steadily dropping to a lower altitude. At high tide, the lower sections of the cave were underwater. Tru mentally calculated when she thought the tide might come in, and though she based her estimate on recent experience, the tide schedule changed, and she wasn't sure how close she was. However, if they wanted to exit at the bottom, she figured they had about six hours left.

She led them through a tunnel that narrowed. When she got down on her belly and shimmied under a low overhang, Jed and Liam followed suit without grunts or complaints. Eventually they emerged on an ovoid rock overlooking a narrow space that widened into the largest room in the cave system. Light came from down below, a sure sign their quarry was near.

Liam and Jed doused their headlamps before lowering to their bellies and peering over the edge. Tru sat, leaning against the wall of the passageway, while they assessed the situation and had silent conversations that consisted of looks, pointing, and FBI sign language.

When at last they scooted back and joined her, they didn't look all that encouraged. Jed exhaled. "Six people. Schatz, Braithwaite, the two men they're meeting, and two bodyguards."

"I can see where the other tunnel enters the room. We're going to have to go in that way and surprise them in the act." Liam handed over his phone. "Record everything, Princess. This is going into evidence."

Though she didn't think she'd get any clear footage, she took the phone. "I'll record everything, but I'm going down there with you."

"Negative." Jed gave her a look that brooked no argument.

He'd rarely exercised his Dominance like this, and Tru responded to it immediately. Her resistance softened and faded. "Yes, Sir. I'll wait for a signal from you."

"Good girl." Liam pressed a kiss to her cheek. "Start recording now and don't stop until I tell you to."

She dowsed her headlamp, army-crawled to the edge, and then she looked down. She easily found the six people Jed had mentioned, and she pressed the button to record. From this position, some sounds reached her ears—an occasional word or phrase out of context. It took some time—twenty minutes according to the video counter—but Jed and Liam eventually came into the room. Their words traveled the distance clearly.

"FBI! Hands in the air."

Words were exchanged, and instead of the bad guys surrendering, the two bodyguards launched themselves at her Sirs. Tru swallowed a cry of distress. The last thing she needed was for them to worry about her when they were fighting for their lives.

It was hard to watch and even harder to film. She wanted to drop the camera and run to help Liam and Jed, but she couldn't disobey their order to stay put and film.

Seconds later, a half dozen more FBI agents clad in SWAT gear bounded into the cavern from the other direction. Tru predicted that Agents Monaghan, Forsythe, and Lockmeyer were among them. In a perfect world, the villains would surrender, but this situation was far from ideal. Soon the agents were locked in hand-to-hand combat with the five men, and Tru noticed Zarah Braithwaite edging back toward the way she'd come. Tru didn't think she'd follow the path that led back to Zangari's Fetish Inn, but that wasn't the only place she could get to by following that path. It branched off to come out on the cliff. If Zarah was good at climbing, she'd be able to disappear into the night.

"Sorry, Sirs, but I'm not going to let her get away." Knowing it would record on the video, she whispered the apology, and then she pressed the pause button.

Though she moved quickly, it seemed to take disproportionally longer to slither down the tunnel and through the tight places than it had taken to get to the ledge. Careful with her footing, she hurried to where she thought Zarah might be headed, but when she got to the point where the tunnel to the cliff branched off, there was no sign of the woman.

Tru stopped and listened. The sounds of the fight filtered down the passageway to where she stood. Just as she took a step toward the branch where she thought Zarah might have gone, a vision flashed through her mind. Trusting the brief glimpse into the future, she turned in the direction of the fight. Fifty paces proved her hunch correct.

Off to the right, another path led to a large, flat outcropping that dead-ended against solid rock that reflected erosion from swirls and waves of a much higher water table. Okay, calling it a path was generous. There was no floor worn smooth by time and many bootlegging feet. It had been years since she'd climbed like this, but if Zarah could do it, then Tru sure as hell could. Parts were sheer, and she felt for handholds and footholds she knew were there. Eventually she pulled herself over the edge of the precipice and onto the flat shelf.

Zarah was there, digging into a metal box, her back turned to Tru. The noise of the scuffle—the thud of flesh meeting flesh and the grunts and shouts of the combatants—was loud here, and that obscured the small sounds Tru made.

As in the alcoves of the last room, this place housed crates of what Tru assumed were guns and drugs. However, Zarah wasn't digging into any of those. On her knees, she dumped the contents of a hard briefcase into another. Sparkles and shimmers reflected in the beams of light from Zarah and Tru's headlamps. Thinking quickly, Tru unpaused Liam's cell phone recorder and panned the scene.

Tru stared at enough bling to stock a jewelry store, and then she noticed the next thing Zarah was doing. She pressed clay into the empty case. That action triggered an alarm deep within Tru's intuition.

"Stop!" Tru didn't have a weapon or real training in a martial art—taking six classes when she was twenty-six didn't count—but she infused her voice with authority and hoped it would work. "Freeze. Put your hands in the air."

Zarah froze, but she didn't put her hands in the air. Instead she slowly turned around. "You. I knew it was too much of a coincidence that you'd be in three of the hotels where I happened to be. You've been following us for months, haven't you?"

Apparently Zarah Braithwaite had not only bought Tru's subterfuge, but she had embellished it in her imagination. She thought that Tru was part of the FBI. Tru pressed her lips together and shot for the moon. "You stole the gems from your bosses, and they killed your husband in retaliation. Isn't that what happened?"

Laughing, Zarah shook her head. "So eager. Trying to move up in an organization is a bitch, and you're not hungry enough to win this. I'm going to kill you anyway, but first I'm going to set the record straight. I killed Angelo. He was a lovely man, but he had no ambition. He thought being a courier and bringing in some extra money a few times a year would be a good side project to pay for extra vacations. He was sweet, but short-sighted. I wanted more. When the opportunity presented itself, I traded up. And now I'm going to do it again. Those men are peons. Yes, they're higher up the chain than I am right now, but that's going to change. I'm about to catapult myself into the upper echelon of The Eye. It's a pity you won't be around to see it." She nodded at the cell phone in Tru's hand. "And you're not going to stop me with that thing."

Tru didn't know anything about this "Eye" thing, but it put the graffiti she'd discovered next to Angelo's body into perspective. She'd known this whole deal was about more than a murder, but she hadn't known that an organized crime syndicate was involved.

"Drop those suitcases."

Zarah's smile turned brilliant. "Oh, sweetie, I will." She threw the one she'd been packing with clay over the other edge of the outcropping and ran toward Tru, knocking her out of the way. Tru scrambled to throw her weight forward so that Zarah's momentum didn't push her over the edge. That would be a nasty fall, and the landing would be deadly. Zarah didn't seem to notice the drop. She jumped.

Tru heard her skitter and slide, but she was too busy trying not to go over backward to see if Zarah had survived the fall intact. As the ground rushed up to meet her and Tru rolled to lessen the impact, an explosion sounded below. It came from where Zarah had thrown the suitcase. Too late, Tru realized the clay had been C4, which was highly combustible according to every TV detective show she'd seen. This was going to make one hell of a blog post.

It didn't set off a spectacular blast, but it did knock loose a rockslide. Tru prayed that Jed launched himself to the right and that Liam stayed put. Safely on the ground, she scrambled down the way she'd come. Well, she scrambled as quickly as she could considering that she wasn't prepared to rappel. Finding places to shove her fingers and feet on the climb down proved challenging with just one headlamp, and Tru found herself frustrated and afraid. What if Liam hadn't stayed put? Her vision hadn't run simulations of various scenarios. It had simply shown her a four-second movie.

Once she was down, she ran toward the cavern. This was her vision come true, and whether they had listened or not, her Sirs needed her right now.

The uneven path to the main cavern widened suddenly, and she found a gun pointed at her face. Already powered by adrenaline, a fear response didn't kick in, but thankfully her common sense hadn't deserted her. She skidded to a halt and put her hands in the air.

A dust-covered Agent Lockmeyer peered behind Tru before lowering her weapon. "Braithwaite ran off."

"She put explosives in a suitcase and tossed it over the side." Tru pointed to the overhang where she had found Zarah stealing precious gems. "I tried to stop her, but she took another case full of diamonds and maybe rubies."

Agent Lockmeyer motioned Tru to follow her. "We have teams waiting at all three entrances, so she won't get far."

Tru hurried after the woman in charge. "There are more than three ways into these caves. They extend for at least a mile down the coast." She doubted Braithwaite knew her way through the system, but it was extensive and riddled with hiding places, so finding her would be challenging.

The main room looked very different. The clearing, chipped away and leveled by generations of smugglers and bootleggers, was covered in rubble. A large section of rock had sheared off and dropped to the floor of the cave. Tru pointed her headlamp in a sweep of the area. Agents Monaghan and Forsythe, along with three agents she didn't recognize, stood over four handcuffed men. They all wore evidence of the chaos Zarah Braithwaite had caused. "Where are Jed and Liam?"

Jed came out from the other side of the wall created by the sheared rock. Blood from a cut on his hairline ran down the side of his face, and he was dirtier and dustier than the others. "I'm here, Princess. I dove right."

Temporarily relieved, she fell into his arms. He hugged her tightly, and then he released her quickly. "Where's Liam?"

"Here. I didn't stay put, but my helmet did."

Tru followed the sound of his voice to find Liam on the other side of the new wall. He leaned against it with his eyes closed, and his right arm hung limply by his side. The layer of dust and grime didn't help, but he seemed to have a grayish pallor. "You're hurt."

"Broken collarbone. It's nothing." He attempted a smile, but it came out more like a grimace. "Probably a concussion. My helmet came off when I was grappling with Schatz, and then the explosion happened. I've had worse headaches."

In her vision he had been hurt on his right side, though she'd assumed his arm was broken. She took a step closer and tripped. Jed caught her, and she looked down to see a pair of feet sticking out from a pile of loose stone. They were clad in an expensive brand of boots marketed to outdoor types.

"I chased him here just before the explosion. If I had stayed put, I'd be in that pile with him."

Blood drained from Tru's extremities. The first time she'd ever used her vision to warn someone away from danger, and it had only worked out for one of the two men she loved. The air suddenly became devoid of oxygen and her legs lost feeling.

Jed caught her, and as he set her on the ground, he pushed her head down to her knees. "Slow down, Princess. You're hyperventilating."

"I almost killed Liam. I've always kept the visions to myself, and now I know why." She gulped air as hot tears scalded her cheeks.

"You said they're not in context." Liam slowly lowered himself to the ground next to her. "I'm staying put now."

She looked at him with tear-distorted vision, and she realized that this moment had been her vision. She removed her waist belt and used the strap and his elbow pad to fashion a sling to keep his arm and shoulder immobile. Poppy had said that six-week course on first-aid training was a useless waste of time, though she'd still gone to each class with Tru because the instructor had been attractive. Right now it was coming in handy.

Jed left her to care for Liam. She heard his voice giving commands to a crew of agents who were being sent to retrieve the cache of weapons and drugs they'd found.

Liam used his good hand to wipe away the wetness on her cheek. "Why are you still crying?"

She shrugged. "I don't know. I guess because I love you, and I'm relieved that you're mostly okay." She finished tying the sling and looked over her work.

"I love you too." Liam's grimace disappeared for a brief moment as he made his declaration. "We told you to stay up there."

"I saw Zarah leave, and I couldn't let her get away." She related her brush with the murderer to Liam. Jed had returned, and he listened to her tale. They laughed when she said that Zarah thought Tru had been tracking her for months.

"It looks like we're going to have to search this whole cave system." Jed frowned thoughtfully as more agents entered the room. "This is a much bigger break in the case than we'd anticipated. If we follow Zarah Braithwaite long enough, she'll lead us to the people, places, and supplies for The Eye. We have a name and a face."

"It's more than we had before." Liam closed his eyes. "Since Tru's cover is blown, it looks like she's going to have to return to her safe, boring career as a travel blogger."

Tru laughed. Her life had been anything but boring.

"I'm serious." Liam cracked open one eye. "I want to know the truth, Princess. I have theories, but no answers."

She had no idea what he was talking about now, but she knew that people with concussions sometimes didn't make sense. "What do you want answers about?"

Jed rejoined them. He sat on her other side as Liam answered her question. "You. Were you an adrenaline junkie before chemo messed with your brain? I read about the way it changes your brain chemistry, especially when you're younger."

Had she always been addicted to thrills? Maybe. "I've always been the person who had to climb to the top of the tree, and I loved walking the ridgeline of the roof at Gram's place. I'm adventurous, a daredevil."

Jed rubbed a hand up and down her back. "Or you think you don't deserve to be alive. After talking with Alex, we figured out that you have put a lot of time and effort into avoiding serious relationships."

Yeah, she had, but only because she thought she'd eventually die. What was the point of putting more people through the pain of losing her than necessary? She faced Jed. "Not anymore. I love you both, and I'm willing to do whatever it takes to make this work." She took Liam's good hand. He opened his eyes, and she continued. "Anything. I know we all travel, and we live 300 miles apart, but we can make it work. I have a ton of airline miles."

Liam's eyes closed again, but this time he was smiling. Paramedics entered from the corridor that led to the beach. Agent Forsythe directed them to where Jed and Tru sat with Liam.

Tru moved back to give the medical professionals room. "I'll come home with you to help you recover from your concussion."

Jed pointed to his head. "I got hit on the head too."

Tru twined her fingers with his. "I hope it's not a concussion. I'd like at least one of you to not have a headache."

"Sex cures headaches," Liam mumbled as the paramedics lifted him onto a gurney. "I might have a headache every day for the rest of my life."

She pressed a kiss to his dirt-streaked forehead. "Me too."

Chapter Twenty-One

The air had turned decidedly crisp, and the gentle breeze washed across the stream and through the trees, rattling the colorful leaves and shaking a few loose. An orange maple leaf landed on the top of the wooden picnic table next to Liam's slice of hot apple pie. He picked it up by the stem and twirled it between his thumb and forefinger. Next to him, Tru's thigh pressed against his as she shifted. She wrapped her arm around his and leaned on his good shoulder.

"It's the perfect day to visit a cider mill." Tru shoved the rest of her sugared donut in her mouth and washed it down with apple cider.

"Yes, it is. Perfect day, perfect companion." He kissed her lips and came away with sugar crystals on his mouth.

This ritual is one Liam had been doing for as long as Joyce Adair had been part of his life. Even when he'd become too old for hanging out at the cider mill with his mom to be cool, he'd kept going. Today was the first time he'd brought anyone else. His mom was on a weekend trip with her new boyfriend, and the foursome had plans to come back to the mill in a few days.

"Want me to feed you?" Tru sat on his left side because his right collarbone was still healing. These past few weeks had been idyllic. Not only was he on temporary desk duty—meaning he got to spend all day with his computers—until his injuries healed, but Tru had kept her promise to stay with him until he was fully recovered. The more time he spent with her, the more he was convinced that she needed to be around all the time.

"Am I not eating fast enough for you? Do you have a hot date tonight?"

She giggled and slung her legs across his. "As a matter of fact, I do."

Jed was due home in a few hours, and the two of them had planned to surprise her with a scene. Though Jed had scened with her since she'd been here, Liam hadn't been able to do much without jarring his broken collarbone. The sex had been decidedly vanilla, which wasn't bad, but it was no longer his favorite method.

Tru picked up his fork and loaded it with sweet, apple-y goodness. "I've never fed anyone before. This'll either be intimate or awkward."

He strove for intimate. "Have I told you lately that I love you?"

Her smile warmed his heart, and the way her eyes softened made him want to scoop her up and find a private place to show her how he felt. "Yes, Sir, but I never get tired of hearing it, so feel free to say it again."

Staring into his eyes, she fed him the rest of his pie, and it was definitely intimate. By the time he finished the pie, Tru wore the same expression she got when he licked her pussy and refused to let her climax. He grinned. "Let's go home."

"I thought you'd never ask." She leaped to her feet. "I want to get more donuts and a pie to take home."

For a change, the line inside the mill wasn't too long. "Go on. I'll clean up here." There wasn't much trash, and he took his time, watching her walk until she was out of sight. Then he gathered his paper plate, their paper cups, and their napkins.

"Nick? Is that you?"

Liam looked up to find a woman approaching. She looked as if she was in her late forties. Her hair was short and blonde, and makeup caked her face. However nothing could disguise the memory of her with long, dark hair and even darker circles under her vacant eyes. "Nope." He tried to turn away, but she reached across the table and grabbed his arm. Pain seared through his shoulder. He wore a sling that kept his arm close to his body, but casting a broken collarbone wasn't possible.

"It is you. God, you're the spitting image of your father. With that thick hair and blue eyes, you always were a handsome devil."

Liam hadn't heard that name since his mom had let him choose a new one. When she'd adopted him, they'd made the change legal. "Lady, take your hand off me."

"I know that tone. You were always such an angry little boy."

"Kids get that way when they have drug-addicts for mothers who care more about scoring their next high than whether their kid is alive." He remembered promising Tru that he'd be nice when the time came, but seeing this poor excuse for a human being dredged up some nasty sentiments.

"Nick, I'm sorry. I'm clean now. I've been sober for twenty-two years."

He had long ago disowned that name. His mother had lit a fire in the backyard, and they'd ceremoniously burned everything that reminded him of the life he'd hated. "I don't care."

"Giving you up was the best thing for you."

Rage burned through his chest. He jerked his arm from her grip. "It was never about me. It was always about you—when is your next high, where are your drugs. And you didn't give me up—I was taken from you and your rights were terminated. You didn't even show up for the hearing." Yeah, he'd hacked into the sealed records and read everything pertaining to Yvonne Eisenberg and her son, Nick. If he was going to owe his life to the government, then he was damn well going to ferret out every piece of data. "Six foster homes. That's what happened to me."

Another hand on his arm, this one with a gentle touch. "Sir? Are you okay?" Tru's voice penetrated the haze of fury, dissipating it with her calming presence.

He looked down at her. "I'm fine. Are you ready to go?"

She held up a bag laden with goodies.

"Is this your wife?"

Tru studied the woman he wished would leave. "You're Liam's birth mother." She gestured to a group of people near the bank of the stream, a father and four children. "That's your family?"

The blood drained from Yvonne's face. She glanced nervously toward her family. "I haven't told them about you."

Liam slung his good arm around Tru. "There's nothing to tell. I have a family, and you're not part of it."

Tru walked with him to the car without saying a word. As they passed the trash bin, she took the crumpled paper products from his fist and tossed them away. With it went the remnants of rage he'd kept all these years. Yvonne Eisenberg had thrown him away, and Joyce Adair had treasured him. The one woman mattered, and the other one did not.

"I'm proud of you." Tru fastened her seatbelt, and then she put the key in the ignition.

"I wasn't nice."

"You weren't mean or unnecessarily cruel. You said nothing you'll regret."

He hadn't. Wearing a goofy grin, he watched Tru as she drove. "I like having you here to look out for me."

She glanced over. "I like being here to look out for you."

The late October sun was setting, and Jed sat in his car in the parking lot adjacent to Dare's apartment building and stared at the ring he'd picked up from the jeweler. For the past few weeks, Tru had been staying with Dare to take care of him. On the days Jed was home, she spent time at his place or with both of them together.

It had been idyllic. Never in a million years would he have thought he'd find a woman who made him want to commit to this level. He loved Tru. He loved her joy and the way she embraced life. He had even come to love her need for adventure. The week before, the two of them had gone skydiving. The experience had been thrilling and awesome. She was the other half of his soul, and never would he have imagined that he'd be okay with sharing her. Six weeks ago, Liam Adair had been a colleague with whom he had a friendly, collegial association that sometimes had a passive-aggressive edge. Now the two of them were closer than Jed was with his brothers.

The ring had three stones, two diamonds and an emerald, to signify their unique relationship. Though she couldn't legally marry both of them, they planned to ask her anyway, and they also planned to let her flip a coin to see which one of them got to do the legal honors.

His phone dinged, and he checked his text messages to find one from Dare. *Ready.*

They'd planned a scene together, their first since leaving Zangari's Fetish Inn. After the scene, when she was doped up with serotonin, they planned to propose. He exited the car.

Kneeling naked on the floor next to the sofa, Tru waited for her Sirs. In a few weeks, Liam's shoulder would be healed, and he'd return to work. Though he was working his cases and trying to find the whereabouts of Zarah Braithwaite, Jed managed to be home most evenings and weekends. They lavished on her a bliss that she'd never imagined. Being with them, serving them, loving them—it had become all she wanted. Part of her dreaded Liam's recovery. She didn't want to go back to Northport except to visit Gram and Poppy, which she'd done last week.

Liam, lounging on the sofa, jumped up at the knock on the door. He greeted Jed with a hand clasp and some pounding on the back. Tru broke protocol to peek and make sure Jed was careful around Liam's injury. The two exchanged pleasantries.

"How was California?" Liam closed and locked the door, engaging two deadbolts and a sliding lock.

"Sunny. Boiling hot in some places and freezing in others. I'm glad to be back." Jed stopped in front of Tru. He ran his fingers through her hair. "I missed my sub."

She had missed him as well, but she swallowed the assurance. He hadn't given her permission to speak.

"Stand up, Princess."

She got to her feet, and he claimed her with a kiss that quickly turned savage. His hand fisted in her hair, pulling hard until the kiss broke, and then he trailed sucking kisses down her neck.

"Talk to me, Princess. Tell me what's on your mind."

"Serving you, Sir. I've missed you terribly."

"Let me see if I can fix that." He palmed her breast, kneading it with harsh pressure until his mouth took over. He sucked her nipple, alternating hard and soft pulls. She peered over his head to find Liam seated in a chair, watching.

Jed picked her up and laid her on the sofa. He ravaged her breasts with his mouth, and with his fingers, he squeezed and rolled her nipples. His free hand roamed her hips and thighs, and she moaned when he dipped his fingers into her pussy. He hiked her leg up so that Liam had a clear view of what he was doing. Tru watched Liam watching them, and his heavy-lidded expression sent extra thrills through her body. Jed fingered her until she cried out a small climax.

Then he kissed her again, urgently this time. "I've missed you, Princess. I've missed touching you, listening to you talk, seeing the way you look at me."

She grinned. "I didn't know you wanted to talk, Sir. Did you hear about what's going on in the legislature this week? It's amazing how many politicians are plain old idiots."

"Not that kind of talk." He rearranged the pillows on the sofa to create an incline leading up to the low arm.

"I bought a new dress."

"You'll have to model it for me later, when I decide you're allowed to wear clothes." He repositioned her so that her ass was on the arm of the sofa and the cushions supported her back and neck. Then he stripped out of his shirt and pants.

"I love your naked body. It's so freaking sexy."

This time he grinned. "Back at you, Princess." He lifted her legs so that they were out of his way, and he fed his cock into her greedy pussy.

Tru looked at Liam to find him watching intently and ignoring the tent in his own pants. She wanted to ask him to join them, but she knew he wanted to watch right now.

Jed set a frantic pace. He'd been away for four days, and he had definitely missed her. He climaxed before she did, and then he withdrew. "Stay put."

Though her legs were in the air, which looked silly without her Sir standing there to hold them up, she didn't move.

Before long, Jed returned with a vibrating wand. "You're going to come, Princess, but you're not going to move. Put your hands above your head." He resumed his place between her legs, giving her something to rest them against, and he drizzled lubricant over her clit.

Tru had heard about the power behind these devices. She'd confided in Jed that she'd always wanted one, and he'd brought her back one. "Oooh, Sir, you remembered. Thank you."

He pressed it to her clit, and the powerful vibrations immediately made her body arch. He plucked at her nipples, playing her like a cheap guitar as he slid the head between the sensitive nub and her pussy. Before long, an orgasm washed over her body. She cried out, thanking Jed for giving her two orgasms.

"You're welcome, Princess." He slowly twirled her left nipple in his fingers, and he left the wand pressed just below her clit. "And we're going to watch you come one more time."

With that thing vibrating powerfully against her pink parts, giving them another show wasn't hard. Her body arched and twisted. She moaned and cried out as it became almost too much. Between her legs, Jed rubbed lubricant into her anus. She surrendered to the pleasure he wanted her to have, and an orgasm pummeled through her core.

Jed lifted her, and his lips claimed hers. He thrust his tongue into her mouth, marking her more than kissing her. Then he sat down on the sofa and pulled her onto his lap. She snuggled against his body, shaking with the aftermath of three orgasms.

Then Liam got up. He shed his clothes, sat back down, and took his cock in hand.

Though it was hot as hell watching him touch himself, Tru frowned. "Sir, please let me do that for you."

Jed kissed her forehead. "Ask the right way."

Tru slid to the floor and crossed the small room. She knelt at Liam's feet, her head bowed. From the periphery of her vision, she watched his hand move lazily up and down his cock.

"Tell me what you want, Princess." Liam paused his masturbation attempt.

She liked that he'd taken to using the same term of endearment. "I'd like to serve you, Sir."

"We already had dinner."

"Very funny, Sir. I meant I want to make you come. My mouth, my pussy, my hands, and my ass are at your disposal. You can even fuck my breasts if you want to."

Behind her, she heard Jed sit forward. "I may take you up on that another time."

She grinned at Liam. "Please tell me what you want."

"Your ass. Get a condom."

They'd stopped using condoms for everything except anal. Both had been willing to wait for birth control pills to kick in, but she'd assured them that pregnancy wasn't an option after all the treatments she'd been through. She scurried to the bedroom for a condom, and when she returned, she knelt at his feet and rolled it over his erection.

She tried to straddle him—due to his injury, she had to be on top—but he stopped her. "Turn around. I'll line it up, and you sit down slowly." She did as he commanded, sitting on his cock slowly so that it penetrated her ass at the pace he decreed.

When he was fully inside, he pulled her back to rest against his chest. With a finger on her jaw, he turned her face to the side and kissed her as he fondled her breasts and played with her clit. Wait. That was too many hands. Liam ended the deep kiss that rocked her senses, she moaned as Jed slid into her vagina. With both of her Sirs inside her body, she fully submitted. More orgasms were in store, probably more than she thought she could handle, but right now, her Sirs slid in and out of her body to a slow-burning rhythm they'd perfected in a few short weeks. She didn't care if she ever came again—she just wanted this feeling to last forever.

"I love you both so much."

"Marry us." Liam's breath whispered over her ear and down her neck, sending shivers in all directions.

Jed kissed the other side of her neck, and then he pulled back to peer into her eyes. "Wear our ring and our collar."

She didn't know how the marriage thing was going to work, but the collar was something for which she yearned. "I would love nothing more."

"Move here." Jed ordered. "We'll get a place together."

She meant to answer in the affirmative, but a powerful climax turned her response into a passionate shout.

"Soundproof," Liam added, but neither of them varied their pace. "So we can tie you up and force you to orgasm until you pass out."

"Yes," she said. "Yes to everything."

If you enjoyed this title, please consider leaving a review at your point of purchase.

Michele Zurlo

I'm Michele Zurlo, author of the Doms of the FBI and the SAFE Security series and many other stories. I write contemporary and paranormal, BDSM and mainstream—whatever it takes to give my characters the happy endings they deserve.

I'm not half as interesting as my characters. My childhood dreams tended to stretch no further than the next book in my to-be-read pile, and I aspired to be a librarian so I could read all day. I ended up teaching middle school, so that fulfilled part of my dream. Some words of wisdom from an inspiring lady had me tapping out stories on my first laptop, so in the evenings, romantic tales flow from my fingertips.

I'm pretty impulsive when it comes to big decisions, especially when it's something I've never done before. Writing is just one in a long line of impulsive decisions that turned out to showcase my great instincts. Find out more at www.michelezurloauthor.com or @MZurloAuthor.

Lost Goddess Publishing

Visit www.michelezurloauthor.com for information about our other titles.

Lost Goddess Publishing Titles

BDSM Anthology/Club Alegria #1-3 by Michele Zurlo and Nicoline Tiernan

New Adult Anthology/Lovin' U #1-4 by Nicoline Tiernan

Menage Anthology/Club Alegria #4-7 by Michele Zurlo and Nicoline Tiernan

Blade's Ghost by Michele Zurlo

Nexus #1: Tristan's Lover by Nicoline Tiernan

The Doms of the FBI Series by Michele Zurlo

Re/Bound (Doms of the FBI 1)

Re/Paired (Doms of the FBI 2)

Re/Claimed (Doms of the FBI 3)

Re/Defined (Doms of the FBI 4)

Re/Leased (Doms of the FBI 5)

Re/Viewed (Doms of the FBI 6)

The Dragon Kisses Series by Michele Zurlo

Dragon Kisses 1

Dragon Kisses 2

Dragon Kisses 3

The SAFE Security Series by Michele Zurlo

Treasure Me (SAFE Security 1)

Made in the USA
San Bernardino, CA
17 March 2018